Patricia Grey w... ... ...n Barnet and coll... ... ...n Hertfordshire. S... ... ...l manner of companies from plastic moulding and Japanese banking through to film production and BBC Radio, eventually ending up as Contracts Manager for a computer company. The background to JUNCTION CUT, her first novel, was supplied by her parents who grew up in Kentish Town.

Junction Cut

Patricia Grey

KNIGHT

Copyright © 1994 Patricia Grey

The right of Patricia Grey to be identified as the author of
the work has been asserted by her in accordance with the
Copyright, Designs and Patents Act 1988.

First published in 1994
by HEADLINE BOOK PUBLISHING

First published in paperback in 1994
by HEADLINE BOOK PUBLISHING

This edition published 2001 by
Knight an imprint of Caxton Publishing Group

10 9 8 7 6 5 4 3 2 1

All rights reserved. No part of this publication may be
reproduced, stored in a retrieval system, or transmitted,
in any form or by any means without the prior written
permission of the publisher, nor be otherwise circulated
in any form of binding or cover other than that in which
it is published and without a similar condition being
imposed on the subsequent purchaser.

All characters in this publication are fictitious
and any resemblance to real persons, living or dead,
is purely coincidental.

ISBN 1 84067 367 2

Typeset by
Avon Dataset Ltd., Bidford-on-Avon

Printed and bound in Great Britain by
The Guernsey Press Co. Ltd, Guernsey, C.I.

Caxton Publishing Group
20 Bloomsbury Street
London
WC1B 3JH

For my parents

Prologue

January 1940

'Station,' Micky Williams sang out. 'Kentish Town Station.'

He was sure the old girl in the squashed purple hat had asked for this stop. He waited, his hand hesitating over the bell. In the dimly lit interior the woman sat rigidly staring ahead. Micky shrugged. What did he care if the bus company lost the extra fare? In a week's time he'd be Private Williams. And he couldn't wait.

With two merry tings the future Private Williams set the bus trundling down Kentish Town Road again, folded his arms and lounged back on the platform contemplating the day when he could wave goodbye to the bus depot for good.

At the front of the bus, Edie Yeovil gnawed her top lip and thought about the call-up with very different feelings. She lived in dread of the day her Ronnie would be taken away, put in khaki, handed a rifle, and sent to God knows where to be shot. Most of his friends had already been conscripted. The ones he'd planned to meet in the West End this afternoon were already old hands, having been in uniform for a whole six weeks. Soon his employers were going to run out of excuses to have his call-up deferred. As Ronnie had said, 'Insurance isn't what you'd call an essential occupation, Mum. In a few weeks I could be in uniform so Phyl and I have set the date.'

I could forbid the banns, Edie thought. Only what was the point? It stood to reason if the law thought Ronnie was old enough to die for King and Country, they were going to think he was old enough to get married without his mum's permission. And, even worse, Ronnie wouldn't see that she'd done it for his own good. That his mum knew best and could see that Phyllis was only marrying him because she was desperate for a husband.

I'd almost rather he got called up now before she can get him to that altar, mused Edie. Then, as the thought entered her mind, she tried to snatch it back before God heard it, as she'd done when she was a little girl. Of course she didn't want Ronnie in the army! Whatever Phyllis did to him, it wouldn't be as bad as having him lying dead on some battlefield hundreds of miles away. She couldn't quite suppress the half-formed prayer that they'd introduce conscription for women too. No one, after all, could blame her for what happened to Phyllis once she was in uniform.

'I hope you get your stupid head blown orf! I hope Hitler does it personal.'

Hearing her own thoughts, spoken aloud like that, startled Edie out of her day-dream. The two girls sitting opposite were struggling to their feet, swaying and clutching at seat backs as the brakes bit.

' 'Course I didn' mean it, but he didn' have no right. Finking I was that sort of girl!'

Edie peered through the windows. On her right, the white walls of the ABC bakery building, reflecting what little moonlight there was, told her she'd missed her stop and ridden on to Camden Town. Seizing her belongings, she rushed down the aisle, clouting shoulders and ears with wildly swinging bags and dragging newspapers on to the floor.

'Steady on, Missus. 'Ere, I'll hold yer bags while you get down.' Micky Williams put out a steadying hand.

'I can manage quite well, thank you,' Edie said frostily. She wondered whether she ought to offer the extra fare, but he'd already set the bus trundling into Camden Road.

Edie stood blinking, trying to adjust to the darkened streets. She shifted her grip on her bags. The string round the brown-paper package containing her gas mask tangled in her gloves. Clutching her suitcase to her chest, Edie struggled free, juggled mask, case and handbag into a more comfortable position, and prepared to trudge back up Kentish Town Road.

Her first step sent an eddy of cold water into the side of her best leather shoes. Edie winced. The shoes weren't really suitable for the wet January night any more than the plum-coloured woollen dress that she was wearing was suitable for fitting corsets in Daniel's Department Store. But she'd ignored the pointed looks of the manager and kept her chin up. She was a corsetry *consultant*, wasn't she? Not a common assistant. And she wasn't going to let Ronnie down by turning up at the Nettleses' house in a black skirt and white blouse looking like she'd come to serve the tea.

A passing car sent a wave of water over the kerbstones. Edie edged towards the shop fronts. A restaurant door opened and closed quickly. The warm meaty smell of gravy drifted across the pavement and reminded her how hungry she was.

'I hope Valerie's started the tea,' she muttered. Then remembered that even if Val had, there wouldn't be any for her. Thanks to those stuck-up, snobbish Nettleses she'd have to make do with some bread and a piece of cheese that she'd got in the larder.

The memory of this afternoon's humiliation added momentum to Edie's flagging steps. Head down against the wind, she battled on up the hill, her tiredness temporarily forgotten. Even with their white-washed kerbs, the edges of the roads were difficult to see. Her eyes started to water from the effects of the cold wind and strain. This whole blackout business was so ridiculous. In the four months they'd been at war with Germany there hadn't been a single air-raid.

The drop from the pavement to Clarence Road caught her by surprise. She half-stumbled into the road and tottered into the path of an oncoming car, its headlights reduced to slits by their cardboard covers.

The squeal of brakes was accompanied by a shouted instruction to watch her step.

Tears filled Edie's eyes. That was what Thelma

Nettles had said when she'd caught her foot in the edge of their rug.

'I know these little Persian rugs are fashionable now but they really are a terrible nuisance, aren't they?'

Edie had agreed. She'd never had a Persian rug in her life. The only rug in Junction Cut had been bought in Daniel's sale four years ago. The large faded patch didn't really show if you remembered not to move the armchair.

Thelma had shown her into a small room to the right of the hall. 'I thought we'd be cosy in here.'

Edie had struggled out of her coat, the mask catching on buttons and tangling in her belt.

'Oh, do you still carry that? We ought to, I know, but I'm afraid I usually forget.' She'd disappeared with Edie's coat and hat and returned with her youngest daughter, Susan. 'We've just finished luncheon so we'll have all afternoon to do our sewing.'

Edie had tried not to let her disappointment show. Her last client had kept her late, dithering over a step-in or back-lacing corset. And then she'd missed her bus. She'd had nothing to eat since a piece of bread and butter at seven-thirty this morning.

Easing Valerie's bridesmaid's dress, carefully wrapped in a sheet to avoid creasing, from her suitcase, she'd smiled brightly. 'How lovely!' At least, she'd comforted herself silently, there would be tea.

There had been tea. Not served by a maid, as she'd expected, with silver bowls and plates of sandwiches and cakes, but a cup placed on the table by her elbow as she crawled on all fours trying to pin up a straight hem whilst that spoilt Nettles girl whined and complained.

Thelma hadn't touched a needle all afternoon. Instead she'd sat there, watching Edie fitting and tucking until the pattern of the carpet was imprinted on her knees and excusing her daughter's bad manners with an indulgent, 'Her fiancé might get leave this weekend.'

Susan stood on tip-toe, nearly pulling the newly fitted waistband of her dress from its bodice. 'It's him. I heard a car.' Wriggling out of the pink satin, she'd dropped it carelessly into Edie's arms, pulled a jumper and skirt on, and rushed from the room. A moment later she'd returned, her mouth drooping. 'It's only Daddy. And Hatty says dinner's ready and if we don't sit down straight away it will be cold and she won't take the blame for it. Dad's gone straight in.'

She brought odours of roasting meat and sweet sauces into the room with her.

The memory of what had happened next brought a flood of embarrassment through Edie's body that was so strong it drove out the damp January chill more effectively than a roaring coal fire and a hot dinner could ever have done. Never, ever, she vowed would she set foot in the Nettleses' house again, speak to Phyllis again, let Ronnie in the house if he married into that . . . that . . . ! The list tumbled round her head whilst her feet, spurred on by bursts of hot anger, drove her up the long hill.

JUNCTION CUT

By the time she reached the sand-bagged entrance to Kentish Town Station, the burst of adrenaline had worn off. The suitcase was dragging on her left arm. She would have liked to rest it for a moment but didn't dare put it down on the puddle-strewn pavements in case the wetness seeped in and ruined Valerie's bridesmaid's dress.

Gritting her teeth, Edie turned the corner, walked the last few weary steps up Fortess Road, and turned into a tiny cul-de-sac of cramped terraced houses.

The last of the fitful starlight disappeared behind massing clouds. Pulling off one glove, Edie groped over the painted wooden door until she located the latch on number four, lifted it and pushed. The door swung inwards for six inches, then stopped.

Edie thrust harder. The door moved a couple more inches, grinding into the soft obstruction jammed in the angle between the hinges and wall, then refused to budge any further. There was a wooden row of clothes pegs on the wall behind the door where they kept their outdoor clothes. It must have fallen off. Edie tutted with irritation. She just hoped it hadn't brought any plaster down with it. It always took months to get the landlord to carry out any repairs. Ronnie wouldn't be home yet but Valerie should be in. Where on earth had she got to? She must be able to hear her.

Rapping sharply on the wooden boards, Edie raised her voice. 'Valerie? Val, are you there?'

The hall passage remained in darkness. Edie could

just see the foot of the stairs. 'Valerie, are you up there? I can't get in.'

Flattening herself against the wall, Edie tried to thrust her way through the narrow gap. Her body wriggled inside the house, but the bags, clasped in her right hand, jammed in the opening. After a brief hesitation, she dropped them outside on the pavement.

The light switch was halfway down the hall. Shuffling into the blackness, Edie located the metal tubing carrying the electric wiring, slid her hand up until she reached the brass roundel and snapped the lever down. Turning, she looked back to see what damage the collapsing coat rack had inflicted on the wall.

The scream that welled up from her stomach caught in her throat and flooded across her vocal chords like a paralyzing drug. Her mouth opened wider and wider until the jawbone ached with the strain, but only a whispering sigh escaped.

Chapter 1

'Ain't this nice, Carey?'

'What?'

'Having a drink like this.'

Carey Meeks sucked a few more inches of best bitter through his straggling moustache before he answered. 'We always have a drink on Saturday night.'

Irene tried to ignore the hunched shoulders and tight jaw. Despite thirty-five years of practice, she found she still couldn't overlook her husband's mood. It dragged her down and spoiled the moment for her. 'Don't sulk, Carey,' she begged. 'It wasn't that bad, what she done.'

'I'm not sulking. I got one opinion, you got another. And if you can't see yours is daft, that's your privilege, girl. I ain't arguing.'

Irene didn't want to argue with anyone. She just wanted to put the troubles of this week behind her and have a good night out before the troubles of the next started. 'It says in the Bible people who live in glass houses shouldn't throw stones.'

'No it don't.'

Irene was stuck. She knew there was something in the Bible about throwing stones but now she came to think about it, she couldn't recall any of them living in glass houses. She sought for some other topic that would take Carey's mind off their current argument. The one that was causing such a babble of excitement in the bar, and had paid for their free drinks, was the only one that came into her head. 'I've never seen two thousand pounds before.'

'You ain't seen it now. That ain't all his winnings – Gus told me. Oggie's going to give him the rest on Monday. Ain't got enough in the house to pay him it all today.'

Irene looked wistfully at the pile of white notes on the bar; whatever the total, it was more money than she or anyone else in Junction Cut had ever seen in their lives.

They'd missed the big scene, but plenty of people had been eager to describe it to them. How Gus Hendry had slipped out into the back, taken off his potman's apron, and re-emerged in his best waistcoat and jacket to take up his place behind the bar. The sight had been unusual enough for most customers in The Hayman to stop drinking and watch curiously. Gus had ignored them all. His massive hands placed flat on the polished bar, he'd stared fixedly at the door curtain.

Intrigued, but sensing some form of entertainment was about to begin, everyone had swung their chairs so they could watch the door too. The silence had been so complete, that for the first time the noisy clicking of the minute hand on the bar clock could clearly be heard. As it cracked noisily on to the 'VI', the heavy faded velvet curtain that divided the bar from the street entrance had stirred gently, indicating that someone had opened the front door.

The drinkers had tensed expectantly. There was a muffled stirring of feet within the lobby that had been created by the hanging of the inner and outer blackout curtains, then the velvet drape was swept aside, rattling back noisily on its brass rings, to admit the local bookmaker, together with two of his heaviest runners.

'You could hear the elephants farting down at the zoo, it was that quiet,' was the way one of the other drinkers had described the moment to the Meekses.

Oggie had stood for a moment longer looking round the room, then he'd walked slowly forward, flanked by his two minders. He wore his normal outfit of long, double-breasted, black woollen overcoat and a bowler hat which sat on the top of his sandy eyebrows. But it was his bag that all eyes were fixed on: a battered Gladstone, clasped lovingly with both hands across his chest. Everyone knew that Oggie paid out from that bag, and that if he'd brought the money personally then someone must have had a big win. Perhaps as much as fifty quid.

Reaching the bar, Oggie had heaved the bag on to the polished surface in front of Gus. 'Where do you want it?'

'Gus swelled up like he was going to burst. And he's a big bloke anyway, ain't he?' the gossiping drinker informed the agog Meekses. 'Then he says, cool as a cucumber, "Just count it out on the bar, please, Oggie. One note at a time, if you please."'

The minders had turned sideways, one elbow on the bar, forming a protective shield around Oggie whilst he drew the first crisp white fiver from the bag.

'On and on they came. Five, ten, fifteen, twenty. I never seen so much money in me whole life. And Gus just stood there, nodding his head up and down and saying, "Thank you, Oggie", every time he put a new fiver on the pile.'

Eventually the show had come to an end. With a decisive snap the bag had been shut. Oggie had wheeled round, faced the room, and announced: 'Oggie always pays, you know that. Never welched on a bet. Never will.' With a nod to left and right, he'd led his minders back into the night in slow funereal procession, leaving a beaming Gus and his dazed wife to enjoy their newly acquired fortune.

Carey contemplated the back view of the plump little blonde leaning over the counter, her black skirt hitched so high it showed several inches of pink slip.

Lily waved a note at her husband. 'Another round on Oggie, Gus?'

'Whatever you say, Lily. Same again all round, Fred.'

A cheer went up.

Someone started playing a well-known tune on the piano. Before long the whole bar was swaying to 'Knees Up, Mother Brown'.

Pints of beer, their creamy heads frothing and spilling around their bases, disappeared from the bar as fast as Gus and Fred could line them up.

Carey's mouth watered. He wanted another drink

but couldn't go up to the bar without getting Irene one too. Eventually he compromised by grunting, seizing her empty port glass, and struggling to his feet.

'Get one for Edie too, she's just come in.'

Carey peered through the thickening haze of blue smoke and saw his next-door neighbour, Edith Yeovil, standing by the door, her handbag clasped across her chest like a shield. 'Ain't never seen her in a pub before.'

'Gus must have asked her. Get her a port, Carey.' Irene raised a hand and shrieked. 'Yoo-hoo, Edie. Over here. 'Ave a bit of my seat.' Using her hip, Irene thrust her neighbours along, clearing a corner of the bench seat.

Returning with his own pint clasped between his palms and two glasses of port balanced amongst the fingers, Carey perched on a stall and lowered his precious burden. 'Got yer a port, Missus Yeovil. That all right for you?'

Edie stared ahead. Two glittering drops slid down her cheeks, leaving a trail like snail slime in the caked powder on her face. As Carey watched, the trickle became a flood which collected at her jawbone, flowed to a point under her chin, and fell in large single drops on to the golden clasp of the handbag.

Carey hastily nudged his wife's ankle, jerked his head in Edie's direction, then buried his face in his pint. Crying females were women's business.

'Wha'ever's the matter? Are you feeling poorly, Edie?'

There was no answer.

'Shall I take you home?'

Taking Edie's arm, Irene tried to get her to stand up. 'Give us a hand, Carey. I can't get out 'til she moves.'

With some difficulty they managed to get Edie to her feet. 'Get through that gap, Carey. Come over queer, did you? I expect it's comin' in from the cold like that. Oi, watch it!'

This last remark was addressed to an enthusiastic songster whose flailing arm had caught Edie's hat and knocked it over one eye. Glancing round, he made some ribald remark about people who didn't know when they'd had enough. It was taken up by several other customers. Irene and Carey finally managed to steer Edie past the double blackout curtains and out into the damp streets to a chorus of good-natured jokes. Throughout, Edith Yeovil hadn't uttered a word.

'What's the matter with her?' Irene asked as soon as they were safely on the pavement.

'Dunno,' Carey shrugged. 'Best get her home. Get the other arm, girl.'

Irene obediently took hold of Edie's elbow again and, their quarrel temporarily forgotten, they steered her back up Fortess Road and into Junction Cut. Carey let out a muffled curse.

'What's the matter?'

'I've banged me leg on something.'

Carey stooped. In the fitful starlight that just penetrated the blacked-out street, they could make out a small suitcase and a brown-paper package tied with string leaning against the front of the house.

'These yours, Missus Yeovil?'

'What she leave 'em there for?'

'May be she got took queer in the street. You'd best get her into bed.' Carey unlatched the door, pushed, and found that it wouldn't open fully.

'What's up?'

'Dunno. Hang on to her and I'll see.'

Carey Meeks was a thin man. A railway porter's pay didn't run to over-eating. Pulling in his stomach, he edged into the gap and made his way along the hall to the light switch.

'Oh, Gawd!'

'Carey? What is it?' Irene thrust her head and one shoulder around the door. 'Oh my lord.'

Wriggling inside, Irene stumbled into her husband's arms. Carey could feel her heart thumping against his chest as he looked over her shoulder at the scene behind the door.

Fifteen-year-old Valerie Yeovil stared back at him. At least, her right eye did. The left was lost in the tide of dark red blood that had erupted from the wounds on that side of her head.

Her brown hair was loose. The right side still gleamed with chestnut lights under the dim hall lighting. The left was plastered to her head, the long tresses caked and tangled into rats' tails by the drying blood. Her face had the appearance of a pantomime mask: one half dead white, the other a rich port that was already turning to liver-shaded. At the top of the red half, where the hair sprang from the wide forehead, the flesh had been pulled and ripped back to reveal splinters of bone.

As the blows had smashed her into unconsciousness, she'd slid down the wall, her bare heels skidding across the polished hall linoleum until she'd come to rest with her legs splayed out at an angle of forty-five degrees. During her descent the back of her dress had caught on the lower hinge of the door, pulling the skirt up round her hips, and showing clearly that she was naked from the waist down. Carey couldn't take his eyes from that curling triangle of dark hair at the apex of her thighs.

A series of small yelps, like a puppy that had got its paw trapped, brought them both back to reality.

'Edie! Oh, Carey, we got to stop her comin' in.'

'She's been in, girl.' Carey pushed his wife back towards the door. 'What do you think she's in such a taking for?'

A hand groped out and seized Irene as she re-emerged on to the pavement. The eerie whimpering sounds continued, rising in pitch.

'Get her inside,' Carey ordered, opening the door of number six.

With her arm round Edie's shoulders, Irene steered her along the hall passage and into her own kitchen. Carey followed.

Irene pulled out a chair. 'Sit here, Edie.'

Edie stared beyond her. Her jaw twisted. Her mouth opened. A thin note emerged. It didn't vary in pitch; it just continued on and on and on.

Irene took off the lopsided hat, drew back her right arm, and hit Edie's cheek with a slap that rattled her jawbone.

Shocked eyes stared blankly into hers for a moment, then Edie said calmly and clearly: 'They'll have to postpone the wedding now.' For a heartbeat longer she stood, poised and triumphant. Then she collapsed into the chair, sobbing loudly.

Irene nodded, satisfied with the results of her first-aid. 'I'll put the kettle on.'

Carey emerged from the scullery wearing his ARP warden's hat.

'What you wearing that for? They haven't bombed her. They bashed her head in!'

Carey couldn't have explained why he'd put the hat on. He just knew it made him feel more in control of the situation. 'You stay in here. I'm going to run down to the police station in Agar Street.'

He went out of the back door, but before he was half way down the yard Irene called him back. Holding the door to behind her, she whispered urgently to him: 'Slip next door and pull her dress down first, Carey.' Her voice slid even lower. 'It ain't nice. A young girl being seen like that.'

He nodded.

It took barely three minutes for him to do as Irene had asked. It took only a minute more to find a constable. Even if it was a woman one.

She was efficient though, he'd give her that. Led him quietly back up Fortess Road, extracting the story from him as they walked. When they reached number four, she left him standing self-consciously on guard whilst she entered the house.

When she squeezed back through the half-open door, Carey noticed the three flashes on her sleeve for the first time.

'I don't suppose any of these houses has a telephone?'

Carey shook his head. 'There's one in The Hayman, miss . . . er . . . Sergeant.'

She walked back the way they'd come. Carey assumed she was going to the pub, but as she reached the entrance to The Cut she stopped and sent three shrill blasts into the night.

Sash windows were flung open all round the little square.

'What's 'appening?'

'Was that a copper's whistle?'

' 'Oo's that? That you, Carey? What's 'appening?'

He could see the sergeant talking to someone. The metallic rim of the man's helmet was just discernible. Carey guessed he was one of the part-time auxiliaries who regularly patrolled the area. He caught the sound of the policeman's heels as he turned quickly in the road and disappeared from the opening.

The sergeant rejoined Carey.

'It *is* a copper! A woman one. Something's happened at the Yeovils', I reckon.'

The sound of half a dozen sash windows being closed was followed by the opening of six doors.

Carey saw, with a sinking heart, that the onlookers included Minnie White, a woman Junction Cut thought ought to be running the Ministry of Information, since she'd spent most of her life in training for the job.

JUNCTION CUT

'What's 'appened?' she repeated. 'Where's Edie?'

That was a question he felt he could answer. 'She's having a cup of tea with Irene.'

Minnie changed course and led her corps towards number six. Watching them filing through his own front door, Carey salved his conscience by telling himself that Irene always liked a bit of company. He found determined women difficult to deal with himself. And so, it appeared, did the CID inspector.

At any rate, he had a job getting rid of that sergeant when he arrived.

'I told Auxiliary Constable Wilmott to let you know that the divisional surgeon would be required, sir. Didn't he?'

'Must have slipped his mind. Now you get back to the station and tell them for me, there's a good girl. And you'd better send the Morgue Wagon as well.'

In addition to his detective sergeant, the inspector had brought a couple of uniformed constables with him. One had been sent round the back and the other was now told to take up position to stop any sightseers wandering into The Cut. 'You go as well,' the inspector added, nodding at Carey. 'You're no use here.'

He didn't like the man's tone, but he'd discovered in the last war that you couldn't choose your officers. So he went. It was a mistake. Minnie must have been hovering behind his own front door. As soon as he moved, she slipped out and scuttled along the two yards of pavement to the Yeovils'.

'Jesus! Look at this!'

No one else had the chance to take up Minnie's invitation because she was firmly escorted back to number six by the detective sergeant. But the damage was done. Excited shrieks and squeals started filtering from the Meekses' partially open door.

Carey reluctantly joined the constable at the entrance to The Cut. They waved through the grim, dark green van that would take the body to the morgue once the doctor had certified that life was extinct. The driver rolled down his window and shouted across to the constable. 'Doctor here yet?'

'No. You've got plenty of time for a fag.'

'Ain't we always?' The noisy crashing of his gears drowned out the sound of Lily Hendry's rapping high heels. She burst into The Cut before Carey could stop her.

'You had no right! No bleeding right.'

Gus puffed into view behind her. 'But, Lily, you can get it back first thing Monday. Look, see, here. Take the money.' He waved a fistful of notes at Lily's retreating back.

'I will! Don't you worry, I will. But you still had no right to pawn me brooch for your stake, you hear? Eh, what you doing?' Her last snarl was directed at the constable who'd stepped into her path.

'Do you live in this street, love?'

'What's it to do with you?' Lily peered past him and saw Carey. 'What's happening, Mr Meeks?'

He waited for the constable to answer. When he didn't, Carey said awkwardly, 'Young Val, she's been . . .' He dried, unable to say the words. Gulping, he tried again: 'Young Val, she's been . . . well, she's dead. The police . . . they're sorting things out.'

Gus caught up with his wife. 'Dead? She was all right this morning. Has she had an accident?'

'Talk sense. They don't have coppers all over the place for an accident.' Lily seized the wadge of notes that Gus had been waving at her and stuffed them in her pocket.

Gus's thinking processes didn't work very fast, but when he came to the inevitable conclusion, his eyes grew larger in his moon-like face. 'Young Gussie!'

He surged towards number two. Lily followed. Caught by the urgency of Gus's tone, the constable veered off after him. Carey decided he might as well go too. Even though by the time he reached the front step, it was obvious there wasn't much wrong with young Gussie. His indignant wails on being woken filled the street.

Over the constable's shoulder, Carey could see Dolly Toddhunter, one of the upstairs tenants at number two, beaming fondly at the squalling bundle.

'I take it the nipper's all right, love?'

'Sounds like it, doesn't it?' Lily flopped on to the bed and eased off one shoe.

Dolly's face turned towards the door. Flickering flames were reflected in her round, black-rimmed spectacles, hiding her eyes. But presumably she noticed that there were both a constable and an ARP warden in the house. 'Is there a raid? I didn't hear the warning... if only someone had come...' Whilst she talked Dolly was attempting to wrap the baby in a blanket and scoop up her gas mask. The dangling straps caught little Gussie across the face. His screams became even louder.

'She's deaf,' Carey hissed in the constable's ear. 'Can't hear a blessed thing. No,' he yelled, 'there hasn't been no raid.' He spoke slowly and loudly as people were inclined to do with the deaf. As a consequence, Dolly failed to lip-read him properly and continued to try to reach the door.

'There's no raid,' shouted Carey. 'Not the Germans, Dolly.' He shook his head vigorously from side to side.

'He must be out. Otherwise I'm sure he'd have warned me.'

'Who must be?'

He'd forgotten to shout. Dolly lip-read that question with ease. 'The German boy. Billy.'

The combination of noise and illegal light spilling out into the street had attracted the detective sergeant. 'What's she talking about?' he demanded sharply. 'What German?'

It was Lily who answered him. She was massaging the toes beneath her black silk stocking, her leg drawn up on the bed giving a clear view of white thigh and pink suspenders. 'He lives upstairs. Same as her.'

'She lives with a German?'

Lily gave a shout of laughter. 'She should be so lucky! Billy's got one of the rooms upstairs. Dolly rents the other.'

The sergeant returned to the street door. 'Inspector Kavanagh!'

The inspector appeared in the doorway, half a dozen inquisitive faces framed in curlers and headscarves behind him. 'Found something, Frampton?'

The sergeant explained. He didn't bother to lower his voice. 'Think the Hun's room is worth a look?'

'I certainly do. Up here, is it?'

He needed both hands on the banisters to get up the bare wooden stairs.

He's drunk, Carey realized.

Minnie and the rest pressed after him, ignoring the attempts of the constable to prevent them. With an almost shame-faced look at the Hendrys and Dolly, Carey joined the back of the crowd. They bumped and jostled each other in order to see over the officers' heads and look at a room that was identical to half a dozen other rented rooms in Junction Cut.

The faded wallpaper had once been white with a pattern of pink roses – their outlines were just discernible as a darker shade of brown amongst the dirty beige shades of the walls. At the end of the room, beneath a window that overlooked the front street, was a slatted wooden bench. A black bachelor cooker stood on the right side of the bench, whilst the left side held a white enamel bowl with a chipped blue rim. Underneath, on a shelf, there was a matching jug, a scrubbing brush – bristles nearly worn to the flat handle – and two iron saucepans. To the side of the bench, a meat safe balanced on a small, green-painted cupboard.

The rest of the room contained a large wardrobe, a small table, a chair, an iron bed and a threadbare carpet.

The excited nasal breathing of Minnie and the rest of the women reverberated in Carey's ear as the inspector strode to the wardrobe, grasped both handles and flung the scarred and battered doors open. Two hangers rocked forlornly in the empty interior.

The inspector looked across at Carey. 'Expecting to go away, was he?'

'No. Yes. Maybe.' How should he know what Billy was planning? But, on the other hand, he was a part-time ARP warden. He ought to know who was in the houses, otherwise they'd waste time searching under bombed buildings for casualties who'd never been in them. That was all very fine in theory, but people didn't want you poking into their private lives.

He finally told as much of the truth as he knew. 'He never told me if he was. And he had a regular job to go to on Monday.'

'Looks like he's scarpered then, don't it?' the sergeant remarked. 'What do you make of that, sir?'

It was Minnie who voiced what the inspector – and everyone else – was thinking. 'He done it. Billy done it.' Her voice rose in an accusatory shriek, ringing down the stairs and into the rapidly filling street. Minnie, who'd never called him anything but 'Billy' in the seven months he'd lived in The Cut, shouted: 'Did you hear? The Hun done it!'

Chapter 2

May 1940

Three and a half months later, in his office at Scotland Yard, Chief Superintendent (C) Roland Dunn said much the same thing. At least he said: 'The German did it, Jack.'

Detective Chief Inspector Jack Stamford looked at the bulky figure behind the desk. The late-evening sunshine flooding in at the window behind the senior officer made it impossible to see his expression but he thought he caught a hint of pleading behind his superior's simple statement. 'Yes, sir?'

Dunn pushed a file across the desk. 'No doubt about it. See for yourself. I know Kavanagh had a certain reputation for... shall we say, taking short-cuts? But this one is sound, Jack. We can't afford to have Zimmermann getting away with it just because the two arresting officers are dead.'

Stamford could see his problem. The Valerie Yeovil murder had caused a national sensation. The press, tired of reporting the so-called 'Phoney War', had seized on the story with delight. As a headliner it had everything they could have ordered: an innocent young girl, a grieving widowed mother, violence, sex and a German villain.

An artist's impression of 'The Hun' had started appearing on news vendors' stands by midday on the Monday following Valerie's murder. On Tuesday morning an alert booking-office clerk at St Pancras had drawn his supervisor's attention to a man asking questions about trains to Liverpool. By the time the police had arrived in response to the supervisor's telephone call, Billy had been recognized and only the presence of two Military Policeman, who'd locked him in the Ladies' Waiting Room and stood guard on the door, had prevented him from being lynched from the iron girders over Platform 1.

Within days the press had whipped the country into a frenzy. Miles of newsprint declaimed the 'proof' that a fifth column had been infiltrated into the country with orders to demoralize the British public by a campaign of rape and murder. These stories had led to a roaring trade in bolts and locks, the formation of vigilante patrols, and a minor boom in the number of assault cases appearing before the Magistrates' Courts.

If Zimmermann were to walk free now due to a mistake or oversight in the police evidence, then the resultant enquiry wouldn't stop at Agar Street station.

Dunn said: 'If Kavanagh hadn't had such a quick result Central would have been called in anyway. So it's not unreasonable for us to be seen to be taking an interest now. Go over the evidence again, Jack. I don't want the Prosecution having to ask for a postponement of the trial. But equally I don't want the Defence getting

JUNCTION CUT

that bastard off on some technicality – some detail that Kavanagh overlooked.'

So much for innocent-until-proven-guilty, Jack thought. 'Is there any further news on Inspector Kavanagh's accident, sir?'

'No. And I doubt there will be. The official line is that Kavanagh swerved to avoid some animal that had run into the road. Car plunged into the canal. He and Sergeant Frampton were drowned. A tragic end for two hard-working officers.' He must have seen the sceptical lift of Jack's eyebrow. 'Yes, all right, we've both heard the rumours. But there are two widows left to consider, Jack. Telling them their husbands were too drunk to see where they were driving isn't going to be much of a comfort, is it? How would your wife feel if . . . ?'

Dunn suddenly lapsed into a coughing fit. Jack waited until the loud throat-clearing had stopped then said, 'It's all right, sir. I don't mind discussing Neelie.'

'Er, yes. I presume her visit will be coming to an end now. In view of this morning's news?'

Despite the subject, Jack couldn't quite suppress a smile. Two years was some visit. 'Yes, sir. I expect Neelie and Annaliese are on their way to England now. My father-in-law too, I hope.'

His initial impulse when the news of the German advance had reached the Yard, had been to try to cross the Channel and collect his wife and daughter. But he'd been trained to think logically. And logic had, as usual, supplied a cold dose of common sense.

It would take Neelie and her father less than twenty

minutes to reach the docks at Rotterdam. To rush into the path of the advancing German army whilst they were already on a ship heading for Harwich wasn't going to help either of them.

'No need to panic, of course,' Dunn was saying. 'BEF will hold them in the East. Won't get anywhere near the Channel.'

'I'm sure you're right, sir. What's the CID strength at Agar Street?'

Dunn seized on the change of subject with relief. 'Apart from Kavanagh and Frampton, there's another sergeant.' He consulted a file. 'But he seems to have been on sick leave for the past nine months. And there should be three detective constables, but one of those positions is vacant at present. You're thinking of using the home team, so to speak?'

'I think so. There doesn't seem much point in assembling a full incident team when the trail is so cold. I'll start with a sergeant and bring in extra officers on a need-to-use basis.'

'Bolton is available.'

'No thank you, sir.' Detective Sergeant Bolton had assisted on his last two cases. Stamford had ended up disliking him more than the villains they were chasing. 'I'd like to get the feel of the place first, if you don't mind, sir. Then perhaps we could discuss staff?'

'Of course, whatever you think best, Jack.' He tapped the Zimmermann file that was lying on the desk between them. 'Just don't let this one get away.'

'I'll do my best, sir.' As the words left his mouth,

JUNCTION CUT

Jack was aware of a cold chill filtering down the back of his neck that wasn't entirely due to Scotland Yard's well-deserved reputation for draughts. Had he been a fanciful man, he would have said that Kavanagh's ghost was standing silently at his shoulder.

His arrival home was greeted by a burst of staccato gunfire, the screaming explosion of what he took to be a grenade, and the noisy barking of a scruffy black and white dog who seemed to be the target of this all-out attack.

'Evening, Sammy. What's the dog done?'

Sammy O'Day scowled. 'He's been trying to get me mum's chickens. I just threw a grenade at him. That's what Brendan says grenades sound like. He ain't got none 'cos the Army ain't given him none yet. Brendan says the generals couldn't organize a . . .'

Jack interrupted before Sammy's piping voice could enlighten the rest of St Leonard's Square as to his elder brother's opinion of the abilities of the British Army's top brass. 'Is your mum inside, Sammy?'

'She's doing your cleaning.'

Letting himself in, Jack removed the Zimmermann file from his briefcase, locked it in a solid black filing cabinet that was bolted to the floor in a discreet corner of the front room, then went in search of Eileen O'Day.

He found her on her knees in the bathroom, employing an ancient tea-towel with vicious energy to buff up the already gleaming copper pipes.

'You don't have to do this, Eileen. I'm very grateful,

you know that, but I could employ someone. You've got enough to do with your own family.'

Eileen levered herself up and sat on the edge of the bath. 'I keep telling you, with three of them gone, I've got plenty of time on me hands.'

Jack stared at her with a mixture of exasperation and affection. She'd taken him under her wing when Neelie left, long before three of her sons had been conscripted, and despite only being four years older than him, had a habit of treating him like one of her six sons.

Leaning over, Eileen rubbed the rag in a desultory fashion over taps that were already so highly polished that Jack could clearly see the worried 'V' shape between her eyebrows in them from where he stood at the door. He waited.

Eventually she said, 'Is it true? What they're saying about Belgium and Holland?'

Jack told her what news had filtered through to the Yard.

'She'll be coming back then?' Eileen had befriended Neelie whilst she lived in Kentish Town, but since she'd walked out, had never directly used her name.

'Yes. They both will. My father-in-law too. I'd better check the top bedrooms.'

'I turned 'em out last week. They only need sheets. I left them airing in the cupboard.' Eileen twisted the rag between her fingers, screwing and threading until the tips grew white from lack of blood.

'What is it?' Jack asked gently.

She burst out suddenly, her black eyes flashing: 'They got three of mine already. Even if the Germans *are* coming, they wouldn't take another one, would they, Jack?'

'Another one?' Jack made some quick mental calculations. 'Maurice isn't eighteen yet, is he?' he asked, referring to Eileen's second youngest.

'Maury? He's sixteen. I ain't worried about him. You know Maury. If he ever gets called up, he'll end up selling them the tanks. Both sides if I know Maury! No, it's Pat.'

'Pat? They can't call Patrick up. Fireman is a reserved occupation. You know that, Eileen.'

'It was,' she sighed. 'But that was when they expected all them bombs to fall. Well, they ain't.' She stood up, thrusting her rag and tin of polish into the pocket of her apron. 'I don't know how I'd manage without Pat.'

Jack wished he could reassure her, but privately he could see her point. The bombers hadn't come, but now it looked as if the tanks might.

With instructions not to put the sheets on the beds until they were needed, Eileen left to get her depleted family their tea.

Jack eased off his tie and looked longingly at the cool, white bath. He'd had it installed when he bought the house. It had caused quite a sensation in the street at the time. He would have liked to fill it to the brim and lie soaking in the tepid water but an ingrained sense of duty drove him back to the Zimmermann case.

Changing into an old shirt and trousers, he carried a chair out into the back garden, tilted it precariously against the house wall, crossed his ankles on top of an ancient water butt, and opened the brown file.

Considering the amount of speculative prose that had appeared in the press on the case, the official account seemed pathetically sparse. Jack flicked through the slim sheaf of paper. Witnesses' statements, suspect's statement, pathologist's report, forensic report from the Metropolitan Laboratory at Hendon, arresting officer's statement. In all they hardly seemed to amount to more than twenty sheets of paper.

Valerie had died from four blows to her skull, one struck from behind, the other three from the front. In addition to the fatal blows, her right arm had been broken by at least two blows from the same object – a heavy bar, approximately two inches broad and probably hooked at one end. Stamford checked Kavanagh's report. The murder weapon hadn't been found. The pathologist put the time of death between six and seven o'clock. His final sentence read: 'There is evidence that the victim had had sexual intercourse shortly before death occurred.'

It wasn't hard to imagine what had happened: Valerie had fled along the corridor, reached the door, but been hit by the first blow before she could open it. She'd turned, instinctively putting up her arm to shield herself, and the murderer had clubbed her down.

Over the garden walls he could hear the voices of his neighbours, busily discussing the merits of broad

JUNCTION CUT

beans and early cabbages, as flower beds were dug up and replaced by vegetable patches. Their chatter became tangled with the sizzle of frying fish as Friday-night teas were introduced to the pan. Jack yawned. Ever since his last promotion, there had been people dropping hints that a detective chief inspector should move to a more 'suitable' area. This working-class district, with its constant noise and perpetual smuts from the railway yards, might be all right for a sergeant, and was just about acceptable for an inspector, but a chief inspector was almost a gentleman. It had been intimated several times that a move up the hill to Highgate or Hampstead would be politic.

Well, perhaps if Neelie hadn't walked out... He pushed the thought away and tried to force his attention back to the file but the words refused to make any impression, dancing around in incomprehensible groupings and forming meaningless sentences. Slapping the file shut, he re-locked it in the cabinet, changed back into his suit and tie, and set out down Malden Road.

Agar Street was a solid, square station constructed at the end of the previous century in the ubiquitous London Yellow brick. His appearance was greeted by the station sergeant with the equanimity of a man who knows he can't be held responsible for the fact there are no CID officers present.

'I believe you weren't expected until Monday, sir,'

he said, with no suggestion of either apology or explanation. He opened a door at the back of the station. 'This is the CID office, sir.'

Standing back, he allowed Jack to precede him into the room.

Jack tried the drawer of one of the filing cabinets. It was unlocked as the door to the office had been. He picked up a document marked 'Confidential' from a desk and dropped it into a drawer at random. Glancing through the rest of the litter on the desk, he found several witnesses' statements beneath a half-eaten sandwich. An ash-tray full of stubbed cigarette butts had overflowed across one of the chairs. Another held two unwashed cups.

Assorted official circulars regarding the flying of carrier pigeons, letting off of fireworks and carrying of cameras and binoculars in Restricted Areas were taped in a haphazard pattern over the wall. A rota next to them informed him that Detective Constable Bell should be on duty. Jack opened an inner door marked 'DI'. The office was in darkness but the room had the same stale nicotine smell.

'You weren't expected until Monday,' the sergeant repeated stolidly. 'Sub Inspector Connolly is still in the station, sir. I'll let him know you've arrived.'

Jack stopped him. It was just a visit to get his bearings. He saw no reason to disturb the uniform branch until his 'official' initiation on Monday. Mentally he scanned the papers he'd flicked through in the Zimmermann file. 'Is Sergeant McNeill on duty?'

'Yes, sir. Came on at four o'clock.'

'If he's in the station, would you ask him if he could spare me a few minutes? I won't keep him more than ten.'

'I'll send *her* down, sir.' The sergeant paced heavily away.

Jack winced. So much for Scotland Yard's powers of observation.

He tried them out on the woman who entered the office a few moments later and stood coolly waiting for him to speak.

She was tall, that was his first impression. He was six foot yet her calm blue eyes were nearly on a level with his brown ones. Her face was oval with a slight elongation at the chin, rather like an inverted egg. The shape was more obvious than it might have been because her brown hair had been drawn back and fixed in a coil on the back of her head, presumably so that it would fit under the very unflattering helmet that she was holding under one arm. He brought his eyes back from the helmet to her face. Some officers would have been embarrassed at this close scrutiny by a senior officer. She obviously wasn't.

'Sit down, Sergeant. I won't keep you long.'

He waited until she was seated, moved the tea cups off DC Bell's chair, sat opposite her and explained his brief to re-examine the Zimmermann arrest. 'You were the first officer on the scene. I'd value your impressions. As I'm sure DI Kavanagh must have done.'

She could not quite suppress the expression that

flitted briefly across her face. Stamford tried to put a name to it. Contempt? Disbelief? Amusement?

She said simply: 'Where would you like me to start, sir?'

'Wherever you think best. What were you doing in the area, for instance?'

'I always make at least one sweep around the area during the shift. I was returning to the station when Mr Meeks caught up with me.' Her voice was low with a curious clipped note at the end of each word, as if she was making a deliberate effort not to cut short the final sound.

Jack found it quite hypnotic as she recited Carey's garbled appeal for help, her subsequent check on Valerie's body and the summoning of the CID officers.

'Did you examine the rest of the house?'

'Briefly, sir. Whilst we were waiting for the DI to arrive. Mr Meeks had already told me the mother was in his house. But there was a brother. I wanted to check he wasn't in the house too.'

'I assume he wasn't?'

'No, sir. I believe he returned some hours later. I don't know. Inspector Kavanagh dismissed me as soon as he arrived.'

Jack noted her choice of word – 'dismissed'.

She sat waiting for his next question, her hands folded in the lap of her heavy blue skirt, her expression non-committal.

Certain that she had more to tell than she was volunteering, Jack persevered. 'Where was the body?'

'Behind the door.'

'Sitting? Lying on her back? Her front?'

He knew the answer. He'd read the report. But he wanted this woman to go back to that night. He wanted her to walk into that house again and see the scene as she'd seen it a few hours after Valerie Yeovil's murder.

'She was sitting, sir. Her back was against the wall.'

He waited. She volunteered no further information.

Jack said mildly, 'When you were looking for the brother, did you notice anything out of place in the house? Something you felt was strange?'

'No.'

There was the briefest flicker in the those calm eyes. If he hadn't been watching her closely he would have missed it. He experienced that prickle of excitement at the base of his spine that always came when he knew he'd made the first breakthrough on a case. 'Did you like Inspector Kavanagh?'

It was an indiscreet question, inviting her to comment on a senior colleague. But he had to do something to shake her out of that shell of protective formality. He knew if she lied and said 'yes' he could never work with her.

She said, 'No.'

Jack waited.

She continued slowly, searching for the right words. 'Inspector Kavanagh thought women should stay in the kitchen – or the bedroom. Lots of policemen do, of course.' She looked directly at Jack, as if she expected to read his own opinion in his face.

He kept his expression carefully neutral.

'The inspector made his views known, sir. It made it difficult for the female officers on this station to work effectively.'

'You believe that policewomen should receive the same respect as male officers?'

'Yes. Don't you, sir?'

'Certainly.' Stamford placed his forearms on his legs, linked his fingers and leant forward slightly. 'Of course, I believe they should also be subject to the same discipline.'

'Yes, sir.' She'd grown wary again. The chink in the protective shell closing.

'For instance, if I suspected that a policeman was deliberately withholding information out of spite towards a dead colleague . . .'

'It's not spite. I told him. He didn't want to know . . .' Her eyes flashed.

'I want to,' Jack said quietly. 'Tell me.'

She took a deep breath. Her eyes continued to sparkle but her voice was steady enough as she said: 'I just thought it strange, sir, that . . .'

The rest of her sentence was lost in a screaming horrific wail above their heads that suggested all the harpies of hell had just landed on the station roof.

Chapter 3

Above the wail of the air-raid siren, Jack was aware of other sounds ceasing; footsteps stopped, voices died away, a braying laugh was roughly hushed by another voice. Sarah McNeill's blue eyes met his across the polished desk. Wordlessly she extended the index finger of her right hand. Jack nodded and her glance dropped again to the simple watch on her left wrist.

Unannounced and unknown to the general public the police had already formulated contingency plans for keeping London's roads clear of refugees in the event of an invasion. If the siren sounded for five continuous minutes Agar Street uniform branch would swing into a well-rehearsed routine, blocking off designated roads to civilian traffic and leaving them free for the fast movement of military personnel to the invasion areas.

Without looking up from her watch, Sarah uncurled her middle finger, then her index finger. Three minutes. The sound was dinning in Jack's head, pushing on his ear-drums from the inside. Slowly her little finger unfolded to join its three long slim fellows. Four minutes. Jack's eyes were rooted to the thumb held flat against her palm.

The station sergeant put his head round the door and bawled: 'Another bloody false alarm, if you'll excuse my French, Sarge. If I could get my hands on the stupid sod who thinks every passing cloud is a German bomber...'

The wail of the air-raid siren stopped and he suddenly found himself yelling into silence. He gulped, blushed, and shuffled backwards again. Jack sat quietly until the reciprocal 'All Clear' had been given. He guessed (quite correctly) that the decision to site the air-raid warning siren on the section of roof directly over the CID office was another oblique statement on the late Inspector Kavanagh's popularity.

Once the final notes had finished ricocheting and whirling around his skull, he ascertained what it was that had aroused Sarah McNeill's suspicions in the Yeovil house and arranged to view the scene with her on the Monday morning.

Junction Cut gave no indication that it knew most of Europe was at war.

Norway and Denmark might already be occupied, France, Belgium and Holland be fighting for their lives, but The Cut had the still, untroubled feel of a street where the men had gone to work, the older children had been pushed reluctantly out to start another school week, and the women were beginning again on the same Monday to Friday routine of washing, ironing, cleaning and baking that had been going on in these houses since they were built eighty years ago.

A black and white cat strolled down the pavement, selected a suitable piece of wall and stretched out, blissfully scratching a troublesome flea on its back against the rough brickwork. A small girl shot out of an open door and made a grab for its tail.

'Queenie, come 'ere! Leave that thing alone. You'll get lousy again. And put yer shoes on, we ain't poor.'

A whoosh of dirty water followed Queenie on to the pavement. Jack paused in mid-step to allow the tide to flow into the gutter. Raising his hat politely to the woman who'd appeared in the open doorway, he continued his stroll. Once out of earshot, he said: 'Ain't they?'

'Sir?' Sarah McNeill's face wore her usual expression of non-committal enquiry.

He repeated his question, re-wording it slightly. 'The people in this street, what sort are they? Poor? On assistance? Fully employed?'

She thought for a moment then replied, 'Mostly employed. They're not well off, but they get by.'

'What about the one who just tried to ruin my shoes?'

'Minnie White. She's got four older girls at school. Her husband works on the railways. Lots of the men around here do.'

As if to confirm its proximity the muffled clank of a goods train passing under the first bridge out of Kentish Town filtered across the roof tops, indicating that the wind was from the south-west and the housewives would have to contend with a plague of soot smuts from the continually shunting coal engines.

'How long have you been stationed at Agar Street?'
'Eighteen months.'
'And before that?'
'I was at Leman Street, sir.'

Jack waited but once again Sarah McNeill was volunteering no additional information. He sighed inwardly and wondered if he'd made a mistake in asking Dunn to arrange for her temporary transfer to CID.

They'd walked the length of the street and reached the flat, brick wall that formed the cross-bar joining the two sides of Junction Cut. Turning on his heel, Jack surveyed the street.

The brickwork had presumably been yellow once, but eighty years of coal dust had aged and dirtied it to the colour of dried mustard which deepened to black in places where the grime had collected along the pointing. None of the houses on his left had front gardens, each springing directly from the paving stones, the position of their slightly recessed front doors marked by a narrow white-stoned step set flush against pavement and wall. Some of those on the right had fenced off handkerchief patches of earth which supported roses, runner-bean canes and minute vegetable beds. All the doors were painted an identical shade of dark green, which suggested that the houses had the same landlord.

The cat had disappeared but Queenie had turned her attention to this new entertainment. Standing on her left leg, the bare toes of her right foot scratching

JUNCTION CUT

at the back of her calf, she stared curiously at the two strangers.

Her mother wasn't quite so blatant. The metal pail, refilled with clean water, was dumped on the pavement. Wringing out her rag, Minnie slapped it on her front window, moving the dirt around in desultory circles.

'My mother always said you shouldn't clean the windows when the sun's out. Leaves smears,' Jack remarked.

'Yes, sir.'

'Are all the houses occupied?'

She replied promptly, 'All but two.'

So you've been taking an interest even if Kavanagh did dismiss you, Jack thought.

'Which two?'

'Eighteen, down this end.' She nodded. 'And number seven.'

'That would be about the middle on this side, wouldn't it?'

'It's opposite number six, sir. The street is a bit uneven.'

They were retracing their steps now. Another door opened. A wooden kitchen chair was dumped outside. A thin woman, clutching a knife in one hand and a saucepan of water in the other, plumped herself down and drew a potato from her apron pocket.

'These would be some of the "informed sources that spoke exclusively to our correspondent", would they?' Jack enquired.

He thought he caught the beginnings of a laugh in Sarah's voice as she replied, 'Yes, sir.'

He glanced sideways. Her profile was still as immovable as ever under the ubiquitous helmet. 'You don't have to wear uniform now you're in the CID, you know. In fact, it would be preferable if you didn't.'

'I'm sorry, but I was only told after I'd come on duty that you'd arranged my transfer with the Superintendent of Women's Police.'

Black mark to me, Jack decided. I didn't ask her first.

'Would you like me to go home and change, sir?'

'No. I'd like you to introduce me to Mrs Yeovil.'

It was a request that proved impossible for Sarah to carry out. She'd hardly reached for the metal knocker on number four before the wash rag was flung unceremoniously into the bucket and Minnie White was across the road and eagerly informing them that Edie was out, but if she could help them at all . . . ?

Before Jack could answer, Sarah said: 'Mrs Meeks will probably be in. Shall I try her, sir?'

Jack hesitated. Good manners, not to mention good politics, meant that Valerie's family ought to be told about the re-investigation before her neighbours were informed.

Sarah misunderstood his silence. 'The houses are the same, sir. I can show you in there.'

Jack nodded. It was unfortunate that Mrs Yeovil wasn't available, but he was going to have to talk to the Meekses at some point. If rumours were going to start circulating, they might as well be based on the truth.

Carey opened the door to admit the two officers, and slammed it shut again with a: 'Morning, Minnie. Mustn't keep you.'

He ushered them down a narrow passage, its paintwork a deep gloss brown and its plastered walls a shade of pale buff. It was a combination that Stamford associated with every Metropolitan police station he'd ever been in. It crossed his mind that someone in the Met might be supplementing his pension by selling surplus supplies by the back door.

'It's lucky we found you in, Mr Meeks,' Sarah said.

'I'm on late shift this week, miss. Don't start 'til two o'clock. In here, sir.' He didn't sound too happy about his late start and when he opened a door at the end of the passage Jack realized why.

The kitchen and scullery stretched the length of the back of the house. The whole room smelt of soap, boiling water and blue bags. Beyond the criss-cross patterns of brown paper strips on the window, the yard was full of lines of shirts, sheets, pillow cases, towels, blouses and – discreetly positioned on a string nearest the house – vests, long johns and pink bloomers, all dancing in the morning breeze.

Carey made the introductions. Irene Meeks's mouth curved into a reluctant smile, whilst her eyes flashed angrily at her husband. 'Whatever did you bring them in here for, Carey? Take them into the parlour.' One hand pushed wisps of damp hair off her forehead, whilst the other struggled with the knotted strings of her flowered overall.

Carey tried to back his visitors into the hall again. His eyes held the haunted look of a man who'd just spent four hours getting under his wife's feet whilst she tried to do the Monday morning wash.

Jack stood his ground. 'I like kitchens.' He glanced upwards. An empty drying rack, its wooden slats swaying slightly in the draught, was lashed a few inches from the ceiling.

'You'll be much comfier in the parlour, sir.' Irene was rolling down the sleeves of her dress. Fingers still red and roughened from the wringing sought and found wrist buttons. 'Show the lady and gentlemen the parlour, Carey. And then come and give me a hand with the tea things.'

Jack realized that if he insisted on remaining in the kitchen, she'd spend the entire visit worrying about the lack of proper ceremony.

He allowed himself to be shepherded back to the front room. It had a cold, unused feel.

Carey whisked back the heavy curtains. 'Irene leaves 'em drawn,' he explained. 'Says it stops the carpet from fading.' He edged out again.

Jack blinked in disbelief. The room was full of the most unlikely collection of ornaments: brass buddhas; wooden boxes inlaid with mother-of-pearl and turquoise; lacquer ones painted vivid shades of black, scarlet and white; carved statues of white bone and yellowing ivory; and painted plates in china, glass and what he thought might be plaited reeds.

Looking round he saw that the walls looked equally out of place in a Kentish Town terrace. Instead of the expected cheap prints or family photos they displayed lace fans, grotesque wooden masks, a ceremonial sword, and two sticks in plaited hide that ended in an exuberant fountain of white animal hair.

His gaze completed its sweep of the amazing decor and met up again with Sarah McNeill's. 'The Meekses' son is a sailor, sir. Merchant Navy.'

Before Jack could reply, the door swung open and Irene struggled in with a tea-tray. Carey followed with a milk jug and a hang-dog expression.

'The inspector was just admiring your ornaments, Mrs Meeks,' Sarah remarked, moving a wooden display case containing a gold pocket watch in order to clear a space for the tray.

Irene beamed. 'Our Joey bought 'em. Brings us something every time he comes 'ome. Don't he, Carey? Been all over the world he has. That watch come all the way from Cape Town. Present for his dad's fiftieth birthday that was.'

Jack accepted a rose-patterned tea cup. 'He must have been at sea for some time?'

'Twenty years. Joined as a boy sailor, Joey did. Wouldn't look at anything else. He's been out there ever since. On the ships. Forgotten more about the sea than some of these conscripts will ever learn, that's what our Joey said on his last leave. That's got to count for something, hasn't it, sir? That an' placing your trust in the Lord.'

She looked appealingly at Jack. And he understood. She was seeking reassurance that, in the event of enemy action, her Joey had a better chance than most. He wished he could give it to her, but he suspected that survival in this war would, as in the last, be based more on luck than experience.

Carey Meeks said abruptly: 'No point in trusting what don't exist. I gave up religion five years ago,' he informed Jack. He made it sound as if he'd signed some kind of Theological Pledge.

'Don't be silly, Carey. You ain't a heathen.'

'Didn't say I was. But if you had any sense, girl, you'd see how daft it is. If everyone who dies goes to Heaven or Hell, that means they must be fair choked with all them cavemen and Ancient Britons and Romans and the like. I ask you, sir. Would you want to be sitting on some cloud sharing a harp with a smelly savage dressed in a mammoth waistcoat?'

'Carey! That's blasphemy!'

Stamford decided it was time to drag this conversation back to normality. 'Do you have any other children, Mrs Meeks?'

'Yes,' she said.

'No,' said Carey.

Their eyes locked. Jack was struck by their resemblance to each other. The grey hair, with a light sprinkling of the original pale brown; the bright brown eyes; the thin faces with their sharp noses; they were almost interchangeable. But Carey Meeks's face was

JUNCTION CUT

already sagging into lines of defeat. Irene, on the other hand, reminded him of Eileen O'Day; they shared the whippet thinness over a core of steel that was characteristic of most of the women in this area. Unemployment, drunken husbands, too many births, too many mouths to feed, world wars – nothing defeated them; they'd grit their teeth and get on with life, holding their families together no matter what life might throw at them.

Irene looked away first. 'Children are a worry, ain't they, sir? Have you got any?'

'A daughter.' At least, he prayed he still had. They'd bombed Rotterdam. He'd dictated a telegram to Neelie then spent the weekend trying to reach his father-in-law's house by telephone. The first calls had gone unanswered, according to the operator. Finally, she'd informed him all lines were unavailable.

Mentally shaking off the panic that was screaming at him to do *something*, *anything*, when logic said there was nothing he could do, he told the Meekses why he'd come.

They received the news of Kavanagh's death with conventional murmurs of regret. And then waited.

'It means that we're reviewing the evidence again.'

A puzzled look appeared on Irene's face. 'You mean Billy never did it, sir?'

'No, I don't mean that. The police charges against Mr Zimmermann still stand. But someone else will have to present – er, explain – the evidence to the Court when he comes to trial. So I'd like to go over it again.

Just to be absolutely certain there are no mistakes. If you don't mind?'

The Meekses didn't mind. Unfortunately, they had nothing to add to what was already in their statements. It was nearly four months ago. The details of that day, which had been just like any other Saturday until the moment Edie Yeovil walked into The Hayman, were already becoming blurred. Irene had seen Valerie in the back yard that morning, but couldn't remember whether she'd seen Billy Zimmermann or not.

'You sort of see people only you don't when you know them. If you know what I mean, sir?'

Jack did. It was one of the reasons witnesses' statements so often contradicted each other.

Carey was sure he hadn't seen either of them.

'You were both home by six o'clock?' He looked at Carey but Irene answered him.

'That's right. Carey come in just before six.'

'And neither of you heard or saw anything unusual?'

They looked despairingly at each other. 'I don't think so,' Irene finally said. 'Like I said, it were just like other days.'

Jack sought for something ordinary, some detail that would take her back to that particular Saturday. 'What did you cook?'

Irene answered immediately. 'Liver and onions. An' baked jam roll. I always do a tea I can put in the oven on Saturdays, so's I can use the pans on top for the water.'

'For our baths,' Carey said.

Irene shifted uncomfortably.

Jack caught Sarah's eye. He lifted an eyebrow in Irene's direction. Sarah took the initiative.

'You had your baths before tea?'

'Irene has hers before I come in,' Carey explained. 'Then she heats me up some water and I get in soon as I get home. While she gets the tea on.'

Now she'd got past the embarrassing subject of baths, Irene felt able to talk freely again. Without Jack asking, she volunteered the information that they'd finished washing up about quarter past seven and walked round to The Hayman.

'Gus stood us drinks. He'd had a big win.'

Carey coughed warningly.

'And you didn't see anyone going into the Yeovils' house, between, say, five and seven o'clock?'

The pathologist's report had put Valerie's death between six and seven, but it was possible the murderer had entered the house earlier.

Both shook their heads. 'I were in the house,' Irene said. 'Except for when I went to get the bath from the yard. And that was earlier. About half-four. After that I was in the house. And I had the blackout up.'

'Tell me about Valerie. What sort of girl was she?'

The Meekses didn't know. Irene eventually suggested she was 'just ordinary'.

'How long have they lived here?'

'About six years, ain't it, Carey? They moved here when Ronnie started work.' She leant forward slightly towards Sarah. 'Got ever such a good job, Ronnie has. Insurance office. Proper pension and everything.'

'Not now he ain't,' Carey muttered under his breath. 'He's been called up,' he explained to Jack. 'A few weeks ago. They gave him a bit of grace on account of his sister but he 'ad to go in the end.' Unconsciously echoing Edie's own thoughts, he said, 'Don't know which his mum thought was worse – her Ronnie wanting to get married or joining the Army.'

'Isn't his fiancée a nice girl, then?' Sarah asked.

'Oh, yes! She's ever such a lovely spoken young lady, ain't she, Carey? She's one of them Nettles girls.' Seeing Jack's blank look, Irene prompted, 'You know, sir. They got the ironmongery shops.'

Jack did know. The blue and white striped awnings of the Nettles ironmongery emporiums were a familiar sight in the Kentish Town-Gospel Oak areas.

'But Mrs Yeovil dislikes her?'

'Well, sir, the fact is I don't think Edie would have liked any girl that Ronnie wanted to wed, them being close like.'

'Was Mrs Yeovil close to Valerie?'

The question made Irene uneasy. She made a pretence of collecting up cups, stacking and rattling china on the tray painted with a view of Madeira. It was Carey who finally answered.

'I reckon she'd rather it had been just her and Ronnie.'

Irene looked anxiously at Jack. 'She weren't unkind

to Val or nothing. It's just . . . well, some mothers ain't close to their daughters.'

'And some are a blessed sight *too* close,' Carey muttered under his breath.

Irene stood up. 'Bring that teapot along, Carey,' she ordered. 'Unless the lady and gentleman would like another cup?'

They both declined. 'We won't keep you any longer, Mrs Meeks. Do you know when we will find Mrs Yeovil at home?'

'She works Mondays, Wednesdays and Fridays. And half-day Saturdays. Drat!' Irene finished. This last remark was directed at the hall wall. A thin, enquiring wail was rising in pitch behind it. 'He's woken up.' She marched off down the hall, the slightly oversized man's slippers she was wearing flapping noisily against the lino.

Carey unlocked the front door. The gouges of fresh wood where the huge bolt had been fitted were still visible against the brown paintwork.

'Shall I tell Edie you called, sir?'

'Yes, please do.' He would anyway, Jack knew. 'And tell her it's nothing to worry about. Just routine.'

'Was the Yeovils' drying rack lashed up like that?' Jack asked as soon as the Meekses' door was closed.

'It was much lower. About . . .' Sarah indicated a spot about six inches above her head.

'And Valerie's slip was on it?'

'Yes. The same pattern as her underwear. I mean, I thought it was odd. She had her dress on. I can't see

53

why the murderer would re-dress her, can you?'

'What did Inspector Kavanagh say when you pointed it out?'

'That she'd probably washed it herself.'

'Was it wet?'

'I don't know. I didn't feel it.'

Jack mentally scanned the report he'd read. 'The rest of her underwear was scattered over the kitchen floor?'

'Yes. And her shoes. He wouldn't have taken her dress and slip off, then put the dress on again would he?' Sarah reiterated.

'No. But he might have let her.' Jack looked into his sergeant's enquiring face. 'If she'd managed to pretend she welcomed what he was going to do, enjoyed it even, he might have let her take her own clothes off. Perhaps she hung the dress and slip over the drying rack.'

'And put the dress back on again afterwards?'

Jack had been standing with his hands in his pockets, pretending he hadn't noticed the growing band of window-washers and potato peelers on the pavement. He caught the incredulous note in Sarah's voice and flicked his glance sideways at her. 'On my first beat I got called to a house fire. Tenement place. When I reached it the lower floors were well ablaze but the upper ones were relatively untouched. There was a woman at one of the windows. We leant a ladder across to her from a neighbouring building, it was only about a three foot gap, and told her to crawl across. Do you think she would?'

'Obviously not.'

'Why obviously?'

'Well, you wouldn't be telling me this story otherwise, sir. Would you?'

Jack grinned.

'Rule number one of being an effective officer, Sergeant. Don't spoil your superior's punch-lines.'

'Yes, sir. So what happened?'

'Eventually I had to crawl across the ladder myself. Know why she wouldn't budge? Her husband had taken the only dress she possessed so she couldn't leave the house whilst he was at work. And she'd decided she'd rather burn to death than be seen outside in her knickers.'

'So what you're saying is that even rape victims can be modest?'

He was glad of her quick understanding. 'Exactly. She waited until he was relaxed, feeling pleased with himself. Then she slipped her dress on and made a run for it.'

'It would take a lot of self-control on her part, wouldn't it? Keeping up the pretence.'

'Yes, it would. I think we need to find out more about Valerie.' Jack considered the street. Given the occupants' obvious interest in the comings and goings at their neighbours' houses, it was hard to believe no one had seen anything out of place that evening. 'Do you know how long number seven has been empty?' he asked.

'No, sir. But I'll find out.'

A tug at his jacket attracted his attention. Queenie peered up at him. 'Please, mister. If yer giv us sixpence, I'll tell yer about the murderer.' Her eyes screwed into narrow slits, Queenie hissed, in a fair imitation of her mother's voice: ' 'E 'ad dreadful staring eyes. It fair givs me the shivers when I fink of them eyes boring into me.'

'Another informed source,' Sarah said.

Jack bent over her. 'Sorry, Queenie. But that's not an exclusive.'

She frowned, wrestling with this unknown word.

'It's been in the papers before,' he explained. 'What I really need to know is something nobody else has found out.'

'Oh,' Queenie lowered her hand. Her mouth drooped with disappointment.

'How old are you, Queenie?'

'Six.'

'Why aren't you at school?'

' 'Ad the chicken pox.' Reasoning that she wasn't going to get sixpence for this piece of information, she wheeled round on her bare soles and scampered back to her mother.

They left Junction Cut aware of a dozen pairs of eyes burning the back of their necks. They were stopped by a loud yell.

'Mister, wait!'

Queenie flew down Kentish Town Road, her fair hair, scooped into bunches, streaming out like swan's wings in the sunlight. She arrived at their sides with

JUNCTION CUT

a panting gasp and garbled out: 'It was the night Billy done it. 'E went then.'

'Who did?'

Queenie sighed audibly at this example of grown-up stupidity. 'Mr Jolly,' she explained. 'Him that lived at number seven. He went away on the night that the Hun done it.' She jerked one finger across her throat in an expressive movement. 'He just disappeared, wivout a word to a living soul. An' me mum says it was bleedin' selfish, 'cos if he'd 'ave said he was going, we could 'ave had the coal out the shed 'stead of that grabbing rent collector.' She finished on a triumphant intake of breath and extended an expectant hand.

Jack felt in his pocket and found a shilling. 'That's two sixpences,' he informed her. 'So you owe me another bit of information.'

Her voice floated back to them as she ran back towards The Cut. 'I'll fink of something, mister.'

Jack turned back to his new sergeant. 'Find out all you can about Mr Jolly.'

Chapter 4

Lily Hendry received the news that the police were taking an interest in that Saturday again with alarm, although she was careful to hide her feelings behind an expression of bored disinterest.

'Waste of time,' she said with a shrug when Irene told them. 'Ain't they got enough crimes to go round now?'

'The policeman said it was just routine,' Irene replied. 'That other one, the ... you know.' Her left hand clasped an imaginary glass and rocked it in front of her lips. 'He's dead. So this new one has to go over everything that we said again.'

'Does *she* know?' Lily's head jerked in the general direction of number four. The movement set the single cabbage rose on her cream straw hat dancing and swaying.

'I knocked about seven, but I couldn't get no answer. I'm sure she's in there though. I could hear her shifting the furniture about.'

'Yeah, well.' Another lift of Lily's shoulders was answered by an understanding nod from Irene. Edie Yeovil had always been a bit odd, even before the murder.

'Cup of tea?' Irene suggested.

Lily looked through into the hall passage. Gus was absorbed in examining the makeshift air-raid shelter that Carey had rigged up in the cupboard below the stairs.

'Go on then. I could do with taking the weight off me feet. They're killing me. The train was packed with soldiers. Thought I'd have to stand all the way from Cambridge but this corporal give me his seat. Gus had to make do with the corridor though.' She gave a private giggle. 'He thought Gus was me dad.'

Irene laid out cups, milk jug and a plate of biscuits. 'Used up our week's sugar ration in me baking. All right without?'

'Carry me own.' Lily produced a flat blue tin from her bag and extracted two sugar lumps. 'Have one on me.'

'Thanks, Lil. I'll pay you back, soon as I've been up the Colonial Stores. How did you get on today? Is this pub the one?'

'No, it ain't. Pond's in the wrong place.'

'But, Lil, surely a pond don't matter that much?'

'It does to Gus,' she said bitterly. 'I can't believe it. Rene. Three and half months since he won that money, and we're still stuck in two rooms in this dump. No offence.'

'None taken. Me and Carey would much rather be in a nice little place of our own somewhere 'stead of paying rent to Mr Bowler. It seems funny Gus can't find a pub he fancies. What's wrong with them all?'

'Nothing, except they ain't the one his parents had.'
'Beg pardon?'

Lily extended her cup. 'His parents used to have a pub in the country somewhere. The daft thing is, he can't even remember where it was, but he's got to have one just like it. Same building, same village street, same duck pond – same bleeding everything!'

'Why?'

Lily checked that the two men were still safely engrossed in their inspection of the stair cupboard. She lowered her voice slightly. 'Last place he was happy, I reckon. His parents died when he was eight and an aunt and uncle in Muswell Hill took him in.'

'That was good of them.'

Lily made a derisory face. 'Had him working in their shop for years. No pay, just keep. And he had to look after them when they took poorly themselves.' Her voice dropped even lower. 'They got really stinky towards the end. You know, couldn't hold it. Gus had to do everything for them. Like they were a couple of babies. And then do you know what they went and did?'

Irene shook her head mutely.

'Never left him a brass farthing. Shop, money, everything, went to some cousin in Scotland.'

'No!'

'God's truth. Gus ended up on the street with just the clothes he stood up in.'

'Well, aren't some people wicked?'

'Who's wicked?' Carey asked, returning to the kitchen.

Lily's foot tapped Irene's shin warningly under the table. 'The Germans,' Irene said, reasoning that nobody was going to argue with that statement.

'Are you ready, Gus?' Lily asked. 'We'd better get Gussie to bed. Thanks for minding him, Irene.'

Back at number two she left Gus to settle the baby in his cot whilst she turned her attention to her shoes. They were brown suede with a smooth kid-leather lining. At the moment the high heels were smothered in dried cow dung interspersed with tiny pieces of chopped hay and around the edges of the soles the wetness had stained an uneven black speckled with green flecks that she suspected were goose shit. She'd bought them on that heady day when Gus had escorted her up West to celebrate his win. There had been these shoes and the matching bag for her, a new shirt for him, and a painted wooden train for little Gussie. And afterwards they'd had tea at The Ritz where a snooty waiter had looked down his nose at Gus's brown shoes. And that had been the last and only good that she'd got from Gus's windfall.

'Bleedin' country,' she muttered under her breath, using the corner of the towel to scrub ineffectively at the mess.

'What?' Gus said over his shoulder.

'Nothing.'

It wasn't, she thought furiously, as if he'd need to spend all his precious money on a flat. You could pick up a short lease on a really cosy place for a song now that the bolters had all deserted to the country. And there'd still be enough left for the pub if he ever found it. But he wouldn't have it. What didn't go into the pub was staying in the Post Office as savings for a rainy day.

'Blimey, Gus,' she'd protested. 'If it ever rains that hard, we won't need a pub. We'll need an ark!'

But he'd remained stubbornly unconvinced and in sole possession of the savings book: each Friday her housekeeping money and the rent was withdrawn and jealously handed over and the dwindling total column fretted over. He was already talking about getting another job so they wouldn't have to touch the savings at all.

Giving up on the shoes, she padded into the kitchen. Unclasping her handbag, she removed the contents and carefully peeled back a section of the suede lining revealing a small rectangular section cut into the base. One scarlet nail probed the tissue-paper packing and gently levered out the contents. Holding a corner of the white paper, she allowed it to unroll until an oval brooch, its design a filigree of gold petals, dropped into the palm of her hand. Taking it between her thumb and forefinger, she held it to the naked kitchen bulb and allowed the yellowing light to play through the green stone at its centre. Even in the dim wattage of the kitchen light, the fire inside flashed with a breath-catching radiance.

Gus surged into the kitchen. From habit she quickly dropped the brooch back into the bag although it was a pointless gesture when he not only knew of its existence, but had actually pawned it to finance his winning flutter with Oggie.

'Anything to eat?'

'There's some sausages if you want to put 'em under the gas. I'm going to bed.'

'I'm not hungry,' he replied. 'I'll come with you.'

From any other bloke she'd have taken that as an invitation to sex, but she knew better when it came from Gus. Lying next to him in the darkness, listening to his wheezing, Lily tried to fight against the natural dip in the centre of the bed that would tip her body against his. She couldn't have explained why she did it. If she'd launched herself at him stark naked, he wouldn't have done much beyond turn over and wish her good night. So when his hand found hers beneath the blanket, she tensed with surprise.

'Lily? You awake?'

She lay still, faking sleep. 'Lily?'

'What, Gus?'

'I'm sorry. About the pub. But it's got to be right. You do understand, don't you love?'

'Yes. I understand.'

Gus squeezed her fingers, then turned away.

'Trouble is,' Lily said, displaying a rare burst of insight, 'we can't get a train to where you want, Gus. It ain't just forty miles up the line. It's forty years in the past.'

She waited for him to argue, but his only response was a deep, asthmatic snore. In the distance the lonely wail of a train whistle moaned into the night. Lily felt a pang of wistfulness. Trains meant work. Sundays changing at Crewe Junction on her way to the next variety theatre and the next stage-hand, musician or box-office manager who was prepared to provide bed and board for a week or two.

Twisting uncomfortably in the double bed, Lily considered the past seventeen months and wondered how things would have turned out if she hadn't got herself pregnant.

The abortionist had been blunt: 'You're more than five months gone. Why didn't you come earlier, you daft cow?'

Because she hadn't known, was the simple answer to that one.

'No sickness?' the woman had demanded.

Lily shook her head. 'And me monthlies was regular. And I weren't putting on weight.'

'Happens like that sometimes,' the woman had said. 'Well, I ain't touching you. It's too dangerous.'

'But I can't have a kid! I'm a dancer. Who's going to employ a dancer with a belly that sticks out further than her tits?'

The woman had looked at her thoughtfully. 'No bloke?'

'No. Not a regular one.'

'Take my advice then. Get yourself one. There's always one soft enough to take on another man's kid. Doesn't have to be for long. Leave the kid with him and take off if you don't fancy him.'

A week later she was living with Augustus Hendry.

Her foot brushed Gus's. Balancing on the furthest edge of the mattress, the hard seam digging into the small of her back, she tried to remember when the plan had started to go wrong.

He'd insisted on marriage for a start. Then she'd felt wretchedly ill for months after little Gussie's birth. Gus had uncomplainingly looked after the baby and her; washing, ironing and cooking without protest.

At first she'd hated the baby. He was no more than a smelly, noisy bundle who'd ruined her looks, trapped her in this miserable lodging and who gnawed at her already sore breasts until she wanted to throw him across the room and scream out her pain and frustration.

Gradually, however, as her looks returned, little Gussie had started to sit up and pull at her hair and clothes. The deepening love that she'd felt for him had taken her by surprise. She'd never cared for anyone before. Sometimes she almost hated him for making her love him. It was no longer a case of picking up her cases and going. Whatever the future held now, it had to include her son. And the only home she could give him at present was with this man, twenty-one years older than her, who was so pathetically grateful to her for giving him a family and so disastrously incapable of increasing it.

Gus was snoring gently. The low buzz acted as a counterpoint to the raised voices filtering through the brickwork from number four. Sounds like Madam Toffee-nose is entertaining her future daughter-in-law, was Lily's last thought as she drifted into sleep.

'Entertaining' was not perhaps the right word for the past few hours at number four.

Edie had spent a week agonizing over the meal. During the course of Ronnie's engagement, she had managed to limit Phyllis's visits to the afternoon. In that way, she'd been able to entertain her in the front parlour. But dinner was different. She knew that what Phyllis meant by dinner was not the midday meal but a cooked tea. By no stretch of the imagination could she see herself serving up shepherd's pie and boiled cabbage to her son's fiancée on the scrubbed wooden table in the kitchen, with its shelves of pots and pans and its uninterrupted view of the stone scullery sink.

All her life Edie had struggled against appearing common. Even when she'd been reduced to one room in Warden Road and handouts from the Assistance Board, she'd always been careful to keep her neighbours at arm's length, keeping the docile Ronnie and the increasingly rebellious Valerie shut in instead of allowing them to play in the street with the other children. 'Wait until we have a proper house again,' she'd urged. 'Where you can make nice friends. People more like us.'

Well, Ronnie had, hadn't he? Everyone said what a nice girl Phyllis was. And you certainly couldn't accuse her of being common. She never said 'fink' or 'gonna' when she meant 'think' and 'going to'. And such a respectable job too. Personal secretary to a solicitor.

Her family had even put an engagement notice in the *Telegraph*. It was almost as good as announcing it in *The Times*.

'No, indeed, you wouldn't find her up against a wall behind the Palace on a Saturday night,' Edie muttered, collecting up an armful of tins from the larder cupboard. A check on the collection of empty cocoa, tea and custard tins that acted as her 'bank' had told her what she already knew – that the only money she had in the world was precisely fifteen shillings and fourpence. A series of embarrassing trips to a pawnbroker in Holborn had raised enough money to buy a second-hand lace table cloth, two soup dishes that almost matched two dinner plates in her own cupboard, two wine glasses and a slightly chipped crystal vase. A bottle of claret and some beef, which the butcher had let her have from under the counter without taking any of her meat coupons, had completed her preparation for a 'proper' dinner party.

Her plans had started to go wrong almost immediately. With the dinner simmering, she'd manhandled the sofa in the parlour against the wall with the intention of putting the kitchen table in its place, only to find that the table wouldn't go through the door. With mounting irritation she'd been forced to drag it back down the corridor, leaving black tell-tale streaks all along the hall lino, and lay it up in the kitchen. The pots and pans had been hastily pushed out of sight in the parlour, but not even the bunch of late tulips she'd arranged in the crystal vase could compensate, in her opinion, for the dreadful sight of the scullery sink with its brown-stained wall where lime-hardened water had dripped for twenty years from a badly fitting pipe joint.

The evening had continued to go downhill from that moment. Phyllis had worn what, in Edie's opinion, was an indecently low-cut dress, considering the whole family was still supposed to be in mourning for Valerie.

On seeing the table she exclaimed: 'Oh, you shouldn't have gone to all this trouble for me.' Thereby implying that Edie didn't normally dine in this style. And she'd refused all but the smallest sip of the claret.

A worry started to niggle at the back of Edie's mind that perhaps she'd bought the wrong wine. She took a mouthful, and then another. It tasted strange to her, but then she didn't normally drink. And the man in the shop had assured her that several of the big houses in Adelaide Road had a regular order for this particular brand.

Conversation was stilted – a difficult minefield for both of them, where neither of them wanted to stray into dangerous subjects which might stir up unexpressed resentments. Phyllis took one false step when she let slip that she'd had a letter from Ronnie and then added, 'I'm sure he'll be in touch with you soon.'

'He doesn't need to write to me every week. I'm sure he's got more important things to do than write to his mother.' But, Edie's resentful tone said, I can't imagine what they could be. She finished her glass and refilled it again. Once you got used to it the taste of claret was really quite pleasant.

When they reached the beef, Phyllis offered a share of her meat coupons. Which, Edie was sure, wasn't done in the best households.

'Certainly not. I hope I know how to entertain my guests properly.'

She hadn't meant to say that, but once the words were out she saw a slight flush staining Phyllis's cheeks, and guessed she was thinking of that disastrous Saturday evening at her parents' house. Edie felt a small thrill of triumph, much like a fencer who had scored the first tentative hit on his opponent.

Swallowing another mouthful of claret, Edie watched her quarry carefully, wondering where else to probe for a weakness.

'There's a reason I wanted to see you this evening,' Phyllis said.

'Good heavens, you mean you didn't just come for the pleasure of my company? Well hie never.' Edie was using what her children would have called her 'shop voice'. A slightly too high-pitched tone with an excess of aitches that she normally reserved for the customers in Daniel's corsetry department.

She gulped more wine. She was beginning to feel quite bold. Not tongue-tied or shy at all.

Phyllis opened her handbag and extracted a letter.

'What's that?' Edie said suspiciously, as Phyllis slid it across the table.

'It's Ronnie's letter. Please read it.'

'I'd rather not, thank you.'

'Please do. There's nothing in it you shouldn't see. In fact, he's had an idea. And he asked me to talk to you about it.'

Edie continued to regard the crumpled envelope as if she suspected it of containing bubonic plague. Eventually Phyllis said: 'He was going to arrange for his paybook to be transferred to me after the marriage. But he thinks – in fact, we both do – that it would be better if you kept the money.'

'Why?' Her heart started beating faster. Paybooks went to next of kin, didn't they? Did that mean Phyllis was resigning the position already? Well, she'd always known the engagement wouldn't last.

A spark glittered in Phyllis's brown eyes. She wasn't an attractive woman, her long-jawed face tended to look more interesting in photographs than in reality. 'Because,' she said, keeping her voice steady, 'Ronnie feels you must be finding it difficult to manage without his wages. Particularly since your husband's insurance policy ceased paying out last year.'

'Who told you about that?' Edie's voice had lost its pretensions.

'Ronnie, of course. We discussed it. Naturally he was concerned that you shouldn't be in financial difficulties when he left home.'

'I'm not in any difficulty, thank you.' Edie pushed the letter back abruptly. A folded corner caught on the lace and jerked the cloth, setting the vase swaying.

Phyllis caught it. 'For goodness' sake, don't be so

silly! I don't need the money. I can manage very well on my wages from the solicitor's office, particularly since Mummy and Daddy have been so generous in helping us with the flat.'

'I should think they would have been. I mean,' Edie gave a shrill laugh, 'they've had plenty of time to save up for your nest egg. It must have been a positive clutch by this time.'

'What!'

'Well, dear, you can't deny most girls marry rather earlier than twenty-eight. I expect your parents were beginning to think you'd never leave.'

Phyllis opened her mouth and closed it again. Her front teeth gripped her bottom lip in an effort to stop it trembling. She attempted to treat the remark as a joke.

'I expect you're right. But then, I was lucky. If I hadn't waited, I would never have met Ronnie.'

'Pity you ever did. Still, I'll say no more on that subject.'

'I think perhaps you should, don't you? You've never made any secret of the fact you dislike me. The least you could do is tell me why.'

Edie was surprised by this direct challenge; but she was also exhilarated. Phyllis wanted a fight. She could have it. 'Oh dear, surely that's obvious? I mean, of course, you can't expect a boy of Ronnie's age to see when he's being made a fool of. No indeed. But, well, we know, don't we?' The shrill giggle at the end of this sentence sounded strange even to Edie.

'Know what?' Phyllis waited.

Edie decided to clear up the table. She was sick of this dinner party. She wanted Phyllis to go.

Phyllis persisted: 'Know what?'

Edie dropped the plates with a clatter. 'That you only got engaged to him because you were desperate. You weren't likely to find another man, were you? Not at your age and with your looks. Not that you didn't keep him dangling on for long enough, hoping that you might. One week you're walking out with him, and the next it's all excuses about extra work and family commitments and heavens knows what, and the next you're back. Well, you may have fooled Ronnie, but you don't fool *me*.'

Phyllis stood up. 'I think I'd better go now, it's getting rather late.'

'You do that.' Edie sensed that she was winning even though she wasn't entirely sure what the object of the battle was.

Phyllis walked quickly to the front door. Edie galloped after her. It was *her* house. *She* was going to open the door. Thrusting Phyllis aside, she struggled with the stiff bolts. The slippery metal knobs kept sliding from her fingers. After several attempts, she leant against the wall and allowed Phyllis to open up and step into the street.

Despite the late hour, it wasn't completely dark. The deep purple of the eastern sky shaded to a pale lilac in the west. A few strands of cloud, like pale grey silk scarves, drifted across the horizon, reflecting the gold of the setting sun in the molten ribbons around their outlines. A yell, followed by the thwack of a ball against orange-box wood, indicated that several of The Cut's children were being allowed to take advantage of the extended daylight hours.

Edie leant against the door jamb and watched Phyllis clip crisply away in the direction of Fortress Road. 'Yes, that's right. Run away.' She recalled the reason she hadn't been at home to protect Valerie that afternoon. 'You know you've got a death on your conscience, don't you?'

Phyllis half-turned. Even in the dim light, Edie could see her face had lost all its colour. Her lips parted, whispering something that was almost inaudible, then she turned and ran.

Edie laughed, excited at the way she'd sent Phyllis scuttling for cover. She attempted to follow the younger woman, but found that the street seemed to be rippling up and down in a strange manner, rather like a sheet shaken prior to folding. She'd have to make do with a parting insult instead. Drawing in a deep breath, she recalled every swear word she'd ever heard, opened her mouth – and let out a belch that could have rattled the windows in Whitehall.

There were hoots of delight from the cricket-players. Holding on to the door knocker for support, Edie peered blearily at them. She tried to tell them to go away and play outside their own houses. Instead of words, a series of violent hiccups burst from her mouth. A couple of the older boys imitated her, hiccupping and belching with enthusiasm. Tears started to run down Edie's cheeks. She'd never forgive Phyllis. Never. She was responsible for the worst thing that had ever happened to her in her life: she, Edie Yeovil, had become common.

Nothing Phyllis could do in the future, or had done in the past, Edie decided, cannoning uncertainly from one hall wall to the other as she negotiated her way back to the kitchen, could be as wicked as what she'd done this evening.

The last image of Phyllis's horrified face swam shakily before Edie's eyes again. What was it she'd said? 'How did you know?' How do I know what? Edie wondered, groping her way to the sink.

Chapter 5

Tuesday 14 May
Jack Stamford's initial plan to visit Edie on Tuesday was frustrated by a summons to New Scotland Yard. The rapidly deteriorating situation in Holland and Belgium had led to an urgent review of police contingency plans in the event of a full-scale invasion – a prospect that was becoming daily more likely.

At the end of a series of meetings where the moods had varied between reckless defiance and unspoken relief that at last something was happening, Dunn caught up with Jack in a corridor and asked him back to his office.

'How are you getting on?' he demanded, as soon as they were once again established on opposite sides of the mahogany desk.

'I've hardly had a chance to do more than review the initial statements and reports yet, sir.'

Dunn cleared his throat noisily. 'Hmmm. There has been a suggestion, in certain quarters . . .'

'The Assistant Commissioner thinks . . .' Jack interpreted silently.

' . . . that in view of the present political situation, we shouldn't bother too much with this Zimmermann fellow. Just let the case stand as it is.'

'You mean, since his countrymen may be arriving by parachute at any minute to break him out of jail, there's little point in my finding out whether he deserved to be in there in the first place?'

'Yes. That is an increasingly prevalent viewpoint.'

'Is it yours, sir?'

'No!' Dunn slammed one hand down on the desk. The brass inkstand and pen holder, presented for twenty-five years loyal service, wobbled dangerously. 'No, Jack. We have to assume we're going to win.'

Stamford recalled stories he'd heard about Dunn. Hadn't there been a couple of brothers who'd died in gas attacks in Flanders in the last war?

'We go on with this investigation, Jack, until stormtroopers are marching up Whitehall. Luckily,' he added unconsciously confirming Jack's suspicions regarding the AC, 'the Chief Constable agrees with me. That's one advantage of having a barrister in the job. He regards the upholding of the law as our prime objective.'

'Rather a novelty in the police force,' Stamford murmured.

Dunn chose to ignore the irony. Visibly making an effort to relax, he said: 'Have you heard from your wife?'

'No.' There had been no response to his telegram.

His reluctance to discuss the matter communicated itself to Dunn, who changed the subject again. 'How's the girl getting on?'

It took Jack a few moments to realize that he meant

Sarah McNeill. 'Fine. She's following up some leads for me at the moment. Possible missing witness.'

'Had a bit of a problem with that appointment, you know. All right using girls on the investigations, of course. I mean, obligatory on juveniles and rape cases. But second in charge on a murder investigation – ruffled a few feathers that. Still I managed to square it. Wartime and all that. Extraordinary conditions. Got to let the women see we appreciate their efforts.'

'I'm sure Sergeant McNeill is grateful for your interest, sir,' Jack murmured. He had a sudden vision of Sarah's cool blue eyes and straight expression and was glad that Dunn hadn't said any of that to his new sergeant – entertaining as the outcome might have been.

He left to discover whether his unwittingly patronized sergeant had managed to make some progress in tracing the elusive Mr James Jolly, the missing tenant of number seven Junction Cut.

Sarah was feeling naked. After years of being on duty in a heavy navy-blue jacket and skirt with attendant heavy shoes and a helmet that must have been designed by a man, she was becoming uncomfortably aware that the uniform had, to a large extent, been a sort of disguise. Once inside it, the real Sarah McNeill disappeared and was replaced by WPS McNeill, attested representative of the Metropolitan Police Force.

Today she was on duty in her own clothes and was

beginning to find the effect disconcerting. She'd selected a pale grey suit with a long jacket and a slim skirt that ended in kick pleats in order to give herself freedom of movement, and a short-sleeved linen blouse with a white background sprigged in a tiny pattern of pale mauve violets. Her thick, naturally wavy hair she'd left loose, but held off her face with a couple of tortoiseshell combs. Finally she slipped her feet gratefully into a pair of plain grey court shoes and kicked the hated boots under the bed.

The effect, she thought, observing her reflection in the passing shop windows, was one of cool businesslike efficiency. She found out it wasn't quite what she'd hoped for when she walked across the rear yard at Agar Street and was greeted by a shrill wolf whistle.

Without appearing to, Sarah's blue eyes swept the yard whilst she continued to walk towards the rear doors of the station. There were several uniformed constables standing around, plus a couple of civilians wearing Civil Rescue armbands, and a burly man in a long drab sandy coloured coat and cap who appeared to be making some kind of delivery to the station canteen. They were all keeping their faces studiously straight, although the youngest constable was obviously having more trouble than most.

'One I owe you, Dave,' she muttered under her breath. Pushing open the rear doors, she made her way to the CID office and found Stamford's message explaining his summons to Scotland Yard and asking her to follow up on the Jolly enquiry. 'It shouldn't be

JUNCTION CUT

too difficult to find the rent collector', he'd written as a final PS.

Sarah had tended to agree with him until she found out who the rent collector was. 'Monk?' she repeated. '*Felonious* Monk?'

'Oh I couldn't say,' Minnie White shook her head. She looked vaguely aggrieved that there was something about Junction Cut she didn't know. 'We always call him Mr Monk. Well, you would, wouldn't you?' She didn't explain, but Sarah instinctively understood, that rent collectors were on a footing with doctors' receptionists and bus inspectors; not really important themselves, but representing authority, so not to be called by their first names.

'Small thin man,' Sarah prompted. 'About fifty.' She nearly added that he normally looked like a ferret that had been caught down someone else's rabbit hole, but thought better of it.

'That's right. That's him.'

Sarah made some rapid calculations, trying to remember when Felonious had last been enjoying His Majesty's hospitality. 'How long has he been collecting the rents?'

Minnie folded her arms and leant against the open door. Her brow furrowed. 'Must be nine or ten months now. Back of last summer sometime he started.'

'So he was here in January?'

'Oh, yes.' Minnie's eyes lit up. 'Do you think he saw something to do with the murder?'

'I don't know. Do you think he did?'

Minnie thought about it for a few minutes, then reluctantly admitted that she thought he hadn't. Otherwise, it stood to reason, she'd have prised it out of him by now. She could, however, provide an address for him, directing Sarah to Leighton Road.

Sarah turned the corner by The Assembly House pub just in time to see a familiar figure emerge from a two-up, two-down terraced house near the Post Office. The narrow head flicked from side to side in a movement that was obviously habitual. Sarah saw it freeze on the third flick, leaving the thin nose pointed firmly in her direction. She stopped. Felonious spun on his toes in the opposite direction and began walking quickly away from her.

Halfway down Leighton Road he suddenly dived across the street and disappeared down Bartholomew Road. If Sarah hadn't been watching him closely, she'd have missed the fast sideways scuttle and lost him altogether. Quickening her pace, she wove round a terrier that was straining and yapping at its lead, and hurried into the entrance to Bartholomew. If he'd gone into one of the houses already she'd have no choice but to retrace her steps to the house and wait for him to return. Which, on Felonious's previous form, could take several days if he thought the police wanted his assistance with their enquiries.

To her relief she spotted him again, his thin upright figure keeping exact pace with a young woman wheeling a pram. His head was bent slightly towards the woman's, suggesting he was listening to something she had to say. The whole picture was that of an attentive father walking his missus and their latest addition in the spring sunshine.

Sarah stepped out smartly. Felonious risked a quick glance over his shoulder and saw her gaining on him. Abandoning his newly acquired family, he increased his pace to a trot and turned into Gaisford Street, doubling back the way he'd already come. Sarah began to realize the advantage of a pair of flat shoes over high heels. Along Gaisford she managed to prevent Felonious increasing his lead but couldn't gain any ground on him. In Kentish Town Road he was forced to halt, dithering on the kerb by a sudden procession of assorted vans bearing hand-painted signs announcing they were 'Auxiliary Ambulances'. It gave Sarah the chance to get within ten yards of him before he darted out amongst the traffic and galloped into Anglers Lane. There she narrowed the gap, and was just about to collar Felonious when he gave one final twist, flicked his shoulder out of her reach and dashed through the door marked 'Men – Second Class' in the Prince of Wales Public Baths.

It was the sight of her own arm, clad in unfamiliar pale grey rather than the normal navy blue, that brought Sarah to an abrupt halt just as she was about to thrust the door open. Flopping back against the wall, she drew a couple of deep breaths and considered what to do next.

In uniform she wouldn't have hesitated to march in and demand that the attendant produce Felonious.

Even if she'd been about to apprehend the light-fingered little crook for yet another dip into an unsuspecting pocket, she'd have had no qualms about entering the men's baths in her civilian clothes. But to ask him about a rent collection? Whilst she was wrestling with the ethics of her situation, two men emerged from the door. One, his pink skin glowing and his hair still damp under his tweed cap, ran an appreciative eye over her and dropped his right eye in a suggestive wink. Straightening up with an angry glare, Sarah swung away and spotted a familiar figure pacing up Prince of Wales Road.

'Dave!'

'Morning again, Sarge.' The young constable grinned. 'Like the new uniform. Are the WPCs going to be wearing it too?'

'Sergeant McNeill to you, Constable.' Quickly she explained the situation.

'Want me to collar him?'

'No. Just go in there and let yourself be seen. I want him flushed out.'

Concealing herself in the doorway of the neighbouring pub, Sarah waited. It didn't take long. Felonious came out of the bath-house door like the ferret he so resembled and flew past her hiding place with such speed that she had no time to trip him with a well-placed ankle. The constable followed him out a second later and raised an enquiring eyebrow, obviously prepared to give chase.

Sarah shook her head. Felonious was her problem.

She didn't want Stamford thinking she was incapable of carrying out a simple questioning without uniform assistance.

He led her along the full length of Prince of Wales Road, and across Haverstock Hill, dodging and ducking amongst the streets between Haverstock and Finchley Road until he eventually emerged into Finchley Road itself. By now Sarah had discovered the trick of running in high heels. Ignoring the stares of the passers-by, she whisked and weaved amongst them, her eyes locked firmly on the back of Felonious's bobbing figure. Occasionally, he'd stop briefly, risk a quick look back, then hurtle forward in a burst of sprinting. Sarah matched him, sprint for sprint. By now she was so angry she was quite prepared to race Felonious until one of them dropped down from exhaustion.

She only spotted the drawback to her tactics when the blue and white sign of Finchley Road Station came into sight. Felonious increased his speed again and for a second she lost him amongst a crowd emerging from the underground. Cursing under her breath, Sarah rushed into the entrance hall and stopped: Felonious was nowhere to be seen.

She hesitated. If he wasn't already on a train, she might be able to pick him up on the platform. If he was, he could emerge anywhere. As she tried to make up her mind, the rumbling whine of a train leaving the station told her she was too late. She'd have to return to Leighton Road and put a watch on Felonious's digs.

Cursing and limping slightly, she started back the way she'd come. For the first time she became aware of a blister on the back of her heel. The doorway of the Sketchley Dye Works was the nearest. One half of it stood open. Hobbling into the gap, Sarah eased off her right shoe and examined the damage. A slight stirring in the blackness behind the closed half of the door caught the corner of her eye. Leaning back, the shoe still clasped in her right hand, she smiled broadly: 'Hello, Felonious.'

Once Sarah's hand was firmly clamped over his forearm, Felonious was prepared to come quietly. Assaulting the police was not his style; his usual mode of obtaining a livelihood gave them too many chances to assault him back.

'I never done it,' he protested, as she led him back up the road.

'Done what?' Sarah enquired.

She felt his inner struggle. Which particular bit of villainy was he supposed to be providing an alibi for? 'Dunno,' he said finally. 'Whatever you're arresting me for. I never done it.'

'Did I say I was arresting you?'

'No.' Felonious shot her a resentful look. 'You mean, you're not? What you chase me for then?'

'Why did you run away if you haven't done anything?'

'I always do when I see a copper on me tail,' Felonious admitted with off-handed candour. 'It's habit like. I'm going straight now, honest. I got a proper job.'

JUNCTION CUT

'I know. That's what I want to talk to you about.' Sarah steered him into a café and ordered two teas. 'I hear you collect the rents in Junction Cut?'

'Collect them on all Mr Bowler's places in that area.'

'Leo Bowler owns the houses in Junction Cut?' Sarah asked. In a way it made sense. She'd been wondering who'd be fool enough to allow Felonious to wander around with a satchel full of rents. But not even the permanently sticky-fingered Fel would dare steal anything from Leo Bowler.

For the past twenty-five years Bowler had been suspected of being at the centre of most of the villainy on the patch. Suspected but never convicted, since it was impossible to find anyone prepared to testify against him. And over the years Bowler had further consolidated his impregnable position by the judicious supporting of local charities and the insertion of his son on to the local council.

'Owns places all over,' Felonious replied, tipping his tea into the saucer and blowing gently. 'Somers Town, Holborn, Hampstead ... Some of them posh folks up near the Heath would be surprised if they knew who owned their fancy houses.'

'Do you collect up there too?'

Felonious returned the brown puddle to the cup and sipped experimentally. 'Nah. Just Kentish Town and a bit of Camden.'

'Including number seven Junction Cut?'

'It's empty.'

'But you knew the former tenant? James Jolly?'

'Wouldn't say I knew him, miserable old bugger.'

'Do you remember the day he left number seven?'

That Felonious did remember. He'd returned from an evening's drinking in The Mother Shipton to find the keys to number seven on his floor, together with a week's rent. 'No note,' he said with an aggrieved frown. 'Just the keys, back and front door, tied up with a luggage label with the address on it, and the money.'

'And that was the night of the Yeovil murder?'

'Suppose so,' he conceded. He'd had to go round to the house to see if it was in a fit state to be let again the following Monday. 'Horrible it was. Full of that real old-fashioned furniture like me gran had. Reckon it had been there as long as the house. Didn't even have a gas cooker. Just one of them old black ranges.'

'And a shed full of coal?' Sarah wasn't able to resist the remark.

Felonious scowled. 'I was entitled to something for me trouble.'

Sarah probed a bit further, but it was obvious Felonious had no idea where James Jolly had gone – or why. He did volunteer the information that Jolly had once boasted he was The Cut's longest-standing tenant. 'Fifty years he reckoned he'd been there. Proud of it he was. Shows a lack of ambition if you ask me.'

'And what's yours, Fel? To lift the Crown Jewels?'

'As a matter of fact, I did pop in to look at them

once,' he admitted, unabashed. 'Hidden them now though, ain't they? Until this lot's over.'

She left him contemplating Hitler's unfair interruption to his next career move and returned, at a slower pace, to Agar Street to write up the report for Stamford's return on Wednesday.

'I'm still asking around,' she reported as he scanned her report without comment. 'According to the neighbours Mr Jolly's wife died years ago. None of them remember her. And he had a couple of unmarried sons who were killed in the Great War. As far as they know he hadn't any other relatives. And he doesn't seem to have had any friends either. In fact, he seems to have been thoroughly misnamed. Jolly was the last thing he was.'

'Was?' Stamford repeated. 'You think Mr Jolly is no longer with us?'

It wasn't something that had occurred to Sarah. She'd used the past tense simply because he wasn't physically in Junction Cut any more. She hadn't intended to imply he was dead.

'Keep on looking,' Stamford instructed. 'If he has no family and no friends, who could he possibly have gone to visit?' He didn't seem to expect an answer. Instead he changed the subject. 'Did you call on Mrs Yeovil whilst you were in The Cut?'

'No. I thought you'd want to be there.'

'Probably best, yes. Pity it's got to be delayed again.'

'Thursday is one of her days at home,' Sarah

reminded him. 'We could see her tomorrow.'

'If we have time,' he replied, adding the neatly written pages to the Yeovil file. 'I've arranged with the prison governor to interview Billy Zimmermann tomorrow.'

Chapter 6

Thursday 16 May

Jack had always prided himself on his ability to see beneath the surface and make up his own mind on any situation. Facing Ebhardt 'Billy' Zimmermann, he realized how tenuous this image of himself was.

After months of reading and hearing about 'the Hun' he'd formed a mental picture of a Teutonic type – blond-haired, blue-eyed – with a hard rasp of Germanic accent around the edge of his words. Even the blurred newspaper photographs, taken as Zimmermann was hustled from the original Magistrates' Committal, hadn't really penetrated his preconceived picture.

But the boy facing him across the battered and scarred wooden table could have been put down in any working-class house across the Metropolitan Police area and not have looked or sounded out of place.

The prison officer left with an unnecessarily loud clashing of bolts and keys. Jack turned back to Billy. He knew from the records that Zimmermann was nineteen but he could have passed for a couple of years younger. He was a good-looking boy; his dark hair – slightly too long – flopped over a thin, high-cheek-boned face dominated by a pair of large brown eyes. His complexion had the translucent pallor that comes from spending too much time inside.

Jack said: 'You understand why we want to ask you some more questions, Mr Zimmermann?'

Billy shrugged his shoulders without raising his head. His fingers massaged the prominent wrist bones that gleamed whitely beneath his skin. Eventually he muttered: 'Don't matter.'

Jack tried again. 'I'm Detective Chief Inspector Stamford and this is Sergeant McNeill. Have you been told why we want to question you again?'

This time Billy's head twisted slightly. He directed a half glance from beneath long lashes at Sarah. 'He's dead, ain't he?' he said. 'So you gotta ask me again. About the murder.' His voice was low-pitched, not unattractive but obviously uneducated. It lacked the nasal twang of a cockney voice, but was definitely a product of London not Berlin. Jack said as much.

'I ain't never been there. Me mum and dad were German. I ain't. Born in London I was. You check. I wanted to join up and do me bit same as everyone else, but they wouldn't have me. Reckoned they couldn't pass me A1 'cos I had consumption when I was a kid. But I reckon it's 'cos they thought I'd go round shooting our side in the back or something.'

The vehemence with which Billy spat out this speech surprised Jack. The boy had straightened in his chair, gripping the sides fiercely, as if he was afraid if he didn't hang on to it he might dive across the table and assault the two police officers. The detached part of

JUNCTION CUT

Jack's mind noted that the translucent skin wasn't prison pallor but the aftermath of tuberculosis.

Billy broke the moment. Suddenly collapsing in on himself, as if someone had just pricked him with a pin, he mumbled: 'Says I'm British on me identity card, don't it?'

'I'm sorry.' Jack looked at the bent head again. Because he was still on remand, Billy was wearing his own clothes: a plain shirt and a pair of brown corduroy trousers which sagged from his waist. The white shirt, with its narrow self stripe, was too big for him. He'd left the top three buttons undone and his present posture allowed the front to fall open. As the boy wriggled in his seat, the left side dragged away even further, and Jack glimpsed the livid red and purple bruising across one rib.

'You're in a cell by yourself, aren't you?' he asked.

'Yeah.'

'Do you ever mix with the other prisoners?'

'Trustee brings me meals.'

'Is there an officer with him?'

'Yeah.'

Jack was aware of the enquiry in Sarah's eyes. Sitting to the right of him, she couldn't see the bruised chest.

Having got this far, Jack persisted: 'What about exercise periods? Don't you mix with them then?'

Billy shook his head. 'Go out after the others. Half an hour round the yard, every day.'

'By yourself?'

Billy muttered something he couldn't catch.

'I beg your pardon.'

'Warders,' Billy said. 'Two of them watch me.'

'They're called prison officers now.'

'Everyone in here calls 'em warders. Or worse.'

'Do they treat you well?'

The question earned Jack another direct stare from Billy. 'Yeah. Fine,' he said. His tongue slid over his lips, moistening the cracked flesh.

Jack realized that if he pushed this line of questioning, it was likely that he'd alienate Billy before they reached the main reason for his visit. He switched tack. 'Why do they call you Billy? Your real name's Ebhardt, isn't it? How do you get to Billy from that?'

Some of the tension eased from Billy's body. 'Started when I was a kid. Other kids started calling me Billy, after Kaiser Bill I reckon, and me mum and dad took it up. Stopped them mixing me up with me dad. He was Ebhardt Heinrich too.'

'Did Valerie call you Billy or Ebhardt?'

'Billy. Nobody calls me Ebhardt.'

'Tell me about Valerie.'

Billy's shoulders lifted and descended again. He resumed his contemplation of the wooden table. 'She was just a girl, you know?'

'No. I don't know. I never met her. In fact, I've never even seen her. Not even after she was dead. I wasn't involved in the original investigation. You tell me about her.'

'Nothing to tell.' Billy slumped even further in his

chair. Linking his fingers, he started to play some kind of cat's-cradle game with them.

Jack wasn't going to help him out this time. Instead he stretched his own legs, tilted his own chair back on two legs and contemplated the depressing decor of the interview room.

It was larger than a cell, but only because it had been built on a square rather than an oblong design. The bottom two-thirds of the walls were covered in dark green tiles whilst the top third had been lime-washed in an off-cream shade. The only light came from a fan-shaped window set high in the wall. Since its small surface was not only bisected by five heavy iron bars but also plastered with brown paper strips to prevent flying shards in the event of an air-raid, the amount of actual daylight penetrating to the floor of the room was insufficient for him to identify the colour of the floor tiles, although Jack guessed they were probably the ubiquitous dirty brown that was used in other non-secure areas of the prison. The whole room had the familiar prison aroma of stale urine and boiled cabbage.

The silence ticked by. Somewhere in the depths of the building bars clashed and clanged, to be followed by the rhythmic marching of feet clattering down a metal staircase. 'Exercise period,' Billy offered. Jack refused to be diverted. He maintained his silence.

Eventually Billy said: 'I liked Val.'

Jack swung his chair upright, faced Billy and said: 'Did she like you?'

'Yeah. Yeah, she did. She was like me, see?'

'How?'

'She didn't have nobody really. Like me.'

'She had a mother. And a brother.'

'She reckoned her mum didn't want her.'

Jack remembered Irene Meeks's statement. She'd said much the same thing about Edie's relationship with her daughter.

'Did she tell you why she thought that?'

'Nah. But you can tell, can't you? If someone don't want you around.'

Despite the fact Jack was asking the questions, Billy's answers were directed at Sarah. She'd bent forward, her hair lifted by the tortoiseshell combs then falling in a heavy curtain either side of her face as she wrote neatly and concisely in the black notebook that lay open in front of her. Jack watched Billy watching her. He hadn't, of course, seen any women for the past three and a half months, so it wasn't surprising that the sight of an attractive one should hold a strong interest for him. But Jack found the fact he couldn't hide it rather discouraging. What if he'd been attracted to Valerie – and she'd rejected him? He put the question to Billy.

'She was just a kid,' snorted Billy. 'At school.'

'She was fifteen. Plenty of girls leave school at fourteen. Lots are courting by the time they're fifteen.'

'Val wasn't.'

'Are you sure? Would she have told you about a boyfriend?'

'Wouldn't have to, would she?' Billy said with some

feeling. 'That nosy cow opposite would have found out and told the whole Cut.'

'Do you have a girl friend?'

'No. I can't talk to girls,' Billy confided suddenly in a rush. 'Don't know what to say to them. They laugh at me.' He blushed and started lacing his fingers together in an even more frantic pattern.

Jack was touched by this revelation. He remembered his own first attempts at courting. Girls whom he'd played with a few years earlier had suddenly turned into remote, sophisticated beings who gathered in huddles with sisters and friends and giggled at a private joke when they saw him approaching, or – even worse – as he was walking away. Had Valerie laughed at Billy? he wondered.

Instead of putting that question to the boy, he said: 'How long had you lived in Junction Cut?'

'About six, seven months. I come there when I changed me job. It was nearer see?'

Jack consulted his file. 'That would be the Pavaria Furniture Company?'

Billy nodded.

'Where did you work before that?'

'On Carter's Fruit and Veg Stall, up the market. Lodged with them too.'

'Queen's Crescent Market?' Jack asked. He knew Stan Carter.

'Yeah. That's the one.'

'Why did you leave?'

'Had to. Mr Carter, he wanted to give me job to his

wife's nephew. But he found me this new one. And he got me new room too.'

Billy appeared to regret his burst of loquacity. He went back to trying to out-stare the table top. Jack mouthed across to his sergeant: 'Ask him about his past.'

Sarah did her best. Each fact had to be prised out of the suspicious and frightened boy. Jack sensed Billy didn't want to talk about his past but, at the same time, wanted Sarah to go on talking to him. Little by little she extracted his story.

His parents had emigrated to England a couple of years after the last war. Why he didn't know, his mother had never told him. At first the family had been comfortable enough. His father had been a skilled carpenter and when he couldn't find work in that field, he'd been willing to turn his hand to anything else to keep them. Then he'd become ill and died. Billy thought he was about seven at the time, he was vague about the exact date.

'That must have been difficult for your mother?' Sarah suggested. 'Alone with a child in a strange country. How did she manage?'

Billy gave a bitter laugh. He crossed his arms on the table and leant towards the sergeant, unconsciously shutting Jack out from the discussion. 'She didn't. Just gave up, me mum did. Copped off from life. Me mum never really learnt the language proper, so she couldn't talk to no one.'

'So how did you live?'

'Hand to mouth' seemed to be the answer to that one, judging by Billy's halting, stumbling description of his childhood. They'd moved from room to room, trailing from one London district to the next. Sometimes paying their way, but more often than not flitting when the rent man became too persistent. Or the School Board man started asking awkward questions about Billy's non-attendance. Sometimes his mother had disappeared for days at a time. 'Used to wander off. Dunno where she went,' he explained. 'If the rent man slung me out before she come back, I'd bunk down in a doorway 'til she come home again. Bit like a homing pidgin she was. Always found her way back.'

Or she had, until one winter morning when he was fourteen. 'She just never come back,' Billy said to Sarah. He seemed to have completely forgotten Jack's existence. 'Said she was going out for a twist of tea. I waited. Over by Covent Garden we were then. I run errands for stall-holders. Dossed down in the doors at night. But she never turned up.'

And after a month, he had gradually accepted that she wasn't coming back this time.

'Did you ever see her again?' Sarah asked softly.

'No. Dunno what happened to her. Maybe they put her in a nut-house. Maybe she died. Don't know.' After that he'd drifted until he ended up in Somers Town, an area he vaguely thought he remembered from his childhood. A series of casual labouring jobs had ended in Stan Carter's stall and finally the Pavaria Furniture

Company. He seemed to harbour no resentment at his final move, accepting without protest that family ties were the strongest.

Having brought Billy's life history to the point where he'd arrived in Junction Cut, Sarah looked at Jack for guidance.

'Tell me about that Saturday. The day Valerie died. Did you see her at all that day?'

For a moment he thought Billy was about to shut down again, but then he said, with a return to his earlier truculence, 'Don't think so. Don't remember.'

'What do you remember about that day?'

Not much, seemed to be the answer. With great difficulty Jack managed to get him to confirm his original statement. He'd gone to the public baths earlier that day, he'd eaten his dinner at a local café and spent the afternoon in his room.

'And at approximately what – six-fifteen that day – you suddenly decided to pack up and move to Ireland?'

'Yes. That's right. Not against the law, is it?'

'Not in the slightest. But you left Junction Cut on Saturday evening, and were picked up at St Pancras Station on Tuesday. Where were you on Sunday and Monday?'

'Around.'

'Around where?'

'Just around.'

The rapport that Sarah had established with the boy was evaporating. Jack could feel the barrier of apparent indifference going up again.

'Did you murder Valerie Yeovil?' He fired the question angrily into the silence.

'No!'

'Then stop being such a berk and help me prove it.'

As an interviewing technique Jack suspected it wouldn't have won much approval at the Police College, but it seemed to have the desired effect on Billy.

Gulping and swallowing back tears with an effort, he said: 'I can't. I told you everything. I never did it. I wouldn't hurt Val.'

'When you were picked up you had three deep scratches on your left cheek, apparently made by finger nails. Blood and flesh were extracted from beneath the finger nails on Valerie's right hand. Did she scratch you?'

'No. I had a fight. In the street. This whore, she wanted to know if I was looking for business. When I told her to get lost, she turned nasty.'

'A button was found in the turn-up of your trousers. When Valerie was found, she was wearing a suspender belt with a similar button missing. How did it get into your clothing?'

'Don't know. Maybe somebody put it there.'

'What about the jumper fibres.'

'What fibres?'

'On the front of her dress. The forensic team found blue woollen fibres, soaked in shellac. You use shellac at work don't you?'

Billy nodded fatalistically.

'And you were wearing a blue jumper when you were arrested?'

'You know I was.'

'But you still say you didn't kill Valerie.'

'Yes.'

'Or see her on that Saturday?'

The hesitation was slight, but long enough for Jack to know the boy was lying when he said he hadn't.

'You left at six-fifteen. The murderer could have been in the house with Valerie at that time. Or going in. Did you leave by the front or back door?'

'Back. I used the passage at the back of the houses.'

'Was anyone else using it?'

'Didn't see anyone.'

'What about before you left the house? Did you see the other tenants? The Hendrys or Miss Toddhunter?'

'Not see them, no. I heard Lily go out. About fifteen minutes before that. And Dolly, she was in the front room looking after the kid when I left. I heard her singing to it. Funny that, ain't it? Her being deaf and being able to sing.'

'Perhaps she wasn't born deaf,' Sarah suggested.

'Did you know Mr Jolly, the tenant at number seven?' Jack slipped the question in quickly.

Billy looked surprised by this change of subject. He said: 'What, the old bloke? Yeah, I suppose so. He used to sit in the front most days. Never talked to me though. Or anybody else. Just grunted mostly.'

Jack waited to be asked why he was interested in James Jolly. But apparently Billy had no curiosity on that point. Jack drew in a deep breath of prison odours, gagged, and decided he'd had enough for today. Perhaps once Billy had had a bit more time to reflect, he might find cooperating with the police preferable to an almost certain drop attached to the business end of a hemp rope.

He said as much to Sarah as they drove away from prison.

'He doesn't trust the police. And, frankly, I can't say I blame him.'

The uneasy ghost of Inspector Kavanagh brushed against Jack again. For a moment the sensation was so real that he could almost see the man's bulky shape swaying on the back seat as he glanced in the rear-view mirror. Repressing the fancy, he said: 'He likes women. That much was obvious. He couldn't take his eyes off you.'

'Yes,' she agreed. 'But he struck me as a bit of a loner. Those sort of men often relate better to women rather than men. He wasn't trying to guess what colour my knickers are.'

The front wheels wobbled dangerously into the kerb as his sergeant succeeded in surprising him again. He glared at Sarah's profile. 'Do you think he did it?'

'No,' she answered immediately. 'Although I don't know why I think it.'

'Neither do I,' Jack said. 'But I agree with you.'

He thought of Billy's final plea as the warder led him back: 'I didn't do it, mister. Make them believe me.'

Feeding the wheel through his hands, Jack turned smoothly into Gray's Inn Road. 'So it looks like we've got a race on our hands. Can we prove Billy's innocence before the invasion arrives and makes the whole question somewhat irrelevant?'

Chapter 7

Friday/Saturday 17/18 May
Jack Stamford made no further progress with the Yeovil case on Friday. Instead he spent the better part of that day getting paralytically drunk.

Holland had surrendered. The last hope of a phone call demanding that he collect Neelie and Annaliese from some south-coast port had gone.

He'd started with one small whisky, drunk from one of the crystal tumblers that someone had given them as a wedding present. He raised it in a silent goodbye to his wife and daughter's images caught by a box camera on Beachy Head the summer before Neelie had left him. When the bottom of the glass showed through the straw-coloured liquid, he'd added another few inches. In the small hours of Saturday morning, he found himself hunched on the window seat of Annaliese's bedroom, dreamily wondering whether the German forces allowed travel between occupied countries?

With the invasion uppermost on his mind, the sudden rapiers of light springing up from the earth to probe the underside of puffy black clouds – turned unexpectedly silver as the beams sought and found them – seemed totally appropriate. He slid the window sash up, allowing the cool night air to play on his face, and listened for a while. But there was no accompanying drone of engine noise or pom-pom from the anti-aircraft batteries. He felt an alcohol-induced petulance at the realization that it was just another training exercise for the searchlight batteries on Hampstead Heath.

He awoke in his own bed, to find an ack-ack gun pounding away in his head and a familiar face bending over him.

'You're lucky you didn't break your neck!' Eileen O'Day informed him from between tight lips. 'If you're planning to make a habit of getting drunk, sit down somewhere safe first.'

'Sorry, Eileen.' His tongue was sticking to the roof of his mouth. Greedily he took the cup of tea she was holding out to him and gulped down the sweet brown liquid. 'What time is it?'

'Four o'clock. Saturday afternoon,' she added with a touch of malice.

'Did you put me to bed?'

'Pat gave me a hand before he went down the fire station. Lucky he was here, otherwise I'd have had to ask the lady. You're too heavy for me to shift alone.'

'What lady?'

'The one who came round this morning to see you. She couldn't get an answer. That's why I used me key. Found you passed out on the window seat. Another inch or so and you'd have gone straight into the garden.'

'What was her name?' Jack asked, with a sick feeling in the pit of his stomach that wasn't entirely due to the warm tea hitting gastric juices still reeling from the onslaught of an entire bottle of Black and White.

'McNeill. She said to tell you she'd be in the office on Sunday if you needed her.'

'Oh God.' Jack winced. On his second attempt he managed to swing his feet out of bed and more or less make contact with the floor.

'It's all right. I told her I'd never seen you this drunk before. Not that that means much – some drinkers can be very cunning. My auntie kept her gin in a stone hot-water bottle. She used to go to bed sober as a bishop and at two o'clock in the morning she'd be sitting up in bed singing "Rock of Ages". But don't worry, I let your Miss McNeill know that you didn't have a hot-water bottle.'

'Thanks, Eileen. That must have settled any doubts for her.'

She was oblivious to sarcasm. 'Don't make a mess of the bathroom. I'll go downstairs and put a bit of dinner on for you. You need something inside you.'

Jack opened his mouth to protest then thought better of it. When he came downstairs half an hour later, the ack-ack guns had retreated over the hill and his stomach behaved itself with reasonable decorum whilst he forced down a plate of mashed potatoes, peas, sweetbreads and gravy. Eileen bustled round the kitchen, not talking but not leaving him on his own either.

'I'll give you something off my ration coupons,' he said when he finally slid the knife and fork down with some relief. 'You can't use your family's meat allowance on me.'

'Sweetbreads aren't on ration. Aren't policemen supposed to know things like that?'

'Probably. But we haven't had to deal with much in the way of black-market traffic yet so I really haven't been keeping abreast of those particular regulations.'

'I expect you will – have to deal with black marketeers soon, I mean. Whether we stop them or not, there's going to be fewer places to get the food from now.' She sat down opposite him and placed the teapot, milk jug and cups in a row. Eileen drank tea after – and often during – every meal. She pushed a brimming cup towards him. As he reached to take it, she clasped one hand over his.

'They'll be all right, love. One woman and a little girl. The Germans aren't going to bother them, are they? It'll be the men they'll be looking for.'

Jack returned the squeeze gratefully but didn't trust himself to speak. Looking at the plucky, dark-eyed little woman trying to cheer him up, he felt bitterly ashamed. Eileen had four sons in uniform: two who could already be in the front line, another risking his life daily at sea, and Patrick who might be called upon to deal with whatever inferno the Luftwaffe might unleash any day now. And yet she was worrying about him.

He tried to put this into words, but Eileen thrust his hand away impatiently. 'What else are friends for, eh? Now don't sit here by yourself this evening, will you? Come over and listen to the radio.'

'I won't if you don't mind. I've got some papers to go through. Don't worry,' he added, catching her anxious look. 'I only get drunk once a war. Anyway, I don't think I've got any more alcohol left in the house.'

'You haven't now,' Eileen said, collecting her handbag. 'I poured it all down the sink. Say hello to that nice Miss McNeill for me, won't you?'

Sunday 19 May

Jack wasn't looking forward to having to say anything to that nice Miss McNeill. Given her previous experiences with Kavanagh, it wouldn't be unreasonable for her to assume he was just another copper who ran to the bottle whenever he faced the slightest pressure and then expected his colleagues to cover up for him. However, it was something he had to face.

He arrived at Agar Street at eight-thirty on Sunday morning to find an unlikely collection of ill-assorted men marching and drilling around the yard at the rear of the station. All ages were represented, from the butcher's seventeen-year-old boy to an elderly silver-haired gent whom Jack recognized as the retired headmaster of one of the local elementary schools. They all wore arm-bands bearing the initials 'LDV' and half a dozen carried rifles. The remainder were making do with broom-handles, garden rakes, a couple of ancient blunderbusses, a cavalry sword and other assorted stick-like weapons. The headmaster seemed to be getting the hang of a Zulu assegai.

'Quick march!' yelled a small compact man, with the broad shoulders and broken nose of a former boxer. 'Left, right, left...'

Thirty pairs of boots tramped obediently forward.

'Left turn.'

Twenty-seven pairs of boots swung left, and three went right. In the ensuing chaos the headmaster managed to hook off the local barber's wig with the tip of his spear.

'God, what a shower. My old sergeant major would 'ave died laughing...'

'The Agar Street contingent of the Local Defence Volunteers,' murmured a voice at Jack's elbow.

He turned and found Sarah had swapped the grey suit for a plain, short-sleeved blue dress. He also discovered that her hair wasn't solidly brown; there were twists of gold within, particularly on the ends where the summer sun had bleached a natural inclination to fairness.

'There aren't enough rifles to go round at present,' she continued. 'So local citizens were asked to hand in anything that might be used as a weapon. It makes you wonder what sort of life some of them must lead normally, doesn't it?'

'It does indeed. Shall we go in?'

He wasn't in the mood for light-hearted chit-chat, and once in the CID office had every intention of plunging straight into an explanation for his unprofessional behaviour.

She forestalled him, speaking quickly and deliberately as if she'd been rehearsing this speech for some time: 'Mrs O'Day told me about your family. I'd say I'm very sorry but it sounds inadequate and anyway you could probably assume that I would be. I don't suppose anything I can say is going to make the slightest difference to the way you feel. But I just wanted you to understand that I know you don't make a habit of getting drunk. And I didn't mind covering up for you this once – everyone else thinks you were off sick with food poisoning.'

'How do you know I don't make a habit of it?'

She looked at him for a moment. It was a considering sort of look, as if she were trying to make up her mind about something. Then she said: 'My dad was a drunk. Believe me, I can recognize one from half a mile down-wind. Do you intend to visit Mrs Yeovil today, sir?'

Jack accepted this closing of the subject with gratitude. 'Yes, I think we must. I should have done it days ago.'

Sarah retrieved a felt hat trimmed with a single strand of dark blue petersham ribbon from the stand. Bending her knees slightly, she squinted in a fly-blown mirror propped against a row of files and adjusted the hat on her hair, tilting it at a cheeky angle over her right eye.

'Sunday best?' Jack asked.

'Second best. My best was bought in Selfridge's sale in a moment of total madness. There's no way it qualifies under the description "plain clothes". I save it for off-duty.'

'I look forward to seeing it some time.'

Preceding him out of the door, she raised an enquiring eyebrow at him. Too late, Jack realized what he'd just said could have sounded like a proposition. He was about to correct the impression when he caught the glint of amusement in her eyes and knew she was teasing.

After a brief struggle with his jaw muscles, he grinned back.

Edie refused to allow them into the kitchen. Thin, determined and immovable in her black mourning dress, she stood resolutely two feet from the open front door and indicated the inner door to the left. 'I receive visitors in the parlour.'

The room had the same cold, unused feel as the Meekses' parlour. It was not as well furnished however, nor as cluttered, although paler rings in the wood of the dresser and mantelpiece suggested that several ornaments had recently been removed from the room. Its scents were a mixture of lavender, copper polish and slightly mouldy linen. But overall there was another smell which was naggingly familiar but which Jack couldn't quite place.

Edie received his expressions of condolence and apologies for the intrusion with composure. 'It has to be done, Inspector. You want me to repeat my statement, I suppose?'

'If you wouldn't mind.'

Taking a deep breath, Edie launched into words. Flatly, almost monotonously, she chanted her original statement, word for word. 'There,' she finished. 'Will that do? Or do I have to come to the station and sign it again?'

'Er, no. We don't need another written statement, unless you decide to change anything in the old one.'

'There's nothing to change. As I said last time, I'm afraid I can't remember anything between being in the Nettleses' house and sitting in Mrs Meeks's kitchen. I can't even remember how I got home. Or finding Valerie's body. Although they say I must have done. The doctor said it is a common reaction.'

Jack contemplated the woman opposite him. She had, he thought, never been beautiful. He wondered whether the shock of Valerie's murder had taken the light from her hair and skin, or whether the faded fairness had started to set in years before. He thought probably it had: the thin lines around her eyes and mouth looked to be the product of years of discontent.

He took her gently through her movements on that Saturday, but she had nothing more to add beyond confirming that the arrangement to visit the Nettleses and alter the bridesmaids' dresses had been made a week previously.

'So other people knew you wouldn't be at home that afternoon?'

'Yes, I suppose I might have mentioned it. Of course I don't speak to the neighbours very much. They're not our sort of people, you see? Mr Yeovil was a bank clerk.' She said it with a slight air of puzzlement. As if this sort of thing didn't happen to respectable, white-collar workers' families.

'How long have you been a widow?' Jack asked.

'Pardon?' Edie appeared to be collecting her thoughts. With an effort she focused on Stamford again. 'Victor, Mr Yeovil, departed this life when Valerie was a baby. I've been on my own for fifteen years.'

'It can't have been easy for you. Alone, with two children.'

Suddenly Edie smiled. 'Yes. Well that's all over now, isn't it? It's just temporary, this house. We'll be moving soon.'

'We?'

Edie looked puzzled for a moment then understood. 'A slip of the tongue, Inspector. I quite forget Ronnie's gone sometimes.'

No mention of Valerie, Stamford noted.

'Your son was at work that Saturday, I understand?'

'Saturday morning. He worked one Saturday morning in three. Well, one has to if one's in a supervisory position. It's expected, isn't it?' Edie's voice was beginning to take on her 'shop tone'.

'And the afternoon?'

'He went out with some of his friends. Up to the West End.'

'He didn't see his fiancée?'

'She was working all day. At least, she said she was.'

'Have you any reason to believe differently, Mrs Yeovil?'

Jack could practically see the temptation to pour out a string of grievances against her prospective daughter-in-law fighting its way up Edie's scrawny neck. She swallowed hard and said: 'No.'

'Could we see Valerie's room, please?'

'You mean my room?'

Jack realized that since these were two-bedroomed houses, mother and daughter must have shared. 'If you wouldn't mind, Mrs Yeovil.'

He thought she was about to refuse, but eventually she led them up the narrow stairs and indicated the room on the left. 'This is mine. The other one's Ronnie's.'

It had been decorated with the same rose-patterned wallpaper as the rooms at number two. The bed counterpane and curtains matched the pink shading in the roses. The room had a crowded, overfurnished feel, induced mainly by the amount of light being sucked up by a heavy wardrobe and a dressing table in the same dark brown wood. On its surface there were several glass jars with silver-coloured tops and a brush and mirror set in the same ornately twisted design. The silver gilt on the handle grips and around the edges of the jars had been worn off by years of handling to show the cheap brass underneath.

Edie indicated an empty bed, stripped to its mattress, across the back window. 'That was Valerie's bed. And she had the little cabinet over there for her things as well.'

Jack opened the cabinet. It was empty. 'And where are they now? Her things, I mean.'

'I gave them away. It seemed selfish to keep all those good clothes when there are so many in need. I gave them to the collection centre for refugees in Camden. One has to do what one can for these unfortunate people, doesn't one?'

'What about books, old magazines, jewellery?'

'The school asked for her textbooks back. The rest I donated to the refugees. She went to St Mary's Convent, you know. Not one of the local schools.'

'You must have been very proud of her. She was obviously a bright girl.'

Edie twisted a handful of her dress, scrunching the shiny material in a tight ball. 'I liked her going there,' she said finally. 'She met our sort of people. Nice girls, you know.'

'What about her special friends. Was there a best friend?'

'Margaret Cave. Her father has a sweet shop off Leighton Road. Although Valerie had other friends too. Nice girls, you know? Several of them had fathers in the professional classes. In fact one of them was the daughter of a solicitor. Maybe you know him . . .'

Jack interrupted: 'Is it likely that Valerie saw Margaret on the day she died?'

'No,' Edie answered immediately. 'She never saw Margaret on Saturdays. Margaret is expected to help her father in the shop on Saturdays. They went out together on Sundays, sketching.'

'Sketching?'

'And painting.' Edie took down a framed painting from the wall and handed it to Jack. 'She did this. I kept it because Ronnie liked it.'

Even in the dim light, Jack could recognize the talent that had produced the delicate sketch. A misty pond, caught in half tints, a few lines suggesting the dragon fly hovering across the rippling water. 'Where is this? Do you know?'

'Hampstead Heath, I expect. They usually went up there.' Edie's indifference was obvious.

Abandoning the bedroom, Jack led the way downstairs again. Edie made to open the front door, but he turned back into the parlour. She hovered in the door for a moment, as if she might insist he leave.

'Just a few more questions, Mrs Yeovil. Why don't you sit down again?'

Reluctantly she did so, perching on the edge of her armchair, fingers linked across her knees.

'How well did Valerie know Billy Zimmermann?'

'Hardly at all. He wasn't our sort of person.'

'Billy seems to think they were friends.'

'That's ridiculous! They couldn't be. I mean, he's so common, isn't he?' Edie produced her argument triumphantly and stood up. 'You must excuse me now, Inspector. Thank you for calling.' She extended her hand, graciously dismissing him. This time Stamford allowed himself to be dismissed.

Back on the pavement Sarah let out her breath in a huge sigh. 'Good heavens! I know grief takes people in different ways, but I've seen rat-catchers show more emotion for their victims than that. Did you notice, sir? There wasn't a single picture of Valerie in the parlour or bedroom.'

'Yes, I noticed.' But that doesn't necessarily mean anything, he wanted to say. He'd put all the photographs of Annaliese away. It made it easier to forget. The association of ideas, of babyhood and sterile nurseries, jogged a memory. He finally identified the strange smell that had been permeating the house behind him; it was Lysol. Edie had scrubbed the lino behind the door with disinfectant until the pattern had worn off.

'What now?' Sarah asked.

Curtains were twitching and doors opening all along the street. Queenie was thrust into the road so her mum could 'keep an eye on her'.

Jack contemplated the busy scene. 'It doesn't make sense,' he said.

'Sir?'

'Jolly,' he explained, nodding across at the empty house. 'Our missing witness. Assuming he saw something that night and the murderer knew it and had to silence him, he'd have had to kill Jolly, put the key and rent through Monk's door, and then move the body on the Saturday. He couldn't be certain that the rent man wouldn't check until Monday. And how the devil could he do that without being seen by this lot?'

JUNCTION CUT

Sarah didn't have an answer, but Jack didn't really need one. He was thinking aloud. 'Has the house been searched?'

'Only by Felonious.' She caught his drift. 'He couldn't still be there. I mean, even if he'd been hidden and Fel missed him, it is three and a half months. We'd smell him in Agar Street in this weather.'

'It is possible. If it was in a position where decomposition had been retarded . . .' Jack made up his mind. 'I think we'd better get a search warrant. Uniform can execute it tomorrow. I want the whole house taken apart.'

Chapter 8

Monday 20 May

The search of number seven unearthed a dead rat in the kitchen, old-fashioned furniture thick with opaque polish, curtains so thin that the light filtered through the much-washed material, and a spare room full of yellowing newspapers, carefully torn into quarters, presumably for use in the lavatory. It did not, however, produce any clue to the whereabouts of James Jolly – alive or dead.

Perched on the stairs, ignoring the resentful looks that were being shot at him by the dirty, sweating uniformed constables, Jack examined as much of the house as he could see from that position. It was a bachelor's home. No pictures on the walls, no vases or knick-knacks on any of the surfaces. No woman's touch to soften the bare necessities of living. Presumably Jolly's wife had died so long ago that all traces of her had rotted, broken or been thrown out.

The uniformed sergeant clattered back down the stairs, carrying a long pole. 'That's it, sir. We've had the floor boards up in both bedrooms. There's nothing under them.'

'What about down here?'

'Solid floor.' The sergeant stamped a well-shod heel to demonstrate his point. 'There's no basement. And we've had a look in the attic. He's not here, sir. And we can't find no clothes neither, nor shaving tackle. Looks like he scarpered.'

'Or the murderer had the sense to take his clothes as well to make us think he did.' Standing up, Jack brushed down his clothes and nodded. 'Thank you, Sergeant. Secure the house again, will you?'

He found Sarah in the kitchen chatting to a young constable who made himself scarce as soon as Stamford appeared. 'Dave's been helping me check out the kitchen, sir. I don't think Jolly was murdered. Unless the murderer was a woman.'

'An intriguing theory, Sergeant. Explain.'

Sarah threw open the doors of the larder and the meat safe. 'No food, sir. Even if Jolly only bought what he needed each day, there should have been something. A mouldy crust. Solidified milk. Rotting vegetables. I can believe a murderer who packs Jolly's clothes to make us think he left of his own accord. But remembering to clear out the larder?'

'What a low opinion you have of our domestic skills, Sergeant.'

'Well, sir. Have you ever cleared out your own kitchen cupboards?'

'Since you ask, no.'

A shrill giggle from the back yard attracted their attention. Beyond the grimy windows, a familiar figure stretched out her arms and squealed: 'Do it again. Again, please.'

Scooping up Queenie beneath the armpits, the constable swung her up and round so she soared out like a fairground ride.

Jack stood on the step and watched. Beneath his feet the deep scoop within the stone showed where Jolly had sharpened his knives for nearly fifty years. On the third spin, they spotted him and ground to a quick halt.

'Hello, Queenie. Have you still got the chicken pox?'

'Na. Me mum finks I got mumps this time.'

'Oh, Gawd.' The constable put her down quickly.

'I think your sergeant is looking for you.' Jack stood aside and allowed the constable to rush back into the kitchen.

Queenie put her hands behind her back and smiled innocently.

Jack tried to look stern. 'Have you thought of anything to tell me for my other sixpence yet, Queenie?'

'Na. I tried though. Honest I did. You ask me mum. I thought of lots of fings about Billy. But she said they was all in the newspapers.'

'What about Mr Jolly? Tell me something about him.'

Queenie rolled a tongue in her cheek, pushing it into grotesque shapes that showed how she was going to look if her mother's diagnosis was correct. Finally she told him that Mr Jolly shouted a lot if you threw the ball against the wall of his house.

'Anything else?'

'He used bad words. And threw his stick at us.'

Jack shook his head. 'I'm afraid if you can't do better than that, I'll have to ask for a refund.'

Queenie looked uncertain.

'He means he'll have to ask for his sixpence back,' Sarah called from the kitchen.

Alarmed, Queenie fled. Jack turned round and nearly fell over his sergeant.

'Sorry, sir.' Sarah rose to her feet, rubbing grease from her palms. 'I was just taking a look under the table. Have you noticed that the furniture in this place is a much better quality than that in other houses in The Cut? There's a maker's mark. Guess who?'

'Tell me.'

'The Pavaria Furniture Co. Billy Zimmermann's employers.'

Sarah's discovery might not mean anything. It was possible that the Pavaria company had supplied furniture to half Kentish Town. But Minnie White proved unexpectedly helpful for once.

'He worked there,' she said promptly in answer to Jack's enquiry. 'Years ago mind. He was already retired when I had our eldest. And she's coming up for thirteen this summer. Is it important?'

Jack could almost see her waiting to absorb information like a sponge. 'It may be. I wonder – you never heard Mr Jolly mention any relatives?'

Minnie sadly admitted that she hadn't. 'Both his lads were killed in the last war. That was a good bit before me and Percy moved here. But I remember me gran telling me about him. She knew his wife too. Put the pennies on her eyes when she died.'

'Is your grandmother still alive, Mrs White?'

'Bless me no, sir. She died when I wasn't much bigger than Queenie. But I've got a good memory. I never forget anything I've heard. You ask anyone round here.'

'I believe you, Mrs White.' Jack lifted his hat and wished her a good morning before rejoining Sarah who was hovering outside number seven.

It was a connection, however tenuous, linking Jolly to the murder, and had to be checked out.

'It doesn't help Zimmermann much though, does it, sir? I mean, if anything it makes things worse. It could be argued that Jolly still had contacts at his old company and he'd found out something about Billy.'

'Like what? If Billy had been boasting at work about what he was doing – or would like to do – to Valerie, don't you think we'd have heard about it by now? No, I don't think we're going to find out where Mr Jolly fits into this puzzle until we find him. In the meantime, let's interview some of the other players.' They'd been walking across the road whilst they discussed Jolly and now stood in front of Zimmermann's old address.

Unlike the other houses, which had disgorged the same quota of window-washers, step-whiteners and vegetable peelers on to the pavement as soon as the police search began, number two had remained incurious, closed and still curtained. Jack's knock brought a shouted instruction to: 'Bugger off.'

'Police. Will you open the door please, madam?'

Lily Hendry was fair like Edie Yeovil. But there the resemblance ended. Lily's fairness had been enhanced to a golden blondeness which bordered on brassy in sunlight. Even on a Monday morning her round face had been carefully made up with powder, rouge and lipstick. She barely came up to Jack's armpit, but she had a way of standing that suggested she knew she was attractive to men. In Jack's assessment she was a sharp little piece.

She led them into the front room. Like the Meekses' house, the downstairs consisted of two rooms, the kitchen/scullery at the back and this small parlour which the Hendrys used as their bedroom. It smelt of dirty nappies and cheap perfume. Unlike number six, a crude arch had been knocked through into the kitchen, making the two rooms self-contained.

' 'S'cuse the mess.' Lily flung an armful of clothes on the floor and indicated a chair. She perched herself on the bed and swung one leg back and forth, tapping out the rhythm of some unheard song. 'Come about the murder, have you? Irene said you'd be round. Don't see what you expect me to say though. We told that other copper everything.'

'I'm sure you did. But perhaps you've remembered something else by now? It's surprising how little things come back to people, often months later.'

'Not to me they don't. Ain't thought about it much.' Lily removed a packet of Capstans from the dressing table and extracted a cigarette. 'Thanks.' She leant forward, dipping the end into the flame of Jack's lighter. Her fingers held the side of his hand longer than was strictly necessary. He kept his expression neutral. After a few seconds, a flicker of anger sparked in Lily's eyes. Inhaling deeply, she blew a long, slow stream of smoke into the air inches from his face. 'So, what do you want to know?'

'Tell me about that Saturday. Did you see Valerie at all?'

'Saw her at the pig bin in the morning.'

'The what?'

'Pig bin. It's out there. In the alley at the back.' After another lungful of smoke Lily explained. 'We all put our waste in it, and a bloke comes round and picks it up every morning. He's fattening up some porkers on his allotment. We're all supposed to get a share when he kills them in the autumn. Val was at the bin that morning. She dumped half a pound of raw liver her mum had left for her tea. She reckoned she couldn't bear the stuff.'

'What time was this?'

'Just before eleven. Gus was going to work. That's how I remember. Soon as he'd gone into The Hayman I fished the liver out. Gave it to him for his dinner. He never complained,' she added, seeing the expression on Sarah's face. 'Never even flaming tasted it. Just shoved it straight down and rushed out again.'

'Rushed out where?'

A wariness descended on Lily's face. Forming an 'O' shape with her mouth, she slid out the tip of a pink tongue. Wavering smoke rings floated into the stale air of the bedroom.

'If it helps your memory, Mrs Hendry,' Sarah said, 'it's illegal for an unlicensed bookmaker to accept monetary bets. But we can only arrest someone placing them if we can catch them in the betting house.'

'That right?' Lily weighed this information. Leaning back against the pillows, she considered. 'All right,' she said. 'He went to see how his bet had done. I knew soon as he come in he'd won. Bursting out of him it was. Like sweat coming out of his skin.'

Jack asked: 'What time did he get back?'

'About four. Paced around here for half an hour 'til I thought he'd wear a hole in the carpet, then dashed out to fix up his big scene with Og... with the bloke who was going to pay out. Made him late for work.'

'Big win, was it?' Jack enquired blandly. He already knew the answer. Even three months later, Gus Hendry's win was still a subject of canteen gossip at Agar Street, hotly discussed by constables calculating the odds on threepenny accumulators.

'Big enough.'

'And you?'

'What about me?'

'What time did you go to the pub?'

'About six, I suppose. I had to wait for Dolly to come back and mind the kid.'

'Did you see anyone? In the street?'

Lily stubbed out the end of her cigarette in a handy

saucer and took another one. Ignoring Jack's lighter, she struck a match and applied it to the tip. 'No. Nobody.'

'What about Billy? Did you see him at all?'

'Can't remember. I told that other copper. I may have seen Billy sometime that day. Probably did. You can't avoid seeing the other tenants when you're all squeezed in like bed bugs.'

'Did you get on with him?'

'Never saw much of him. He never bothered me if that's what you're getting at.'

She was equally unforthcoming about Valerie. Whether she genuinely had no opinion of the dead girl or whether she just didn't want to get involved it was hard to tell. After eliciting that her husband had taken the baby out and Dolly Toddhunter had left for her part-time job half an hour ago, Jack decided he wasn't going to get any further with this witness. At least not today.

'Would you mind if we used the back entrance?'

'Help yourself.' Instead of going through the kitchen, Lily opened a small half door squeezed between the stairs and the wall of the scullery. It had shiny metal bolts fixed across old paintwork. 'You can get through here.'

Ducking down, Jack found himself in a shallow porch. A narrow brick-built building stood a few feet from the entrance. The wood plank door ended a foot from the concrete floor.

'Bleedin' draughty in the winter,' Lily remarked,

pushing her way ahead of Sarah. 'Wind whistles right up your drawers.'

'Very uncomfortable.' Jack sensed he was the one who was supposed to feel uncomfortable. He strode forward and peered out of the back gate. The alley behind the houses was barely the width of his shoulders. Two people using it at the same time couldn't avoid seeing each other. Unless, he supposed, one ducked into a yard. On the other hand, the wooden fence on each side of the alley was well above his head. And the upper windows of the houses would probably have had their blackout curtains drawn. So if the murderer had been lucky enough to find the alley empty, he could have slipped in and out of the Yeovils' without anyone being the wiser.

To his right the alley curved in a dog's leg, its access to the road concealed at this angle. To his left it appeared to come to a dead end. A metal bin stood in a sort of make-shift shrine of bricks and wooden planking against the end wall. Walking down to it, he lifted the lid and was almost overwhelmed by the stink of vegetable peelings.

Sarah had remained behind talking to Lily. They stood, half in, half out, of the Hendrys' yard, blocking the narrow alley. Jack opened his mouth to call a question and found himself about to address Minnie who was bearing down on him with a crust of loaf in her hand. Sarah and Lily had disappeared.

Jack braced himself for another interrogation, but it seemed he wasn't Minnie's quarry this time. Barely glancing at him as she dropped the bread into the pig bin, she uttered a quick instruction to be sure to put the lid back properly – 'Otherwise the cats get in' – and hurried back the way she'd come. Opposite Lily's yard, she wheeled right and took hold of the gate latch. The gate remained stubbornly shut.

'Lily? Are you in there, love?' A sharp rattle brought no response. 'Lily? Could I have a word?'

Obviously Lily had decided that Minnie had quite enough words of her own without the necessity to collect them from other sources.

Jack strode forward until he was within a few feet of Minnie, giving her the option of squeezing to one side or returning the way she had come. After a second, she backed away. A few more steps and she decided it was easier to proceed in a frontal direction.

'Has she gone?'

Jack guessed that this question, hissed through a gap in the back fence, was directed at him. 'Yes, she's gone.'

'Good.' Lily whisked the yard gate open and jerked an inviting head. 'Sorry about that, but she's got a pig bin her side of the street.'

Jack realized he was missing something. Fortunately Lily was in a mood to moan. 'Got no reason to come round our back, has she, unless she's after something?'

'And what is she after?'

'Money, of course. They're all at it. Ever since Gus got his winnings. They come round here more regular than they go round Uncle's. God knows why. I mean, if I can't get it out of him, what chance have they got?'

'A careful man, is he, your husband?'

'Pig stubborn,' Lily said frankly. 'Got this dream about a little pub in the country with the wife and kids. The neighbours have got more chance of getting Hitler to stick a couple of coats of white-wash on their 'ouses, than of getting a fiver out of Gus. 'Course, it's his own fault. He should never have given Irene that fifteen quid to get her old man's watch out of pawn. Now they all think they're going to stick their hands in his pocket. Still, at least they ask. Instead of helping themselves when we're out. Not like that lot in Litcham Street, eh?'

This last remark was addressed to Jack but accompanied by a sly smile in Sarah's direction. Beneath the tilt of her hat brim, Jack saw his sergeant's eyes harden. An icy light glazed her azure irises. 'I would have thought that depended on the person, Mrs Hendry. Rather than their address,' Sarah replied.

'Mud sticks,' Lily responded. Her mood seemed to have lightened. 'You know what they say – once a Litcham Street girl, always a Litcham Street tart.'

Jack decided it was time to leave. He allowed Sarah to precede him along the back alley. The swish of her hips and the stiff angle of her neck radiated a clear message: 'Don't you dare ask.'

As they burst out into Fortress Road again, he cleared his throat.

'Yes?' Her voice could have stripped flesh off bones.

'Can we discuss the case? Or should I get my tin helmet first?'

For a moment he thought she was going to hit him, then abruptly the tension drained out of her body. 'Sorry, sir. I didn't mean to react like that. It was a bit of a shock. I can't believe I didn't recognize her before.'

He fell into step beside her. 'From Litcham Street?'

'Yes. I grew up there. We both did, me and Lily. Lily Thomas she was then. Her mum was a prostitute. I don't know how I could have missed her for so long, except that her hair wasn't blonde when she left.'

'When was that?'.

'When she was fourteen. She's a couple of years younger than me so that must have been...' Sarah counted on one hand. 'Nineteen twenty-eight. I remember that morning.' To an appreciative chorus of cat-calls and whistles from open windows, Lily had sashayed down the centre of the road in a tight dress four inches above her knees and her mother's red high-heeled shoes. 'Her mum was yelling out the window: "come back, you little cow, them's me best pair!"'

'And I presume she got quite a lot of inventive suggestions on how to detach her best pair?'

Sarah laughed aloud. 'Yes, she certainly did!' They were approaching Agar Street station. Sarah stopped and turned to face him. 'Look, sir, about Litcham Street...'

'Could we leave Litcham Street for now, Sergeant? Unless it has any bearing on this case?'

'In a way it does. Indirectly.'

'How?' Litcham Street was generally considered to be an open sewer by the police authorities of Kentish Town. Sometimes the eccentric drainage systems of the tenement houses literally ran with excrement, but more often they disgorged violence, alcoholism, incest, despair and pain – both self-inflicted and administered with intent. The local Housing Society had attempted to improve the area by building new flats, but the hard core of the troublemakers remained. However, up until now, he hadn't considered the possibility that Valerie's attacker had come from the most obvious criminal catchment in the area. Was it really that simple? A random victim selected by a known villain?

'When Lily was teasing . . . well, gloating I suppose,' Sarah was saying, 'about recognizing me from Litcham Street, she started to say that it wasn't much different here really. Meaning Junction Cut.'

'You mean somebody in that street is known to the police?'

'I don't know about known, sir. But she implied that someone in Mrs Yeovil's family had done something that was against the law. The exact quote was: "We've all done something that would put us in the clink at some time, ain't we? And that stuck up lot at number four are no better than the rest of us."'

Chapter 9

Tuesday 21 May

'I've never felt I knew a victim less.'

'Can you know a victim at all?' Sarah asked.

By mutual consent they'd abandoned the CID office at Agar Street. The whole uniform branch, including the auxiliaries who until now had been regarded as excess personnel, hindering rather than helping the regular constables, were once again bracing themselves for the expected invasion. The French line had been broken; Churchill had made a radio broadcast warning of the approaching Blitzkrieg; at last something was starting to happen. The station vibrated with the same air of suppressed excitement and expectancy that had filled the country in the first weeks of September 1939, before the anti-climax of stalemate and too many police doing too few jobs had set in. Being caught on the edges of this whirl of activity, with nothing to contribute to it, had made them both uneasy. Eventually Jack had suggested a walk might clear their heads.

Sitting side by side on a bench in Regent's Park, they contemplated a newspaper picture of Valerie Yeovil. The plain white blouse and square-necked grey gym-slip suggested it had been taken from a school photograph. She'd worn her hair in one plait. The thick skein lay over her right shoulder, covering one breast and falling below the bottom edge of the picture. A plain black velvet band framed her oval face and gave her the appearance of a madonna. Jack stared into the dark eyes. They looked back: bland, uncommunicative, giving away nothing about the person behind. He moved the cutting closer, but she dissolved into a thousand printer's dots.

Sarah said: 'I don't see how you can *know* a victim. I mean, all you have to go on is other people's impressions, haven't you?'

Jack remembered that this was her first murder investigation.

'Yes, you do,' he agreed. 'But you can build up quite an accurate picture of a person from what others tell you about him or her. You can tell who liked them, loved them, hated them, envied them. And that's usually where you get your first clue to the most important element in a murder case. The motive. But this girl . . .' He gestured hopelessly with the cutting. 'What on earth do we know about her?'

'She was clever,' Sarah offered. 'Not many girls from that area go on to take their matriculation.'

'Anything else?'

Sarah gnawed her bottom lip. The promise of another brilliant summer was already evident in the bursting flower beds and warm sunshine. The first of the summer flies buzzed self-importantly round her face. Raising a hand to swat it away, she knocked her hat sideways. Jack tilted it back into position over her eyebrow.

'Thanks. Er, no. I mean, I can't think of anything we know about Valerie. Apart from the obvious: that her mother doesn't appear to have liked her very much and neither did anyone else as far as I can see. At least, if they didn't dislike her, they seem to have been fairly indifferent to her. Except for Billy, of course.' She knew she was babbling and caught her bottom lip with impatience.

'Yes.' Jack's eyes met hers. He was puzzled when she slid her gaze away, focusing instead on a bed of nodding purple pansies. 'It all comes back to Billy again, doesn't it?'

'So where do we go from here, sir?'

'The best friend. The one whose father keeps a sweet shop off Leighton Road. What was her name – Margaret something or other?'

'Cave. Margaret Cave, sir.'

Jack checked his watch. It was nearly four o'clock. 'She's probably still at school but if we take a slow walk up there we shouldn't have to wait too long. Is that all right with you?'

'Fine, sir. I like walking. Miss all that pounding the beat, I suppose.'

'No. I mean, I know you've been on duty since eight. And by the time we've finished with Margaret it will be gone six. If there's anyone you'd like to call? Someone expecting you this evening, I mean?'

'No, sir. That's quite all right. Shall we go then?'

She set off determinedly down the gravel paths, leaving Jack to follow and wonder why he seemed to have been relegated back to 'sir' every other sentence.

Leighton was the first road past Kentish Town Station. In order to reach it they had to pass the entrance to Agar Street station again. As they drew level with it, the uniformed constable who'd unknowingly risked a dose of mumps the previous day burst out and called urgently: 'Sir!'

Jack waited whilst the constable shot up the road trying to temper a natural inclination to run. 'Inspector Stamford, sir. There's someone waiting to see you. Ding Dong – I mean Detective Constable Bell – has been trying to find you. But nobody's clocked you since dinner. She's been here a couple of hours.'

'Who has?'

'Mrs Cohen. She came here before. The night they pulled Billy Zimmermann in. Wanted to speak to him.'

'Then why is this the first I've heard of it? There's no visit report for her. In fact, according to the records Zimmermann didn't receive any visitors during the time he was held in the cells here.'

'I forgot.' Sarah had retraced the few steps she'd been keeping between herself and Stamford and now stood in front of him again. She looked stricken. 'There was so much chaos that night, what with the reporters trying to get in and the relief change over taking place at the same time.'

'So Mrs Cohen saw Zimmermann in the cells that night?'

It was the constable who answered: 'No, she didn't, sir. Inspector Kavanagh wouldn't let him have no visitors.'

Jack felt a prickle of excitement. 'All right, I'll come back to the station and see her. But I think you'd better go round to Leighton and see Margaret, Sarah. Find out all you can about Valerie. I want a better description of that young lady's personality than "just ordinary". And time's running out.'

The woman who was waiting in his temporary office was the sort he'd once heard a former sergeant describe as 'red hat and no knickers'. Except this woman wasn't wearing a hat, unless you counted the scrap of lace stabbed on to the back of her crimped hair. Despite the heat, she wore a mink coat clasped round her ample figure by plump fingers which sparkled with diamond rings. A knuckle-duster of carats was extended towards Jack. He took it and found himself looking into a pair of shrewd eyes.

'Vulgar, ain't it?'

'I beg your pardon?'

'This lot. The diamonds and the fur in the middle of summer. Bet that's what you're thinking?'

'On some it would look vulgar. On you it looks right.'

She gave a shrill burst of laughter. 'Bet you got that out of a film!'

'I did, Mrs Cohen.'

'Call me Bea.' Flinging back the coat to reveal a tight-fitting costume in royal blue crêpe, Bea settled back in the chair and ran an appraising eye over

Stamford. 'I like a good-looking fellow,' she said frankly. 'Don't mind me staring, do you? Blokes do it all the time.'

'Help yourself.'

Bea availed herself of the invitation for another minute, then raised a pair of twinkling black eyes to Jack's face and grinned.

He grinned back. 'So, how can I help you, Bea?'

'It's me who can help you. I can tell you the truth about Billy.'

'Which is?'

'He didn't do it. Rape that girl. He didn't have any reason to. He was getting plenty of that from me.'

Jack looked at the face in front of him. She'd covered it thickly in powder, the rounded cheeks emphasized by globes of rouge. Even with the light behind her, it was obvious she was in her fifties.

'Fifty-three next birthday,' Bea offered without being asked.

'And how long have you and Billy been lovers?'

'Since just before Christmas. Couple of months after Stan Carter asked me to take him on.'

Jack's head jerked up sharply. 'You own the Pavaria Furniture Company?'

'As good as. It's my old man's business but he's . . .' One finger weighed with a two-carat diamond described circles an inch from Bea's forehead. 'Not his fault, poor love. We had a good run. And I got him in a posh private nursing home now. But he's never going to be a husband to me again.'

'I'm sorry.'

Bea shrugged. 'Maybe he's luckier than Billy and me. If the Germans do invade, I reckon those of us who don't know what's going to happen will be happiest. Less time to brood, see?'

'Us?' A thought occurred to Stamford. 'Is Billy Zimmermann Jewish?'

"Course he is, love. Not practising, mind you. Shouldn't think he's been near a synagogue since his pa died. But that doesn't matter to most folk, does it? Once a Jew, always a Jew, that's the way they see it.'

Jack didn't feel qualified to comment on this remark but there was something he had to ask Beatrice Cohen.

'No,' she said promptly, 'I was away that weekend. The factory here is too small. I was looking at a new place in Harpenden. Got a big contract from the War Office and we needed the space. Didn't get back until Tuesday afternoon. By the time I'd got myself a smart lawyer and got him in to see Billy it was too late. That boozing inspector had got him signing all sorts of lies.'

She was becoming agitated. Small veins stood out like purple cobwebs beneath her jawbone. Fumbling in her pocket, she drew out a gold cigarette case, embossed with the initial 'B' in diamond chips, and extracted a long brown cigarette. 'Turkish.' She extended the case in Jack's direction. He shook his head.

Bea clicked it shut with a one-handed flick. 'Another vulgar little toy. But I can afford it. I can afford anything I like. Fancy house, servants, clothes from posh designers. And a lover young enough to be me son.' She blew a cloud of fragrant smoke. 'Men,' she added, staring Jack straight in the eye, 'call them private secretaries.'

'Why did you come to see me, Mrs Cohen? It wasn't just to shock me with details of your private life, was it?'

'If it was, I ain't succeeded, have I?' Bea gathered her coat around her again. 'I came because Billy told his solicitor that you treated him decent. Not like just another dirty little foreigner. I'm trusting you to get him out. I thought you'd do it quicker if you had all the facts.' She rose and offered her hand. 'Nobody else knows about me and Billy. If he hangs, see, I've still got to live here. Billy understands that. If things go well for him, he'll move in with me. And if they don't . . .' She shrugged. 'I'll just be the ex-employer.'

Jack clasped a handful of rings. 'They won't hear from me unless it's essential to the case. Thank you for trusting me.' There was one more question he needed to put to her.

'Jolly?' she said. "Course I remember him. Miserable old bugger! Retired about fifteen year back. Didn't want to, but we didn't have the work coming in so Mr C. had to lay him off.' She thought it unlikely that he still had any contact with the other workers at the yard. 'Never had any friends when he was there. Can't see anyone bothering to keep in touch once he'd gone. I'll ask around if you like?'

Jack agreed that he would like. 'I need a current address.'

'Leave it to me, love.' Bea gathered her coat around her again and surged to her feet as the constable reappeared in answer to Jack's call.

The door had barely closed, leaving a fragrance of scented smoke and even more pungent face powder, when something occurred to Stamford. Poking his head out of the door, he called after her departing back: 'Mrs Cohen, what exactly are you making for the War Office?'

Bea Cohen turned. The bustle of the corridor had stopped briefly. Her answer carried clearly: 'Coffins, love. Thousands of them.'

Sarah's expression as she marched across Kentish Town Road and along Leighton caused several citizens who knew her and who held a relaxed attitude to the current war-time regulations to flinch out of her way and wonder which particular breach the police had uncovered. Sarah was oblivious to them all. She walked automatically, unseeing and aware only of the emotions whirling around in her head and heart.

She had been totally unprepared for the effect the touch of Stamford's hand, brushing her hair as he adjusted her hat, would have on her. The nature of the job she'd chosen made intimate relationships difficult, if not impossible. If a man didn't become fed up with the irregular working hours, then he became embarrassed and defensive about his friends' reaction to her uniform. All the WPCs dealt with the situation in different ways. In her own case the problem was compounded by her connection with Litcham Street.

In addition to the small core of professional prostitutes, it was known that some of the other women were happy to oblige the rent and tally men if it meant keeping a roof over their heads and food in their kids' mouths. It had made her wary of her own reactions. What might be an innocent smile from another woman could be interpreted as a come-on from a Litcham Street girl. As a probationer she'd been aware of the speculative looks being cast in her direction by some of the older regulars. Her solution had been to give up any hope of finding a man and throw all her energies into her career. Now she'd started jumping like a virgin schoolgirl when a man touched her in a perfectly innocent way. And not just any man, but a married one and a senior officer in the police force.

And, if you're truthful, my girl, she scolded herself silently, one who probably hasn't even noticed you're female. Now get a grip and get on with this investigation.

On this bracing thought, she marched into the Caves' shop and was directed by the proprietor to the flat above where his daughter was doing her homework.

'French,' Margaret explained, pushing away a lined notebook. 'I hate French. They all laugh at my accent. And I don't see the point of learning it anyway if I'm going to be a doctor. French people would want to go to French doctors, wouldn't they? Would you like a bun?'

'No, thank you.'

Despite the heat a fire was burning in the fireplace. Margaret led the way to the two armchairs either side of the hearth. Settling herself in one, she took the brass fork from the carousel, speared half a currant bun, and held it to the flames. 'I like them toasted. If you're too hot you could sit on the other side of the table.'

'No. I'm fine.' Sarah tucked her ankles out of the direct blast of the heat.

Margaret was still in her school uniform; the same white blouse and grey gym-slip that had appeared in Valerie's photograph. But there the resemblance ended. Margaret had none of her friend's wide-eyed promise of future beauty. She was what could politely have been described as sturdy. Her round face, which could have been her best feature, was surrounded by a pudding basin of mousy hair and partially hidden behind wire-rimmed glasses.

'What made you decide on a medical career?' Sarah tried, unsure how to open this conversation.

'I didn't. It's what Dad wants me to do. He's very keen on women's education. *His* mum was a suffragette.' Margaret lashed margarine on to the smoking bun and took a large bite, smearing fat across her cheeks. 'I wish she'd just been normal.'

'Do you? Why?'

Margaret masticated a mouthful of hot bun and margarine. 'Because then I could just do what I liked instead of having to have a proper career. I mean, it's all right if that's what you want. But what if you just want to stay home and get married and have children? You can't, can you? My gran says women who settle for that are traitors to the movement.' She sighed heavily and speared the other half of the bun.

Sarah felt it was time to bring the conversation round to the purpose of her visit.

'What do you want to know about her?' Margaret said when Sarah asked for information about Valerie.

She thought. What did she want to know? She knew all the basic facts. What she – and Stamford – really needed was to grasp the elusive girl beneath the 'just ordinary'. 'Why did you like her?'

'I didn't much.'

'Pardon?' Sarah blinked. 'I thought she was your best friend?'

'She was.' Margaret retrieved a jar of jam from the hearth and added a generous dollop to the toasted bun. 'You've got to be friends with someone, haven't you? Even if you don't really like them. We had to be friends, see, because we were the two Lady Agneses.'

'The whats?'

'Lady Agnes students.'

'Who's Lady Agnes?'

'She's not anyone now. She's dead. She was another rotten suffragette. She endowed a scholarship at the convent. For two "poor female students who would not otherwise be able to take advantage of the scholastic opportunities open to their more fortunate sisters".'

Margaret had recited this liturgy in a high-pitched tone that vibrated with scorn. She returned to her normal tone to add that it paid for school fees, uniforms and textbooks. 'But not all the other things you need to go to a place like that.'

'Such as?'

'Servants, cars, money . . . all the things the other girls have got and pretend they think you must have too. Even though they know very well you haven't.'

Enlightenment dawned on Sarah. 'And Valerie was the only other pupil who came from the same background, so you stuck together?'

'That's right.'

'Did she hate the school too?'

'I don't think so. If she did, she could have got out. Dad made me go, but Val put herself up for the scholarship. To spite her mum.' Margaret licked off the last of the jam. 'She wanted Val to go out to work.'

Sarah digested this information whilst Margaret carried out the same operation on the bun. Something Edie Yeovil had said niggled. 'If,' she asked, 'you didn't like Valerie, why did you spend your Sundays with her? Her mother said you used to sketch together. Isn't that true?'

For the first time Margaret's air of mildly truculent boredom slipped. She looked uneasy. 'Yes. Up on the Heath mostly. We took a picnic and stayed up there all day.'

'You must have done a lot of painting in that time. I saw some of Val's work. Could I see yours?'

Margaret shrugged. 'If you like.' Heaving herself out of the armchair she left the room and returned with an armful of cartridge paper. 'These are mine.'

Sarah examined each sheet with growing respect. Even she, who had little interest in art, could tell they held the beginnings of an exceptional talent. When she said as much to Margaret, the girl's plain face lit up. 'Do you really think so? I mean, I always thought they were quite good, but there's no one to ask. We only do still life at school. Bowls of fruits and things. And I'm really best on landscape and figures.'

'Yes, I do. They're wonderful, Margaret.'

She blushed and produced a small artist's sketch pad. 'I did pictures of Valerie. If you'd like to see?'

The first sketch was a head and shoulders charcoal drawing. The madonna of the newspaper photo was just discernible in the oval face, but the rest was a different Valerie. Her hair was loose, fanning out in a dark cloud across the paper. The dark eyes beneath the straight black brows held an unmistakable challenge, as did the slightly mocking smile on the full lips.

'There's a pencil sketch overleaf. You can see more of her in that,' Margaret said.

Sarah flipped the sheet and caught her breath. Margaret had been speaking literally. Valerie was sprawled face down on a bed, the leg nearest the artist bent slightly towards her waist. Her arms were hugging a pillow on which she cradled the upper part of her body. Her face, the chin resting on the top edge of the pillow, held the same mocking challenge as the previous sketch. But this time the reason was obvious: she was stark naked.

'She asked me to draw her like that,' Margaret explained. 'She wanted to see what she looked like without her clothes on. There's another one. See.' Margaret thumbed over the sheet. Reclining on one hip, her body supported on one elbow, Valerie displayed her full breasts and slightly rounded stomach with no apparent sign of embarrassment.

'I thought it would be all right.' Margaret's voice started to shake, the animation dying. 'Rubens did it, didn't he?' Doubt crept over her face as Sarah remained silent. 'I haven't shown anyone else.'

Sarah found her voice. 'I think you have an extraordinary talent, Margaret. I wonder, could I keep these? Just for now. You'd get them back.'

'All right. You can keep them if you like. And one of the others.' Rather shyly Margaret pushed the other sketches forward. 'You could frame it. If you wanted to.'

Sarah selected a paint-washed scene of small boys and toy sailing boats by Hampstead Ponds. It reminded her of something else she'd seen recently. 'Valerie's mother showed us one of her sketches. Do you know, Margaret, you have a very similar style. In fact, they could almost have been painted by the same person.'

The flood of colour that shot from Margaret's neck to disappear beneath the lank fringe told Sarah her guess was correct. 'What did Valerie really do on the

Heath, Margaret?' she asked quietly.

'Nothing.' Margaret stared at her feet. 'She wasn't there. Not all the time anyway. She made me give her some of my paintings to show at home so they wouldn't wonder where she'd been.'

'And where had she been?'

'Edgware. She used to get the tube in the morning and come back and meet me later that day. If anyone saw me alone, I had to say she was sketching on another part of the Heath.' Sarah waited. Margaret dragged her gaze from the floor. Tears diverted round the grease smears on her shiny cheeks and fell in large plops on the carpet. 'I should have said, shouldn't I? Only I didn't see what it had to do with that German boy. And nobody asked.'

Sarah put an arm round the plump shoulders. 'It's all right, Margaret. How often did this happen?'

'Six, seven times. She went in the holidays. And a couple of times after the war started. Then she stopped.'

'Do you know what she was doing in Edgware?'

Margaret bit her lip. 'Yes.'

'Yes?' Sarah prompted.

'She was meeting a man.'

Chapter 10

Wednesday 22 May

'Bloody hell! was Stamford's uninhibited comment on being presented with Margaret's sketches. He'd reported on his surprising conversation with Beatrice Cohen and Sarah had trumped him by producing Margaret's handiwork. 'Where were these done?'

'In Margaret's bedroom. Valerie went round after school sometimes. Ostensibly to do her homework.'

'And she kept them in the flat? Where her parents could find them?'

'Margaret's mother died when she was three. And her father prides himself on respecting his daughter's right to individual privacy. His mother was a suffragette.'

Jack looked up from the sketches. His sergeant's face wore the expression of non-committal detachment that had marked the first days of their relationship. 'You make it sound on a par with being a werewolf.'

'It's how Margaret says it.'

Ding Dong Bell entered the office under the excuse of collecting a copy of Daily Orders from the In Tray. His eyes dropped to the sketches and he barely managed to choke back a whistle of surprise. On leaving, he scuttled over to the other DC's desk and started talking animatedly. 'Well, at least we seem to have re-awakened the rest of CID's interest in this case,' Jack remarked ruefully. 'Are you sure Margaret doesn't know who this man is?'

'No. I'm sure she doesn't. Val talked about meeting "him", but that's all she'd tell her. According to Margaret though she was always excited for several days before each expedition. And – to quote Margaret – looked like she'd swallowed a pint of cream when she got back.'

'A lover?'

'I think it's quite feasible, don't you, sir? I mean in the light of . . .' Sarah indicated the sketches. 'She said she wanted to know what she looked like without her clothes. Maybe what she really wanted to know was what she looked like to someone else?'

Jack looked at Valerie's face in the drawing. There was no denying Margaret's talent. In a few pencil strokes she'd captured the provocative glint in the eyes and the challenging curve of the half smile. Jack would have bet a year's pay that this girl hadn't been a virgin prior to the attack in Junction Cut. He picked up the phone and gave the operator the telephone number of the pathologist who'd carried out Valerie's post mortem.

When the man was eventually persuaded to come to the receiver he was infuriatingly vague. 'Well, I wouldna like to say yes. But then, I wouldna say no either.'

Jack suppressed his impatience: 'How about a definite maybe?'

'Oh, aye. I think I could say that.'

'Valerie Yeovil may not have been a virgin prior to the attack in Junction Cut?'

'Yes. Yes. That's a possibility.'

'A definite possibility. Or a remote possibility?'

'Oh, bordering on the definite, I'd say.'

'And you didn't think to mention this before, doctor?'

'Nobody asked. It's no the sort of thing you throw into a casual conversation is it?'

Jack reminded him that his report had led the police to draw the conclusion that the victim had been raped.

'Well, that's up to the police, is it not, Inspector? If you'll check the wording of my report you'll find I said there was evidence of sexual intercourse. Not forcible sexual intercourse.'

Jack drew a deep and audible breath of annoyance. 'So you don't think she was raped?'

'I wouldna say that.'

'Then what the hell are you saying?'

'I'm saying, Inspector, that since it is my experience that post-coital bliss is usually accompanied by a slow smoke rather than a fast clout over the head by a sharp instrument, I didna see any reason to quarrel with the generally held view of Valerie Yeovil's last moments. Now if that's all you wanted to know, I've a floater from the river that I'd like to deal with before he makes this place smell any more like the hold of an Aberdeen trawler.' With a click, the line went dead.

After Stamford had reported the gist of the pathologist's conversation to her, Sarah said: 'It ties in with your theory then, sir. She could have faked enjoyment. Taken her own clothes off. I mean, it might not have been that difficult if it was someone she'd already had sex with on a regular basis.'

'Mmm.' Jack frowned into the distance over her head. 'You say the visits started last July and stopped in mid-September. Why?'

'Margaret didn't know. I suppose he might have been called up?'

'And didn't get any leave until late January? When he comes looking for Valerie. And . . . what?'

'She didn't want anything more to do with him. So he loses his temper; she gets frightened, pretends to agree, then he panics and kills her when she makes a run for it. She was under-age, remember. So even if we couldn't prove rape, we could have got him for intercourse with a minor.'

'Which fits in with the facts, except for one thing.'

Sarah mentally reviewed the evidence. 'The suspender button?'

'Exactly. Zimmermann might have been telling the truth about his facial injuries. Maybe he did meet a bad-tempered whore. You could even come up with a reasonable excuse for the jumper hairs on Valerie's dress. But her suspender button in his turn-up? How the devil do we get round that?'

'Planted?'

'How? According to Billy's statement he was in his

room until he had this sudden overwhelming urge to visit the Emerald Isle. The murderer would have had to follow him and drop the button whilst he wasn't looking. Which seems a bit of a long shot.'

'I wasn't thinking of the murderer, sir.'

Her blue eyes had darkened. They looked directly at Jack. 'What are you . . .' Then he understood. It wasn't him she was looking at. It was the chair he was sitting in. 'Kavanagh?'

'It's a possibility, isn't it?'

Jack let his breath out in a gentle sigh. 'Yes. I'm afraid it is.'

Her mother was the most likely person to provide information on who Valerie knew, or had known, in Edgware. But Edie worked Wednesdays. Having decided against interviewing her at Daniel's Department Store, Jack was forced to kick his heels until the next day. Enforced inactivity always irked him. And today, for personal reasons, he found it more unbearable than usual. He started to prowl the main office, pulling out files, checking and re-checking. From the corner of his eye, he was aware of three covert gazes following him; quickly dropping back to desks and typewriters whenever he tried to catch their eye. At midday he picked at a meal in the station canteen, his sense of isolation increased by Sarah who, having spent the morning avoiding him, carried her meal to a table for four which was already occupied by two WPCs and the station Matron, leaving him to eat alone.

That afternoon he instructed her and the two detective constables to start a check on the inhabitants of Junction Cut. 'I want to know if any of them was known to the police prior to the murder.'

'I can tell you that, sir,' Ding Dong volunteered. 'Uniform have a couple of regular Drunk and Disorderlies. Percy White often comes in on the cart Saturday nights.'

'Well, you won't mind checking Criminal Records anyway, will you Constable? Just in case there's anything else.'

Ding Dong's expression suggested he could think of better ways to spend a summer afternoon. 'Waste of time, if you ask me,' he hissed to the other DC as soon he thought Stamford was out of earshot. Unfortunately for him, Stamford wasn't.

'And when you've finished that, Constable, check where they all were on the afternoon of the murder.'

'All of them?' Bell's voice rose in disbelief. 'The whole street?'

'That's the idea,' Stamford agreed. 'Any news on Jolly?' he asked Sarah as she put down the phone after another abortive call to the local Food Office.

'No, sir. No trace at all.'

Jack gave an exclamation of impatience. 'For heaven's sake! This whole country has been issued with identity cards, ration books, and various other assorted pieces of paper that the Government finds indispensable to the correct running of a war. And you're telling me we can't find one old man?'

Sarah bristled. 'It takes time for address movements and ration re-registrations to be returned and filed by the correct departments. But if you think you can do it any faster, perhaps you'd be good enough to show us some of Scotland Yard's infallible techniques!'

The two detective constables bent over their desks, apparently having acquired a sudden passionate interest in month-old Alien Registration returns.

They were in the main CID office. Jack said quietly: 'Come into my office, Sergeant.'

He waited until she'd seated herself opposite him and then said in the same deceptively mild tone: 'Now, is the problem in this relationship me or you?'

Sarah blinked. Her mouth compressed and for a moment he thought she was about to say she didn't know what he was talking about. Finally, however, she said: 'I'd say it was six of one and half a dozen of the other, sir.'

'Agreed.' Jack extracted a crumpled envelope from his breast pocket. 'This is my excuse. What's yours?'

Sarah fingered the thin paper doubtfully. The address had been boldly printed in black ink, the neat gothic script directing the letter to Stamford c/o Scotland Yard.

'Read it,' he offered.

Uncertain what to expect, Sarah extracted a single sheet of paper and held it to the light.

Sir,
I have the honour to be the neighbour of your

father-in-law, Piet de Vos. Today the boy tried to deliver your telegram but found this impossible as the de Vos family are not at home. I have therefore taken the telegram and have opened it. I hope you will forgive my presumption in reading your private correspondence but in these extraordinary times, extraordinary manners are sometimes necessary.

I should tell you that your father-in-law has not been in good health for some months. Two weeks ago he suffered a mild stroke and was advised by the doctor to take a rest. He closed the bakery and took his daughter and granddaughter to stay with friends in France, possibly near the coast. Regrettably, however, I am unable to tell you their name since I do not believe I ever heard it.

I now know, as do many of my countrymen, that our Government's policy of neutrality has ensured that our country will be over-run by the German Army at any hour. I am too old to do more than stay here and wait for the inevitable, but I intend to give this letter to another neighbour who is young enough still to believe he can make a difference and who intends to try to reach England. He has promised me that if he should do so, he will post this letter for me and I will trust to the efficiency of your famous postal system and Scotland Yard to ensure it reaches you.

Please forgive my garrulousness but I have always admired your language and could not resist this chance to indulge what I believe will be my last chance to write in it for many years.

I hope we shall have the opportunity to meet in happier times.

Pray for us.

Else Deetman

Sarah turned the envelope over. The smudged postmark showed it had been posted in Harwich two days previously. 'He made it then, this younger neighbour?'

'Looks like it, doesn't it? The Yard sent a car round with this last night.'

'Nothing else? I mean, no note from the person who posted it?'

'No. Just that.'

Sarah refolded the letter and passed it back. 'What will you do? Go to France?'

'I don't see how I can. Apart from the logistical problems of getting there, I've no idea where to start looking. I've never heard of my father-in-law having friends in France. Neelie certainly never mentioned them. I don't even know which coast we're talking about – Mediterranean or Atlantic. I've contacted the Embassy in Paris. Now all I can do is sit here and wait. And I feel so bloody useless!'

'Don't,' Sarah said. 'At least they know they've got a home waiting. It's more than most of the refugees coming here have. I'm sorry I lost my temper earlier. Put it down to women's problems – they usually do. I'll get back to checking criminal records.'

Thursday 23 May
Central eventually disgorged the information that Billy Zimmermann had been tenuously connected to a prostitution racket four years previously.

'Over Limehouse way,' Ding Dong said, reading off his notes. 'Couple of lascars bringing in girls for sailors' comforts, if you know what I mean, sir. They got four years apiece and deportation afterwards. Zimmermann had a room in the boarding house where one of the men lodged. No suggestion he had anything to do with the case.' Regret tinged his already lugubrious voice.

'Anyone else?'

Sarah's connections at Leman Street produced one conviction for soliciting under Lily's maiden name of Thomas. But it was the Meekses, the one family Stamford would have bet had had the least connection with the police, who produced the biggest surprise.

'Scannell? Edgar Scannell!'

'That's him, sir.' Ding Dong was pleased at the reaction he'd provoked. 'Doing time in the Scrubs for that Post Office job in Camden last year. His missus, Pearl, is the Meekses' daughter.'

'I remember that job. They beat up the postmistress with a pick-axe handle. He was lucky to get such a light sentence.' It explained, Stamford realized, Carey Meeks's refusal to admit he'd got a daughter.

'Does it help us?' Sarah queried.

'It wouldn't seem so at present. But nothing about this case is as straightforward as it seems,' Stamford replied. 'There's nothing on any of the Yeovils?'

The three officers shook their heads.

'So whatever Lily Hendry knows – or thinks she knows – about one of the Yeovils, it looks like they got away with it.' He reached for his hat and spoke directly to Sarah, excluding the two DCs from his invitation. 'Let's go and see Mrs Yeovil again and see if she can shed any light on Valerie's mystery man. At least now we know who's done what, we can look at Junction Cut with a fresh eye.'

When they turned the corner into The Cut, Stamford and Sarah discovered that everyone was looking at the street with fresh eyes. It would have been difficult to do otherwise. The little close appeared to have been the scene of a major disaster. Bodies lay in all directions: sitting on the kerbs, lying on the pavements, propped against the houses. Some were bandaged and splinted into immobility, others nursed broken arms, legs and heads, a couple were being stretchered unsteadily to a waiting ambulance.

Jack bent over the nearest body, an elderly woman lying outside number two, and turned over a buff label tied to her cardigan. He discovered her neck had been broken by falling masonry.

An eye opened, gleaming through the polished lens of her spectacles with interest. 'Are you a doctor?'

'No. I'm a policeman.'

'How interesting.' Dolly Toddhunter levered herself into a sitting position against the step.

The movement brought a shriek of protest from a tweedy woman in a WVS outfit who'd been applying a wadge of cotton dressing to an elderly man's eye. 'No, no dear. Don't move. You're dead. You have to wait for the live casualties to be transferred to the Casualty Clearing Station first. Then we deal with you.'

Dolly did not react to this instruction. Jack remembered she was deaf. Speaking directly into her face, he said: 'Apparently you're a corpse. You're not supposed to sit up. Or speak, I imagine.'

Dolly glared round his back at the outraged WVS woman. 'I'm communing from the other side.'

'You can't do that. This is an official Civil Defence Exercise. Casualties are expected to behave responsibly. No, wait, come back. I haven't finished with you yet.' This last remark was addressed to the walking wounded she'd been bandaging, who'd taken advantage of her distraction to nip round Dolly and through the open door of number two.

'Gone for a pint,' Dolly explained, leaning herself comfortably against the step. 'Have you come to question me?'

'As a matter of fact, I was hoping to speak to Mrs Yeovil.'

'She's out. Went off early, so she wouldn't be asked to take part in this exercise, I imagine. A very silly woman. If only she'd realize that if she laughed *with* us, people wouldn't laugh *at* her.'

JUNCTION CUT

Jack hesitated. He was reluctant to waste another day. Dolly watched him. Her bright black eyes reminded him of a robin's. 'Do you think it would be all right for a corpse to sneak off for a drink?'

Dolly beamed. 'This one would love to.'

Scrambling to her feet, she led them into number two, through the kitchen and across the narrow alley into the back yard of The Hayman. The casualty who'd lost his eye passed them at the back door, wiping froth from his lips with a guilty grin.

Their emergence from the private quarters and into the public bar caused a momentary stir, but the mid-morning customers soon relapsed into their normal muttered conversations. Life was strange enough these days. Why shouldn't two coppers be drinking in The Hayman with an elderly spinster who'd been labelled as if she was due for despatch on the night train?

The May sunlight was slanting through the Victorian stained-glass windows, sending elongated lozenges of red, green and blue in abstract patterns across the scrubbed floor and supping customers. Dolly wore a coronet of ruby diamonds across her forehead and over the thick coils of hair that wound round her ears. Despite her age, there was no trace of grey amongst the black locks. Sipping at the whisky he'd just bought her, she cocked one bird-bright eye in Jack's direction and waited for him to speak.

'You must have known Billy Zimmermann well,' Stamford suggested. 'Since you shared a house with him.'

'We roomed in the same house, that's not quite the same thing. I wouldn't say I knew him well – I doubt if anyone did. He kept himself to himself. Making friends is an art that requires practice like any other. And I do not believe Billy ever acquired the necessary skills. He seemed to me a rather solitary young man.'

'No visitors?'

'None that I ever saw. Unless you count Valerie.'

'Valerie visited Billy?' Stamford's voice had risen involuntarily. It had no effect on Dolly, but several other heads turned. He pulled his stool at a sharper angle to the room, presenting his shoulder rather than his face to the on-lookers. He repeated the statement, turning it into a question this time. 'Are you certain?'

'Yes, I met her on the stairs once or twice. She was attempting to teach him to read. More from a desire to escape her mother than from any wish to impart learning to the less fortunate I imagine.'

'Billy Zimmermann was illiterate?'

'And still is, I assume. Unless they've introduced remedial reading in His Majesty's Prisons?' Dolly finished her whisky with evident enjoyment. 'However, I don't think illiterate is quite the right word. It implies stupidity. And Billy isn't stupid. He simply can't read. I encountered children like that when I was teaching. They are perfectly intelligent, exceptionally so in some cases, but they are unable to recognize letters and word shapes for some reason. Billy was like that.'

'You were a teacher?' It was Sarah who spoke, for the first time since they'd reached Junction Cut.

JUNCTION CUT

Maybe it was the expression on her face, or maybe Dolly had grown used to the effect this statement had on her listeners. 'Yes,' she said, straightening her backbone. 'Before I got this in Flanders.' She touched her left ear. 'A shell exploded right next to my ambulance. Came round in a field hospital without a scratch on me, except the world had gone silent. Were you there?' She addressed her question to Stamford.

Jack nodded. 'Last six months.'

'Then you'll understand. In a way it was a blessed relief, not to hear any more. I could still see, of course, but at least the screams were gone. I considered myself fortunate. Then.' She smiled. 'It was different when I got back to Blighty. No one wanted a deaf teacher. No one wanted a deaf anything. Eventually I obtained a part-time book-keeping job in a laundry. You are, in fact, extremely fortunate to find me at home today. Normally I work in the afternoons, but today my employer has permitted me a whole half day's holiday. It is, so to speak, my last day of freedom before I commence full-time employment next week. The other lady in the office has just obtained a new position as an omnibus conductress – what they call a clippie, I believe – and I am to do both her job and my own from tomorrow. This is not a tribute to my efficiency, it is a tacit acknowledgement by the skin-flint who employs me that he is unlikely to get anyone else to work for the money he pays.'

Her tone was sarcastic but there was no bitterness in it. Jack had a sense of intelligence going to waste.

He asked: 'Did you see Billy at all that Saturday?'

'In the morning. I walked back from the public baths with him.'

'How did he seem?'

'Perfectly normal. I imagine most murderers do.'

'And the Yeovils? Did you see them?'

'No. No. I didn't see the Yeovils.' There was the slightest break in the smooth flow of her well-modulated voice. It invited him to probe further. So he did.

'But you saw someone. Someone you didn't expect to see?'

Dolly Toddhunter was a decisive woman. Having made up her mind, she didn't bother to prevaricate. 'I thought I saw that girl Ronnie Yeovil is engaged to.'

'In Junction Cut?'

'Not at first, no. It is my habit to eat my Saturday tea in the Weaver's Cafe. It is my one treat. I'd just finished eating and was paying my bill when I thought I saw her sitting at a table by the door. But when I turned back, she was gone.'

'But you saw her again?'

'I thought I did. As I came home, I think she left Junction Cut just as I got there at approximately a quarter to six. But I could have been mistaken. It was very dark by then.'

Chapter 11

Friday 24 May

Edie's absence throughout Thursday, coupled with CID's continuing failure to locate James Jolly, did nothing to improve Stamford's already stretched nerves. Sarah watched him struggling to maintain a façade of calm professionalism whilst his mind was obviously across the Channel.

After a fraught morning, when the three junior CID officers did their utmost to keep out of Stamford's way whilst appearing to be doing their jobs to the best of their abilities, his decision to change his mind and question Edie at the department store was greeted with a heart-felt sigh of relief all round.

Leaving the station by the rear entrance, they encountered yet another drill by some of the Agar Street LDVs. This time, however, the effect of a week of practice was impressively demonstrated in the synchronized marching ending in a slamming 'halt' with rifles smartly sloped over new khaki tunics. As the final echo of heels meeting cobbles died away, the stocky broken-nosed LDV instructor with the handmade sergeant's stripes permitted himself a quick smile which turned to a scowl as a wolf whistle sounded from the direction of the station garages.

A police driver who'd been lounging against one of the wireless cars straightened up, obviously ready to make some facetious comment, spotted Jack and Sarah on the steps and hurriedly reapplied himself to polishing the already gleaming paintwork of the bonnet.

'Impressive performance, Sergeant,' Jack remarked, nodding at the contingent who stood staring stonily ahead. 'You must have put in a lot of hard work to bring them to that standard so quickly?'

The bruised face cracked into a smile. 'Thank you, sir.' Leaning forward on his toes, he hissed, 'Tell you the truth, they're a good bunch. Wouldn't tell them that, but I reckon we can give Hitler a good run for his marks. Got to, ain't we? All in it together now, sir.'

'Do you think we are, sir?' Sarah asked as they left the sergeant abusing his red-eared contingent and turned out into Kentish Town Road. 'All in it together, I mean?'

'Don't you?' Stamford seemed genuinely surprised by the question.

'I suppose so. But, I mean . . .' What did she mean? Sarah struggled to put it into words. 'Well, if the Germans do invade and everyone fights, then who keeps order? And if they win, do we leave it to them to run the police force? What if they want us to do it? Wouldn't it be better if we did? At least we know the people. What will you do if that happens, sir?'

She thought he was going to ignore the question.

The silence went on for so long that she became uneasy. Had she given him the impression she was a Quisling like that Norwegian minister? It wasn't what she'd intended. 'What I meant was . . .' she finally said.

He interrupted with fierce abruptness. 'I know what you meant! You do have a way of making people face things that they'd rather avoid, you know.'

'Sorry.'

'No. It's a fair question – interesting too. When does cooperation become collaboration? I suppose it's something that everyone in an official position might have to face sooner or later. Not just us. I think the answer in my case is, no, I wouldn't work for them. Would you?'

'No.'

'That's two of us for the Resistance then,' Stamford remarked, pushing open the doors to Daniel's. A female lift attendant, smartly groomed in maroon livery, shut the brass doors, and carried them up to the corsetry department on the first floor.

The department, like the rest of the store, had an empty air. Assistants in crisp white blouses and black skirts huddled together in the middle of the sales floor, broke apart at the sight of potential customers. One hurried forward, her face wreathed in an eager smile.

'May I help you, sir? Madam?'

'We'd like to speak to Mrs Yeovil, please.'

'The corsetry fitter?' The assistant's eyes flicked from Sarah to Jack and back again. Sarah saw the woman take in the ringless third finger on her left hand. Only years of maintaining an outward air of calm competence whilst in uniform prevented her blushing fiercely. At least Stamford's warrant card wiped the knowing smile off the assistant's face.

Sarah's embarrassment was nothing compared with Edie's. Her expression of dismay when she recognized the two officers was so intense that they could almost believe she'd been caught red-handed after slaughtering the entire department single-handedly. 'I don't think . . .' she flapped, her hands flicking agitated fingers, as if she were shooing starlings from newly sewn seeds, 'that this is appropriate.'

'This is a murder investigation, Mrs Yeovil. In my opinion it is entirely appropriate. Is there somewhere we might talk privately?'

Edie looked round helplessly. Behind the high polished counter, backed by floor-to-ceiling drawers of brassières, slips, stockings, suspender belts and corsets, the supervisor stood in all her malicious authority. 'I think,' she said, 'the fitting room would be convenient, Mrs Yeovil. You will remember, however, that you have a client in ten minutes?'

Flustered, Edie led the way through a set of curtains and ushered them into a small room thickly carpeted in gold. The mirrored walls picked up their reflections, each caught and miniaturized by mirrors within mirrors, so that a dozen Sarahs, Jacks and Edies receded into the distance. Jack leant against the door, leaving the two plush upholstered chairs for the women.

For a moment Sarah half-expected him to produce the nude sketches of Valerie. Instead he asked her about Edgware.

Edie appeared to be genuinely puzzled by the question. And angry when Jack disclosed the reason. 'A man! I don't believe it. No. Not my Valerie. I brought her up to be a decent girl.'

Her hands gripped the chair arms. Instinctively, Sarah laid her own hand over the nearest. She became aware of the smell of alcohol overlaid with the scent of violet cachous. 'That's not what the inspector's saying, Mrs Yeovil. There may be a perfectly innocent reason for Valerie's trips. An old family friend, perhaps? Someone she knew when she was younger?'

'No. No. There's no one. I don't believe it. That wicked girl is lying.' Even to Sarah's ears, there was a half-heartedness about Edie's protests. She was going through the motions, protesting for the sake of protesting, but in her heart she believed what they were saying.

'You've no idea who this man could be?' Jack demanded.

Edie shook her head. In the mirrors, a dozen Edies denied their daughter's deception.

'There was nothing in the possessions you threw out? An address? A letter?'

'No. There was nothing like that. Valerie didn't get letters. It was just books and clothes and some make-up from Woolworths.'

'Was the slip that matched the underclothes

Valerie was wearing on the day she was killed amongst them?'

'I think so.'

'It was an expensive set, wasn't it? Not the kind of clothes you'd expect to find a schoolgirl wearing?'

'Tea rose, artificial silk. Eighteen shillings and sixpence the set including staff discount.' Edie's professional training took over, spilling the words from her white lips without any conscious effort from her brain. 'But she didn't wear them for school. They wouldn't have allowed it. Just at the weekends. You know how young girls like pretty things.'

'Especially when they're meeting their boyfriends.'

Beneath Sarah's hand, Edie's twisted, her fingers seeking to interlock. In response to a frown from Stamford, Sarah loosened her clasp. Evidently it was get tough with Edie time. Certainly he put his next questions aggressively, demanding to know why she hadn't told them about Valerie giving Zimmermann reading lessons. Making it clear he didn't believe her claim that she knew nothing about them. 'This is a murder investigation, Mrs Yeovil. That means if Billy Zimmermann is found guilty they'll pull a hood over his head, put a rope round his neck and drop him through a trap-door. Normally the drop breaks the prisoner's neck, but just occasionally they get it wrong and he swings there choking to death.'

Edie gave a low moan. Fumbling in the bosom of her dress, she drew out a lace-edged handkerchief and pressed it to her lips.

'Do you want that to happen to an innocent man, Mrs Yeovil?'

'No, no. But I don't know... We're a nice family. Junction Cut is just temporary. We don't belong there. Please, I have my client. Please go. Leave me alone!' She sprang up, pushing Stamford away from the door and running out into the shop floor, scattering the group of assistants who had no time to pretend they were doing anything but eavesdropping outside the fitting room.

'You think I was too hard on her, don't you?'

'Yes. No. I don't know.' Sarah bit her tongue with annoyance. She sounded like a real ditherer.

They'd returned to the CID office in order to allow Stamford to re-read the witnesses' statements. He looked up now from the file and said: 'She's hiding something. Look at this statement. She left the Nettleses' house at five forty-five or thereabouts. It shouldn't have taken more than half an hour to reach home. That puts her in Junction Cut around the time the murder took place. Yet your notes show Carey Meeks didn't summon help until gone eight o'clock. Where was she in that missing hour and three quarters?'

'She was in shock. She could have been anywhere. Wandering around. Passed out in number four. You don't think she's protecting the murderer! Why should she?'

'She didn't like Valerie. We've got several witnesses

to that fact. She loved the brother. Where was he during the fatal hour? And why isn't there a statement from him?'

'I don't know. Inspector Kavanagh took one. I remember Ronnie coming into the station. I expect it wasn't written up because Ronnie didn't have anything to say. He was out all that afternoon and evening in the West End. With four friends who were on leave. They went to the first house at the Palladium. Inspector Kavanagh checked.' For the first time Sarah felt a spurt of warmth towards the dead inspector. The alternative didn't bear thinking about. She'd come across cases of incest during her work with uniform, of course, but she'd never become hardened to it — and the idea that it should lead to rape was particularly stomach-churning.

The idea seemed to take Stamford by surprise. 'I hadn't thought of that,' he admitted. 'I was toying with a scenario of Ronnie returning home, finding his sister with this mystery man, and losing his temper.'

'With Val? Isn't it more likely he'd attack the lover?'

'Perhaps he took the opportunity to make a run for it while brother and sister were fighting. Anyway it's all just speculation if Kavanagh checked out his alibi. Even,' he muttered under his breath, 'if he was too damned slap-dash to write it up.' He yawned and stretched his arms above his head. 'In which case, I suggest we check out Edie Yeovil's alibi, Sergeant.'

* * *

The Nettleses lived in one of the roads that ran between Highgate Cemetery and Hampstead Heath. The three-storey houses radiated a feeling of prosperous middle-class smugness which was only slightly marred by the mobile barrage balloon that had taken residence at the end of the street.

The poor might be just down the hill in Kentish Town, but the only way they'd set foot in these enclaves of post-Victorian respectability was to polish the brass, serve the dinner, sweep the carpets and deliver the milk. The poor, each white-washed step, gleaming knocker and immaculate curtain intimated, were obviously lazy and had no place in this street of self-made prosperity. Which made it all the stranger that Ronnie Yeovil should even have met one of the daughters of the house, let alone become engaged to her. Susan, the youngest Yeovil daughter, solved the first part of the mystery.

'I introduced them,' she explained. 'Ronnie and I work at the same office. Insurance. It's deadly dull but Daddy wouldn't give me a decent allowance so I had to get a job.' Taking a lacquered cigarette box from the side table she offered it first to Sarah then Stamford. They both declined. 'Why?' she said, clicking fruitlessly at a table lighter. 'Is it important? Damn, this thing needs filling.'

Stamford produced his own lighter. 'Not at all, I was just curious.'

Susan sat down and indicated the sofa. 'Not our sort you mean? Oh, it's all right. I don't mind your saying it. Even Phyl could see that. Can I offer you a drink? Whisky? Sherry?'

Stamford accepted a small whisky and soda, which enabled Sarah to feel free to take a sherry. Susan joined her.

The Nettleses' lounge exuded the same feeling of well-bred opulence as the exterior of the house. The tenderly buffed brass fender enclosed a tasteful flower arrangement in place of the winter fire; polished surfaces were covered with delicate porcelain ornaments; a grand piano displayed a collection of silver-framed photographs ranging from sepia-tinted portrait studies of grim-faced Edwardians to more recent family groups – less suggestive of incipient rigor mortis thanks to faster shutter speeds but equally po-faced.

Susan poured the drinks herself. 'We had a parlour-maid, but she left last September. Joined the ATS. And Daddy won't let Mummy engage a new one. He says it's wrong to take a young woman from war work. And Mummy and I should do more in the house as our bit for the war effort.'

'What's his contribution to the effort?' Sarah couldn't resist asking.

'He was on the local ARP roster, and now he's got himself appointed a part-time Captain in these new Local Defence Volunteers. He was fitted for his uniform today. Bespoke, of course.'

'I didn't know they had ranks,' Sarah said.

'I think he commissioned himself,' Susan admitted.

'And designed his own uniform.'

They'd already established that the newly appointed Captain Yeovil and his wife were dining out. But since Susan had been at home that Saturday evening, there seemed no reason why she shouldn't supply the answers they needed. An exercise in which Susan seemed only too ready to participate.

She was a pretty twenty-year-old, wings of dark brown hair framing a lively face of the traditional English 'peaches-and-cream' colouring. Her blue eyes sparkled with life as she answered the two detectives' questions.

'The Christmas before last,' she said in answer to Stamford's question regarding Phyllis and Ronnie's first meeting. 'Nineteen thirty-eight. I was having a few people round for drinks and dancing to the gramophone, that sort of thing. One of the men let me down at the last minute so I invited Ronnie. There aren't that many spare men to go round at Christmas and I couldn't find anyone else at short notice.'

She hadn't met Edie Yeovil or Valerie until the following June. 'At the engagement party.'

'Did you like them?' Stamford asked.

'Well,' Susan drew another breath. She tended to need a lot since all her words were delivered on a breathy stream of air.

'No,' Susan breathed, 'I can't say I did. She ... Mrs Yeovil, I mean ... was odd. She kept telling us all how her family had once worked for a vicar. And how the Junction Cut house was only temporary. It was embarrassing. Quite honestly if she'd have just said, "Look, I'm dead common, but my son's marrying your daughter, so you can just lump it", we'd all have liked her better. Do you see?'

The two detectives did see. It wasn't hard to imagine Edie fluttering around in this rarified middle-classness, so desperately not wanting to show up her son. 'What about Valerie? Did you like her?'

'To tell you the truth, I'm not sure. I mean, she obviously didn't give a damn whether we liked her or not. Which was a sort of plus point for her, if you see what I mean. I only spoke to her once. About insurance. She seemed to think it was a wonderful job because I got to handle loads of money. I had to disillusion her, tell her that we used cheques rather than actually filling envelopes with five pound notes.'

'And what about the Saturday she died? Tell me about that day.'

'She'd come to fit the bridesmaid's dress – Mrs Yeovil, that is. Not Val. Another one of Daddy's attempts at saving resources.' Laying the smoking cigarette in a handy ash-tray she bounced to her feet and fetched one of the silver-framed photographs from the piano. It was a wedding group: a pretty, dark-haired bride, clutching an enormous bouquet of roses and lilies across her stomach, and flanked by two bridesmaids simpering into the camera lens. The youngest girl, her hair bound in a rose coronet, was just discernible as Susan.

'That's my sister Jane's wedding. Five years ago.

She's got two children now. Daddy decided we could re-use the dresses. Not the bride's, of course. Mummy put her foot down on that one. But the bridesmaids' outfits, God help us. Valerie was supposed to wear my old dress and I was going to have Phyl's.' She tapped one manicured finger on the older bridesmaid.

It explained a lot, Sarah thought, staring into the grainy black and white faces. Two younger, prettier sisters, one already married, the other, she noted, engaged. And Phyllis, the oldest and plainest of the three girls. In her late twenties and no man in sight. Was that why she'd tied herself to a man nine years younger from a social class that plainly wasn't going to be acceptable to her family?

'Do you expect Miss Nettles home soon?' Stamford asked.

'Miss . . .' Susan looked nonplussed for a moment. 'Oh, you mean Phyl? She doesn't live here any more. She's got a flat in Maitland Park.'

'But she was living here when Valerie Yeovil was killed?'

'Yes. Although she wasn't actually *here*. She was at work all day. She didn't get in until gone eight.'

'On a Saturday?'

'She'd been sick for most of that week,' Susan said. 'Apparently one of the old boys had a lot of important typing to be done and Phyl volunteered to go in Saturday and do it. She's like that. Very conscientious.'

Stamford said abruptly: 'Have you any idea why Mrs Yeovil finds that visit difficult to talk about?

Did something happen? Something she'd rather forget?'

A coil of ash, fragile and soft, fell to the ground, shattering into grey flakes on the silk carpet. Susan put her cigarette down hastily. 'Damn! Mummy will be furious.' She attempted to scoop a fingerful of the offending dirt up. It disintegrated, smearing her with grey dust. Stamford waited. One eye flicked in his direction. 'You're not going to let me duck that question, are you? All right. I suppose you might as well know. You see, Mummy had a meeting of her First Aid Committee at seven that night, so she asked Hatty to serve dinner early . . .'

It wasn't what Sarah had expected. Quite simply Susan and her father had seated themselves in the dining room in response to Hatty's summons. 'It had four places laid because I was expecting my fiancé that weekend. Anyway Mummy was showing Mrs Yeovil out, at least we thought she was, only then she – Mrs Yeovil – just appeared and sat down at the table and started babbling on about how much she was looking forward to dinner.' Susan looked appealingly at the two officers. 'We didn't know what to do. I'd just decided to sit tight and pretend we'd expected her to stay, when all of a sudden Mummy came in with her hat and coat, and you could sort of see her realizing that she'd made a dreadful mistake.'

The following scene had been ugly. All Edie's resentments at imagined insults and slights had poured out. 'It was horrible. I mean, she was practically foaming at the mouth. And then she just grabbed her things and ran out.'

'Nobody went after her?'

'No. Mummy wanted to, but Daddy said it was best to leave it.' Susan shrugged. 'I know it doesn't put us in a very good light, but honestly it wasn't done as a deliberate snub. We just didn't think.'

'Which do you think she's blotting out, sir?' Sarah asked as they left the house. 'The murder? Or the humiliation?'

'I think it would take a psychiatrist to answer that one. She does seem obsessively concerned with what others think of her.' But who knew what way shock would take people? 'By the way, didn't you have a gas mask with you?'

Sarah clamped a hand to her side with an exclamation of annoyance. 'I left it on the arm of the chair.'

'Go back. I'll wait out here.'

Stamford was whiling away the time watching the relief crew for the barrage balloon being initiated into the mysteries of the winch when she came out again. A large, round-faced man, his LDV uniform falling in baggy folds over equally baggy folds of flesh, was being urged to put his back into it by the regular corporal he was relieving.

Stamford cocked an eyebrow as Sarah arrived at his elbow and said: 'Yes?'

'Sir?'

'You're obviously bursting with news, Sergeant. What is it?'

Sarah was momentarily thrown. If her face was that easy to read, what else had he seen there? Swallowing hard, she said: 'The cook, Hatty I suppose, answered the door. She just let me find my own way to the lounge.'

Susan had been on the phone, unaware of the other woman in her soft-soled shoes moving across the thick carpet.

'They've just left,' she'd said, the breathy delivery replaced by a straightforward, well-rounded tone.

A babble of indistinct chatter had crackled from the receiver.

'No. They were asking about Mrs Yeovil. I told them about . . . you know . . . her having hysterics.'

Chatter again.

'No. No. I said you were at work all day.'

Static.

'I'm not using a tone. Listen I rang you that evening. Once at five and again after that old bat had left to warn you she might cause you trouble with Ronnie. You didn't answer.'

More static.

'Oh come on, Phyl. You can hardly have been in the lavatory both times.'

Silently hooking the leather strap of her gas-mask holder, Sarah had crept out.

Chapter 12

Phyllis arrived just as Hatty was preparing to serve the dinner. Unlike Stamford, who hadn't visited this street since his days in uniform, she could see the subtle changes the past nine months had brought.

The basement areas, once enclosed by spikes, were now open to the pavement, their perimeters defined by stone copings indented at regular intervals by crumbling holes where the railings had been set until the Government had ordered them to be torn out for scrap iron. Highgate had complied with patriotic fervour and now the houses resembled elongated faces with bottom jaws thrust out to display toothless gums still showing the unhealed holes where the stumps had been drawn.

Hatty opened the door to her. 'They never told me you were coming tonight, Miss Phyllis,' she grumbled with the familiarity of a cook who had known her since babyhood and was well aware that she was indispensable. 'I've not cooked dinner for you.'

'It doesn't matter, Hatty.' Phyl kissed the older woman's cheek. It smelt of flour and jam and safe childhood escapes to the kitchen when her mother wasn't looking.

Hatty wasn't going to be baulked of a good grumble. 'I can't be expected to stretch rations for four to rations for five unless I'm told.' She shuffled back down the hall towards the baize-covered door that led to the kitchen. 'Miss Susan's already sat down. You'd better join her.'

Even though she was the only one eating at home tonight, Susan had taken her normal place to the left of the long dining table. The idea of usurping either of her parents' positions at the head or foot would never have occurred to her. She greeted Phyllis's entrance with a simple: 'Thought it would be you. Is Hatty feeding you?'

'She says not. But you know Hatty.'

'Convinced we'll starve to death once we have to look after ourselves,' Susan suggested.

'Exactly.' Phyllis pulled off a green felt hat decorated with a jaunty feather and slipped off the swagger jacket of her chartreuse-coloured costume. Crossing to the sideboard, she opened one of the drawers, selected spoons, forks and knives from the polished silver cutlery, and laid herself a place opposite Susan.

'What else did they say?' she asked.

'Just what I told you on the telephone. They were interested in the Yeovils, not you. What did you . . .'

Susan broke off as the door crashed back on its hinges and Hatty staggered in bearing a large soup tureen.

'It's only vegetable. I can't be expected to do more. There's a war on you know. Makes the butchers lazy.'

'I'm sure it will be delicious,' Phyllis said, taking two soup dishes from the sideboard. 'You don't need to stay. We can serve ourselves.'

Hatty heaved an ample bosom into place in a way that would have made Edie Yeovil beg her to reconsider her brassière fitting and announced that they'd have to because she had the fish to see to and did they expect her to do everything in this house?

'What do you think the butchers have to do with it?' Phyllis asked, tipping the massive china tureen so that her sister could spoon up the half inch of soup at the bottom.

'I don't think they keep the best bones for her any more. She used to use them for stock. I suppose they sell them now.'

Both women sipped in silence, spoons trawling stray lumps of carrot amongst the translucent liquid and carrying them to lipsticked mouths.

'Where were you?' Susan said finally. 'That afternoon?'

'I told you, at the office.'

'Oh, come *on*, Phyl. Look, I didn't say anything last time, did I?'

'The last time?' For the briefest moment, Phyllis's spoon paused between bowl and mouth. Then her voice rose. 'It's not *that*! You surely don't think I'd be stupid enough to get caught twice?'

Whether Susan did or not had to wait whilst Hatty provided plaice in a cream sauce, potatoes and peas.

'I didn't think you'd be that stupid once. I could

understand a grand pash if he'd looked like Clark Gable, but Stephen looks like Daddy. In fact, a couple more years and a few less hairs and you won't be able to tell them apart.'

'It's not about looks. Is that why you're marrying Johnny? For his looks?'

'Well...' Susan twisted her ring, letting the light sparkle from the solitaire diamond. 'They certainly help. And don't you think he looks dreamy in his RAF uniform? I just hope he doesn't get burnt. If he gets shot down, I think it would be better if he just died, don't you?'

'Susie! That's terrible.'

'No, it's not. It's what Johnny says too. One of his squadron got burnt in a training exercise and Johnny says he'd rather die than go on living like that, so there!' Her blue eyes flashed angrily. 'At least we're honest with each other.'

'Yes.' Phyllis laid down her knife and fork, the fish half eaten.

Susan was instantly subdued. 'Sorry, Phyl. I didn't mean that. It's just, well... I don't understand. Honestly, I never did. What was it all about?'

Phyllis pushed her plate away and stared blankly at the framed colour portrait of Their Majesties' Coronation and struggled to remember what it *was* all about.

It had been about being fed up with being the one who had to be found a partner at the tennis parties. About pretending that she was engrossed in her conversations with elderly aunts at the Town Hall dances and didn't really want to dance. About smiling until the muscles in her jaw ached with the pain at Jane's wedding and pretending she didn't hear all the whispered questions and nods in her direction.

Not, of course, that Stephen could ever be seen in public with her. But she'd understood that. Respected his desire to nurse his dying wife to the end. It wasn't, she'd reasoned, really adultery. His wife had had all of Stephen that she'd needed during the last two years of her life. The part that he'd given to her was no longer of interest to his wife. But it had meant everything to Phyllis. Suddenly she was no longer the dull, boring, eldest daughter. The one whose chances of catching a husband became less and less likely with each party she attended. She was Stephen's mistress.

She'd rolled the words around in her mouth, savouring the taste. It was a delicious secret that had allowed her to laugh at all those strait-laced bearers of malicious sympathy at her descent into spinsterhood.

Ordinary acts had become erotic: sitting decorously in the office taking dictation during a meeting and remembering how the previous evening she'd been lying on this very carpet whilst Stephen's hands and mouth had explored her naked body. Catching his eye, knowing he was remembering the same things, and wondering if he was becoming as aroused as her. Handing him papers in a certain way so that the hairs on the back of his wrist would brush against the soft vulnerable underside of hers. Hurrying to retrieve ancient files bound in pink tape from cavernous archives, feeling the tightening of excitement in her stomach as his footsteps had paced slowly along the racks, and the agony of frustration when someone else entered the room. Stephen had made her feel desirable, beautiful, magical. And eventually, ugly.

But she couldn't explain all that to Susan. She took refuge in a half-truth: 'Stephen and I were in love. And now we both love other people. It's as simple as that.' The effort of remembering had brought a hard lump to her diaphragm, killing her appetite. 'I don't think I want any more of this.'

Hatty had made jam sponge for pudding. Escape was impossible. 'It's made with margarine, not butter. But you'll not notice the difference.'

It was an order. The two women ate meekly. Afterwards they carried a coffee tray to the lounge and sat in silence listening to the news on the Home Service. 'Have you seen him since?' Susan said after the last well-modulated, reassuring vowels of the announcer urging them not to listen to defeatist rumours of imminent invasion had died away.

'Why should I have?'

Susan knew her sister well enough to recognize an evasion. 'When?' she demanded.

There was no point in stalling. Susan would niggle and worry until she'd dug out the truth. That was how she'd found out about the affair in the first place. Phyllis admitted: 'Last August. He asked me to meet him. To clear up any misunderstandings.'

'What is there to misunderstand, Stephen?' she'd asked. 'You spent two years telling me we'd be married as soon as your wife died. And ten weeks after the funeral you marry someone else.'

Trusting idiot that she was, she'd been sympathetic about his desire to take his wife's body back to the York church where they'd married. Had borne his weekend trips north to sort out her affairs with equanimity, understanding his need to maintain a show of grief for the sake of his wife's family. Respecting his wishes that their engagement shouldn't be made public until a decent interval had elapsed. Even on the last day, she'd had no suspicion that her world was about to fall apart. A telephone call in the middle of Susan's pre-Christmas party. The unexpected thrill of hearing his voice. And afterwards?

The next hour was blurry to her still. She remembered putting down the receiver: the bakelite casing appeared to be made of lead, so heavy that she could scarcely hold it. Afterwards she'd walked back into the lounge, her feet unexpectedly loud on the polished floor where the carpet had been rolled back. Somebody had put a record on the player; a quickstep melody, light and bright, urging feet to spin with the rhythm. They were all in twos again. Except for one boy – a gauche, nervously ill-at-ease boy who hung back near the radiogram and cast desperate glances at the door as if hoping to make a bolt for it. Clamping one arm round his waist and seizing his hand, Phyllis had dragged him into the mêlée. Cold rage had given her the confidence and vivacity that had always eluded her. She and Ronnie had danced every dance, often to the delighted applause of the other guests. And she'd determinedly forgotten all about Stephen, until that day in Hyde Park, in August.

'You're engaged, I understand?' Stephen had said, his glance going to her gloved hands.

'Yes. I met Ronnie last Christmas.' Let him see how easily he was forgotten, her mind had urged defiantly.

'I'm glad. You deserve someone decent, Phyllis.'

'Shall we walk?' She stood up quickly, biting her tongue on the obvious comment.

'Of course.' He'd taken her elbow out of habit and she hadn't withdrawn it.

They passed slit trenches dug into the browning grass of the park. She'd waited for him to speak. When he hadn't, she'd finally said: 'What are you doing in London, Stephen? Have you left the practice in York? Your father-in-law's practice?' It hadn't been intended as a barb, but she was pleased to see him wince.

'Yes. I have. I'm on my way to Bristol, Phyllis. I've got a position with the Frazer and McKenzie Far Eastern Trading Company. As a legal adviser. I catch an Imperial Airways flying boat at the end of the week.'

The air was clammy, prickling at her skin, threatening a summer storm. Tremors generated by another sort of electricity had started to crawl over her body.

'I had to see you before I went, Phyllis,' he'd pleaded. 'To explain. I never intended to hurt you. It was just –

a madness. You can see that, can't you?'

Of course she could see it. Already her mind had begun to turn to a tropical bungalow – long and low, silhouetted against a blood-red Eastern sunset with herself and Stephen relaxing on the verandah. When the first heavy drops of rain had plopped on to her light summer dress, spreading until they merged and turned the primrose voile into egg-yolk yellow, she'd accepted his suggestion they return to his hotel.

The receptionist at the Alexandra Hotel had barely glanced up as he handed over the key. She hadn't understood the significance of that until it was all over. Until Stephen had stripped off her wet clothes, pushed her on to the bed and lain eagerly on top of her, thrusting and panting with an urgency that was reminiscent of those desperate fumbles in the old archive room. Only after, when he'd rolled away with a groan and told her how happy he was that she understood about Mary, had she begun to notice that this was a double bedroom. And then the reason the receptionist in this respectable family hotel had made no protest at a guest taking a woman to his room had hit her with sickening clarity.

'Where is she now?' she'd asked, already beginning to feel the vomit rising in her throat.

'Shopping with her mother. You wouldn't believe the amount of kit that's necessary for a tropical posting. Especially now, in view of Mary's condition. Don't worry, they won't be back for hours yet.'

'She's pregnant?'

'Mmm.' Stephen had nuzzled at her nipple. 'That's why I accepted this job. You don't think it looks like a blue funk, do you, Phyllis? I mean, you understand, don't you? I can still join up out there if I'm needed. But I want Mary and the baby out of Europe. Away from the bombs. You do understand?'

'Yes. I understand, Stephen.' He'd wanted absolution. A pardon for the way he'd treated her. And once she'd given it, she'd been rewarded with a quick session in bed for being a good, understanding girl.

His weight had been pushing on her diaphragm, forcing the bile into her throat. Thrusting him away, she'd rushed for the bathroom. The last thing she'd heard him say before she retched into the basin, was: 'They'll be safe in this new posting. There won't be any war in Singapore.'

She gave Susan an edited version of the meeting, her account heavy with the implication that she'd used Stephen for one final fling before her wedding to Ronnie.

Susan tucked her legs up, hugging her ankles with one hand. 'Phyl,' she said suddenly, 'what's it like?'

'What's what like?'

'Well, you know . . . doing it. The whole way, with a man?'

'You mean you don't know? I thought you and Johnny . . .'

'No. Not the whole way,' Susan burst out angrily. 'How can we? There's nowhere to *go*. You remember last October, when Johnny got a forty-eight hour leave and I went to stay with his parents in Surrey? We were going to then, but they never let us out of their sight. Johnny swears they'd loosened a couple of the floor boards on the landing so they could hear if he tried to get into my bedroom.' With an apparent switch of subject, she said abruptly: 'Do you think they'll bring in conscription for women?'

'I don't know. Why should they? Most are doing their bit now. And they've just passed this Bill to mobilize the nation, which means they can direct us where they want us. So I don't see why they need to conscript us into the forces.'

'I hope they do. Shall I tell you something?' Susan rocked forward, her face flushed. 'I'm going to join the WAAFs.' Lowering her voice, even though there was little chance of Hatty hearing anything in the kitchen, she giggled and confided that she'd already made enquiries.

'But why?'

Susan gave an exclamation of impatience. 'You should know, Phyl. Because I'm fed up with being stuck in this prison. I want to be free. I don't want Mummy or Daddy always knowing where I am every hour of the day and night. Or to be transported everywhere in Daddy's damn motor like a prisoner under escort. I love this war, it's given me the chance to escape. Before, Daddy would only let us leave if we were going to be delivered safely into some other male's domestic prison. Like Jane – and you. You know he's only helping with the flat because you're preparing a little nest for Ronnie's homecoming. When is that, by the way?'

'He finishes his basic training on Thursday. He should get seven days' leave, but the way things are . . .' She made a hopeless gesture with one hand as if trying to brush back Hitler's panzer divisions from the lounge carpet.

'Last chance then,' Susan said. 'You can't expect another murder to get you out of it.'

Phyllis stiffened. 'What do you mean?'

'You know, Phyl. You looked like you'd been reprieved from the firing squad last February. Val's murder was a godsend to you. Perfect excuse to delay the wedding – again. You won't be able to wriggle out of it this time. It'll be a special licence and congratulations Mrs Yeovil unless the old bat strangles her precious Ronnie first to save him from the wicked, designing witch.'

'In the circumstances, Susie, don't you think that remark is in rather bad taste?'

'Why? Oh yes. I see what you mean. Still the police don't suspect her of braining Valerie, do they?'

'I've no idea what the police think. I should have thought you were in a better position to know that than me. You met them.'

'Yes.' Susan sighed, hugging her knees. 'Now *he* was rather scrummy. I could understand someone having a pash on him. Which reminds me, you didn't answer my question. About what it's like.'

'No, I didn't. And I'm not going to. You'll just have

to find out for yourself. I'm not staying, give my love to Mummy and Daddy.'

Once again the skies were light, stained with mauve and copper streaks as Phyllis made her way back to the flat. Her move was still so new that she thought of the house she'd just left as 'home' and Maitland Park as 'the flat'.

One aspect of its convenience was the separate entrance. Instead of having the other tenants watching her comings and goings, the basement flat was relatively private, the front door being reached from the street. Holding on to the metal banister that had escaped the scrap collection, Phyllis carefully negotiated the twisting staircase and descended into the pool of blackness in the area. Her key was already in her hand. Fumbling forward she located the lock and tried to insert the key. Her clenched hand slid through apparent solidness and razor-sharp pains seared across her knuckles.

With a gasp of surprise, she snatched her hand back, scraping more skin on the broken shards of glass. She heard the muted tinkle as the key fell through the broken pane and landed on the hall floor.

All the newspaper reports of Valerie Yeovil's death came flooding back. Her first impulse was to run back to the street and bang on the main door of the house screaming for help.

Footsteps hurried along the pavement. Phyllis looked up as a couple, heads bent close together, arms entwined, walked past. They didn't notice her but she could still see them clearly against the lighter sky. Reassured that help was within calling distance if she needed it, she pushed at the door and felt it swing away from her fingertips.

Glass scrunched under her feet as she located the light switch and clicked it down. The flat was a small one: bedroom, dining room, kitchen and bathroom. All four rooms had suffered the intruder's attentions. The polished dining table, a present from her parents, had been scoured with ugly gashes. Bent and disfigured cutlery lay across its surface, prongs and blades bent out of shape as they'd been gouged into the wood. A lamp, once a delicate shepherdess, now lay in a dozen fragments beneath the shattered mirror it had been flung at. The kitchen had escaped relatively lightly with just a few cupboards turned out. But the bedroom had been attacked with an almost frenzied ferocity. Clouds of goose down lifted and swirled in the draught from the open door as Phyllis surveyed the devastation: slashed pillows had disgorged their contents over a shredded counterpane; powder and rouge trailed in drifts over the dressing table, mixing with smashed china pots; the brocade curtains, pinched and pleated by the seamstress into columns of immaculate evenness, now hung in lopsided fragments. Picking up her own carving knife from the floor, Phyllis moved to the bathroom, the blade held against her stomach, as if to fend off what she might find.

After the bedroom it was almost a relief to find the damage was confined to the polished wood bath panel.

JUNCTION CUT

A glass bottle of perfume had been smashed to carry out the feeble scratching. Its remains lay in the bath, the smell of lily-of-the-valley overpowering in the small room.

And there was something else, curled like a snake, on the bottom of the white enamel. With fingertips, Phyllis shook it free of the broken bottle and wound it slowly around her free hand like a bandage. For the first time she became aware that her grazed knuckles were bleeding.

The voice behind her caused her to spin round with a cry of fright. A dark shape filled the open doorway to the street.

'Sorry, miss. I didn't mean to give you a fright. But you're showing a light and it's dusk.' The constable moved a little further into the hall, his boots grinding the broken door pane into smaller fragments. 'Everything all right, is it, miss?'

She was silhouetted against the light. Phyllis realized that he couldn't see her properly. Quickly she dropped the knife and stepped into the hall, pulling the bathroom door shut. 'Yes. Everything is fine, thank you, officer. I forgot my key and had to break a pane to get in. I'm afraid I cut my hand.' As proof she held out the crudely bandaged fist. 'I'm sorry about the light. There.' She snapped the switch off, plunging them both into darkness. 'I'll draw the curtains. Thank you for telling me.' She moved forward, forcing him back.

'You want to get that door fixed, miss,' was his

parting shot. 'I'll keep an eye out when I come past on me beat until you do.'

When he'd gone, Phyllis returned to the bedroom and sank on to the bed. She felt desperately weary. A drifting feather floated past and stuck to her lips. Clumsily she drew the back of her injured hand across them. It left a trail of blood. She could taste the salt mingled with the tang of lily-of-the-valley. Almost dreamily she pulled off the makeshift bandage and watched the blood dripping on to the white cover.

Raising her hand to her lips, she licked the warm liquid. It was comforting somehow, the warmth of her own tongue. A sense of well-being started to creep through her tired body. She looked round the devastated room with growing pleasure. She'd been punished. It was what she deserved for what she'd done.

Chapter 13

If Phyllis Nettles had had a disastrous Friday, then Lily Hendry's could have been described as relatively successful.

She'd persuaded Gus to join the Local Defence Volunteers a few days earlier. He had, by mutual arrangement with the landlord, started working at The Hayman again on a part-time basis. But it still meant he was at home too much for Lily's comfort. He got on her nerves. There was no other way to say it. It made her feel guilty.

'If he talks to me, it makes me want to scream. If he don't talk to me it makes me want to scream. He treats me better than any other bloke I've ever met, but I can't stand to be in the same room as him most days,' she'd moaned to Irene Meeks. 'Ain't I a bitch?'

Straightening her shoulders to relieve the arthritic twinges that her two loaded shopping bags were causing, Irene matched her pace to the younger woman's, and said comfortingly: 'We all feel like that about them sometimes, love.'

They halted at the kerb's edge, waiting whilst a bus crawled slowly past, its pace dictated by the marching parade of men taking up half the road.

'What about this lot then?' Irene suggested. 'Local Defence Volunteers. Let him do his bit for the war effort.'

As usual, he'd done what she wanted without argument, and had returned home with the news that his unit was to man a mobile barrage balloon. 'Just at night,' he reassured her, kneeling by the kitchen chair where she was carefully painting her nails, peering into her face in a way that always set her teeth on edge. 'And we take it in turns, so I'd only be away a couple of nights a week. It would just be until we find our pub. I told them that. It's not like the regulars. You can leave. That'll be all right, won't it?'

Lily assured him it was very much all right. 'Got to be seen to be doing your bit, ain't you, love?' In a burst of relief that he'd finally be out from under her feet, she dropped a kiss on his head.

He put his hands round her waist and pulled her forward, snuffling kisses on her face. 'Get off. You'll smudge me polish. Leave off, Gus.'

He shuffled backwards immediately. 'Sorry, Lily.'

Friday was her first day of glorious freedom. The drill that Stamford and Sarah had encountered in the yard of Agar Street station had been confined to those of the LDV who had no other calls on their time during working hours. 'I was excused too,' Gus had told her, 'because I'm on the barrage balloon training rota for tonight. But I think I should go, show willing, don't you?'

It had taken thirty minutes for Lily to push him out

of the house, strap little Gussie in his pushchair, tilt her cream straw over the cloud of blonde hair she'd already piled on top of her head, and head for Oxford Street.

There were hats to be tried on in Bourne and Hollingsworth, evening shoes with diamanté buckles to consider in John Lewis and silk negligées to be fingered in Selfridge's. It didn't matter that she only had her housekeeping money. Just breathing in the atmosphere was enough. After months of having Gus clamped to her shoulder, droning endlessly about the need to save money for their dream pub, the joy of being free to spend in her imagination was heady stuff. She wheeled the docile toddler from Marble Arch to Tottenham Court Road and back again. Only after her second visit to Selfridge's perfume counters did she start to become aware of an ache in the back of her calves and the need to sit down.

The Lyons Corner House was busy but an obliging nippy found her a corner table where the pushchair could be placed without tripping other customers or the scurrying staff.

'Pot of tea for one,' Lily ordered. 'And a buttered tea cake.'

'You can have more if you have margarine instead of butter,' the nippy offered.

'Bring the marge then.' Gussie whimpered and reminded his mother to order a glass of milk for him. She was bending over the chair, tipping the liquid into his greedily gulping mouth with one hand and trying to mop the drips with the other, when a pair of flat black shoes announced the return of the waitress.

'Excuse me, madam. But would you mind sharing?'

Lily was a sociable girl who was happy to talk to anyone. 'Pleased to,' she said. 'Have a seat, love.'

'Gee, we ain't even been introduced yet and already I'm your love. And to think they warned me you British were real standoffish.'

Lily straightened up quickly and found herself gazing into a pair of laughing brown eyes. A quick scan confirmed that the rest of him was just as interesting. About thirty years old: thick dark hair, cut short; a tanned, square face; broad shoulders above a wide chest. And all of it wrapped up in a crisply pressed khaki uniform.

The accent puzzled her. 'Has Roosevelt decided to join the war after all?' she asked.

'Not that I know of, ma'am. I'm from Canada, not the States.' He thrust a hand across the table. 'Joe Minsky. Pleased to make your acquaintance.'

Lily found her own hand being vigorously pumped. 'Lily Hendry. Pleased to meet you too, Joe.'

'That's swell, I like that. The way you call me Joe straight off. Most folks I've met since I landed, they call me Mr Minsky. Or Sergeant. Should I call you Lily? Or Mrs Hendry? I guess it is Mrs? You aren't just minding the kid for a friend?'

'It's Mrs,' Lily agreed. 'But you can call me Lily.'

'Swell.' Joe beamed his satisfaction.

By the time he'd munched his way through a plate of Welsh rarebit and treated her to another tea cake, she'd learnt that he was stationed in London acting as a liaison officer between the War Office and the Canadian forces.

'Reminding them to write home to Mom every week and telling them how to avoid a dose of the clap,' he explained frankly.

By the time he'd finished his coffee, he'd somehow gained the impression she was a widow and she had a date to meet him that night at Jack Straw's Castle on Hampstead Heath.

'What's that? Some kind of stately home?'

'It's a pub.' Lily made a few calculations and added. 'See you there about eight o'clock?'

'Whatever you say, honey.'

The evening was a great success. Joe loved cute English pubs. He also loved cute English girls. He even loved their cute English kids. And to prove it he'd bought a brightly coloured spinning top for little Gussie. 'He just puts it on the floor and pushes the handle down like this, see.' He demonstrated on the polished bar, to the accompaniment of indignant shouts from the locals.

'Sorry, folks,' Joe apologized, instantly abashed. 'Just wanted you to know I understand that you and the kid come as a package,' he told Lily, steering her to an empty table. 'I like kids.'

He told her about his childhood in Alberta. About his farm that an uncle was running for him at the moment. And about the hotel he was planning to build after the war.

'On the farm?' she asked.

He burst out laughing. He had a hearty, joyful laugh that brought several heads turning in their direction, beaming in sympathy. 'Hell, no. I aim to have a place in Montreal or Quebec maybe. Somewhere with a fancy restaurant and a classy night-club on the roof. I danced in a place with that once. Real stylish. All the walls had these big windows so you could see over the whole city. You like to dance, Lily?'

'I love it.'

'That's great. How about you and me showing them how it's done tomorrow then? I hear there's a good place in Leicester Square. You know it?'

He pronounced it 'Lie-chester'. 'Lester,' she corrected automatically. 'Yes, I know it.' Lily thought quickly. Gus had said he'd be manning the balloon on 'a couple of nights'. But did that mean two nights together? Over Joe's shoulder she saw a couple of girls in VAD uniform sipping gin and lime and eyeing Joe's broad back with interest. Throwing a proprietorial glare in their direction she said: 'Yes, that would be smashing, Joe. I'll meet you there. About eight again?'

'I'll pick you up at home.'

Lying her way out of difficulties came easily to Lily. Now she rested a row of polished nails on Joe's arm and lowered her voice. 'You can't, Joe. See, the fact is . . . I live with my mother-in-law. In fact, she's minding little Gussie for me tonight.'

'So?' Puzzlement puckered at Joe's good-natured face.

Lily gave a despairing shrug. 'She hasn't really accepted my husband's death yet. I had to tell her I was going out with an old girlfriend tonight. You do understand, don't you, Joe? I can't hurt her.'

Joe was instantly full of sympathy. Of course he understood. He'd see her in 'Lester' Square at eight o'clock. 'No problem.'

Saturday 25 May
There were plenty of problems as far as Lily was concerned. Her relief when she found out Saturday was Gus's second night on the balloon detail was tempered when he informed her he wouldn't have to leave so early today.

'Last night was the first time for everyone so we got there early so the regulars could show us the ropes . . .' He broke off suddenly, his moon-face lightening with laughter. 'Hey, did you hear that? I made a joke. Anyway the regular lads said not to come till after they'd had their break tonight. Said we was too keen by half.'

'So what time will you be going?' Lily asked, holding her breath.

'About half six, I suppose.'

Lily groaned inwardly. Eventually she managed to get him out of the house by six. That's when her next problem arose. Pounding up the stairs, she rattled

Dolly's door-handle vigorously until the older woman opened the door to her room.

'Can you mind little Gussie for me again, Doll? He's settled in his cot. Shouldn't be no bother.'

'No.'

'What?' Lily was already descending the stairs. She paused with one hand on the banister, an expression of dismay on her face.

'I said no. I'm afraid it's not convenient.' Dolly came out a few steps on to the landing, jabbing a pair of knitting needles into a large ball of khaki wool and winding a shapeless sausage of knitting in the same shade around the bundle.

'But why?' Lily's voice rose in a wail.

If Dolly couldn't lip-read the words, she could interpret the expression. 'Because I'm going out. For a drink. With the ladies of my new WVS group. I have been asked to give a lecture on my experiences with the ambulance service in the last war.'

'But you don't drink!'

'Only because I'm never asked.'

Lily experienced a wave of frustration, closely followed by another of pure hatred. She was almost tempted to rush across the back close to The Hayman and buy the old girl a bottle of gin. Except the old girl had already stepped back into her room and shut the door.

Galloping downstairs, she bundled the sleepy baby into his blankets and hurried out of the back passage and into the Meekses' yard. The back door of number six was unlocked. With a perfunctory knock, Lily stepped in and was greeted by a warning shriek from Irene who spun around from the cooker where she'd been pouring water from a saucepan into a blue and white enamel jug.

'Oh, Lord, I could have sworn I'd put the bolt across,' Irene moaned.

Lily looked round blankly, puzzled as to what the Meekses' kitchen could contain that wasn't for her eyes. It all looked the same to her, except for a wooden clothes horse, draped with blankets, that had been set across the scullery end. A tell-tale wisp of steam drifted from above the blankets, and Lily understood. She bit her bottom lip to prevent herself from laughing out loud.

'Sorry, Carey. Didn't mean to interrupt your bathtime. I just came to see if Irene could mind Gussie for me this evening? I've arranged to meet a friend. Girl I used to dance with.'

Gussie wriggled and kicked. Lily set him on his feet and he toddled determinedly for the passage door.

Irene was red from the heat of the stove and the exertions of her own bath. The scarlet shade became even deeper as she hurried across the kitchen and set the jug on a wooden stool pushed next to the clothes-horse screen. 'I don't know. We were going out. Pub. Here's your water, Carey.'

A thin arm groped through the blankets, located the handle, and drew the jug carefully out of sight. The sound of cascading water filled the kitchen.

Irene blushed with even more ferocity. Lily was tempted to tell her not to worry. That it was unlikely Carey had anything she hadn't seen before. But she needed Irene on her side. 'Please, Irene. I wouldn't ask but this girl, my friend, she's just joined up ... Land Army. Probably my last chance to see her.'

'Oh, well, if it's like that ... I suppose Carey could go on his own.'

'Thanks. You're a real mate.' Lily planted a kiss on Irene's hot cheek and was already halfway out the door when a crash followed by an agonized scream made her pause and put her head back in the kitchen.

Discovering he couldn't open the passage door, Gussie had toddled over to the clothes horse instead and pulled on all those interesting blankets. Carey Meeks, his knees bent to his chest and water dripping from his partially soaped head, sat hunched in his tin bath in all his glory.

'Oh, Carey. Oh, well, I never,' gasped Irene, gazing at her husband's naked body for the first time in thirty-five years of married life.

With a shriek of laugher, Lily fled.

She changed in the ladies' toilets under Leicester Square. The locals eyed her suspiciously. Sliding top lip over bottom to smoothe out the thick raspberry lipstick, Lily caught one of the girls' eyes in the fly-blown mirror and said: 'Don't worry, love. I'm not poaching on yer patch. The only fellow I'm picking up tonight is me own.'

Her dress was only cheap satin but it showed off

the right bits, Lily thought complacently. The bodice tied behind her neck, leaving her smooth white shoulders free. From the nape, the shiny black material fell in two ruched drapes to the waistband. The gap between parallel drapes left a good proportion of Lily's heavy breasts open for inspection. Glancing down to examine the finished effect, Lily frowned. The dress was a relic from her show-business career, when it was taken for granted that the show-girls would be available to entertain the theatre owner's friends. Instinct told her that Joe was the sort of bloke who wouldn't want his 'honey' looking that available.

Bolting herself in a cubicle, she hitched up her skirt. Her stockings were secured by a pair of blue ruffled garters. Twisting over the right one, she carefully unpinned the brooch that she'd attached to the inner surface. Holding the slashed bodice close across her breasts, she secured it in a more modest closure.

Bundling her day clothes into a shopping bag, she dropped it on the attendant with a casual: 'Watch that for me, love. Be back in a couple of hours.'

The woman's protest was quickly silenced by a half-crown and the promise of another when Lily returned.

She touched the emerald brooch for luck as she approached the entrance to the night-club. It was the first time she'd worn it in public. Well, the first time on show like this. It had always been on her somewhere, ever since the night she'd stolen it from one of those blokes who'd availed themselves of the theatre manager's hospitality.

Big bloke he'd been. Pillar of the local community; owned some kind of fish business. He'd stunk of cod oil and had black whiskers that rubbed her skin raw whilst he rocked rhythmically back and forth telling her how frigid his wife was. 'Gone to stay with her sister in Blackpool for a month,' he'd panted. 'Lucky for us, eh?'

It might have been lucky for him, Lily had thought. God knows why they imagined she enjoyed these sessions. Suppressing a yawn, she managed to turn it into a moan of passion.

Afterwards when he was lying on his back, snoring his head off, she'd slid silently from the bed and prowled the bedroom, opening drawers and wardrobes and fingering the clothes. They weren't her kind of thing: heavy brocades and thick tweeds, chosen for their durability rather than their style. Idly she'd drawn out a fox-fur stole, its beady eyes glaring redly in the glow from the gas light filtering through the window. The brooch had been caught in the thick russet fur, hanging half open from one boneless limb.

It had been with her ever since. All through the years of second-rate sea-side shows, clubs where police raids were a weekly hazard, and spells where she'd slipped her last couple of bob to the barman to mind her bag whilst she worked the bar and found herself a bed for the night. It was her security: no matter how tough things were, she never *had* to go with a bloke. Whilst she had the brooch, she always had a choice: sex or a trip to Uncle's.

Of course, the Uncle she had in mind was the sort of bloke who didn't ask too many questions about where a girl like her got emerald brooches. Not a flaming straight-as-a-die bloke like Gus had taken it to. She could still remember the stab of horror she'd felt when she realized what he had done. And the agonizing Sunday she'd spent imagining the brooch being compared with the Stolen Property List.

She'd been first in the queue at the pawn shop that Monday morning, ahead of the gaggle of women clutching the best suits and table cloths that went in regularly at the start of every week and were reclaimed on pay day. Expecting any second to feel a hand on her shoulder, she'd slapped the pledge down, handed over her money, and fled from the shop. And then, after all that, the police had started snooping again.

But nothing had come of it. That inspector bloke hadn't even asked about the brooch. Blissfully unaware that the whole district – including the Agar Street station – thought that she'd been over-paid for services rendered she had started to relax. Maybe it wasn't on the stolen list? Maybe the fish merchant had never reported it? Perhaps it had been easier to replace the brooch than have his frigid missus warm up in a divorce court? Whatever the reason, Lily decided, it was the sort of thing Joe would appreciate his 'honey' wearing.

She'd summed him up right.

'Well now,' he drawled, 'look at you. Say, don't you

look swell?' Almost shyly he produced a single red rose from behind his back. 'Bought you this from one of them old girls in Piccadilly Circus.'

Stripping the leaves and thorns, she snapped the stalk three inches from the tightly folded petals and pushed the bloom into her cleavage, balancing the velvety head against the golden fastening. 'How does it look?'

'Swell, just swell,' Joe assured her. His voice had acquired an almost slurred quality, as if he were hypnotized.

Hooked him, Lily thought triumphantly, taking a muscular arm and leading him towards the dance floor.

He was a good dancer, leading her into the rhythms of foxtrots and quicksteps with easy skill. When the band struck up a tango, she half-expected him to suggest they sit it out. English men that she'd danced with had never taken to 'that dago dance'. Instead Joe clasped her to his chest and struck out with confidence. When they got to the dip, he dropped her a broad wink before whipping her upright again.

Lily giggled and pushed herself closer as they promenaded down the floor.

'Let's show them,' Joe whispered, spinning her out in a showy twirl.

Delighted to dance to an audience again, Lily dipped and swayed with confidence. Several tables started applauding. The sound echoed hollowly in the half-empty room. Spinning again, Lily identified a lack that had been evident ever since she'd left

JUNCTION CUT

Kentish Town. The streets, once so full of khaki, had suddenly been taken over by civilians again. Black and white dinner jackets flashed across her gaze like a shifting kaleidoscope, with only the occasional interruption of khaki and air-force blue. 'Where have all the soldiers gone?' she asked, as she hit Joe's chest again with a breathless thump.

'Regrouping for the invasion,' he said under his breath. 'Shouldn't really tell you that. But I guess you ain't no Mata Hari.'

'What invasion?'

'Could be a push any time now.'

'We're going to invade?'

Joe laughed under his breath. 'Other way round. Krauts could be here in a matter of days. They're in Boulogne now.'

Lily faltered, missing her step.

Joe's arms tightened. 'But don't worry, honey, I'll take care of you and little Gussie. First sign of trouble and I'll put you on a boat for Canada. Even send that ma-in-law of yours if you want.'

Lily stared blankly. She'd forgotten her mythical mother-in-law for the moment. She moved automatically to the pressure of Joe's body. I've got to get the baby away, was her first thought. Lily had never taken much interest in politics, but she'd read all the atrocity stories in the dailies, all those things that the Germans had done to innocent kids in the Great War, and there was no way they were sticking any bayonets in her Gussie.

When the music stopped and Joe led her back to their table, signalling for another bottle of wine, she was already starting to make her plans. Joe, she realized, was essential for their success. Never mind waiting for the flaming Germans to land on the beaches, they had to go now. While there were still places left on the boats. Once the invasion started, it would be every woman for herself. She realized he was speaking: 'So does this ma-in-law of yours ever go out?'

Lily could see where the conversation was leading. 'No, never,' she said firmly. 'She's a real recluse.' Joe's face fell. 'What about your place?' she asked.

'They billeted us in a hotel. They got kind of quaint ideas about women in the rooms. Of course, there's other hotels . . .' He let the question hang in the air.

'No,' Lily said. 'I've a better idea. Can you get away in the day time?'

'Sure.'

Lily extended a palm across the table. 'Give me a telephone number.'

Taking a pen from his pocket, Joe held her wrist and wrote in the white flesh. 'What's the plan?'

'I know someone . . . with a flat. She won't mind us using it in the day. I'll fix something for Monday.' She'd have to risk leaving him on his own for one day. But twenty-four hours of anticipation should sharpen his appetite.

'Swell,' he breathed, his appetite already obviously well whetted. 'You sure there won't be any problem about us borrowing this apartment?'

'I'm sure. She'll be pleased to lend it to us.' Lily's full lips twisted in a secret smile. Whether she was pleased or not, Phyllis wouldn't say no. After all, she, Lily, had kept her mouth shut. And one bad turn deserved another.

Chapter 14

Stamford made a note of the conversation that Sarah had overheard at the Nettleses' house and stored it in the Zimmermann file. There was nothing else he could do with the information at present.

'All we've got is the fact that Phyllis Nettles didn't answer a telephone at work, which may or may not mean she wasn't in the building.' He glanced at his watch. 'And at this time of a Friday evening I doubt if anyone else will be there. So we can't check out her alibi until Monday morning.'

'Miss Toddhunter saw her in Kentish Town that evening,' Sarah reminded him.

'Miss Toddhunter thought she saw her,' Jack said. 'I doubt she'd be prepared to swear it in a court of law. There's nothing about it in her original statement.'

'That's probably because Inspector Kavanagh thought deaf was spelt D-A-F-T, sir.'

'You think Miss Toddhunter deliberately withheld evidence from a sense of spite? She struck me as having more integrity than that.'

'Me too,' Sarah admitted. 'I don't think it was like that. The case against Billy was presented as watertight practically from the first hour. I don't suppose she thought Phyllis was important. But it does mean she had the opportunity, doesn't it?'

'Possibly. But opportunity isn't much use without motive. And we don't have one.'

Wishing Sarah good night, he walked home.

The house smelt of Brasso and beeswax. Friday was Eileen's polishing day. As he approached the kitchen another, meatier smell twitched at his nostrils. He found a pan simmering on the stove and a note from Eileen on the table: 'Chicken stew on hob. Leave it until after nine – a tough old boiler.'

Jack's lips twitched. He knew she was referring to one of the O'Days' Rhode Island Reds which had presumably laid its last egg; he also knew she'd phrased it that way deliberately to make him laugh.

It was nearly seven. There were two hours to kill and no notes to read or write up. He decided to walk up to Queen's Crescent and have a word with Stan Carter.

The market stalls were still reassuringly full. True a lot of stock was now hidden in boxes beneath the stalls – to be negotiated for rather than offered for sale – and there wasn't the variety there had been the previous summer, but the general impression was still of sufficient for everyone.

The housewives, their eyes and ears peeled for bargains, had already started to congregate. Hessian bags at the ready, they waited for the costers to admit defeat and start selling off the perishable produce

JUNCTION CUT

cheap. Jack wandered between them, listening to snatches of conversation.

'Not enough coupons for bacon she says. Well, I said to her, if you waste bacon on the kids, what do you expect? I never give it to mine. Makes them grow and then I've got to let their clothes out again.'

'They say tea might go on ration. I don't think I could cope without my cuppas. It's not natural. If God hadn't meant us to have tea, he wouldn't have let Tetley's discover it, would he?'

' "We'll be having oxtail stew instead of roast beef this Sunday," she said. "It's only patriotic. Saving the good meat for the fighting men." She must think I'm dim as a Toc-H lamp. If she has roast beef every Sunday, why's she not got any dripping on Tuesdays, eh? Go on, tell me that?'

'It's all I've got, Pearl love. I'm sorry, but you know how things are. Your dad don't bring home much now, not even with his overtime. People just don't tip like they used. And I haven't been able to find a lodger since Mr O'Brien went back to Dublin last September.'

The last remark made Jack pause. Searching amongst the clusters of women and children he located the speaker. Lost in a black coat that was too big for her, Irene Meeks was peering up into the face of a younger woman who was automatically rocking a pram back and forth.

'But, Mum,' she wailed. 'I ain't paid the rent for two weeks. And Tyrone needs new shoes. I 'ave to keep him in the pram 'cos he's got nothing to go on his feet.'

219

As proof she flicked a faded blanket back and displayed the grubby feet of the toddler who was strapped inside. Three little girls, bright-eyed but too thin and shabbily dressed, shuffled closer to her. 'Just another ten bob, Mum, please.'

'I can't, love. You've had all I managed to put by from me housekeeping.'

Still arguing, mother and daughter moved out of Jack's earshot. Thoughtfully, he made his way to Stan Carter's stall.

Stan was busy serving, but he passed the customer on to a sturdy, freckled boy when Jack appeared. 'Be about Billy would it, Mr Stamford?' he said in a lowered voice. 'Heard you was trying to prove he didn't do it.'

It wasn't quite Jack's brief, but he asked Stan outright if he'd been surprised by Billy's arrest. 'You could 'ave knocked me down with a head of celery,' Stan said frankly. 'Especially when I heard what he was supposed to have done. I mean, he never showed any interest in girls when he lodged with us. Got on better with older women, like the missus. But only in a friendly way. If there'd been any of that sort of business I'd have thrown him straight out.'

'But you did get rid of him?'

'Had to. The missus's nephew needed a job. And no one else would give him one. I wouldn't meself if I hadn't had me ear bashed by the missus. Look at the clumsy lump!'

Jack looked. Potatoes leapt from the boy's hands as

if they had a life of their own and rolled across the sawdust-covered street.

Jack asked about Billy's move to Junction Cut. 'I understand it was your doing?'

Stan nodded. 'Didn't do him much of a favour, did I? But the missus wanted to give Billy's room to the nevvy, said it was too far for him to travel in from Colindale every day and I mentioned it to the bloke who collects the rents – not Felonious, the one before him – and he said Mr Bowler had a room going in one of his other houses. Mr Bowler don't like to let his tenants go, once he's got them. So we fixed it up.'

'And a new job as well, with Mrs Cohen?'

Stan's face lit up. 'She's a peach, Bea. Been one of my regulars for years. Still likes to do her own shopping. In fact, talk of the devil . . .' He nodded behind Jack.

'Speak of angels and hear the beat of their wings if you don't mind, Stan Carter,' Bea Cohen said, dumping a wicker basket on his stall and prodding a pile of greens. 'Have you got my pineapple for me?'

Stan winked. Diving beneath the stall, he pulled out a box and delved inside. 'There you are, last fresh pineapple in England until we lick Hitler, I reckon. Take good care of it.'

'I want to eat it, not nurse it,' Bea said tartly. She twisted the shrivelled fruit at nose height. 'Looks like it needs it though, I'll grant you that. Put it on my account, Stan. And give me two pounds of greens.'

Stan plunged his hands amongst the piled leaves.

Bea touched Jack's arm, drawing him out of earshot. 'Any news?'

'We're carrying out a full investigation, Mrs Cohen.'

It didn't fool her for a second. 'Still got bugger all to clear Billy then, have you, lover? Well, I've done my bit. I was going to bring it up to the station tomorrow.' Taking a flat purse from the shopping basket, Bea fumbled it open with her heavily ringed fingers and extracted a slip of paper. 'There you are.'

Jack read: 'Cranleigh Farm, Nr. Chartham, Kent.'

'James Jolly,' Bea prompted. 'That's where he moved to.'

'You found him!' Jack blinked. A sense of relief that James Jolly hadn't been tipped into the canal somewhere by the murderer was tempered by a mild sensation of annoyance that Bea had so effortlessly produced information that the combined resources of Agar Street CID (such as they were) had been unable to locate. 'How!'

'I remembered my old man started a pension scheme years ago. He paid in a bit for each employee. Didn't last long, but they couldn't get it out until they retired. We've been paying old Jolly half a crown a week for the past fifteen years. And since February we've been posting it to that address. Does it help?'

'It certainly does. Bea, I love you.' He planted a kiss on her cheek to the amusement of the neighbouring stall-holders.

'Go on,' she laughed, pushing him off. 'You know I'm spoken for.' In a lower voice, so that no one else

JUNCTION CUT

could hear, she pleaded. 'And I'm relying on you, lover, to get him back for me.' For a moment, her pose cracked, and he saw the lonely woman beneath the vulgarly determined cheerfulness.

'If he didn't do it, I'll prove it,' he assured her.

And if, as the evidence still seemed to indicate, Zimmermann had done it, then he'd have to prove that too. But he thought Bea understood that. She wanted the truth. And she had faith that the truth was going to prove Billy's innocence. She wasn't asking him to change the facts, just find out what they really were.

'Trust me.' With a reassuring squeeze of her hand, he hurried back to the house to telephone the station and ask for a car and Sergeant McNeill to be available at Agar Street tomorrow morning. After a moment's thought, he also asked for the nearest police station to Chartham to be contacted. He wanted Jolly found and told to stay put until the London detectives arrived.

They left early, an elderly driver sitting stiffly to attention in the front seat and Stamford and Sarah swaying and bouncing on the slippery leather rear seat. The appetizing smells of newly baked bread, warm from the ABC ovens, drifted into the open windows as they sped towards Camden. Sarah's stomach growled audibly.

'Sorry,' she said. 'I didn't have time for breakfast.'

The driver lifted a box from the front passenger seat and waved it over his shoulder. 'Would you like my sandwiches, miss? Fish paste. The wife always makes something up if I'm going on a long drive.'

'I don't really like . . .' Sarah began.

'Go on, miss. Take them,' the driver urged. 'I hate fish paste. She only put it in because we had a row last night.'

With an amused look at Sarah, Stamford took the box and passed it to her. The pungent aroma of pilchards mixed with the scent of the warm leather upholstery as they rattled down Eversholt Street.

At the corner with Euston Road, the driver was forced to brake sharply to avoid a collision with another Wolseley. The uniformed chauffeur's eyes stared coldly at them for a moment: they were the strangest eyes that Jack had ever seen in a man; their opaqueness reminded him of clear marbles. His stare lasted for ten seconds, then long black lashes swept down over the colourless irises and he returned his attention to the road. The single passenger in the back acknowledged their presence with a gracious nod of his head. From the top of his elegantly coiffured silver hair to the tips of his expensively leather-clad fingers which lay across the handle of an ebony walking cane clamped between his knees, he exuded an air of well-bred benevolence.

'Bowler's out early,' Jack remarked. 'I wonder where he's off to?'

'Probably off to supervise the eviction of some tenant who's a week behind with the rent,' Sarah mumbled through a mouthful of paste.

Instead of turning east as Stamford expected, the

driver negotiated his way down Tottenham Court Road, threaded his way amongst the back streets of Soho, where the appetizing smells of frying breakfasts mingled with the pilchard sandwiches, drove past the barbed-wire entanglements along Whitehall and finally crossed the Thames at Westminster Bridge.

'Faster this way, sir,' he called back over his shoulder in answer to Jack's query. 'All the roads near Chatham and Rochester have got a lot of military traffic on them. I reckon we'll make better time sort of sneaking up on Chartham from the south. Should be there in a couple of hours at this pace.'

It soon became obvious that the driver's forecast had been over-optimistic. By the time they'd cleared the southern suburbs of London, they'd already been forced to stop at an observation post where barricades erected to check on traffic entering London were doing an equally effective job of preventing traffic flowing in the opposite direction. Once the sight of their police warrants released them from the bottle-neck, the driver sped forward again, cutting confidently down a narrow country lane just past Sevenoaks which he assured them was a short-cut he'd used the previous summer when he'd taken the grandchildren to the seaside. Rounding a bend, he found himself staring at the back of an army truck which was crawling along the one-car track at an agonizingly slow pace.

'Try and attract the officer's attention, sir?' the driver asked hopefully. 'Official police business?' His hand hovered over the bell.

'No,' Jack decided. 'It's not an emergency call.'

After five frustrating miles the road widened out again, and the driver was able to negotiate a careful passage between the camouflaged vehicle and the high-banked hedgerow. Clearing the front of the truck, they saw for the first time that it formed the tail of a line of mounted guns being towed in convoy.

'Frenchies. Converted to eighteen-pounders,' the driver said knowledgeably. 'See the wheels?'

'What about them?' Sarah asked.

It was Stamford who replied. 'They're wood. That's why we've been travelling at five miles an hour. Any faster and the axles swell up with the friction.' He felt a cold numbness at the realization that these museum pieces were all that stood between them and the advancing German Army.

The driver accelerated past the head of the convoy with a showy clashing of gears.

After another two hours, it finally dawned on them that the driver had almost no sense of direction. He took them on a tour through blossom-filled countryside where deserted orchards had grown crops of camouflaged vehicles and khaki-clad figures would suddenly emerge from ditches to wave them down and ask for identification.

Eventually they rolled wearily into Cranleigh Farm at three o'clock, and climbed stiffly out of the car to admire the distant view of Canterbury to the east. Like other farms in the area, Cranleigh had been commandeered as a billet for the army. Unlike the rest, however, the owners had been allowed to remain in the farmhouse instead of being evacuated to a safer area.

'That was Uncle James's doing,' Fran Jolly explained. 'Said they'd have to burn him out. He's that cussed, just like all the menfolk in this family.' She said it with an air of pride, her plump, weather-reddened face glowing with affection as she looked at the old man who sat opposite her across the scrubbed farmhouse table. 'Now you make yourself at home, my dears, and I'll get your teas.'

For once Jack wasn't inclined to protest that she didn't need to bother. Gratefully he and Sarah devoured fried eggs, home-cured ham and slices of home-baked bread. As they ate, he attempted to draw out James Jolly's story. Drawing hen's teeth would have been easier. The old man begrudged each word, letting it through his whiskered lips only after he'd weighed it and found he couldn't get any change from it.

'Yas,' he eventually admitted. He minded the day he'd left Junction Cut.

'Why didn't you tell anyone you were leaving, Mr Jolly?' Sarah asked.

'Why should I?'

Jack said: 'You must have read about the murder in Junction Cut. Didn't it occur to you that the police might want to question you?'

'No.'

'It just never came into our heads, sir.' Fran Jolly

lifted a massive iron kettle and poured a stream of boiling water into a brown earthenware teapot. 'Once we read they'd caught that German boy, we thought, that's that. We said a prayer for that poor girl's family in church the next Sunday, didn't we, Uncle? And the vicar said one for forgiveness for the murderer. But then I suppose vicars have to do things like that. I couldn't do it myself. An eye for an eye, that's what the Bible says, isn't it, sir?' She drew a large carving knife from a drawer, its blade worn paper thin from years of sharpening. 'If an animal goes bad and starts attacking his own kind, you put him down. Only thing to be done with a mad beast.'

'You think Zimmermann's mad?' He wondered if she'd got this idea from Jolly.

Apparently, however, her convictions were her own, formed long before Uncle James had returned to the fold. 'Has to be, hasn't he, sir? I mean, human life's sacred. They teach you that at Sunday school. It's not for us to start taking it away.'

Jack would have liked to ask how that tied in with her convictions about 'putting down mad things', but Sarah slipped in first. 'You agree with the conscientious objectors then, Mrs Jolly?'

It was James who replied with a scorn. 'None of my family has ever been conchies! Hold your tongue, woman, chattering on like that and smearing muck over this family's good name.'

Fran ignored him. 'The war's different,' she said confidently. 'The German Army is fighting for an evil man. It's all right to destroy the ungodly, the Bible says that.'

'Was Valerie ungodly?' Jack interjected his own question before the discussion could become any more abstract. And don't say she was just ordinary, he prayed silently.

'Sly, that's what she was.'

This was certainly a new angle on Valerie Yeovil.

'Came round pretending she wanted to run errands. Get me shopping and the like. Told her to bugger off. Haven't lost the use of me legs yet.'

'And how does that make her sly, Mr Jolly?'

'Asked me if the assistance knew about me pension from Pavaria, didn't she? I could see what she was after. Told her I'd never claimed charity in me life and I put me stick across the back of her legs to see her out.' He chuckled reminiscently at the memory then added unexpectedly, 'Mind, I liked her better than that mother of hers. Daft as a brush she is.' His watery eyes jealously watched the next forkful of egg being lifted to Sarah's mouth. Jack wondered if they were going to be presented with a bill for the tea when they left.

He smiled at Fran Jolly as she plumped down a plate heavy with slices of fruit cake. 'Thank you. Are you sure you can spare it?'

'Oh, yes, dear. Me and the regimental quartermaster has come to an understanding.' She gave a sudden girlish giggle. 'Listen to me. It's lucky my John's not alive. Otherwise he'd be turning in his grave!'

Jack caught Sarah's eye. She pushed another

mouthful of food in to stifle the laughter. Grinning, Jack extracted some more of the family's story from the woman.

The farm had belonged to her husband and her father-in-law. 'That's Uncle James's brother. They quarrelled something bad nigh on fifty years ago. About a woman, I think.'

It was hard to imagine, but judging by the smug expression on the old man's creased face, it was probably true.

'Anyway,' Fran continued, 'Uncle James took himself off to London and said he wouldn't set foot on the farm again until my father-in-law died. And he didn't. I wrote him on the Friday soon as I'd buried Old John. Said I'd come down to London and fetch him on the Saturday.'

Which no doubt explained why he hadn't had time to dispose of his coal, Jack thought wryly. He turned his attention back to James Jolly. 'What time did you leave Junction Cut that night, Mr Jolly?'

Fran jumped in again. 'I can tell you that. It was a bit after half-past seven. It was my fault. I got lost. I'd never been to London before and it took me that long to find Uncle's that I was all for staying the night and making an early start next morning. But Uncle James wouldn't have it, would you, Uncle?'

The crumpled face rolled and chewed on another mouthful of syllables before spitting one out: 'Rent.'

'You'd have had to pay another week's rent if you hadn't left on Saturday night?' Sarah interpreted.

JUNCTION CUT

The expression on Jolly's face could almost have been approval. "S right. One week's rent instead of notice, that's all I paid. Shouldn't even have left that by rights. She made me leave me linen and furniture behind. Worth more than a week's rent that was.'

'Oh, Uncle, them sheets was worn clear through. And what would we have done with more tables and beds? Best leave them for some poor soul who couldn't afford decent bits and pieces. We put the key through the collector's door before we got the bus to the station,' she informed Jack.

Stamford looked at the old man. Despite his age, the eyes were bright enough, with no sign of the milkiness of cataracts that often afflicted the elderly. 'Did you see any strangers in The Cut that evening, Mr Jolly? Say between five and seven?'

'Saw a woman.'

'When?'

'Five-forty exactly.' Jolly produced a large silver turnip watch from his waistcoat. 'I know because I looked at this. Thought that niece-in-law of mine had finally arrived.'

'What was she like. Old? Young?'

Jolly couldn't say. It had been too dark. He thought she walked young. 'Had a scarf on. Couldn't see her face. Wasn't from The Cut though. I know all them.'

'Did you see where she went?'

Once again Jolly hung on to his words until the last possible second. 'Number four or number six,' he eventually allowed between his lips. 'Don't know which.

231

I was looking at the watch.'

'Then how do you know she went in either?' Sarah said, finishing the last morsel of ham with an audible sigh of satisfaction.

Jolly glared. 'Didn't come on past me. Didn't go back the other way, I looked. Only places she could have gone.'

'Did you see her leave again?'

'No.' Jolly seized the last lump of cake from the plate just as Sarah was reaching for it, and bit into it with a possessive snap.

Jack handed her his own untouched slice then asked: 'Did you know Billy Zimmermann, Mr Jolly?'

'No. He was a kraut, weren't he? Like them that killed my boys. Don't talk to krauts.' Taking offence at Stamford's silent rebuke on his manners, Jolly pushed himself to his feet and shuffled away across the kitchen to nurse his sulks in the fireside settle.

'Thank you for your cooperation,' Jack said, rising to his feet. 'We'll be in touch if we need to question you further.'

A pig-like grunt floated over the high wooden back of Jolly's seat.

'Don't mind him, sir,' Fran said, showing them back to their car. 'My hubby and his father were just the same. And my son is too. It's just the family's way.' She glanced back to the kitchen door and reassured herself it was empty. 'I didn't like to say it in front of Uncle, but – well, I don't know I'd set too much store on what he says. You see, he was fast asleep by the window when I got there. And he dreams something wonderful. Some mornings he swears he's seen his brother, or my late mother-in-law, walking around the farm at night.'

A rumble of sound rolled across the farmyard. Instinctively the two police officers glanced skywards.

'It's not thunder,' Fran said. 'It's the guns at the coast. They're at it all the time, day and night now. You get so you don't notice them after a time. Same with the planes.'

Jack squinted against the tear-inducing brightness of the sky. Over the horizon, he saw three black dots growing larger, their progress marked by the herringbone vapour trails that streamed behind them.

'Hurricanes?'

'Could be, sir. Can't tell the difference myself. They're ours. That's all that matters, isn't it?'

It was Sarah who answered her. 'Yes. That's what matters.'

Jack saw her involuntary shiver. 'We'd better get moving. Given our driver's navigational abilities, we could be in for an extended tour of the Cinque Ports whilst he tries to find London.'

Contrary to Stamford's expectations, they made good time back to London. Abandoning his so-called short route, the driver took the direct road back, re-crossing the Thames at London Bridge and wending his way through the near-deserted City.

During the journey they reviewed the progress they'd made on the case so far. Jack was forced to the conclusion that Zimmermann was still the most likely, in fact the only, suspect.

'But what about Phyllis Nettles?' Sarah protested. 'We've got evidence against her surely?'

'What evidence? An unanswered phone call? A possible sighting by Miss Toddhunter which can't be confirmed? Jolly didn't even suggest it was her he saw. He can't, in fact, identify the woman at all, since he didn't see her face.' Bars of shadow were flashing across Sarah's face as the car passed from street to street. He caught the beginnings of impatience in her eyes and guessed what she was thinking. Why bother to go to all that trouble to find Jolly, then ignore what he has to tell us?

'It's a temptation, I know, to decide on your suspect and then twist the evidence to suit a case against them.'

'I'm not . . .' Sarah bit back the rest of her sentence. 'Yes, all right, I am. But who else could it have been? None of them – the Meekses, the Hendrys, Miss Toddhunter – mentioned a visitor that evening. She must have gone to see Valerie.'

'Doesn't mean it was Phyllis Nettles. What about Valerie's mysterious man friend? Maybe he had a jealous wife.'

'I'd forgotten about him,' Sarah admitted. 'Do you think we've got any chance of tracing him?'

'I don't know. But tomorrow is Sunday, and Valerie always made her excursions to Edgware on a Sunday. So tomorrow, Sergeant, you and I are going to retrace her footsteps.'

He became aware that Sarah was no longer looking at him, but at something outside the nearside window.

'Stop!' she said suddenly. 'Pull over.'

The driver was making the final turn before steering the car into the vehicle sheds at the back of Agar Street but in response to Sarah's order, he obediently braked. Scrambling across Stamford, she lowered the window and called out: 'Margaret. Did you want to see me?'

The girl came reluctantly across the pavement. Her plump body was encased in a grey siren suit which strained at the seams as she bent forward to look in the car window. 'They said you were out. It doesn't matter if you're busy. I'll come back another day.' She was already backing away from the car.

'Don't do that.' Stamford leapt out quickly. 'It's Miss Cave, is it?'

'I suppose it is. Nobody's ever called me that before.' She looked uncertain whether she wanted to be Miss Cave or not.

Sarah got out of the car too. 'This is Chief Inspector Stamford, Margaret. He's in charge of the case.'

Jack smiled reassuringly at the girl. 'Did you want to tell me something, Margaret?'

She looked relieved that he'd taken the initiative. 'Yes. At least, I want to give you something.' She extended a shopping bag. 'It's Valerie's. She kept it hidden at our flat. She said I was never to tell anyone about it.'

Chapter 15

They took Margaret back into the CID office. Jack set two chairs opposite his desk and, after a second's hesitation, perched on the front of it. His intention had been to put Margaret at her ease; Margaret, however, showed no signs of needing reassurance as she stared curiously round the office.

'My grandmother's been in lots of police stations. She used to get arrested. Often. Once she knocked out a policeman with her umbrella.' A wistful look passed over Margaret's face. 'I wouldn't have minded being that sort of suffragette. It's all this education I hate.'

Jack's lips twitched. He remembered what Sarah had told him about Margaret's future plans. 'Why be a doctor if you don't want to?' he asked. 'Go to Art School instead.'

Margaret pouted. 'Gran won't let me. I've got to be a surgeon and challenge the medical establishment.' She raised her legs in front of her. 'She made me this siren suit. It's to demonstrate that it's acceptable for women to wear trousers in public.' She looked gloomily at the two detectives. 'I look like a barrage balloon, don't I?'

There was no comforting answer to that question.

Luckily Margaret didn't seem to expect one. Instead she thrust her hands into her pockets and watched Stamford. Delving into the shopping bag he produced a brown cocoa tin decorated with oval pictures of the late King George V and Queen Mary. The silver script around the edge announced it was a souvenir of Their Majesties' Silver Jubilee.

After watching Stamford struggling with the lid Margaret finally said: 'Here, you have to twist it in a certain way. Let me.'

With a vicious yank, she dragged the lid free of the tin and tipped the contents on to Stamford's desk. A shower of coins and bank notes scattered over the polished surface. Finally a small, red-covered notebook, curled into the shape of the cylindrical canister, flopped out.

'Valerie's Savings Bank,' Margaret explained, slapping flat palms on the desk to stop spinning coins from hurtling themselves over the edge. 'She couldn't keep it at her house because she shared a room with her mother. So she left it with me.'

'Why didn't you hand this in before?'

He knew he'd been too sharp even before the defensive expression flitted across Margaret's face. Sarah saw it too and leapt into the breach.

'Did you think Valerie would get you into more trouble, Margaret?'

It was inspired phrasing. Margaret was only too eager to put the blame on Valerie.

'I was going to give it to Mrs Yeovil. I tried to speak

to her at the funeral but everybody was listening. The whole school had to go, and all the Holy Sisters. I thought if they knew I'd been keeping it for her, I'd get into trouble. Then, afterwards, when I went round to Valerie's house, Mrs Yeovil acted really strangely. She kept telling me they'd be moving soon and she wouldn't listen to anything I said about Valerie. It sort of gave me the creeps – so I left. Then the longer I had the money, the more I thought it might look like I was trying to steal it. I tried to put it in the poor box at St Barnabas.'

But even that plan had run into difficulties. 'I started with the small coins. And every time one went in the box, it made this dreadful loud "clang". People started looking round.' Margaret huddled further into the enveloping siren suit. 'Well, nobody gives that much to the poor box, do they?' Eventually embarrassment had driven her out.

'How much did you put in?' Jack asked.

'Not much. About two shillings, I think. But it was all in farthings and halfpennies.'

Jack ran a quick eye over the pile of coinage and notes on his table. There was something over twenty-five pounds he guessed. 'Do you know where Valerie got this money from, Margaret?'

She pointed. 'It's all in the book. Valerie always kept accounts. She said it was important if she was going to start her own business.'

Jack picked up the small book in his right hand and rifled through the pages. They were ruled into two columns; one headed 'Credits', the other 'Debits'. 'What business did she want to start?'

'She was going to open a brothel.'

Jack just managed to stop himself falling off the edge of the desk. 'What!'

'A brothel,' Margaret repeated. Her tone was casual. She just might have announced that Valerie had plans to open a hat shop. 'You know, a place where men can go to ... well you must know. Don't the police raid places like that?'

Jack stared wildly at Sarah. She was looking straight ahead, refusing to meet his eye. However, a tic in her left cheek suggested she was desperately trying to keep a straight face. He wasn't going to get any help from that quarter.

Margaret seemed to realize she'd said something odd. She attempted to set the record straight. 'Not an ordinary brothel. I mean, not just a couple of rooms like in Litcham Street.'

Sarah winced.

'Valerie was going to have a really elegant place. She had this book, you see. She bought it in Chapel Street market. *Memoirs of a Lady of Pleasure* it was called. She used to lend it out to the other girls at a shilling a time. Anyway, it had a brothel in there. It sounded wonderful. Glass fountains full of champagne, rooms furnished with silks and special mirrors that let you ...'

'Er, yes. Quite,' Jack interrupted. He saw Sarah's tic becoming more pronounced and wondered briefly if

Margaret was indulging in an elaborate joke, but one look at her disingenuous face convinced him she was perfectly serious. He doubted if she had the faintest idea of the grim realities of a prostitute's life – common or elegant – and obviously saw nothing wrong in her friend's ambition.

He ran an eye down the meticulous columns of figures in Valerie's notebook. The book hire was carefully entered, each shilling recorded against a set of initials. There were over fifty, some appearing several times he noted with a certain amusement. The first hire charge was approximately two years before Valerie's death. For some time they were the only entries, apart from the odd five or ten shillings in late-December – presumably Christmas presents. In the late summer of 1939, however, the pattern changed. With mounting excitement, Stamford saw the entries for August and early September; for seven weeks, against the annotation 'D.', there were deposits of ten pounds. He flicked the page over. In October the pattern altered again; from October to mid-January, ten shillings or one pound each week were credited against 'P.'. The last and largest amount, however, was attributed to 'G.D.' Fifty pounds had gone into the cocoa tin on the fourteenth of January – a week before Valerie's murder.

Jack examined the 'Debit' column. It was far shorter. The underground train fares to Edgware occupied seven lines, followed each time by the puzzling 'E.T. – 2s 6d'. A debit for eighteen shillings and sixpence in

November against 'S.U.' he attributed to the Tea Rose underwear set. Apart from those entries, the only money Val had withdrawn was small amounts in sixpences and shillings. Jack made a rapid calculation. 'There's over a hundred pounds missing.'

'I know.' Margaret huddled even further into her suit, as if she was hoping to retract her limbs and curl up inside well out of the detectives' sight. 'That's another reason I didn't want to hand it over. I thought everyone would think I'd taken it.'

'And did you?'

'No.' Margaret looked at Sarah for support. 'I didn't. Honestly.'

Jack squeezed the girl's shoulder lightly. 'It's all right, Margaret. We believe you.'

'You do?'

Jack found himself hoping that Margaret Cave wouldn't need to take the witness stand in the Zimmermann case. Or any other. She had a way of presenting information that suggested she fully expected to be disbelieved. 'Yes,' he said firmly. 'We do. Who else had access to this tin?'

Margaret chewed a doubtful lip. 'I kept it in the bottom of my wardrobe, so anyone who came to the flat really. I mean, it's not locked up or anything.'

'And who did go into the flat between say . . .' Jack checked the last entry. 'The fifteenth and the day Valerie died.'

Margaret thought. 'Dad, of course. And Gran. I think Mr Crossland the greengrocer came on Wednesday evening. He comes every week to play chess with Dad. And the rent man. The milkman comes too, but he always collects his money from the shop. He doesn't come up to the flat. I don't remember anyone else.'

Sarah had straightened up at the mention of the rent man. Now she asked his name.

'Monk,' Margaret said. 'Mr Monk.'

'Was he alone in the flat at all?'

Margaret struggled to remember. Jack knew it was asking a lot for her to recall the exact events of a particular week all that time ago. 'Yes,' she said finally. 'I remember now. Val came round to collect me for school, and then Mr Monk turned up.' He'd been too early and there hadn't been enough money in the flat to pay him. 'So I had to go down and ask Dad to make it up from the till.'

'And you left Mr Monk in the flat? Alone?'

'Yes. But I was only gone a minute.'

'All he needs,' Sarah muttered under her breath.

'What day was this?' Jack asked.

'Friday. That's why I didn't have enough money. Normally he comes on Saturdays.' She looked between the detectives' considering faces. 'I like him,' she said. 'He makes me laugh.' She sought for some other piece of information to help the little rent collector whom she'd inadvertently got into trouble. 'Anyway, I don't know that the money went that week. I didn't look in the box for nearly a fortnight after Val died. It could have been taken any time.'

It was a valid point. 'Do you know who "P." is?' He

showed her the entries. 'Or this "D.".'

'No. Val didn't tell me things. I just had to keep the tin for her. I wouldn't have dared look inside before she died. She'd have known. She knew things about people, Val did. She liked knowing things about them.'

'All right, Margaret.' Jack scooped the money back into the tin and locked it in his desk. 'Thank you for bringing this in. You did the right thing. Have you told anyone else about this?'

'No.'

'Could you continue to keep it just between us? For the time being. Sergeant McNeill will show you out.'

When Sarah returned to the office, she found Jack perched on the desk again, re-examining the account book.

'I don't see Felonious as a murderer, sir. I mean, it's possible he stole the money. Fel's always been tender-hearted when it comes to lost, lonely, homeless valuables. He gets this irresistible compulsion to give them a warm home – in his pocket. But he's never been violent.'

'You like him, don't you?'

She did. The little thief had given the force plenty of exercise over the years, but there was no animosity in him. He took his arrests and imprisonments in good part and bore no grudges against those who brought his spells of incarceration on him. 'Fel would have taken the lot,' she said. 'He's not very subtle. And besides, surely Val's accounts provide a better lead?'

Jack raised an eyebrow in her direction. 'I suppose

you're going to tell me that "P." is Phyllis?'

'It makes sense, doesn't it, sir? And it gives us a motive. Valerie was a blackmailer, wasn't she?'

Stamford sighed. 'Yes. I'm afraid she was.' He walked over to the board where he'd pinned the newspaper photograph of Valerie. The solemn face, with its madonna-like innocence, stared back at him. Knowing what he knew now, he could almost see her composing her features into that bland expression, carefully hiding the mocking smile that Margaret's sketches had caught so well. 'But is that what got you killed, I wonder?'

'Don't you think it is?'

Jack turned back to face his sergeant. 'Phyllis, assuming "P." is Phyllis, paid her, what – twenty pounds? Would you kill someone for the sake of twenty pounds?'

'May be she was killed because she wanted more? Or she'd decided to tell what she knew.'

'But about who? There's more than one suspect in that notebook.'

'D.?'

'Mm. Who do we have in this case who answers to "D."?'

Sarah wrinkled her forehead. 'There's Dolly Toddhunter,' she said doubtfully. 'Only somehow I can't see Miss Toddhunter as a blackmail victim. I think she'd rather enjoy having a salacious past.'

'So do I. Although, of course, it might have been different if she had something criminal in her past.

But, on the other hand, I don't believe Miss Toddhunter ever had seventy pounds to pay to a blackmailer. So I think we can rule her out. Which leaves us with the mysterious man friend.'

'You think she was blackmailing him?'

'Maybe she was making him pay for it. Early practice for her future career. What did you make of that, incidentally?'

'I think it was probably a bit of bravado. She and Margaret were different. Scholarship girls. The ones who had to rely on charity for their education. Children can be cruel. They'll pick on the one who shows any weakness. Margaret deals with it by keeping quiet and trying not to be noticed. I think Valerie probably went to the other extreme. She was so outrageous she kept the class entertained. You don't stone the clown, do you? Mind you,' she added reflectively, 'if she had opened a brothel, I think she'd probably have made a fortune.' After a pause, she asked: 'Why do you think the boyfriend's money is payment for services rendered rather than straightforward blackmail?'

'A bit of both would fit the pattern,' he said. 'D., and I'm assuming that's a surname, pays out ten pounds a session last summer. Then he gets called up. In January he re-contacts Valerie, but she's discovered a better way of making money by then. She demands fifty pounds or she'll talk. She was under age, remember. And maybe he's married.'

'So he pays up the first time,' Sarah said, following Stamford's line of reasoning. 'But the second time, he's had enough and decides to shut her up for good.'

'Given up on Phyllis Nettles already, Sergeant?'

'Just exploring possibilities, sir. Isn't that what you said we had to do? Why do you think "D." is a surname, by the way?'

Jack put his finger on the final entry. 'G.D. – fifty pounds. He got full billing this time.'

'G.,' Sarah mused. 'Gordon? Gregory?'

'Graham, George, Geoffrey . . .' Stamford continued. 'It should be a piece of cake tracking him down in Edgware.'

'We're still going then?'

'We certainly are, Sergeant. I'll see you nine o'clock tomorrow morning, Hampstead Tube Station. In the meantime, I suggest we both go home. It's been a long day.'

Sarah gratefully collected her hat and preceded Stamford through the bustling corridors of the police station to the back entrance. The sight of two prisoners, securely handcuffed and being led into the cells area, reminded her of something. 'What about Felonious, sir? Are you going to pull him in?'

'No. He'll keep. I doubt he's gone far.'

'You can say that again, sir.' Holding back one of the swing doors into the back yard, Sarah stood slightly to one side so that Stamford could see out.

The two wireless cars were still parked under the overhanging sheds that covered one side of the yard. They'd been joined by a London taxi, especially adapted to tow the fire pump that stood next to it, and an old-fashioned, horse-drawn milk cart that had a hand-painted sign hanging over one side designating it: 'Local Defence Volunteers – Agar Street Division'. The skewbald horse in the shafts lifted its head and shook vigorously, dislodging an annoying fly from its shaggy mane.

'Stand still, you mangy brute. Hold still now,' a voice familiar to Sarah ordered.

'Felonious,' she whispered over her shoulder. 'Don't tell me he's joined up.'

Apparently he hadn't. The broken-nosed LDV sergeant emerged from a side door carrying two framed maps and ordered Felonious to stand away from the horse's bridle. 'He knows what he's doing. He don't need yer taking the weight off yer plates of meat and leaning on him instead.'

'I'm only trying to lend a hand.'

'Well, don't. Push off! Fight yer own battles.'

'It ain't my battle.'

'Don't fight it then.' The sergeant heaved the heavy maps into the cart.

'I don't want to. That's what I keep telling you. Couldn't you just give me a little hint like? Just something I could tell Oggie's heavies? Just so he don't lose a packet like last time.'

'Yer. All right.'

From the shelter of the doorway, Stamford and Sarah saw the little man's ferret features brighten.

'Tell them,' the sergeant said, heaving himself into the driving seat and taking up the slack reins, 'that if

Mr Bowler finds out Oggie's trying to fix the odds, he'll do a lot worse than set you on them. Walk on, boy.'

In response to the last command the horse trundled obediently forward, leaving Felonious to leap backwards just as his toes were about to be crushed beneath the back wheel. Returning to earth, he caught sight of the detectives watching him from the partially open door. By the time his feet hit the cobble-stones, his legs were already pumping. He overtook the horse and cart before it had turned out into the road.

'It's habit, sir.' Sarah said. 'He always runs when he sees a police officer coming after him.'

'We haven't moved,' Jack pointed out.

'He doesn't like to take any chances.'

The back of the cart was just swaying out of sight round the next corner when they reached the road. Felonious had completely disappeared. 'Does Leo Bowler run a horse?' Jack asked.

'Not that I've ever heard, sir. It's more likely to be a dog. Or dogs.'

'Does he also run our LDV sergeant?'

'I think he used to work for him on a casual basis. Handyman, gardener . . .'

'Debt collector?'

'Probably. Although no one ever complained officially.' Sarah hesitated at the open gates.

'Have you forgotten something?'

'I think I'll just . . .'

The young policeman, Dave, had emerged with a mug of tea from one door and was walking carefully across the open yard, trying to avoid slopping any of the precious liquid. 'I just want to have quick word with Dave.'

Felonious was sharp, but he was no match for the bookmaker's heavies if they cornered him. It might be prudent to ask uniform to keep a discreet watch on the little thief.

'I'll wish you good night then. And see you at nine o'clock tomorrow. Sorry if you had any other plans for Sunday.'

He raised his hat and walked quickly away. It took Sarah a few minutes to realize that he thought her interest in Dave was personal. She opened her mouth to call after him, then shut it with a snap. What did it matter if he did? Their relationship had returned to its old equilibrium of part mutual respect, part liking, and part reticence. There was no sense in disturbing it again. She sent a silent wish after him that he'd find news of his family waiting when he got home and then hurried back into the station to locate Dave.

Chapter 16

Sunday 26 May

Annaliese was trapped in never-ending mud flats where blackened tree stumps dotted the landscape like spent Roman candles. The lowering evening sky was obscured by the clouds of drifting gun smoke which clogged the lungs and burnt his nose lining with the acrid smell of cordite. Sometimes it was too dark to see beyond the strands of the first barbed-wire barricades. And then the shells burst in the air overhead, briefly lighting the world in their yellow light, and Jack could see her.

She was huddled near the edge of a crater, curled into a small ball, her arms hugging her chest. He couldn't hear her above the pounding gunfire, but he knew she was crying. He wanted to go to her but someone was pulling him back into the dug-out. He tried to struggle free, but the duck-boards in the trench were rotted and broken. They parted under his weight and he sank ankle-deep into the cloying mud which gripped his feet like iron manacles.

Desperately he flung himself against the sloping sides of the trench, pulling with his bare hands at the slimy walls. It was no good, he couldn't move. Over the edge of the trench, the sounds of Annaliese's sobbing carried clearly now that there was a lull in the heavy artillery, her hiccuping gasps of terror mingling with the moans of the men trapped on the barbed wire. He looked round for help. Dolly Toddhunter was coming towards him, ringing a large brass school bell. 'There,' she said. 'Now do you believe it's better to be deaf?'

Jack groaned. He reached out to grasp the trench side again, but it crumpled beneath his fingers, turning into a warm woollen blanket. Dolly dissolved and became the side of the wardrobe. But her bell rang on. Struggling out of the warm fuzziness of sleep, he groped across the bedside cabinet and slammed a balled fist hard down on the clanging alarm clock.

Stumbling into the bathroom, feeling tireder than when he'd gone to bed, he filled the basin with cold water and threw it into his face until he was fully awake. Smothering his chin in lather, he shaved with an ancient cut-throat that he'd inherited from his father.

He needed a haircut, he realized, pushing a hand through the thick mop and seeing where the sunlight had lightened the dark auburn to a warmer copper in streaks. It had also added a pale golden sheen to his skin which was most notable in the 'V' shape that his open shirt had left between his throat and breast-bone.

'Not bad for an old man,' he muttered. At least, too good to be messing around with a civilian murder case when most of the men in the country had more important things to worry about.

Mentally he shook himself. He couldn't think like that. He'd resolved not to when the call-ups had started. At forty he was at the far end of the eligible age band for conscription anyway. But nonetheless he had experienced niggling feelings of guilt when other officers at Scotland Yard with reservist obligations had been called up in the first few weeks of the war.

After pulling on a pair of slacks, a sports jacket and a fresh shirt, he stepped out on to pavements which gleamed from the effects of an early morning shower.

The two youngest O'Days were already up and about.

Maurice burst from their house as Stamford was locking his own front door. Resplendent in a pin-striped suit, white spats, and a snap-brimmed trilby hat, he swaggered to the gate and offered an arm to a pretty dark-haired girl in a mauve flower-sprigged summer dress and straw hat.

'Hitch on, doll,' he drawled in a mid-western American accent. 'And I'll show you a good time.'

The girl giggled, ducked her head coyly, murmured: 'Oh Maury, you are a card!' and took the proffered arm. Walking close together they set off to find what Sunday Hampstead had to offer in the way of good times.

As Jack watched, Sammy ran into the road and extended an arm to his chief partner in crime, another small, knee-scraped eight-year-old whose socks lived in permanent huddles round his ankles. 'Hitch on, Piggy, and I'll show you a good time.'

With a girlish giggle, Piggy placed one hand on his hip, the other through Sammy's arm, and squealed: 'Oh, Sammy, ain't you the one?' Hips swaying in exaggerated imitation of Maurice's swaggering gait, they bounced off after the other couple. The last Jack saw of the four, they were disappearing into Malden Road, with Maurice mouthing furious, but silent, promises on Sammy's fate over his right shoulder.

Sarah McNeill also seemed to have been infected by the holiday mood. She was already waiting for him at the entrance to Hampstead Station in front of a poster headed 'War Emergency' which informed the public that underground stations must not be used as air-raid shelters.

The Sunday-best hat had been pressed into service; a large-brimmed, flat-crowned creation decorated with a spray of flowers in a shade Stamford seemed to recall was called Marina Blue after the present Duchess of Kent. 'I wasn't sure what the plan was,' Sarah explained, seeing the direction of his gaze. 'I thought, if we were supposed to look like ordinary day trippers, I'd better dress the part. What is the plan, sir?'

'I'm not sure exactly,' Jack admitted. 'I want to follow Valerie's route as far as we can.' He drew a cylinder of papers from his breast pocket. 'I had a police artist reproduce Margaret's sketch of Valerie – the head and shoulders view. I think we can reasonably assume that she must have met this man in Edgware. Perhaps he picked her up at the station. In any event, I think we start with the station staff there.'

JUNCTION CUT

It was not a promising beginning. The booking-office clerk was new, the ubiquitous conscription having transported the regular clerk to an RAF station somewhere in Yorkshire. Breathing heavily in adenoidal gasps, she squinted at Valerie's portrait and suggested that 'the regulars' might know. 'Bunaway ib she?'

'That's right,' agreed Jack.

'Terrible bot deese young girls geb up to, isn't ib?' the clerk, who was all of twenty, remarked. 'Next, blease.'

'What now, sir?'

Jack looked round. Despite the current situation, and the Government pleas only to travel if your journey was really necessary, the tiled station was full of families clutching picnic baskets, fishing rods, shrimping nets and cricket bats. Most were pushing eagerly towards the entrance. There were several shouts of 'It's here, Mum' and 'Hurry up, we won't get a seat.'

'Let's see what's out there.' He hoped for a regular bus service. Preferably one with a driver who'd been sitting outside this station each Sunday last summer when Valerie had streamed out with the rest of the crowds. Emerging into the bright light, it took a minute for his eyes to adjust after the gloom of the booking hall, and then he caught his breath with disbelief. Surely it wasn't going to be that easy?

Sarah had seen it as well. A single-decker green and cream coach parked against the kerb, a chalked blackboard by the open door offering: Excursion Trips – Adults 2s 6d. Under twelves 1s 6d. 'E.T.,' Sarah breathed. She turned to Stamford, her eyes wide under the hat brim. 'It's got to be, hasn't it?'

Stamford reflected ruefully that she'd probably think ever after that clues simply flung themselves into CID's path. Hardly worth leaving his desk at Scotland Yard, in fact.

'Let's see.' They joined the back of the queue. Apart from a few single travellers who'd headed purposefully away along Station Road, the majority of the tube passengers were shuffling forward in an orderly queue, whilst a middle-aged man in a peaked cap fished change from a leather satchel at his waist, extracted tickets from his belt, and heaved the odd elderly passenger up the high step into the bus.

'Weren't sure you'd be here,' the woman in front of Jack said. 'You weren't last month. Come up all the way from Belsize Park we did and you never showed up.'

'Don't blame me, missus. Blame the Government. Commandeered the bus for an auxiliary ambulance one week, then give it back the next. Mind the step. Two is it, sir?'

Jack said: 'Where does this bus go?'

'Allingham Lake, sir. Local beauty spot. Rowing boats, swimming, teas. Your young lady will love it.'

'Is it a regular service? Was it running last summer?'

A certain wariness crept into the man's manner. 'Might have been. Why, sir?'

'A friend told us all about these lovely trips she'd had last August,' Sarah said quickly. 'But we weren't quite sure we'd got the right place.'

The man perked up immediately, whipping out two tickets and clipping them with a flourish that suggested he was probably working on commission. 'Bound to be, miss. Step up now. You'll have a smashing day.'

They got the last two seats. With the older children swaying in the aisles, holding tight to the seat backs on either side, and the toddlers and babies wedged on their mothers' laps and held fast by shopping bags bulging with sandwiches, lemonade bottles, swimsuits and towels, the bus jolted forward and turned right at the end of the road.

The journey took forty minutes; mainly because the little bus was brought to a virtual standstill by the gradient of the two steep hills it had to negotiate to reach its final stop. In response to muttered imprecations by some passengers as the bus hung suspended halfway up the steepest of these hills, the driver growled over his shoulder that the regular chap couldn't have done any better and the problem lay in the difficulty in getting spare parts for the gear box: 'There's a war on, in case you haven't heard. It'd go quicker if you got out and walked to the top.'

This suggestion was howled down on the grounds that they'd paid for a seat, and a seat they were going to have. Even if it wasn't going anywhere. Eventually with a great deal of coaxing and the silent willing of forty minds, the bus dragged itself over the crest of the hill and sped down the other side with a swoop that drew yells of encouragement from the rocking children who rated it as good as a fair-ground ride.

When they started the same routine again on the next hill, Jack braced himself for a repeat roller-coaster ride. It didn't come. At the brow of the slope, the road flattened off and threaded its way through a small village of shops, cottages and public houses. The bus drew in opposite one of these and the driver reached across and flung open the door: 'There you are. And they're not even open yet.'

The crowd surged to its feet and started to file off. Jack pressed Sarah's arm, indicating that she should wait. Once the rest of the passengers had disembarked, he took out the pencil sketch and approached the driver, who was fussing with his change satchel. He stuck to the runaway story.

And once again he was frustrated by the call-up. 'Glyn, the regular bloke, joined the army last September,' the man explained. 'In the terriers. One of the first to go. Normally I just help out in his dad's garage. You should have said that's what you were after at the station, sir. Could have saved you the trip.'

Stamford persisted. 'We believe she may have visited the village last summer. Was the excursion bus running then?'

'Runs all summer normally. Easter to end of October. Guv'nor reckons it's a good earner. They don't just own the garage, see? They got the pub next to it and a tea shop down by the lake. So once they got the trippers here, they got two other chances to empty their pockets.' He took the sketch of Valerie from Stamford's hands and looked doubtfully at it. 'There was a girl young Glyn was a bit sweet on. But I ain't sure.'

'What about his parents, would they recognize her?'

'Might do. But they ain't here today. Went off early this morning. Taken the two younger lads to visit Glyn since he can't get leave to come and see them.' He saw Stamford's frown of impatience and added helpfully. 'I reckon your best plan would be to ask Miss Davis. She's the aunt. Runs the tea shop. Just walk back the way the bus come and take the first right. Lake's about a couple of hundred yards down the road.'

Stamford thanked him for his advice, but didn't take it immediately. Instead he led Sarah along the broad village street. The place had a distinctly holiday air. The early morning rain had been replaced by brilliant blue skies, coupled with the warm sunshine. It drew out the scents of burgeoning greenery from every garden and overwhelmed the small, tangible signs of conflict with an air of pre-war normality. Posters inviting attendance at Civil Defence meetings and soliciting used clothing for refugees were already yellowing and curling in the strong sunlight, leaving the hand-painted signs offering 'Teas' and 'Cut Flowers' to claim the visitors' attention.

The village was a mish-mash of conflicting architectural styles. Pseudo-tudor black and white timbering gave way to eighteenth-century weatherboarded cottages which, in turn, were crowding against brick-built houses whose sagging roofs and leaning chimneys showed that their foundations had spent several centuries comfortably bedding into the thick clay soil. At the end of the street a solid, square, white-painted public house, its walls covered in luxuriant ivy, abutted on a single-storey hangar, fronted by a double set of wooden doors tall enough to admit a petrol bus. The wrought-iron sign over the entrance to the forecourt confirmed that they'd found 'Davis's Garage'. A hand-painted notice swinging from one of the two petrol pumps on the forecourt announced that the garage would re-open at eight o'clock on Monday morning, another announced that petrol would only be served to those tendering the correct coupons.

'What now?' Sarah asked. The road in front of them had started to dip again between green fields where rows of pink horse chestnuts stood sentry, their rosy candles just beginning to shed drifts of confetti-like petals across the deserted road.

'Lake.' Stamford wheeled again and set off briskly in the opposite direction.

'Sir,' Sarah asked after she'd managed to catch him and fall into step again, 'is it all right for us to be asking questions here?'

'In what way all right?'

Sarah placed one hand flat against the crown of her hat, which was threatening to blow off. 'I mean, should the local CID office be informed? Since we're outside our area.'

JUNCTION CUT

'I doubt you'll find one on duty on Sunday. Anyway, we're still within the Met.'

'Are we?' Sarah stared at the country scene in front of her, contrasting this peaceful rural idyll with the cramped noisy streets of Somers Town and Shoreditch where the air was so laden with smoke some days that it could almost be weighed in the hand.

Stamford had walked on a few paces. He stopped, looked back at her, and grinned. 'Thinking of applying for a transfer?'

'I don't think so. I mean, it's all right for a visit, but I don't think I'd want to live in all this . . .' She waved her hands as if trying to grasp the correct word out of thin air. Eventually, she finished lamely. 'All this *openness*.'

'I'm glad to hear it. I'd miss you.'

'Would you, sir?' She was unsure how to take this remark. Did he mean personally or professionally? And which did she want him to mean?

'It's hard work, training up a good sergeant. And it's frustrating to get it right and then see all that good work wasted on another section.'

A wave of relief swept over her at the realization that he was referring to their working relationship, followed by a small glow of pleasure that he thought she was a good sergeant, and a tinge of annoyance at that word 'training'. It made her sound like a well-schooled labrador – bright, eager and acquiescent – when she suspected that some of her views on this case not only didn't accord with his, but would probably shock him if she ever voiced them. 'I'm only on temporary transfer to CID, sir,' she reminded him.

'I'm only on temporary transfer to Agar Street. I was brought in to sort out this particular case, remember.'

She had forgotten. He'd started to seem like a regular part of the Agar Street contingent. She knew from canteen gossip that the CID constables and the uniform branch had begun to regard him as one of their own.

Following the driver's instructions they descended another road at right angles to the main street and, after a couple of hundred yards, glimpsed the gleam of water between the trees. The chattering and laughter intermingled with the sounds of squeals and splashing became louder as they branched off down a smaller lane and found the entrance to the lake.

There were perhaps two hundred people crowded around the banks. The earliness of the year meant that the water was too cold for swimming except for the hardiest bathers – which seemed to consist of assorted small children in sagging woollen bathing costumes and a couple of grizzled old men whose skins had tanned and hardened to the texture of cured leather. The rowing-boat concession, however, was doing brisk business. Jack looked at the scene for several minutes trying to work out what was wrong with it. Then it hit him. Over half the rowers were young women. It was something that would never have happened before the war.

There was, thankfully, only one tea shop, a one-storey wooden structure with a shaded verandah which sloped towards the lapping waters. Despite the new paint and the colourful baskets of flowers hung at regular intervals along the verandah's balustrade, the restaurant had an impermanent air, as if it might only be used in the summer months. Miss Davis confirmed that his impression was correct.

'We normally close at the end of October. It wouldn't be worthwhile opening in the winter. I give my sister-in-law a hand in the pub then. Never any shortage of customers there.' Manoeuvring the tray of tea and scones that they'd ordered on to the table, she wiped her hands on her flowered apron and took the sketch of Valerie. 'Last summer, you say?' She shook her head, sending a kiss curl swaying across her forehead. 'The trouble is we get so many young girls here in the summer, and you've really not time to look at their faces. I remember the regulars by their orders – Miss One Weak Tea; Mr and Mrs Cold Ham Salad; Mr Pork Pie and Mustard. Tell me what she ate and I could place her.'

They couldn't do that. And the news that her nephew had been attracted to Valerie merely brought a smile to Miss Davis's face. 'Young Glyn likes to play the ladies' man but that's just to impress his friends. Truth is, he'd run a mile if any of the girls took him up.'

'He's not married then?' Jack could see his murdering blackmail victim theory sliding inexorably away as Miss Davis's smile broadened.

'No,' she agreed. 'I expect he'll end up wedding young

Florrie from the Post Counter. She's had her eye on him since they were in Mixed Infants together.'

An argument at the cash till claimed her attention.

'He's got the right initials,' Sarah offered without much hope. 'G.D.'

'Not much of a motive though. Unless he thought young Florrie from the Post Counter would throw him over if she found out about Valerie. Which,' Stamford concluded, 'doesn't seem very likely when he doesn't even know he's engaged to her yet.'

Sarah poured two cups of strong tea. 'What now?'

'Legwork.' Jack passed her another copy of Margaret's sketch. 'You start with the queue for the rowing boats. I'll go round the other side. Meet back here. Stick to the runaway story.'

It proved to be hot and sticky work. The flimsy sketches became more tattered and smeared with picnic lunches as they were passed from hand to hand. Most of the trippers were anxious to help, but that in itself caused problems since the ones who had no definite information tended to dredge up long, involved stories about missing children who'd miraculously reappeared. They also seemed to feel they had to justify their day excursion to the police in view of the grim situation across the Channel. Sarah lost count of the number of times she was defiantly informed that, as this might be their last chance to enjoy themselves for years, they were spending their savings.

The ones who had – or thought they had – information offered conflicting stories. By the middle of the afternoon, Valerie had variously been seen with tall, thin, yellow-haired men; short, fat, dark-haired men; nondescript men of uncertain age; and a suspicious-looking, bald-headed man, with a limp in his left leg and a German accent.

'What accent did the right leg have?' Jack asked, when Sarah completed her report.

She laughed. She'd taken off the Sunday-best hat and it rested on the grass beside her, together with her shoes. Squinting against the sunlight glinting off the still sheet of water in front of them, she said: 'Do you know, sir, plenty of them thought they'd seen Valerie, but not one of them recognized her as the Zimmermann murder victim.' She drew her knees up into her arms and rested her chin on them. 'Do you think this is where she came? Or have we been chasing some other girl?'

Did he? Stamford weighed the question. The half-crowns for the excursion tickets, so meticulously recorded by Valerie, led him to believe that they were on the right track. 'But there's no reason she should have come to the lake,' he said, half-thinking aloud. 'She could have gone to one of the houses in the village. Or even somewhere within walking distance.' They'd passed several farms on the ride here. He came to a conclusion, standing up and brushing clinging grasses from his trousers.

Sarah followed suit.

'We'll have to organize a house-to-house.' He saw Sarah's expression. 'Don't worry, I wasn't expecting you to do it. We'll have to draft in help. Let's find the local nick.'

As he had predicted there were no CID officers at the solid red and white building with its 'Metropolitan Police' legend engraved over the door lintel. Instead there was one startled sergeant who attempted to rub the remains of his lunch from his chin, take the remaining copies of Margaret's sketches and salute Stamford at the same time.

Jack scribbled a telephone number. 'Ask your senior officer to ring me as soon as he comes on duty. I'll explain what I want from the enquiries.'

The sergeant made to take the scrap of paper, and discovered he was one hand short. He tucked Margaret's sketches under his chin. 'Yes, sir. Is there anything else I can do?'

'Do you know what time the excursion bus returns to Edgware?'

'Eh?' A tide of suspicion flowed over the man's sagging features. Stamford could almost see him considering whether he should phone Scotland Yard and check out this so-called inspector's credentials.

Jack dropped one eye in a slow wink. 'Undercover,' he murmured.

'Ah.' A small flush of gratification that he'd been included in a Scotland Yard inspector's confidences spread over the man's cheeks. 'First bus leaves at three o'clock,' he said smartly, unconsciously straightening to attention. 'Or there's a later one at six for those who want to make a whole day of it.'

JUNCTION CUT

It was a minute to three by the clock on the station wall. Sprinting back to the main street, they found that the green and cream bus was already parked opposite the pub, its noisy engine belching petrol fumes into the warm, scented air. A small queue was shuffling into the open door opposite the driver. They reached the step just as the last passenger mounted and the bus's engine gave one final despairing cough and died.

'Won't be two minutes,' the driver said. Descending from the front seat again, he made his way to the back of the bus, opened a small cubicle and returned with a crank handle. To the accompaniment of groans and derisive comments from the passengers, he inserted it in the front of the engine and swung heavily. The engine issued a bronchial gasp, then collapsed into silence again. Another cloud of pungent petrol fumes rolled across the pavement.

'Phew,' Sarah complained, waving her hat vigorously. 'By the look of this rattle-trap, it would be quicker to walk – on our hands.' She became aware that Stamford's attention wasn't on her or the red-faced bus driver. Instead he was staring fixedly across the road. 'Sir?'

Stamford looked back at her. She was amazed to see his face splitting into a grin. 'Sergeant, I think we've found our first break.'

'Have we?'

'Tomorrow I want you to . . .' The rest of Stamford's sentence was drowned out by a triumphant roar from the bus's engine.

'All aboard,' the driver sang out, swinging himself into the seat. He started to roll forward, leaving his final two passengers to leap into the bus and pull the door hastily shut behind them.

'You want me to what?' Sarah enquired, as soon as they'd sunk breathlessly into their seats.

Stamford repeated: 'Tomorrow I want you to go to Somerset House and start checking out the Register of Deaths.'

Chapter 17

The vicar of St Barnabas reflected that there was a lot in the old saying that every cloud has a silver lining. Not that the war could be described as a 'cloud'; it was more properly a blight. But it was a blight that had a silver and copper lining as far as his collection plate was concerned.

Over the past eight months his congregation had quadrupled; everyone, from the atheists to the I-don't-need-a-church-to-pray brigade, had decided it wouldn't hurt to have God on their side after all, and were prepared to invest prayers and hard cash to that effect. Today the cold pews had been even more packed than usual as people who wouldn't normally waste a Sunday morning in church had crowded in to do their bit for the National Day of Prayer and lend a bit of spiritual support to the beleaguered army across the Channel.

He placed the three women and one man who now emerged blinking into a damp Kentish Town Road into that category. Shuffling forward to shake his hand, they murmured thanks for his sermon.

'I don't believe in God myself, Vicar,' Carey Meeks said, wringing the cleric's reluctant hand. 'But I suppose it can't do no harm, praying to something that ain't there.'

'None at all. I think the harm would only arise if God didn't believe in you.'

'Personally,' Miss Toddhunter remarked, drawing on her gloves, 'I have always felt Prince Leopold had the right attitude on that matter.'

Unexpectedly the vicar recited: ' "O God assist our side; at least, avoid assisting the enemy and leave the rest to me." ' He shook Dolly's hand with rather more enthusiasm. 'An eminently practical viewpoint, madam. Let us hope the Commanders of the Expeditionary Force share it.'

Carey was obviously prepared to argue this statement, but his wife seized his arm and dragged him away. Dolly and Lily fell into step behind, Lily pushing the sleeping Gussie.

'Do you know anything about this evacuation scheme the Government are trying to get going, Dolly? The one where they send the kids to America or Canada?'

'Not a lot, I'm afraid. It was hardly likely to be of interest to me. Why? Are you thinking of sending Gussie?'

'Maybe.' Lily gnawed her bottom lip, removing globules of the pale pink lipstick she'd applied for the church visit. 'Would they let the mums go too?'

'I don't believe so, not under the scheme. Although, of course, there is no reason why they could not book passage on the ship, providing they have an exit permit.'

'Permit?' Lily had never been abroad. She had always assumed it was the same as getting a train to Crewe. You just told the bloke in the ticket office where you wanted to go and whether you wanted First, Second or Third Class, and he punched out a ticket for New York, Paris or Timbuctoo. 'How d'you get one of these permits then?' she demanded. 'Can anyone have one?'

'I believe it depends on whether your activities are considered subversive. Or prejudicial to the country's security.' There were times when Dolly couldn't resist showing off her superior vocabulary. Pride was about the only vice that she was still in a financial and physical position to indulge. She knew perfectly well that 'subversive' and 'prejudicial' were beyond Lily. Taking pity on her, she advised her to try Thomas Cook's in Berkeley Square. 'Has Gus decided to purchase a public house in the Americas now?'

'No,' Lily said quickly. 'Gus doesn't know anything about this. I just want to know how to do it. Just in case. Don't mention it to anyone else, Doll.'

They'd stopped walking, facing each other across the pavement, so that Dolly could lip-read with ease instead of having to interpret half-snatches of conversation from Lily's profile. The sunlight sparkled on the older woman's glasses, hiding her eyes, but the twist of her mouth suggested she had a shrewd idea of what was behind Lily's pleading. 'Very well,' she said eventually. 'Shall we catch the others up?'

'You go on. I ain't going straight home. I've already got the dinner ready to go in. Thought I'd take Gussie for a walk. Get some fresh air into him.'

Miss Toddhunter wished her good morning then and continued on her way up Kentish Town Road, nursing her own opinions on Lily's sudden conversion to church attendance and domestic skills.

Lily crossed the road and made her way along Prince of Wales Road, following the route that Sarah had taken when chasing Felonious Monk the previous week. However, when she reached Haverstock Hill, instead of crossing as Sarah and Felonious had done, she swung sharp right.

Phyllis's flat was halfway up the street on the opposite side to the park that gave the road its name. Lily viewed the steep metal staircase down to the basement area with annoyance. She'd have to unstrap Gussie and carry him down. Which meant that he'd probably wake up and be fractious whilst she was applying a bit of feminine blackmail to Phyllis.

The noise had the effect of attracting Phyllis's attention.

'Lily? What are you doing here?'

'Invite me in and I'll tell you. Had an accident?' she asked, indicating the broken pane which was now covered by a layer of brown paper.

'I locked myself out. In here.'

The damaged table had been covered by a lace table cloth, and the remains of the smashed lamp and mirror were now in the dustbin.

'Is it Mrs Yeovil? Has something happened?'

'Edie?' Lily flopped down in an easy chair. 'No.

Ain't seen her for a few days. I've come to ask you to do me a favour. Seeing as how I did you one a few months back.'

She saw Phyllis stiffen warily. Nonetheless, the other woman took the seat opposite, smoothing down her plain beige skirt over her knees and folding her hands in her lap. The suggestion of relaxed composure was only spoilt by the thumb and forefinger of her right hand, which continually spun the ring on the engagement finger of her left. There was a rime of frost on the sibilant tail of her 'Yes?'

Lily took it as an invitation to proceed with her request, rather than a query as to the truth of her last statement. 'Tell you what it is, Phyl. I want to borrow your flat. You ain't here in the day, so it won't bother you.'

'What for?'

'What do you think?'

Phyllis's employers did not handle many divorce cases, but she'd typed up enough co-respondent's statements over the years to know that hers was about to become 'a flat belonging to a third party'. 'No. It's impossible.'

'No it ain't. Got a spare key, ain't you? We'll be gone long before you get home.'

'Ronnie may be getting leave soon.'

'That's no problem. We'll have a system, see? Leave a vase in the front window if the flat's being used. What do you say?'

'No.'

Lily's eyes narrowed. 'You owe me a favour, Phyllis. I've kept me mouth shut – so far.'

The band of chipped diamonds and gold was still. Phyllis twisted her fingers together. 'You couldn't prove anything.'

'I know you saw her. If I told – well, you know what they say, about there being no midden without the muck?'

Phyllis's eyes were fixed on some point mid-way between herself and Lily. 'Things are changing,' she said. 'The war, it's altering things.'

Lily took a packet of cigarettes from her pocket. Without bothering to offer them to Phyllis, she lit one and flicked the spent match carelessly into the empty fireplace. 'The war ain't altered some things, Phyl. The law's still the law.' Phyllis leant forward and picked up the still-smoking match. 'Manners,' she admonished.

'You're getting to be as prissy and finicky as your future ma-in-law,' Lily said, watching Phyllis search for an ash-tray.

Afterwards, when she thought about the conversation, she decided it was that remark that had swung things in her favour, rather than her attempted blackmail.

Phyllis went over to a curved wall table, took a key from the drawer and handed it over. 'There are clean sheets in the cupboard in the hall. Please change them after you've . . . been here.'

'Be a pleasure. Thanks Phyl. I knew you were a pal.

Can you loan me twopence? I've got a phone call to make.'

With the two coins jingling in her pocket and a swing in her walk, Lily wriggled off to find a telephone and tell Joe it was all fixed for Monday.

From the basement window Phyllis watched her go with mixed emotions. Her initial reaction to Lily's proposal had been anger and disgust. Now, walking back into the bedroom with its repaired pillows hidden beneath new pillow cases, and its temporary curtains, she felt a frisson of excitement at the thought of what was going to happen here.

She tried to imagine herself on the bed with a man. Firstly Stephen. Was that significant, she wondered, putting Stephen in bed with her first? It didn't make any difference. The idea, she found, turned her stomach. Slipping off her shoes, she lay on the blanket and conjured up Ronnie beside her. It was harder since she had no memories to draw on: Ronnie had respected her pleas to 'save themselves' for marriage.

She lay still for ten minutes, turned on one side, staring unseeingly at the side of the bed where the naked Ronnie should be. At the end of the ten minutes, she sat up and slipped the ring off her engagement finger.

Monday 27 June

It seemed to be the first thing that the police inspector noticed. He said nothing, but she was certain his eyes dropped to the ringless hand half hidden behind the pleat in her skirt as she showed him into her employer's office on Monday morning.

Mr Phipps sent her out again to bring sherry for his guest, his designation of the decanter with the silver collar telling her that he wanted only the third-rate vintage. 'And bring a glass of lemon squash for the young lady,' Mr Phipps chirruped as an after-thought.

'Please don't bother. I'm really not thirsty,' Sarah said.

It took a while to decant the inferior sherry into the slim glass vessel. By the time she returned to the office, Mr Phipps was assuring the red-haired inspector that she was a paragon of all the secretarial virtues and, yes, he had no doubt she'd spent the whole of that Saturday working in the office.

The inspector swung his chair to face Phyllis. 'Is that true, Miss Nettles? Were you here all day?'

Something in his tone and the quizzical look in his eyes warned Phyllis that he knew at least part of the truth. She could, when the occasion demanded it, be quick-witted. Now she calculated what he was most likely to have found out: 'No,' she said. 'It's not entirely true. I went out for perhaps an hour and a half.'

The inspector looked at her over the rim of the sherry glass. She saw his nose wrinkle at the bouquet of the ruby liquid. 'Where did you go?' he asked.

'I took a taxi to Kentish Town.'

'Why?'

'I'd decided to visit my fiancé, Ronnie Yeovil. Then, on the way, I half-changed my mind. At least, I decided

JUNCTION CUT

to think about what I wanted to discuss with him. So I asked the driver to drop me in Kentish Town Road. I went into a restaurant and had a cup of tea.'

'Your fiancé wasn't at home that afternoon, Miss Nettles. I assume we are talking about the afternoon?'

Phyllis agreed they were. Between half-four and six o'clock. 'I didn't know Ronnie was out. I assumed he'd be at home in Junction Cut.'

'What did you do after you left the restaurant?'

'I came back here and finished my work.'

'You didn't go on to Junction Cut?'

'No. I changed my mind.' The police inspector held her gaze. The woman police officer was bent over a black notebook assiduously writing down her statement. She looked very cold and efficient in her plain grey suit. 'The moving finger having writ...' came into Phyllis's mind. She was suddenly glad she'd chosen the long-sleeved white blouse and calf-length black skirt today; they hid the goose-bumps crawling over her skin.

Mr Phipps hadn't invited her to sit down. There were, in any case, only two spare chairs in his office. In the piping voice that, more than anything else, had prevented him from becoming a barrister, he now said: 'Do you have any further questions for my...' From force of habit he nearly said 'client', but changed it at the last second to 'assistant'. He was sorry he'd done so when the inspector suggested that perhaps Miss Nettles would prefer to hear his other questions in private, and she agreed. Spluttering warnings about legal representation, Mr Phipps found himself being ushered from his own office.

The inspector drew out his own chair and invited her to sit down. Rather than manhandle the solid mahogany throne that soothed Mr Phipps's inferiority complex if not his bottom, the inspector perched himself on the edge of the solicitor's desk and produced something from his pocket.

'Do you recognize this, Miss Nettles?'

'No.' Phyllis was genuinely puzzled. It looked like a cheap exercise book.

'You never saw Valerie Yeovil with this book?'

'I don't think so . . .' Phyllis hesitated, assuming it was one of Valerie's school books.

The inspector disillusioned her. 'She didn't record the blackmail payments at the time they were received then?'

Her skin was rippling with cold again, although the wooden panelled office was already pleasantly warmed by the golden shafts of light flooding through the windows behind the desk and catching the dancing motes of dust in their slanting beams. 'What blackmail payments?' She knew, as she said it, that she'd left too long a gap between question and answer.

The inspector rifled through the pages, detailing all the weekly ten-shilling and pound notes. 'Over twenty-five pounds between October and January, Miss Nettles. And all recorded against your name. What hold did Valerie have over you? Why was she blackmailing you?'

JUNCTION CUT

Blackmail? Phyllis thought. You obviously never met my late, not-so-dearly-departed, nearly sister-in-law. Val had been far too subtle for anything so crude. The first time she'd simply waited until they were alone, opened Phyllis's handbag as it lay next to her on the Yeovils' sofa, removed a pound note, and put it quite deliberately in the pocket of her own cotton dress. Beneath the half-closed eyelids, her toffee-coloured eyes had challenged Phyllis to say something. She hadn't. The following week, when she'd handed her coat to Ronnie to be hung on the pegs behind the door, there had been another pound in the pocket. And when she left it was gone. After that, it had become a pattern, those weekly tea and hush-money parties. But you couldn't really claim it was blackmail, could you? Not when Val hadn't asked.

She felt that perhaps the inspector would not appreciate the semantics of the situation. So she lied: 'None. Those were presents. I felt sorry for her. Her mother hadn't any money to spare and Val was at an age when she needed pocket money for... well, women's things. I'm sure I don't need to go into details, Inspector.'

'I can't find any evidence that you were particularly fond of Valerie. In fact, no one appears to have liked that young lady very much. So why should I believe that you wanted to make her presents of money?'

'Because I have just told you so, Inspector.' Phyllis started to wish she'd ask Mr Phipps to stay. But to do so would have implied she'd done something that warranted legal advice.

'What were you going to discuss with Ronnie that Saturday?'

The change of subject startled her. Unable to think of a convincing lie, she resorted to the truth: 'I was going to break off my engagement.'

Obviously the inspector could recognize the truth when he heard it. 'But you changed your mind. Why?'

It was a relief to tell the truth. Rather like going to confessional. 'Because I'm a coward, Inspector. Have you met Ronnie's neighbour, Miss Toddhunter?' A brief nod of his head indicated that he had. 'She was in the restaurant. I don't think she saw me, but I saw her. The cook was giving her some fish scraps for her cat.' Phyllis looked between the two uncomprehending police officers, and elaborated. 'She doesn't have a cat, Inspector. Miss Toddhunter is an intelligent and educated woman, but she's been reduced to living in one room and feeding herself on kitchen scraps. I'm twenty-nine, and not particularly attractive. I decided that a husband with prospects and a pension, even one I didn't care for, was better than no husband at all.'

'And now you've changed your mind again?'

So he had noticed the ringless finger. But Ronnie deserved to be told first. She owed him that much at least. 'I've lost weight. My ring keeps slipping off. I have to have the shank adjusted.'

'Ah.' It was a sound charged with scepticism. But instead of pursuing the question, the inspector changed tack again. 'You're quite sure you didn't go near Junction Cut that afternoon, Miss Nettles?'

'Quite certain, I told you. After I saw Miss Toddhunter in the café, I went outside and tried to find a taxi. But there weren't any. So in the end I took the bus. I was back here by six o'clock.'

'What were you wearing?'

'Wearing?'

'It was a cold day, Miss Nettles. I presume you had a coat? And a hat?'

'I had my camel wool coat on.'

'And your hat?'

'It's dark brown felt. Trilby-shaped. It pulls over my right eye.' Phyllis's fingers unconsciously drew the absent hat into position.

'And you were wearing it when you took the taxi to Kentish Town?'

Why did he keep going on about her hat? It was disconcerting. She wrinkled her brow, thinking hard, and eventually said: 'No, I wasn't. I remember now. It was a damp afternoon. I wanted to protect my hair. I wore an old scarf I keep at the office. Why?'

Instead of answering her, the inspector stood up, nodding at his colleague to do the same. The black book was snapped shut, sealing away Phyllis's words, truthful or not. She would have to stand by them now.

'I wish you good day for now then, Miss Nettles. If you do decide there is anything else you'd like to tell us, either myself or Sergeant McNeill can be contacted at Agar Street station.'

She promised to get in touch if she remembered anything of significance, knowing full well that that wasn't what he meant, and showed him to the door.

'So she is the "P." in Val's book,' Sarah said as they emerged into another perfect summer day.

'I don't think there was ever much doubt about that. I wonder if we'll ever find out what it was Valerie knew about her?'

'Do you think it's important?'

Jack shrugged his shoulders. Across the road, his driver leant out, one arm on the lowered window, uncertain whether this was a signal to bring the car round.

The offices of Messrs Branham, Dempster and Phipps were located in a three-storey porticoed building at the lower end of Grays Inn Road. Being solicitors not barristers they were not actually in the Inns of Court, but their brass plate was sufficiently close to those legal rookeries to suggest they rubbed shoulders with King's Counsels on a social basis.

Jack glanced at his watch. It was nearly eleven. His and Sarah's paths now lay in opposite directions. 'You take the car to Somerset House. I'll get back under my own steam.' He whistled the driver, who executed a 'U' turn that wouldn't have disgraced a London taxi driver and slid smartly into the kerb. 'I want to know as soon as you've found the answer,' he instructed, seeing Sarah into the back seat.

She was mouthing 'Yes, sir' through the back

window as the driver took off again with a screech of tyres.

Jack had intended to spend the afternoon at Agar Street. But once he'd returned to the gloomy office, he found he couldn't settle. His sense of uselessness was increased by the buzz of excitement amongst the uniform branch as they executed several new 18Bs, the forms which authorized the detention of enemy aliens or, indeed, anyone else considered prejudicial to the country's security.

He'd spoken on the telephone to the Metropolitan inspector responsible for the Allingham area before checking out Phyllis Nettles's alibi this morning. To his relief the man had shown no resentment at finding Scotland Yard had been tramping all over his patch. Instead he'd promised to organize an immediate house-to-house with Margaret's sketches and to call Stamford back as soon as they obtained a result. Jack had half hoped there might be a message on his desk when he returned from Messrs. Phipps etc. But to be fair to the man, it was a large area to cover, particularly if you included the outlying farms. He couldn't reasonably expect to receive any news until tomorrow. And he probably wouldn't hear from Sarah for several hours.

Retrieving his hat, Stamford left his home number with the switchboard operator, together with strict instructions that all callers were to be given it, and went back to St Leonard's Square. On the way he overtook Lily Hendry, who responded to his raised hat with a dimpled smile and a wiggle of her hips that suggested wherever she was going, she was looking forward to it with a great deal of pleasure.

Sheets and shirts were billowing in his neighbours' gardens. His own would be on Eileen's lines by now. He wondered if the station would receive any calls about fifth columnists signalling passing aircraft with a suspicious combination of knickers, nightdresses and flannel vests. It had become a favourite symptom of the terminally paranoid every Monday recently.

Since he had no reason to open a packet of Persil – he hadn't, in fact, bought one for over two years, he realized guiltily – he had to find some other way to work off the energy that was boiling up inside him and threatening to explode at any second. Stripping off his work clothes, he donned an old pair of trousers, rolled up his shirt sleeves, and located the spade amongst the collection of debris in the garden shed.

'Dig for Victory' the Government had urged. He'd never taken much notice of the instruction himself, but now he attacked the garden as if it were a panzer division. Beds of wallflowers were up-rooted; the remains of late tulips, their petalless stems like wire sculptures, were grubbed from the earth; daffodils were dragged unceremoniously from the soil by their dead foliage and scattered across the lawn. When the beds were clear he slammed the spade into the heavy clay, twisting, turning and slashing until it crumbled into sticky lumps.

He'd left the doors propped open so he could hear the phone. It rang twice. The first caller was Dunn, confirming the rumours that had reached Scotland Yard the previous day: the falling back of the BEF in Belgium and France had turned into a full-scale retreat.

'What about civilians?' Jack asked.

'Roads are full of them,' Dunn said frankly. 'They'd do better to stay put. They're just preventing the troops moving at present and they're vulnerable to Luftwaffe attacks while they're mixed up with obvious military targets. We've got to stop that happening if the Germans land here.' He seemed finally to realize what Jack was really asking. 'No news then?'

'No.' He had put down the receiver hastily, not trusting himself to say anything further.

The second caller was the inspector from Allingham. 'Several possible sightings and one definite. I think you know where, don't you, sir?'

Stamford agreed he did.

'I did wonder if there was any connection at the time,' the other man said, his voice crackling apologetically from the ear-piece. 'But when the Hun was arrested so quickly, I didn't think the matter warranted any further enquiries on my part. Sorry, sir.'

Stamford assured him it wasn't his fault. He hadn't, after all, been the investigating officer. 'Could you have him in your office at ten-thirty tomorrow? And do it discreetly. No need to cause more grief than is necessary.'

Sarah arrived at the end of the afternoon. 'I thought it would be better to come round rather than phone,' she said uncertainly, taking in his sweat-stained appearance.

'It was,' Jack agreed. 'I'm in the back garden.' He became aware that his lips were cracked and his throat was burning. 'Would you like something? Tea?'

'Yes, please.'

She was examining his gardening efforts when he carried the two brimming cups out.

'I'm turning it over to vegetables.'

'Which ones?'

Stamford had to admit he hadn't the faintest idea. He'd never taken much interest in them until now. 'Any tips?'

'None. I've never had a garden. I live in a top flat.'

It was only the second personal confidence she'd offered him during the course of the investigation. He realized he'd like to know more about her, but this wasn't the time. Dragging out two kitchen chairs, he sat her down and asked for her report.

'You were right, sir. I checked all the entries from nineteen twenty-four to nineteen thirty. I didn't think there was any point in going beyond that date. Valerie would have been five by then. And Mrs Yeovil did say she was a baby at the time.' Resting her tea cup, she flicked open the pages of the black notebook. 'There are three deaths registered in that surname during the period. One an infant, one a female in Yorkshire and one female in Somerset. But there's no Death Registration for Victor Yeovil.'

'Good.' Stamford knew he ought to be pleased but

instead he felt a sickness in his stomach at the misery he knew he was about to unleash on several innocent people.

'There's something else, sir.' Reaching in her jacket pocket, Sarah extracted a folded sheet of paper and held it out. 'It's the reason I was so long. I had to wait while they raised the Certified Copy. I'd never have seen it if the Yeovils had been Smith or Brown, but there aren't that many surnames beginning with "Y" and "Z" so they're listed on the same page in the ledgers.'

Mystified, Jack opened the sheet and found himself looking at a Death Certificate. He scanned the details with a growing sense of incredulity.

The certificate was dated July 1924. It recorded the death of Ebhardt Heinrich Zimmermann, aged four. Cause of death, tuberculosis. The death notified by E.H. Zimmermann, father.

He looked up. Sarah's eyes were fixed on his face. 'I don't know who we've got locked up, sir, but our chief suspect has been dead for sixteen years!'

Chapter 18

Tuesday 28 May

He was waiting for them in an interview room painted the ubiquitous gloss brown and buff.

'Told his wife it was a mix up over the petrol allocation,' the Allingham inspector said.

There was a glass partition in the upper part of the door. Through it Jack examined the man sitting within. Even though he must have been aware that he was being watched, Victor Yeovil sat impassively, his hands linked on the table, his eyes fixed on the wooden-rimmed clock fixed to the wall between the two windows.

He must, Jack calculated, be about fifty: a round-faced man, tanned and red-cheeked, with a slightly monastic look thanks to the tonsure of dark hair which still clung around his ears and neck. As Jack opened the door and went in he said simply: 'I knew you'd come one day.'

They'd set out two more chairs on the opposite side of the table. One plain wood, the other polished with a padded seat, which suggested it had been hurriedly commandeered from a local police house. Jack waved Sarah to the padded seat. 'You didn't think to come forward yourself, Mr Yeovil?' he asked.

'No.' The man shifted in his seat, easing his right leg out stiffly as if it might have cramp. 'I knew. But I prayed you wouldn't.'

Jack took the red notebook and placed it on the table, swinging it so that Yeovil could read the entries for the previous summer. 'Are those your payments?'

'Not much point in denying it, is there? Yes, I gave her those, the blackmailing little bitch!'

His eyes were defiant but his mouth, beneath the suggestion of a moustache, was trembling. The sound of the door re-opening made him jump violently.

Jack looked round impatiently at the fresh-cheeked constable who'd just put his head round the door. 'Sorry, sir, miss. The inspector wants to know whether you'd like tea for you and the prison—er, this gentleman?'

'Yes. Thank you. We would. And can we get some air in here?'

The constable sprang on to the window ledge with a spriteliness that brought a tug of envy to Jack's heart. Gripping the wooden cross-bar two thirds of the way up the pane, he tugged the upper part of the sash window open. A welcome breeze fluttered the pages of Jack's notebook, bringing with it country scents of newly unfurled leaves and dew-rich grass. Springing backward without a glance, the constable landed with bent knees, stretched back to full-length, and marched smartly out of the room.

Victor Yeovil remarked, 'Always hanging around the

local aerodrome when he was a kid. Wants to join the RAF. Become a pilot. Couldn't get in before. Wrong accent. Perhaps the fly boys won't be so choosy after the news this morning.'

Jack was reluctant to rise to this obvious attempt to divert the course of the interrogation. Nonetheless, he couldn't stop himself asking: 'What news?'

Yeovil looked surprised. 'Haven't you heard? It was on the wireless, eight-thirty this morning. The Belgium King, Leopold, has surrendered. Let's hope the Frenchies hold out long enough for our boys to get out. Though God knows, they don't owe us much after the mess we left behind last time.'

'Were you part of the mess?'

'Went right through.' Yeovil unhooked a walking stick that Jack had missed from the back of his chair. He tapped it sharply against the stiffened leg. A metallic clink reverberated around the room. 'Got this. And Edie.'

'You met your... Mrs Yeovil... in France?'

Yeovil shook his head. 'Convalescent Home in Hampstead.' Settling himself more comfortably against the hard-backed chair, he continued, 'She was a ward maid. Took me under her wing, I suppose. See, I was a sergeant really. Got commissioned a couple of weeks before I copped a Blighty one. They put me in an officers' hospital. I felt like a mongrel in a pack of hunting hounds. Edie used to come and sit with me at visiting time. I'd no family. And this,' he banged the tin leg again, 'gave us something in common. See, Edie, she'd always felt she was marked. Did you know she was illegitimate?'

Stamford's reply was cut short by the arrival of the constable, carrying a wooden tray containing three cups of tea, three cubes of sugar and a plate of biscuits. 'Sergeant's wife made those,' he informed them. 'Raisin. They're good.' He eyed the crumbly brown discs with undisguised hunger.

'Be sure to thank her for us,' Stamford remarked, passing the plate to Yeovil, who shook his head.

Waiting until the door was securely closed, Jack prompted the man again. 'You were saying, Edith Yeovil is illegitimate?'

'Her mother was housekeeper to a vicar. Paid her nothing but board and keep and allowed her to dress herself and Edie in the cast-offs his parishioners gave for the poor. If that's Christianity, give me the heathens every time.' He cleared his throat noisily. 'Anyway, Edie was brought up to understand she was different. "Tainted by sin" was the way that blessed vicar put it. She felt the shame of it. Wanted to be respectable. And I was her ticket. A wounded war hero. Even had a commanding officer who was prepared to recommend me for a job in that bloody bank. Didn't know it then, of course. Thought she'd fallen for me.' Even after all these years, the anger still throbbed in his voice.

Jack prompted, 'It wasn't a happy marriage?'

Yeovil snorted. 'You can say that again! It was purgatory for me. Maybe for Edie too. I don't know. We didn't talk much. We didn't do anything much, except share a table and a bed. After young Ronnie was born, I just didn't bother any more.' He glared at Jack. 'I reckon I'd have been entitled to find some comfort elsewhere, but I didn't.' Taking one of the raisin biscuits, he snapped it in two with a vigour that suggested he wished it was his wife's neck.

'Go on.'

'Have you any idea what it's like to hate every minute of your life? I'd no one to talk to at home. Even the kid was *her* kid; she'd never let me take him out up the Heath for a game of football or to sail a boat on the ponds. And as for work...!' He took a hasty swallow of tea. The cup rattled as he returned it to the saucer. 'I still can't go into a bank without getting a feeling like I'm choking. It's the smell I can't stand: dusty paper, ink, and sealing wax. I smelt that damn smell every day for six years. Thirteen thousand hours.'

He'd forgotten the two officers were there; his eyes grew darker and more hollow as he recalled those years of purgatory when all his hopes had died and there was only loneliness and frustration ahead.

But then a miracle had occurred. Out of the blue a letter had arrived from an old army pal who'd emigrated to Australia. He'd started a small engineering business. Nothing too grand – just a shack really with a couple of rooms above it – but it had started to turn a profit and he needed a partner. He remembered Victor had always had a knack with engines. Would he be interested?

He'd written back immediately. Started to make

enquiries about the cost of the passage. And that was when Edie had dug her heels in. There was no way she was going. Or letting Ronnie go.

'I thought at first it was the idea of the voyage that frightened her. Should have known better.' He spread out his hands for their inspection. Square, blunt-tipped fingers with a rime of grease beneath the nails and trapped in the cuticles. 'That's what she couldn't take. The idea of being married to a man who got his hands dirty. If I'd been offered a bank manager's job in the middle of the sodding outback, she'd have rowed to Australia. But manual work was common, and Edie wasn't going to be dragged down.'

'Is that why you left her?' Jack asked.

'No. I knuckled under like a good 'un. Married her for better or worse, hadn't I? And I couldn't force her on the boat. So I went on catching the eight-ten every morning and dying a little bit at each stop.'

It had gone on like that for another two years, with the slump growing worse all the time and ten men standing in line to grab your job if you were fool enough to leave it. Then, unexpectedly, the manager of one of the bank's northern branches had died and massive discrepancies in his customers' accounts had been discovered. Victor had been one of those drafted from Head Office to sort out the mess.

'Took three months in the end. I was in digs up there. Came home a couple of weekends, but really there was no point. It didn't make much difference whether I was sitting in my room on my own up there or at Edie's. I'd started to think of it as "Edie's" by then, see? I felt like the lodger.'

Then another apparent miracle had occurred. He'd returned home to a warm and loving welcome. 'She was after me for it. Couldn't keep her hands off me. Like an idiot, I thought absence had made the heart grow fonder. Didn't even bother me when she went off me again a couple of months later. Put it down to her feeling poorly with Val.'

'Go on,' Stamford said, although he thought he could guess what was coming.

'I came home one night when she was seven months gone and found they'd called in the midwife. Edie'd fallen down the stairs. Banged on the wall until a neighbour heard her.' It had been a long labour. He'd lain on the sofa all night, listening to Edie screaming and cursing and crying up above him. Then just after dawn a loud persistent scream of indignation at its rude arrival in the cold, bright world had told him the baby had been born. 'Ten minutes later they came down, told me I had a daughter.' Yeovil's eyes held their far-away look again. He was no longer in the police interview room, he was in the bedroom of his small claustrophobic terrace house in Hampstead. Edie lay in the bed, white-faced and exhausted. And scared. The neighbour had ushered Ronnie away. The midwife had bustled around, fussing with soaked towels and blood-stained rags, refusing to meet his eye.

'Let me see,' he'd demanded, attempting to separate

the noisy bundle from the swathing of blankets they'd wrapped her in.

'I knew,' he said, his voice shaking with the memory. 'Soon as I set eyes on her. She was a big baby, Val. Ten pounds. Lots of hair. And all her finger and toe nails. There was no way that was a seven-month baby.'

'So you left her?' Stamford prompted.

'And your son?' The addition was Sarah's. There was a distinct accusation in her question. A feminine revulsion for anyone who could abandon their own child.

'It wasn't like that. When I walked out that day, I never intended it to be for good. I wasn't thinking straight. I just had to get away – from Edie.'

So he walked north, without any clear idea where he was going. After a while it had started to rain. 'I'd nothing with me. Not even a coat.' He'd got soaked to the skin. But still he'd ploughed on, the water lashing in his face, the needles of cold pricking at his fingertips, lips and ears. Leaving North London, he'd limped through the new dormitory suburbs along wide roads lined with spacious houses constructed to resemble Tudor manor houses, and out into country lanes banded by ancient thicket hedges where horses watched incuriously as he stumbled past, the amputated leg sending jolts of protest through his body at every step. It was the leg that had stopped him eventually. The hardened skin over the stump had blistered and ruptured under the friction of the unaccustomed exercise.

'I'd no idea where I was. Hadn't more than a few shillings in my pocket. I knew I had to get inside somewhere.' So he'd gone into a pub and bought a pint. 'Didn't want it. But my leg was giving me such gyp by then, I had to get the weight off it. May, my missus, she was behind the bar. She could see something was wrong.'

She'd given him a room for the night. But he'd woken in the morning drenched in sweat, with his leg stump on fire and the beginnings of a fever pounding through limbs that had turned to lead. 'Three weeks she nursed me, though she didn't know me from Adam.'

'The real Mrs Yeovil didn't know where you were?'

'No. I told May I'd no family. She was a widow then, bringing up young Glyn on her own. She and her sister-in-law ran the pub and her father-in-law had the garage next door. He's dead now, God rest his soul. When I got on my feet again, I gave him a hand mending a couple of motors. Pay for my keep as it were. Then one day he asked me if I'd like to make it permanent. There were plenty of men on the roads in those days. Just hitching from town to town picking up work where they could. They took me for one of those.'

For the first time it had occurred to him that he didn't need to go back to Edie. That he could be free to start all over again. 'I told them I'd left some things at my old digs. Borrowed the fare back to London against my first week's wages and got my stuff from Edie's.'

'Did you tell her where you were going?' Stamford asked.

'No. Just told her we were finished. I'd send her money each week for Ronnie, but that was all. She could get her fancy man to keep her and the baby.'

Despite the defiant tone of his voice, he seemed to feel a need to justify his actions. 'I wouldn't have cared so much if things hadn't been like they had been between us. I mean, I'd have been angry. Maybe I'd have thumped her. But if she'd been a loving wife to me, I reckon that in the end I'd have just put it down to a bit of a mistake on her part and made the best of the baby. But after the way she'd treated me . . .' His voice choked and he drained the cold dregs of tea from the bottom of his cup.

Stamford prompted: 'So you came here. Why didn't you change your name?'

'I told you, didn't I?' Yeovil's voice took on a touch of impatience. 'I hadn't intended to leave permanently. When they asked me my name, I told them. Had no reason not to. Don't think I haven't regretted it plenty of times over the years.'

'How did you keep in touch with your wife . . . with Mrs Yeovil.'

'I didn't. We were finished.'

'Don't lie to me, Mr Yeovil.' Jack's voice hardened. 'Your wife has moved at least twice to my knowledge since Valerie was born. Possibly more. How did she let you know her new address?'

The faint drone of heavy aircraft engines carried

through the gap in the window. Yeovil's eyes turned towards the blue rectangle enclosed by the wooden window frame. His face must have held just such a wistful expression when he'd sat in the bank, watching the clock hands reeling away his life. Reluctantly he returned his attention to Jack's question. 'I collect spare engine parts from a place in Dunstable about once a month. I told her to write care of the Post Office there if she ever needed to get in touch.'

'And then you married again, without bothering to divorce your first wife?'

'Don't make it sound so cold-blooded. It wasn't like that. I didn't set out to marry May. We were just friends at first. The loving crept up on us. And when I realized she felt the same as me — well, she's not the sort of woman to live over the brush. I knew it had to be marriage or nothing.'

'You could have obtained a divorce on the grounds of your wife's adultery,' Sarah pointed out.

'How? Edie never told me the bloke's name. And I'd come home a couple of weekends from the North, remember? I knew nothing had happened between us, but I couldn't prove it, could I?'

'Wouldn't she consider divorcing you?'

'No.' Yeovil gave a mirthless laugh. 'I told you, what mattered most to Edie was respectability. She'd put it about she was a widow. That was respectable. Divorced wasn't. Maybe if the fancy man had still been on the scene and ready to make an honest woman of her, she'd have gone through with it. But he'd scarpered, hadn't he, so it suited her to hang on to me. I was her insurance policy.'

'Did she know about your second . . . about your present domestic arrangements?'

'No. I told her if she ever came looking for me I'd stop Ronnie's money. And I'd make sure everybody knew why I'd walked out in the first place. She'd had her chance, now I was having mine.'

'So you married May Louise Davis, and applied for a licence to sell wines and spirits?'

Yeovil's mouth twisted in a wry smile beneath the moustache. 'That how you found me? That damn sign over the pub door. I didn't want it. Licence used to be in the wife's name. She made me apply when she was expecting our first boy. Wanted to be sure things would carry on as normal if anything happened to her at the birth. She's like that, my May, not afraid to face up to the worst.' He seemed to realize what he'd said. His lower lip trembled again but he caught it firmly whilst he drew a wallet from his inner pocket, extracted a photograph, and pushed it across the table.

Two boys squinted into the camera. The older, dark-haired and round-faced, showed his paternal inheritance clearly. The younger, a square-jawed, stolid child, with a decisive jaw and an air of being prepared to take on the whole world, presumably took after his mother. 'Those are our two. Colin,' Yeovil stabbed a finger on the bruiser, 'he's ten now. And young Matthew, he's twelve. Bright as a button, young Matt is. He's just passed his scholarship. But they won't take him in if it comes out he's a . . .' His voice faltered on the word 'bastard'. He changed tack. 'This is going to kill May. Does it have to come out? Please, I'm not asking for me, I'm prepared to face my medicine. But can't we do it quietly? May and the kids, they haven't done anything and it's them that will be left here to face all the sniggers and pointing fingers.'

Jack felt a twinge of sympathy for May. And a deep anger with Victor for trying to pin the blame for any hurt caused to her on him. The fact that it was his own actions that had precipitated the coming horrors seemed to have been conveniently overlooked. In any event, his hands were tied. Bigamy was a criminal offence. He'd have to submit a report and what happened after that was up to his senior officers and the prosecutor. He told Yeovil as much.

Victor's shoulders slumped. 'All right,' he said, with resignation. 'I understand. You've got your job to do. What happens now?'

'Tell me why you stopped sending the money for Ronnie? You did, didn't you? Last summer.'

'I saw the engagement notice. In the *Telegraph*. Gave me quite a turn seeing it in print like that: "Ronald Edward, only son of the late Second Lieutenant Victor Edward Yeovil . . ." Luckily no one else noticed it. I wrote to Edie, told her if the boy was old enough to marry, he was old enough to stand on his own two feet and she shouldn't expect to hear from me again.'

'Did she reply?'

'Not exactly. But a few weeks later that little bitch

turned up.' Yeovil looked at Sarah, who'd lifted her head from her notebook at his outburst. 'I know that sounds bad, talking about a fifteen-year-old like that. Especially one who's been killed like – well, like she was. But you don't know what she was like.'

'So tell us,' Stamford invited. 'How did she find you?'

'From the postmarks on the letters. And then the same way you did. She saw that damn licensing sign. I don't know how she suddenly got on to me after all those years.'

'Ronnie's fiancée's sister told her insurance money isn't paid in cash. She realized that your payments to her mother couldn't be from an insurance policy.'

'Oh.' Yeovil digested this information. He said: 'Do you want to hear something funny? I liked her before I knew who she was.' She'd been just another pretty girl from the excursion bus. 'She looked nothing like that picture they printed in the paper.'

'We know,' Stamford said, his mind returning to Margaret's uninhibited sketches.

'That first time, she hung around the garage when the other passengers left. Pretty little thing she was. Started talking to me about the business. And then we got on to the family. She wanted to know all about my kids. How old they were, where they went to school.'

'Didn't you think that was rather odd?'

'To tell you the truth, I thought she was a bit shy.' She'd leant against the open garage doors, watching him struggling with an engine slippery with black oil, her long hair partially obscuring her face. 'She was on her own, see? The way I saw it she'd come on the excursion bus by herself and now she was too shy to go down to the lake. I was even about to suggest I get young Glyn to walk her down and introduce her to a few of the young people.'

And then she'd told him her name. 'Same as yours? Funny that, isn't it?' she'd said.

He hadn't been sure at that point whether it was just coincidence. She'd soon disillusioned him. Moving further into the garage, and pulling the door closed behind her, she'd recited other facts: her mother's name, her brother's name, her place of birth, where her father had worked.

'She didn't spell it out or anything. I mean, there was no "Pay up or I'll tell your wife". In the end, I just pushed ten quid in her hand and thrust her out the door. Prayed I'd never see her again.'

'But you did.'

'Every Sunday. I dreaded that bus arriving. Felt sick to my stomach whenever I heard it. But I didn't dare not be here. I tried offering her a lump sum. Fifty quid to go away. But she wasn't having it. She liked coming each week. Liked watching me squirm.'

'Did you tell her you weren't her natural father?'

'She said she didn't believe me. Didn't make much odds in the end, did it? I mean, it was bigamy she'd got me on, not abandoning my kids.'

'The payments stopped in September.' Jack pointed to the last ten pound deposit in Valerie's accounts. 'Why?'

Yeovil stared across the table as if he suspected Stamford might be playing an elaborate joke. Eventually, he said: 'They declared war. Did you miss it?'

Jack resisted the temptation to reply in kind. He contented himself with a mild: 'And what effect did that have on Valerie's blackmail?'

'She couldn't get here. They classed the bus as private transport. The petrol ration wasn't enough, not the way that thing was drinking it. So we stopped the excursion run mid-September last year. Started again at Easter once I'd got a new petrol tank fitted.'

'Isn't there a public service?'

'Curtailed on Sundays. I thought she'd write,' he said. He sounded almost aggrieved. 'I dreaded the postman's knock. But she didn't. Don't know why. Never heard from her again.'

'Or saw her?'

Yeovil didn't bother to pretend he hadn't understood the purpose of Stamford's question. 'I didn't kill her,' he said simply. 'If I was going to do it, it would have been last summer. Why should I have waited until the winter, when I'd not heard from her for four months?'

It was a valid point and Valerie's accounts seemed to corroborate his statement. But there was that final fifty pounds. Moving the book slightly, so that Yeovil could see the entry, he said: 'G.D. Fifty pounds. Any ideas?'

Yeovil looked blank. He hadn't followed Stamford's

train of thought this time. But Sarah had. She played devil's advocate.

'Glyn would have known what this news would do to his mother. He must have realized how desperately upset and ashamed she'd be if it came out she'd been living with a man who wasn't her husband.'

'No!' Victor Yeovil lurched to his feet, using the table to draw himself up. 'No, I'll not have that. Glyn had nothing to do with this. Don't you go spreading rumours like that, you bitch.'

'Sit down!'

Stamford hadn't moved. He remained to all intents relaxed and at ease in his seat. But his eyes held Yeovil's and it was Victor who looked away first. Mumbling his apologies he sank back in his chair, repeating that Glyn had nothing to do with the murder.

'How do you know?'

An expression of triumph spread over Victor's face. 'Because,' he explained, 'he was under arrest at the time.'

Almost gleefully Yeovil told them that Glyn and a couple of Army pals had gone up to London on leave. 'They got drunk. Middle of the afternoon, would you believe? Decided to collect a souvenir. Had to be a copper's helmet, didn't it?' He gave a half rueful, half proud smile. 'Glyn lost his identity papers in the scuffle. I got a call from Rochester Row to come up and identify him.' He grinned more broadly this time. 'Held over in custody until he came up before the Beak on Monday morning, the silly sod. They got fined, and fourteen days in the glass-house when they got back to camp. So you see, Inspector, Glyn's got the best alibi in the world.'

'And what about you, Mr Yeovil? What time did you arrive in London?'

'I caught the five-twenty train.'

'From Edgware?'

'No. There's a steam service from the next town. I took that.'

'Which station does it go into?'

Victor stared in despair between the two officers. 'St Pancras,' he said eventually.

'Just a step down the road from Kentish Town, right?'

'Yes, all right, I could have done it. But I didn't. I got out at St Pancras and caught the tube to Rochester Row. I didn't go anywhere near Junction Cut.'

'Do you think he did?' Sarah asked when they were once more on their way back to London, leaving behind a crushed and broken Victor Yeovil preparing to face his wife. Or rather the woman he'd loved and respected as his wife for the past thirteen years.

Stamford said: 'There's no evidence to suggest he did. But by not coming forward at the time, he's made things much worse for himself.'

Remembering what now lay ahead of Yeovil when he reached home, Sarah privately doubted that. And what good would it do in the end to prosecute him? She'd frequently noted in herself an inclination to uphold some laws rather more than others. She'd never allowed it to get in the way of her duty. But one day she thought that she just might.

She became aware that Stamford was watching her and suspected he knew what she was thinking. Well, so what? She hadn't sold her soul to the Metropolitan Police yet. 'Why do you think Valerie didn't write to him, sir?'

'I suspect Yeovil's assessment was correct. Part of the fascination of blackmail for Valerie was watching her victims suffer.'

'So what now?'

'Now?' Stamford removed Billy Zimmermann's death certificate from his pocket and studied it again. 'Now we start finding out who the hell Billy Zimmermann really is.'

Chapter 19

Tuesday – Friday
At Jack's request they saw Zimmermann in his cell this time.

'We can't keep him on the Remand Wing. He's in solitary. It's easier all round that way. For him and us,' the officer explained, leading the way along echoing landings where the sound of their footsteps was lost in the high brick walls and then bounced back at them from metal staircases. Warily Sarah looked over the iron railings that protected the open side of the walkway. Two identical landings ran below them. The tramp of feet seemed to match their own on the lower landing, but perhaps it was just a trick of the acoustics.

The officer stopped opposite the last heavy metal door and inserted a key in the massive lock, twisting it viciously at the same time as he slid the bolt open. From the other cells the murmur of voices, chanting rhythmically, increased.

'Shut that row,' yelled the officer.

The voices increased in volume, the words still indistinguishable but the chanting now accompanied by a menacing drumming as something metallic was slammed against the backs of the doors.

'Pack it in or you'll be on report.' The officer dragged Zimmermann's door open and jerked his head. 'I'll leave the wicket open. Shout when you want out, sir. I'll not be far away.'

'Couldn't you leave the door open?'

'Against the Governor's orders.' The officer jingled his keys. 'All doors in this area have to be secured.'

Stamford sensed a sort of grim satisfaction in the man's tone, as if he wasn't entirely sorry to have received such an order. But it wasn't worth arguing about. 'All right. We'll call when we're ready. Thank you.'

With a clash and wrench of keys, they were locked in.

Zimmermann was against the far wall, beneath the barred window. He didn't move as they entered. Jack sat on the bed without being asked and motioned Sarah to sit next to him, leaving Billy to perch on the solitary wooden chair which was the only other piece of furniture in the narrow oblong cell, apart from a shelf screwed along one wall.

Despite the fact he'd spent several more weeks in prison, he looked better than at their last meeting. The pallid cheeks had acquired a sheen of colour and his eyes had a livelier glint.

Jack asked: 'How are they treating you, Billy?'

'All right. Better.' This time his attention stayed on Stamford instead of drifting towards Sarah. 'You tell 'em to?'

Stamford had, in fact, asked Dunn to have a discreet

word with the Prison Governor after his last visit. Obviously it had had the desired effect; Billy was no longer getting a dose of kangaroo court justice from the other inmates. Or perhaps they'd just switched from physical to psychological abuse? The wordless crooning, accompanied by a rhythmic beating against cell doors, had started again. Ignoring Billy's question, he said: 'What's that about?'

Billy surprised him. Indicating Sarah, he said: 'It's for her.'

'Me?' Sarah exchanged a blank look with her boss.

Billy continued to address Stamford. 'The Governor stopped the exercise period. He said he wouldn't take the risk while there was a woman in the prison. Everyone's got to stay locked up until she's out of here.'

'That's ridiculous! What are they supposed to do, riot at the sight of me? Go mad with lust? They must have female visitors. Wives and sweethearts?'

'Yeah, they do. But not in this section, miss. Only woman who's ever been on the landing is the Governor's wife. And they say even he doesn't fancy her.'

He was talking more freely than before, Stamford noted. And there was a relaxed, almost light-hearted air about the boy.

Stamford said: 'Have you had any visitors since we last met, Billy?'

'Only me solicitor. I don't have no other visitors.'

'But you've heard from Mrs Cohen, haven't you?'

Billy nodded. He couldn't keep the sparkle of

happiness out of his eyes. 'Yeah, yeah. I heard.'

And what he'd heard, he liked. 'Did she tell you I was going to get you off this charge?'

'Said you had a lead. Said you were pursuing enquiries, that the right word?' Without waiting for an answer, Billy gabbled on. Now he'd found his tongue, he wanted confirmation that everything was going to be all right, just like Bea had promised. 'Bea said you were going to get new evidence. Something that would clear me? That right?'

'Well, we've certainly found fresh evidence, Billy. Although whether it clears you is something only you can tell us. Show him, Sergeant.'

Sarah passed over the Death Certificate. Uncertainly Billy stared at the document, a frown creasing the forehead beneath his flopping fringe. His lips moved silently as his eyes scanned the sheet. It wasn't the reaction Jack had been expecting. For a moment he was lulled into believing that they'd made a mistake. That the whole thing was just an unbelievable coincidence. Then he remembered: Billy couldn't read.

As the thought struck him, Billy looked up. 'I know that's Zimmermann,' he said, one finger tracing the name on the paper. 'I know that. But I don't, I can't . . .' He struggled to admit his ignorance. 'I can't read, see? Does it say something about me?'

'It says you're dead, Billy.'

He stared between the two officers. His expression suggested he was searching for evidence that this was some kind of elaborate joke they were playing on him. He extended the paper towards Sarah. 'What does he mean?'

Jack leant across her and took the certificate. 'According to this Death Certificate, Billy, you died in the District of St Pancras on the fourth of December nineteen twenty-four. Aged four years. The death was reported by Ebhardt Heinrich Zimmermann, father. Any comment?'

The haunted eyes flickered from Stamford, to Sarah, to the brick walls of the cell and down to the floor. Then Zimmermann lunged forward towards Sarah.

Jack sprang up, ready to restrain the boy. But instead of attacking the sergeant, Zimmermann groped under the bed, dragged out a bucket and retched violently.

The pot already contained stale urine. Its ammoniac smell mingled with the pungent aroma of vomit.

Jack stood by the door, waiting impassively while Billy gagged into the filling pot. He was kneeling on the floor, blocking Sarah's escape route, so she was forced to draw her legs up and huddle against the back of the bed.

Stamford raised two fingers to his lips and drew them slowly away in the manner of someone drawing on a cigarette. Sarah shook her head regretfully and shrugged, extending open hands. She didn't smoke, although she could fully appreciate that the scent of burning tobacco would have helped in the fetid cell. As it was, there was nothing to do but wait until Billy had finished and drawn himself shakily back on the chair.

'Better?'

Billy nodded, drawing his sleeve across his lips. A shudder ran through his thin body.

Stamford manoeuvred the bucket back under the bed with one foot, and sat down again. Gingerly Sarah joined him. 'So,' he said. 'Do you feel up to telling us your real name?'

'It is Zimmermann, honest it is.' Billy choked back a miserable sniff. 'Wilhelm Zimmermann.'

'Not Ebhardt?'

'No.'

'Perhaps you'd better tell us the whole story. And I want the truth this time. I'm tired of being messed about, do you understand?'

Billy was doing his best to regain control of his voice, but it still shook with misery. 'Yeah, I understand.'

It had started in Germany in 1920. 'We were living just outside Lübeck that summer. You know where I mean?'

Stamford did. He'd visited North Germany on the motor-bike tour that had eventually taken him into Holland and introduced him to Neelie. He remembered the area around Lübeck as a bleak land, full of isolated communities with an intrinsic distrust of strangers.

'Me dad, he was a carpenter, did I tell you that?'

'Yes, you did.'

'Yeah, well, he moved around doing a bit here, a bit there. And that summer he got a job in this farmhouse, fixing up the barn and cow-byres. It was a big job, took several weeks. Then at the end, the farmer only gives him half the money they'd agreed. Said the work wasn't any good. My dad argued with him, and the man tried to throw him off the farm.' Billy looked Stamford up and down. 'My dad was a big bloke. Bigger than you. But my mum said he swore he never meant it to happen. He just hit him once, and the bloke went down, straight on to a pitchfork.'

'He killed him?'

'Yeah. He come running home and told me mum to pack up quick.'

'But why?' This was Sarah. 'If it was a fight, he could have pleaded self-defence.'

'The farmer's brother was the local mayor and me dad was an outsider. Who'd you think they'd believe?'

Whatever the rights and wrongs of the matter, Zimmermann senior hadn't waited to find out, he'd fled with his wife and young son to Hamburg with the intention of getting an immigrant's passage to America.

'Only he couldn't, could he?' Billy said. 'Me mum she was . . .' He held out his arms, as if hugging a ball resting on his stomach. 'The Immigrant Officer told him they don't take pregnant women. In case they drop an imbecile or a cripple. Or die. He told me dad to wait until she'd had the kid then try to get on the quota again.'

Only, of course, Ebhardt Zimmermann couldn't afford to wait. He was already paying out for lodgings for his family and bribing the landlady to falsify the register so they didn't appear on it. He needed to get out of the country. The landlady had a friend, first mate on a tramp steamer whose Captain was too drunk to notice that one cabin was kept locked throughout the voyage to the Port of London.

'He took most of their money and he didn't tell them about the Aliens Act 'til they were at sea and it was too late to turn back.'

Stamford saw the question on Sarah's face. 'It restricted the categories of immigrants allowed to settle in England,' he advised her. 'I forget the criteria exactly, but I doubt an out-of-work German carpenter with a dependent wife and son qualified. Isn't that so, Billy?'

'Dunno. Me dad didn't try to find out neither.' The mate had smuggled them off the boat and left them to their own devices in Silvertown. 'Me dad, he spoke a bit of English, else they'd have been picked up straight away.'

As it was they'd managed, finding a room and, by an incredible stroke of luck, temporary employment with a cabinet-maker. And a couple of months later, Ebhardt had been born.

'The landlady offered to show me dad how to register him, and he thought it would look funny if he refused.'

The registration had been accepted without comment. 'Reckon they thought if we were here, we must be legal.' So Ebhardt had acquired a British Birth Certificate and the family had settled down to follow the jobs Zimmermann senior picked up, moving around

London like gypsies from one set of lodgings to the next. Until the autumn tuberculosis had struck at the family.

'Me and Ebhardt both got sick. But I got better and he didn't.'

For a moment, Sarah was aware of the qualities that had attracted Beatrice Cohen. It was hard not to put her arms round the vulnerable figure in front of her and hug him better. 'Do you remember him?' she said gently.

'Sort of. I remember playing with him. I never had nobody to play with after that. I remember me dad better. He died a couple of years after Ebhardt. I can still see me mum sewing him into a sheet she'd nicked off the landlady's bed 'cos we couldn't afford a proper funeral. All her fingers were bleeding where she kept jabbing the needle in them, but she never noticed.'

After that terrible day, his mother had started wandering in both mind and body. And the rest of his life had followed the pattern he'd already described to them on their previous visit.

'Funny, ain't it?' he said. 'Me dad brought me here to get us away from a murder. And if he hadn't, I wouldn't be mixed up in one now. Think it's a sort of punishment? Like somebody up there was watching what happened in Germany and decided to get me for it instead?' In the half light of the cell, his face seemed to twist into a grin, the teeth gleaming whitely against the dark shadows of his face. Then they realized he was holding back a sob. It burst from him in a gasping, shuddering paroxysm of despair. 'I thought you'd come to get me out,' he wailed. 'I thought it was going to be all right.'

He scrubbed ineffectively at his cheeks with the back of his sleeve.

Silently Jack passed across his own handkerchief. He waited until the noisy hiccuping had subsided before asking: 'When did you start using your brother's identity?'

Billy gulped down a final sob and muttered: 'When they started the Registration Cards.'

'Why?'

'Ain't it obvious? I didn't want to be sent to an Internment Camp. I ain't German. I ain't never been German. I didn't want to be in no camp with them. I wanted to fight, for England. So I told 'em I was born here.'

'Did anyone else know about this?'

Emotions skitted across the hollows of Billy's face. He wanted to lie, he really did. But he knew it had all gone too far for that. 'Val,' he said. 'Valerie knew. I told her.'

'Why?'

'Dunno. She was good at getting things out of people.'

Sarah recalled something Margaret Cave had said: 'And she liked knowing them.' She was doing no more than thinking aloud, but as soon as the words left her mouth, she knew what they suggested.

Stamford saw too. 'Was she blackmailing you, Billy?'

'No.'

'Were you lovers?'

Billy slid a moist tongue over his lips. 'She was only fifteen.'

'That's not an answer. Were you having sex with Valerie Yeovil, Billy. Yes or no.'

'Yeah.' Blowing his nose vigorously into Stamford's handkerchief, Billy sat up, straightened his shoulders, and prepared to justify his actions. 'It was her idea. I mean, she came to my room saying she'd teach me to read.'

'Did you want to learn?'

'No. I can't. I've tried. But it was nice to have someone to talk to, so I left her sitting on the bed and I went to borrow a paper from Dolly. And when I come back she was just standing there – stark naked.' His voice rose in a crescendo of indignation and disbelief. 'Honest, it wasn't my idea. She just come over and put her arms round me and started nuzzling up to me, sort of running her hands over me.'

'So you made love to her?'

'I couldn't stop meself. I mean, she wanted it. She did, honest. She'd even brought a . . .' Billy's voice dropped to a whisper. He leant towards Stamford, as if he could somehow exclude Sarah from the confidence. 'She'd brought a French letter. And she put it on when I couldn't. I mean, nice girls aren't supposed to do things like that!'

His voice shook slightly at the memory. She'd shattered all of his illusions about nice girls. But there was worse to come. 'I thought she wanted me to be her feller, her steady feller, I mean. I wanted to take her up the Gaisford cinema Saturday night. But she laughed. Said she just wanted to know what it was like. She didn't want us to start courting or anything stupid like that.'

'When was this?'

'Last October.'

'But the, er, reading lessons, went on, didn't they, Billy? Even if she didn't want you to be her steady feller.'

'Yeah. Well, like I said, she liked it.'

'And you didn't?'

'It was all right.'

'So how often did you see her?'

'Once, sometimes twice a week.'

'Did the relationship continue after you and Mrs Cohen became intimate?'

'Yes. But it wasn't the same.'

'Why was that? Was Valerie jealous?'

'No. I mean, she didn't know . . . then. It's just that once I started doing it with Bea, it felt all wrong with Val. I didn't know it could be like that.' With Bea he'd experienced tenderness and a sense of being loved. 'She cared, Bea, she really cared that she was making me happy. She wanted me to feel good.' Unlike Valerie who, he realized, had no interest in anything but her own satisfaction.

'You said Valerie didn't know then. When did she find out?'

'On that night.'

Stamford clarified the statement. 'Valerie had sex with you on the day she was murdered and you told her about your relationship with Mrs Cohen?'

'I told her it was the last time because I was going to live with Bea.'

'Was she upset?'

'Not at first, no. She wanted to know all about Bea. But she wasn't angry.'

'So when did she start getting angry?'

'When I told her Bea was better at making love than her.' His voice had taken on a defensive edge again. 'It was her own fault. She asked me if it was better with Bea.'

'And you said yes?' Stamford felt the glow of enlightenment flaring and growing within him. He could almost have described the following scene to Billy. But he let Zimmermann go on.

'She went crazy. Pulled my hair and scratched my face.' His hand went automatically to the cheek, long since healed, which had helped to trap him in this nightmare. 'Said I'd be sorry if I liked some fat, frumpy old woman better than her. I don't know why she was so mad. I mean, she didn't want me, so what was she so angry about?'

His bewilderment was genuine; his experience of women so limited that he couldn't understand how badly he'd bruised Valerie's ego. With an older woman, Stamford reflected, it wouldn't have mattered so much. The rejection would have been shrugged off philosophically. But Valerie, for all her scheming, was only fifteen. And she'd reacted with a child's spite when she was hurt.

'She started to get dressed,' Billy said miserably. 'She put her suspender belt on and tried to fasten one of her stockings.'

'And one of the buttons snapped off?' Jack asked.

Billy nodded. 'I laughed,' he admitted. 'It made her even angrier. She pulled her dress on and bundled all the rest of her stuff up in her arms.' And then, as she'd reached the door, she'd turned and spat out her threat. 'She said she'd tell the police about me lying on the National Registration and about what we'd been doing. That they'd arrest me because she was only fifteen. And I'd be convicted and sent to jail.'

'But only for a year or so,' Stamford expostulated. 'Surely that would have been preferable to hanging for a murder you didn't commit? Why the devil didn't you tell us this earlier?'

A memory nudged at the corners of Sarah's consciousness. Something about Zimmermann's previous record. Only he hadn't got a record. He'd just been connected with a case. Then it came to her. The lascars in his rooming house who'd been convicted of living on prostitutes' earnings. 'Deportation,' she burst out. 'That's it, isn't it? You were scared that you'd be deported?'

'What?' Now it was Jack's turn to look bewildered.

Billy said: 'Yeah. That's what they do with foreigners when they commit a crime, ain't it? They put you in jail, then when you've done your time, they sling you back where you come from. Only I never come from Germany. And I ain't going back there. Bea read me about their camps. There was a bit in the *Telegraph* about this place they put Jews. Called Dachau it was, I remember that. I ain't going there. I'd rather be hung here.' His voice was rising to an almost hysterical scream.

'We're at war with Germany, Billy. How on earth do you think this country could deport someone there?'

Clearly Billy hadn't bothered about the logistics. 'They could do it,' he asserted.

'But, Billy,' Sarah protested, 'just because you're German doesn't mean you'd automatically be expelled or even interned. The country's full of German refugees.'

'They're kids. Or fancy professors with fancy friends. Not ordinary blokes like me.'

Which, Stamford thought silently, was probably true. Even amongst the higher echelons of Scotland Yard there had been mutterings against letting refugees flood, unchecked, into this country, whatever the conditions in their homelands. 'Wastes our time monitoring them and takes jobs away from our own people,' was the general theme. It seemed unlikely however, not to say completely impossible, that they could deport anyone to Germany.

'So,' he said, 'you panicked and ran for it. Which way did you go out, front door or back?'

'Back.'

'Did you see anyone?'

'No.'

'Did you go into number four and shut Valerie's mouth for good? Before she could report you?'

'No. No!' Billy saw his dilemma. Telling the truth hadn't cleared him, it had simply provided a different motive. He rushed on, anxious now to provide as much detail as possible so that the police could see that he was telling the truth. He'd spent Saturday night and all of Sunday hiding out at Pavaria's premises. 'There's a dicky catch on the side door,' he explained. 'You can slip it with a knife if you know where.'

His intention had been to try and see Beatrice Cohen on the Monday morning. But she hadn't come in. And the factory was filling up, he couldn't stay out of sight any longer, so he'd slipped out and starting walking the streets. 'I thought I'd come back later, try and see Bea.' But then he'd seen the artist's impression on a newspaper vendor's placard.

'Did you know you were being sought in connection with a murder?'

Billy shook his head. 'I thought Val had told. Honest, I didn't know she'd been done in.'

Too frightened to go back to the Pavaria premises or approach Bea Cohen's house in case the police were waiting to pick him up, he'd slept rough on the Heath that night desperately trying to decide what to do next. Eventually he'd settled on a flight to Ireland.

'I thought I'd get someone to write to Bea for me from there. Thought she'd know how to fix things for me.'

'Do you realize how much police time you've wasted by failing to tell the truth at the outset of this investigation?'

'That other copper didn't want to hear the truth,' Billy snapped. 'He wanted me to say I'd done it. But I never said I did it, and I'm still saying I didn't.'

'Well, as I said, that remains to be seen.' Stamford stood up and put his hat on. A shout brought the prison officer back with suspicious swiftness. He must have been hovering a few yards along the landing.

Doors and gates were unlocked and locked as they proceeded back through the prison and out into the light.

'Do thank the Governor for his concern for my safety,' Sarah said sweetly just before the gate was closed behind them. 'The thought of it will keep me warm next time I'm on a night patrol in Limehouse.'

'Sarcasm doesn't become you, Sergeant.'

'No, but I enjoy it.' Sarah clambered into the passenger seat of the waiting car and waited for Stamford to take the wheel. 'He's still a suspect, isn't he?' she said as they pulled away into the traffic.

The clatter of a passing tram drowned out the beginning of Stamford's reply: '... but there's always the possibility he did hit her to keep her mouth shut. Who else have we got?'

'Phyllis Nettles.'

'Opportunity. But slim motive. She'd been paying out for nearly four months, why strike then? It's a pity we can't find out what it was Valerie had on her.'

'We know what she had on Victor Yeovil. And he had the opportunity.'

A phone call to Rochester Row that morning had confirmed Yeovil's story that he'd gone there to identify Glyn. But it had still left him plenty of time to visit Junction Cut. 'But there's still the time lag.' Stamford slammed one balled fist against the centre of the steering wheel. 'Why wait all those months. If he was going to do it, why not last September?'

'Perhaps it was just a combination of circumstances. He found himself in the area because of Glyn. Called at Junction Cut on an impulse because he couldn't stand the suspense of not knowing when Valerie would get in touch again. And found her alone in the house.'

'Hmm. Perhaps. But James Jolly didn't see a strange man calling at number four. Which means that the murderer probably used the back route. And that argues someone who knew the street. Yeovil had never been there.'

'According to him.'

'Yes.' Stamford sighed. He was tired. He hadn't slept well again. May Yeovil and her two sons were on his conscience, but whichever way he played it, he couldn't think of any way to spare them from the consequences of Victor's actions. 'There is one other possible suspect, of course.'

'G.D.?'

'Who, if he isn't Glyn Davis, could, I suspect, be Valerie's true father.'

'But there's only one person who could have told her that!'

'Exactly,' Stamford said grimly. 'I think it's time we interviewed Edie Yeovil again.'

It proved to be an impossible ambition. Despite calling twice at number four that afternoon, they were unable to obtain an answer to their knocking.

On Wednesday, Stamford decided to corner his reluctant witness at work again, only to be informed by the supervisor at Daniel's that Edie had been fired with a week's wages in lieu of notice the previous Friday. The supervisor informed them that Mrs Yeovil had become unwell after their previous visit. Gladys, the lift girl, was more forthcoming, and gleefully described how Edie had consumed most of a bottle of wine she'd hidden in her locker and ended up calling an account customer a fat, stinking old cow.

They tried Junction Cut again on Wednesday afternoon, but there was still no sign of Edie.

'I couldn't say. She don't like people just popping round,' one of the neighbours offered when asked if she knew whether or not Edie was in.

'Don't come round to us either,' another called across the road. 'Too grand for the likes of us.'

Lily Hendry provided the most likely explanation for Edie's disappearance. 'I expect she nipped out the back when she saw you two coming. She don't like talking about the murder.'

Given Edie's previous behaviour under questioning, Jack acknowledged that that made sense. He asked the uniform patrols to try to raise some response at number four at regular intervals. 'As soon as you see Mrs Yeovil's in, let me know.'

'She can't,' he added to himself, 'stay out for ever.'

But it seemed she could. By Friday evening they'd still failed to raise any response from number four. It was only after he'd telephoned Phyllis Nettles and spoken to the neighbours again, that Jack started to realize nobody had actually seen or heard from Edie Yeovil for nearly a week.

Chapter 20

Joe hadn't been able to get away on Tuesday so Lily had put the time to good use by taking Dolly's advice and visiting Berkeley Square. At the time Stamford and Sarah were questioning Billy she was in Thomas Cook's taking her first step towards a new life in Canada. The young male clerk had been particularly helpful once she'd dimpled helplessly and flirted a little from beneath her curled lashes. He'd even filled out application forms for exit visas and passports for herself and the baby. The half-completed documents were hidden under some old underwear in Lily's battered suitcase. They showed that Lily Jane Hendry (née Thomas) was a widow and that her infant son, Augustus, was commonly known by his middle name: William. Their address was given as Maitland Park Road.

On Wednesday Joe met her at the flat again. Their lovemaking had been perfunctory. He'd come at her almost as soon as the door was closed, barely pausing to push little Gussie, still strapped into his pushchair, into the dining room.

'Mind me stockings,' Lily squealed. 'They're me last silk pair.'

'I'll buy you a new pair.' He gave a grunt of pleasure as he penetrated her. 'Hear the news?' He jigged back and forth, panting excitedly. 'The boys over there, they're really getting stuck in. Fighting those bastards for every inch. God, why didn't I come over here, 'stead of signing up back home? I could have been there in France, seeing some real action, 'stead of fighting a desk in London.'

Lily lay listening with disbelief. He's getting off on the frigging fighting, she thought. Not me.

Joe rose above her. She responded to his cry of triumph with a half-hearted moan. The whole thing had taken under two minutes.

At least Joe seemed to realize his performance had been less than impressive. Pulling her across the bed, so that her chin rested on the buttons of his jacket, he stroked the back of her neck and apologized. 'Other things on my mind. Don't mean I love you any less.'

'Me too, Joe.' She wriggled further up his recumbent figure until she could peer directly down into his face. 'You've not forgotten that you're taking me and Gussie to Canada?'

'Sending, honey. Sending. Can't go myself. But you'll be safe enough with my Uncle Walt 'til I can come for you. He'll look after you.'

'On the farm?' Lily's heart sank. Not more countryside. 'Is it near a town, this place of yours?'

'About fifty miles to the nearest.' His arm tightened around her waist. 'But you can always go stay in a hotel in Montreal if you want to do some shopping. I got a bit put by in the bank. Don't expect you to spend all your time playing chequers with Uncle Walt.'

In a rush of gratitude, Lily encircled his chest with both arms. She waved one bent leg languorously back and forth as she planted her lips on his and pushed her tongue invitingly between his teeth.

Joe responded with a deep kiss, smacked her on the bottom, and rolled her off. 'Don't reckon I'll be much use to you for a while. What say we go get you those new stockings?'

'Whatever you say, Joe.' Retrieving her knickers from the floor, Lily smoothed the bed clothes, reasoning it was hardly worth changing the sheets.

She'd expected him to take her to the West End. Instead he flagged down a taxi and looked inquiringly at her: 'Where's the nearest department store, honey?'

'Daniel's,' she said. It slipped off her tongue before she could stop it and the driver had already pulled away, heading down Prince of Wales Road, before she could formulate a protest. 'Joe,' she hissed, one eye on the pedestrians who flashed past the windows like frames from a magic lantern. 'Couldn't we go up West?'

'Haven't time. I've got to report back in an hour. They'll have stockings at this store of yours, won't they?'

It wasn't their stock levels that worried her. It was their clientèle. 'My mother-in-law . . .' she started to say.

Joe put one hand on her knee. 'She's got to know some time. I appreciate your feelings but you've got to put it to her straight. You and the kid will be safer in Canada. I told you I'd stand her passage money as well, if that's what you want. You want me to come round and face it with you?'

'No! No, Joe. I know you're right. But it's best if it comes from me. Give me a few days.'

'Sure. Take all the time you like.' Paying off the taxi, Joe lifted the pushchair out and wheeled it into Daniel's.

A floor walker oozed towards them. Could he perhaps direct sir and madam?

'Stockings. Where'd we find them?'

'First floor, sir.' A peremptory finger was raised to the lift attendant who was hovering by the open brass cage. 'First, Gladys.'

Gladys looked like she would welcome the ride. The store still had an underused air, with staff outnumbering customers. Stepping out, she waited for Lily and Joe to enter. Lily had her face buried in bolts of sheeting that was advertised as suitable for dying into blackout curtains.

'What do you want that for? You can fix up the farm when you get to Canada. No sense shipping stuff with you.'

Joe hadn't acquired the British habit of reserve. He saw no reason to moderate his voice so that only the person he was speaking to could hear him. Several other heads turned.

'Just browsing,' Lily explained, hustling him into the lift.

JUNCTION CUT

The first floor was even more nerve-racking. It was Wednesday. She was sure that was one of Edie Yeovil's days. And the stockings, wouldn't you just know it, were in the corsetry department.

With one eye on the neighbouring counters, as if she half-expected Edie to pop up from beneath the wooden tops like a jack-in-the-box, Lily fidgeted, her stomach tightening with nerves, as Joe discussed stocking sizes and colours with no apparent trace of embarrassment.

'We'll take six pairs of the black and a couple of the white. And, what do you call that shade?'

'Tea beige.'

'Maybe six of those too. That be enough, Lily?'

'Yes, yes. That's wonderful, Joe.' She just wanted to get out of here. Instead she was forced to stand yet again whilst the assistant explained that unfortunately they had had to raise their prices just a fraction since French silk was in such demand right now. And then, when the price had been negotiated, the bill and cash had to be inserted in the metal canister and sent winging across the floor on its pulley of wires to the cashier's box on the far side of the floor.

Hurry up, prayed Lily silently, whilst trying to maintain a casual interest in a display of children's vests. She wandered a little further towards a tailor's dummy draped with a woman's coat.

Another assistant materialized immediately. 'An investment for the winter, madam. Cashmere and silver fox.' Whilst she talked, she picked the coat up by its shoulders and held it invitingly open for Lily to slip her arms in. 'And just madam's size, I think.'

'I don't want . . .' Lily began. A middle-aged woman, thinly clad in white and black, with fair hair fading to grey, drifted across the corner of her eye. Lily spun round, offering her back to the store. The assistant flicked the coat expertly into place.

She was right, it was Lily's size. Hugging the soft mist-coloured wool round her body, she ran appreciative hands down the collar, burying her fingers in the thick silver pelt.

'It suits madam.'

Lily twirled, admiring her reflection in the mirror. Sliding her fingers under the collar, she pushed it up, allowing the soft fur to caress her cheeks. It was beautiful. It was the sort of thing Gus ought to be buying for her, instead of saving up for his blasted pub. The middle-aged woman appeared again, carrying a bolt of lace. To her relief it wasn't Edie. She caught Joe's eye in the mirror. He winked.

'Winters can get kind of bitter in Canada. I guess you'll be needing something warm to wrap up in.'

'I was just trying it, Joe. I don't expect you to splash out any more.' Don't push it, an inner voice warned. He'll think he's got a gold digger.

But Joe was already examining the ticket, grumbling about the British custom of pricing in guineas. Another deal was struck and the cash canister made a further trip across the high wire, much to little Gussie's delight.

Lily looked at the bulky coat with dismay. How the hell was she going to explain this to Gus? 'I wonder,' she smiled hopefully at the assistant, 'could you keep it for me? I've got a few more things to do. I'll pick it up later.'

The assistant assured her that would be no trouble at all. Madam could collect her purchase any time. Unless madam would like it delivered?

It was the last thing madam wanted.

The change returned, the bill was receipted, and the three of them left in a glow of mutual well-being.

A woman emerged from behind a rack of children's clothing and approached the assistant. 'How much are the children's siren suits. The six-to-nine size?'

'Fourteen shillings and eleven pence, madam.'

'I'm not paying that! I'll cut down one of your sister Betty's coats,' she informed the small girl scuffing her shoes along the edge of the display cabinet.

'But, Mum, it was her gave me mumps.'

'Well, now she can give you one of her coats. Come on, quick. I want to get home.'

Seizing Queenie's hand, Minnie White dragged her daughter towards the exit, her eyes alight and two small spots of excitement glowing in her cheeks.

Since meeting Joe, Lily's marriage had slid unobtrusively into reverse. She'd always been the one who snapped and complained. Even during the early days, when Gus had been waiting on her hand and foot, she'd felt no obligation to make any effort, sure enough of her hold over him to take whatever was offered and give nothing back. Now the nudgings of conscience made her kinder.

Watching his big, clumsy body easing itself round the two rooms that evening, delicately avoiding obstacles in case he woke the baby, she felt a burst of affection.

'You're a good bloke, Gus,' she said unexpectedly. 'A good dad too.'

Gus's round face flushed with pleasure. 'I want to make you happy, Lily. You and Gussie. You're all I've got. All I've ever wanted.'

'Except the pub.'

'Except that,' he agreed. 'But that's for you too. We'll be happy there, you'll see. It'll be just like it was before, when I was little.'

Sitting down beside her on the bed, he placed one arm awkwardly round her shoulders and hugged her into him, moulding her body against his. She could feel the rolls of flesh at his waist and around his thighs. But for once it didn't revolt her. She put her own arm as far round his waist as she could and they sat in companionable silence until the rattling hiss of the saucepan lid announced the potatoes were boiling over.

He wasn't wanted in the pub that evening, nor was there an LDV meeting so she cooked tea for him. It wasn't a skill she'd ever had to practise much before, but he ate the underdone stuffed roast mutton, lumpy boiled potatoes and watery greens without complaint.

He should have married a nice middle-aged widow,

she thought to herself, watching his plump face shining with grease and goodwill. One with a handful of kids.

She opened a tin of peaches for his afters. Gussie woke up and whimpered, rattling the bars of his cot until she went in and picked him up. Returning to the kitchen, she sat the warm, sleepy bundle on her lap, chopped a couple of peach slices up one-handed with the edge of a spoon and poured some condensed milk over. Gussie sucked up the juicy offering with giggling slurps.

'Gus,' she said, 'have you ever thought about evacuating little Gussie?'

'To the country? But we're going there soon as we find our pub, Lil. You know that.' Reaching across the table cloth, he captured her hand. 'Don't worry. If the bombing starts, we'll go to one of those country hotels. We've got money, don't forget that.'

And much good it's done me, Lily thought to herself. Aloud she said. 'I wasn't thinking about this country. I thought maybe – abroad. Lots of kids have been sent to America and Canada. No chance of bombers reaching him out there.' Her grip tightened on Gussie, who'd grown tired of his snack and was now drooping against her breasts, his small fist knuckling closing eyelids.

Her husband stared at her blankly. 'Abroad? He can't go abroad. Who'd take care of him?'

She wanted to say: 'I will. You stay here and I'll go with Gussie.' And, after a few months, she'd write a kind, reasoned letter telling him she'd always be fond of him but their marriage was over. Instead she compromised with a vague statement that parents were allowed provided they got the right visas. And there was always someone prepared to sign a bit of paper if the price was right.

Only Gus wasn't having it. There was no way his son was going abroad. Things weren't that bad. It stood to reason if there was a real danger of invasion the papers would have told them. Just because they were evacuating the army from France didn't mean the Germans were coming after them. 'We'll stick it out here, Lil. Can't be called chickens, can we?'

Personally Lily felt she could put up with being called a Lesser Spotted Newt if it meant Gussie and her could start afresh in a new country where they'd both have a chance of a better life. But she knew that stubbornly petulant look that was forming on Gus's wet lips. Dropping a kiss on his head, she said resignedly: 'If you say so, Gus. I'll put him back in his cot.'

The Governor at The Hayman asked him to work Thursday morning. Lily used the opportunity to collect her coat from Daniel's. With the parcel stowed in the seat, a blanket folded over the top of it, and little Gussie perched precariously on top of the whole, Lily wheeled her prize home and, after some deliberation, took down her old suitcase, folded the coat in the bottom, and replaced the case on top of the wardrobe.

She'd barely stepped down from the chair when there was a sharp knock at the front door. Opening it she found herself facing the two coppers who reckoned

JUNCTION CUT

Billy hadn't done what the whole street knew he had.

They wanted to know if she knew where Edie Yeovil might be since she no longer worked at Daniel's. Her first reaction was indignation. If only Edie had told her, she might have spared her all that anxiety when she was shopping with Joe!

She took her brief spurt of anger out on the police officers by suggesting that Edie had nipped out the back to avoid them, and shut the door in their faces before they could ask any further questions.

Turning back after sliding the door bolts home, she was surprised to find Gus in the passage behind her.

'What were they doing here?' he asked.

'Asking about Edie. Told them she probably don't want to speak to the coppers. It's funny though, because now I come to think about it . . .'

Her voice died away as she looked at his face. It was grey. 'What's the matter? Are you feeling queer?'

He rocked on his heels as if he might fall, then threw his shoulders back. 'Yes. Came over a bit funny at work. Think I'll lie down.'

'Do you want me to fetch the doctor?'

'No need. I'll be all right by tomorrow. Got to be. I'm on the barrage balloon detail in the morning.'

'I thought you was only going to man the balloon at night?'

'Special duties. The regulars are wanted elsewhere.'

The following morning Gus seemed to have recovered. At any rate, he insisted on 'doing his bit'. Bundling Gussie into his chair, Lily hurried down to the public box and telephoned Joe.

'Be there before you, honey,' Joe assured her, his warm brown voice tingling against her ear. 'I got a little surprise for you.'

He was perched on the bottom of the metal staircase when she reached the flat. 'You'll have the neighbours thinking my friend's carrying on behind her fiancé's back. And him away fighting too.'

She meant it as a joke but an expression of dismay clouded his brown eyes. 'Say, I didn't mean to do that. I sure wouldn't want to cause trouble like that. I reckon you can't get much lower, stepping out with another guy while yours is risking his butt.'

'She won't mind. She understands the situation.' Inserting the key in the lock, Lily dragged the chair in and parked her son in the dining room. 'What's this surprise you've got for me?'

Joe reached into his jacket and extracted several booklets, folded in half. Smoothing them flat, he handed them to her. They were timetables. 'I've got it all figured out. There's a Portuguese ship sailing from Southampton in two weeks. And from Lisbon you can take the Clipper to New York. After that there's a train runs up over the border into Canada. I'll cable Uncle Walt to meet you at the other end. You just say the word and I'll book the berths.'

'Portuguese?'

'Neutral flag. It's safer.'

'Oh, yes. I see. What's the Clipper? Another boat?'

'It's a flying boat. Twenty-eight hours non-stop

across the Atlantic. No danger from U-boats, see?'

Lily stared down at the flimsy booklets. For the first time the move stopped being a pleasant day-dream, like a brief excursion into the films on the cinema screen, and started to take substance. In a few weeks she could be in another country. Away from the grimy, soot-ridden streets of Kentish Town, and on a farm somewhere in the middle of Canada. With the promise of a fancy night-club in the future, when Joe came back from the war. If Joe came back. The thought sent an involuntary shiver across her skin.

Her eyes were still fixed on the shipping list, but one hand automatically sought his chest, clinging to a lapel for comfort. He drew the paper from her hand, laid it on the hall table and scooped her into his arms. His mouth clamped over hers, preventing her from breathing, whilst his left hand kneaded her buttock beneath the thin cotton of her dress.

An hour later, lying exhausted and sated on top of the bed-covers, Lily drew her lips over Joe's naked chest, tasting the sheen of sweat beneath the curling hair, and told him to book the passage.

'Do I get a berth for your ma-in-law?'

'No.'

'You won't regret it, honey, I promise.' He raised his arm, catching the light on the face of his watch. 'I got to go. You coming?'

'No. You go ahead. I'll stay here and tidy up.' This time it was worth changing Phyllis's sheets.

Pulling on his clothes, he combed his hair in the

dressing-table mirror, giving her an appreciative wink as she sat up and started to draw on her stockings.

'Go on,' she laughed. 'Get back to work. I don't want to be charged with enticing the troops from their duty.'

With a final kiss, he sauntered down the passage, whistling loudly.

Lily grasped the sheet and stripped the bed with one quick movement. She'd barely gathered the discarded clothes in her arms when there was a cry of surprise from the hall, followed by the sound of something heavy hitting the floor.

Rushing out, she found Joe sprawled on his back, blood pouring from his nose. A familiar figure loomed over him, fists clenched and a snarl of rage twisting his usually amiable features.

Joe was younger, fitter and better trained than Gus. Surprise, and the fact he'd collided with the hall table, had sent him sprawling from Gus's first punch. Now he recovered his wits and his wind and scrambled to his feet. Lunging after Gus, who was attempting to drag his son's pushchair from the dining room, he grabbed the older man's arm and spun him round, driving his fist into the rolls of flesh around Gus's midriff.

Gus grunted but remained on his feet. Getting a hand beneath Joe's chin, he pushed his head up, forcing Joe to retreat until he collided with a standard lamp which fell to the floor. The men's scuffling feet trampled the shade. The light bulb disintegrated into a powder of splintering glass.

Breaking the other man's hold, Joe slung a right hook. Gus staggered against the mantelpiece. His elbow caught a clock, knocking it from the shelf. Catching it as it fell, he flung it at Joe's head. It missed and gouged a lump from the wallpaper before hitting the floor and shattering in a disembowelled mess of cogs and springs.

'Stop it! Stop it, Gus!' Struggling into her dress and shoes, Lily pulled the pushchair clear and rushed at her husband. He flung her to the floor as if she were a doll. Picking up one of the dining chairs, he used it to force Joe back into the corner.

Joe got a grip on two of the legs, shoved back, and succeeded in wrenching the chair from Gus's grasp. 'Say, take it easy, buddy. You know this guy?' he demanded.

With a roar of rage, Gus windmilled into him again. His flailing fists landed several ineffectual punches on Joe's ribs. 'You're not taking them,' he snarled. 'They're mine.'

'What's he talking about?' Joe demanded over Gus's shoulder, his arms and body swerving and blocking with the skill of a boxer. 'Who is this guy, Lily?'

It was little Gussie who answered. He was too scared to yell any more but he'd recently learnt to talk and now he used it to appeal for comfort from the person he'd learnt to expect it from. Extending his arms to Gus, he whispered: 'Da-da.'

'What!' Joe lowered his guard and received another blow to the chest. He scarcely appeared to notice it.

'That true, Lily? Is this the kid's father?'

'No.' Lily looked between the two men and knew it was useless. Joe would never take her to Canada now. 'But he is my husband.'

For a few seconds the two men's expressions were indistinguishable. Then Joe's melted into disgust. Picking up his discarded cap, he banged it against his hand to shake off the dust, muttered 'Sorry, bud,' and left.

Gus slapped Lily once, very deliberately, across the face, then lifted the pushchair up the metal staircase and walked away. She had no choice but to follow.

'Gus, wait!' she panted, catching up with him. 'Let me explain.'

He ignored her. Blood streamed from a cut on her lip. Wiping it away with the back of her hand, she tried again. 'Gus, please. Stop.'

He stopped. 'You were going to Canada. Taking Gussie away from me.' He dragged the half-completed forms from his pocket and waved them under her nose.

'It was the evacuation, Gus. I told you, it will be safer for him.'

'I'm not stupid, Lily. Don't take me for stupid. After all I done for you. Well, you're not leaving me. You're my wife, and little Gussie, he's mine too. You hear? Now you come along home.'

Clasping his huge hand over one of her wrists, he dragged her down the Prince of Wales Road. Halfway down a coalman stepped down from his cart in answer to her cries for help. 'She's my wife,' Gus said.

'Oh, sorry, mate. Didn't realize.' The black greasy cap, its neck guard solid with years of coal dust, was lifted politely in Lily's direction, revealing a white strip between hair and eyebrows, and the man went on about his business.

It was the same with the young constable. As soon as he realized it was a domestic dispute, he stepped smartly back, saluted Gus, and advised Lily to keep the noise down or he'd have to book her for causing a disturbance.

Lily gave up. If she'd had a dad or a brother maybe he'd have spoken up for her. But no other bloke was going to come between man and wife. A slapping for what she'd done was what she could expect. And what most folks would consider she deserved. She may as well get it over with.

Thankfully he used the back entrance so there was no one to see her being dragged into the house. He settled Gussie in his cot first. Lily was half-tempted to run, but what was the point? She'd nowhere to go.

'Gus, look. It's not like you think,' she tried one last time, wetting her lips and summoning up a smile. 'I ain't done nothing wrong. Not really.' She could taste the salty blood from the cut lip.

Gus ignored her. Slowly he unbuckled the thick leather belt from his waist. 'Get into the kitchen.'

She understood. He didn't want to do it in front of Gussie.

Lily backed into the passage and through the kitchen

345

door. Gus followed her, the belt swinging loosely from one hand.

Lily tensed.

He took her right wrist and whipped the belt round it, fastening the buckle tightly so it gripped like a bracelet. 'Sit down. There, by the cooker.' As he talked, his other hand pushed down on her shoulder, making her crouch on the floor.

'What are you doing?'

She tried to pull back, but he threaded the belt round one leg of the cooker, clamped her other wrist, and bound her tightly to the metal.

'You'll not leave me, Lily, you hear? You'll stay there until I get the pub sorted out.'

'Gus! Don't be daft, love. Let me up.' Lily wriggled. The straps bit into her flesh.

Gus walked out and shut the door on her.

Chapter 21

The decision to break off her engagement had acted as a catharsis for Phyllis.

'It's like somebody has slipped the bolts on the cell door,' she told Susan.

'You were the one who turned the key in the first place,' Susan reminded her, forking up another mouthful of mashed potato. They were lunching together, Susan having taken the Friday morning off work.

'You look different.' She examined her elder sister across the checked table cloth. There was an almost carefree air about the other woman: everything from the little straw hat tilted at a rakish angle over one eye to the impractical ice-pink high heels suggested a woman contemplating a summer holiday rather than another stuffy afternoon in Gray's Inn Road.

'I feel different. I don't know why. It just happened. I got up and thought, that's it, Phyllis. From now on you can do anything you want to.'

'And can you?'

'I don't know. But I'm not frightened to try any more. It's not *not* being able to do things that stops you, you know, Susie. It's being scared of what might happen if

347

you can't do them. Does that make sense?'

'Sort of. What are all these things you've decided to do?'

'Change my job for a start. Have you told Father that you want to join the WAAFs yet?'

'Two days ago. He went berserk. But as I pointed out to him, other families have sons to send to war. He's only got daughters, so it's only patriotic that he sacrifices one of us. Which, I must say,' Susan said ruthfully, wrinkling her nose, 'could probably have been put better. But he saw my point. To tell you the truth, I think he's a bit jealous. He'd love to be in uniform instead of selling nuts and bolts.' She examined the printed menu card. 'Shall we risk the apple pie and custard?'

Once the two thick white plates, brimming over with creamy custard heavily scented with vanilla, and pie slices perfumed with cloves, had been set down and the waitress had retreated out of earshot, Susan said curiously: 'Are you considering joining up, Phyl?'

'Might do. Haven't decided yet. But I just feel...' She waved a pastry-smeared fork as if trying to spear words from the air. 'I feel I've got to do more for the war. I can't waste any more time typing endless briefs to overpaid barristers so they can sort out the estates of a load of greedy so-and-sos whose even greedier relatives are now squabbling over the bones.' She finished on a flourish of apple chunk, popping it accurately between her lips and chewing with relish.

Susan signalled for coffee. 'What about Ronnie? I

take it, since you're ringless, that's finished?'

'Yes. For his sake as much as mine. I wasn't being fair to him, Susie. Ronnie's a good man, despite his relatives. He deserves better than me.'

'That should please La Yeovil. Have you seen her?'

'Not for a week. As a matter of fact, that police inspector telephoned me this morning to ask if I knew where she might be. Apparently they've been trying to speak to her for a few days.'

'Probably rushed off to console her precious Ronnie and tell him what a lucky escape he's had, getting away from the wicked witch of Highgate.'

'He doesn't know he has escaped yet. It didn't seem right to put it in a letter. If he doesn't get leave at the end of his basic training, I'll try to visit him.' Retrieving her handbag from the floor, she dropped the five shillings for the set menu on the table and added a shilling tip. 'Must dash, I'm going to break it to Phipps this afternoon that he'd better start advertising for a new secretary.'

Mr Phipps took the news so well that, if she hadn't been buoyed up on a raft of defiance and recklessness, Phyllis could have been offended.

'I envy you, Miss Nettles,' he piped in his ridiculous treble.

'Do you, sir?'

'Yes, indeed. I have never been fortunate enough to be called on to serve my country. In the last war I was deemed unfit to serve.' His voice sank to a conspiratorial squeak. 'Shingles, Miss Nettles. A painful, debilitating disease, with no visible signs. If one is fully clothed, of course.'

'I'd no idea, Mr Phipps.' Phyllis caught her bottom lip with her top teeth.

'Yes, indeed. To all intents and purposes I was an able-bodied man. But not in uniform. I collected enough white feathers to re-thatch the Christmas Goose, Miss Nettles. My poor mother was mortified. In the end she obtained a certificate from our physician and had it published in the local paper. It was, as you can imagine, exceedingly embarrassing for me.'

'It must have been, sir.' Phyllis swallowed desperately, trying not to laugh. This wasn't quite how she'd expected the conversation to proceed. She'd pictured Mr Phipps protesting, praising her work, perhaps even offering a raise in pay. But the spirit of self-sacrifice that was growing in the country with each day of the Dunkirk evacuation seemed to have entered Mr Phipps's soul.

'I wanted to go, you know. To Dunkirk,' he said. 'My brother-in-law has a launch. He's gone. Went down the Thames to Dover on Sunday. I said to him, "Let me come." I've been known to take a turn at the wheel, Miss Nettles. I could have done my bit.'

Phyllis had a sudden picture of the little man wading into the surf in his pin-striped suit, his trousers rolled up and his feet bare as if he were paddling at Southend. It should have made her laugh, but instead she felt a lump growing in her throat and her eyes pricked. 'I expect he thought it was one more space for a fighting

JUNCTION CUT

man if you weren't there, Mr Phipps.'

'Do you know, Miss Nettles, those were his precise words!' He beamed at her. 'But you see why I understand your desire to serve. You are not alone, Miss Nettles. I salute you.'

She half-expected him to do precisely that. But instead the hand was extended and she found her own being warmly wrung. She left work with assurances of assistance with references and time off for interviews ringing in her ears.

If her employer's reaction to her news was unforeseen, Ronnie's turned out to be unbelievable.

She'd been nerving herself for the confrontation all Friday, reasoning that if his training came to a conclusion on Thursday, he'd probably commence his leave on Friday. He was based in East Grinstead, so assuming he called on his mother first (and wasn't that always his order of priority?), he'd probably be at the flat by mid-afternoon.

Since he didn't have a key, she braced herself to tackle a familiar figure hanging around the basement area, no doubt with the usual expression of puppyish devotion on his face.

Rehearsing kind but firm speeches of farewell, she clipped briskly up the hill to her flat and peered down into the basement.

It was empty.

Negotiating the iron staircase with its cunningly placed holes that invariably grabbed unwary heels and wrenched them off, Phyllis inserted her key in the lock, walked into the hall, and screamed. A bulky figure, his face lost in the gloom of the hall, was advancing on her.

'Phyl! It's me. Ronnie.'

With a thumping heart, she gasped for breath. 'You scared the life out of me!'

'Sorry. Come and sit down. I'll get you a drink.' He led her into her own sitting room and poured a brandy. 'Drink,' he ordered.

She drank. As she sipped, the state of the room, with its smashed standard lamp and overturned furniture, impinged on her brain. 'What on earth . . . ?' she breathed.

'Looks like we've had burglars, Phyl. The door was open when I got here. You ought to be more careful.'

'Burglars! It's not flaming burglars!' Spirit, both alcoholic and metaphorical, was coursing through Phyllis's veins. She wasn't a woman to use the mildest swear word normally, but this was too much. 'It's that damn mother of yours. She's crazy, you know.'

'Yes, I do.'

'Pardon?'

'I do know she ain't all there sometimes. Why'd you think she did this?'

Phyllis gulped down the rest of the brandy in one mouthful. She felt the hot spirit slipping down and exploding into her stomach. This was it. There would be no more prevarications, no half-truths. Straight out with it, that was the best way. 'Wait here,' she ordered.

Going to the bedroom, which thankfully seemed to

have escaped Edie's vengeance this time, she delved into the wardrobe cubicles and drew out a long silk scarf patterned in yellows and browns.

Ronnie was attempting to re-right the standard lamp when she returned to the sitting room. 'Recognize this?' she demanded.

Twisting the soft material through his hands, Ronnie didn't answer at once. 'What are these marks? Looks like blood or something.'

'It is. Mine. I cut my hand. She smashed the front door, together with just about anything else she could lay her hands on, last week. I found this in the bath. You do recognize it, don't you?'

' 'Course I do. Bought it for her last Christmas, didn't I? She say she did it?'

'I haven't asked. As a matter of fact, I haven't seen her since. I wanted to tell you first.' Phyllis came to a full stop. Once again things weren't going as she'd imagined. In her imagination, this scene, played and re-played as she tossed in bed, had had her standing over a heart-broken Ronnie. She'd be in control of the situation; firm, kind, and reasonable.

Instead Ronnie seemed to have taken charge. It was *their* flat. He'd helped himself to *her* brandy. A couple of months ago, he'd have stood on the doormat waiting for her to tell him to come in. Phyllis looked at her fiancé properly for the first time since she'd arrived home.

They'd cut his hair – sheared it might be a better description – and added a dash of sunburn that was just darkening to tan over his nose and cheekbones. And he looked thinner; even allowing for the badly fitting uniform which drooped over his army-issue boots and hung over his wrists, there was a definite impression of lean efficiency rather than the slightly chubby clerk she'd kissed goodbye to at Victoria six weeks ago.

'Terrible fit, ain't – I mean, isn't it?' he said, seeing her looking him up and down. 'Mind, you should have seen the first one they issued me with. The quartermaster was blind as a bat. We looked like Fred Karno's army after he'd finished issuing the kit. 'Ad – I mean, *had* to change with other blokes. It were a right lark, a hundred blokes all climbing out of their trousers in the middle of the parade ground. Coat's still a bit of a squeeze.'

He nodded at a great-coat she hadn't noticed before lying across one of the dining chairs. The movement exposed the soft nape at the back of his neck which had previously been covered by hair. She saw the red mark where the harsh khaki had rubbed against his tender skin. The sudden impulse to touch it took her by surprise.

'The haircut doesn't really suit you, darling.' What on earth was she calling him 'darling' for? 'There's something we have to discuss. Something I need to tell you.'

'You want to break off the engagement?'

Hearing him come straight out with it like that took the wind from her sails. 'How did you know?'

'You haven't written for three weeks, Phyl. I guessed something was up. Is it another man?'

'No, of course not. If I could have found another man, I would never have . . .' Phyllis stopped, colour flooding her cheeks. She hadn't meant to be unkind. She certainly didn't want to hurt him.

He finished impassively: 'You would never have become engaged to me.'

'I don't. I didn't . . .' Phyllis floundered. Why did men have to be so damn difficult? First Phipps and now Ronnie. Why couldn't they stick to the script she'd assigned to them in her imagination?

'It's all right, Phyl. I always knew you'd only accepted me because your Jane was already wed and Susan was getting engaged. And that other bloke had let you down.'

Phyllis found her legs wouldn't support her any longer. She felt the edge of the sofa against the back of her knees and sat down blindly.

'Don't squash me cap,' Ronnie said. He slid one hand under her left thigh and extracted a folded forage cap.

Phyllis jumped up, startled by the intimacy of his touch. He pulled her down beside him. 'Steady on. I didn't mean to upset you.'

'How did you know? About Stephen?'

'How'd you think? I work with Susan, remember?'

'She said she hadn't told anyone!'

'Just about fifty of her closest friends.'

Phyllis groaned.

Ronnie slid an arm round her shoulder and pulled her against him. 'It's all right, Phyl. I don't mind. I just thought, if I stuck with it long enough, you'd maybe get used to the idea of being Mrs Yeovil. Bit of an inconvenience, weren't it, Herr Hitler starting this war and getting me called up?'

'Perhaps we should have asked him to postpone invading Poland until after the wedding.'

'Pity you didn't think to mention it earlier, Phyl.'

Phyllis became aware that she was cuddling a man she was supposed to be purging from her life forever. She had to take charge. 'Ronnie, I've decided to change my job. I might join up. The WAAFs.'

'Good for you, Phyl. I'd be proud of you.'

'I don't want you to be proud of me!' Phyllis's voice rose indignantly. 'I want you to have an argument with me. I want you to hate me. I want you to storm out and tell me you never want to see me again.'

Twisting round, she punched his shoulder with the arm he wasn't holding. He responded by tightening his grip and locking his lips firmly on to hers. His kiss was fierce, demanding; unlike his previous tentative fumblings. Surprised but intrigued, Phyllis found herself responding. Sliding his other arm round her waist, Ronnie pulled her into a more comfortable position, and pushed an exploratory tongue into her mouth whilst his free hand slid over the curve of her breast and hip.

It was Phyllis who eventually called a halt to the grappling. Holding him off with the flat of her hands, she started to say the first thing that came into her head. 'Have you had another woman?' He'd never tried to make love to her like that before. Like a man who knew what he wanted . . . or what he was missing. But what right did she have to question him? It wasn't her business any more. 'Have you seen your mother yet?' she finished lamely.

'No. And I don't want to. Not until we're straight, Phyl.' He edged closer, forcing her against the far arm of the sofa, and captured both her hands. 'Look, Phyl. I know you ain't, *aren't*, in love with me. But I love you, see? And you like me, don't yer?'

Phyllis nodded silently. It seemed the least she could say.

'So why can't we give it a go?' Squeezing her hands tightly, he rushed on. 'I been thinking about it a lot, Phyl. Marriage, I mean. And I reckon it's not all that romantic tosh like they put in the films. I mean, if it was, I'd be leaping on the table now and doing a tap dance while some orchestra played away in the background. And you'd be sitting there with lights going on round your head and a soppy expression in your eyes. But it's not like that, is it?'

By now he was bending over her. Phyllis couldn't do any more than shake her head.

'It's more about caring about someone. And being prepared to work together to make something of your lives. Well, I'd take care of you, Phyl. I want to look after you. To make you happy.'

By now his lips had got very close to hers again.

The tip of his nose brushed hers. It tickled. It was really quite pleasant.

This time he was the one who pushed them apart. Holding her shoulders, he said: 'I'm not like some of the blokes at camp, Phyl. I ain't telling you you should do this because I might catch a packet from Jerry and how'd you feel if you'd denied me my last chance at a bit of happiness? I'm not interested in having you before I die, I want you if I live. As my wife. For the rest of our lives. Say you'll marry me, Phyl?'

He'd never been this decisive before. Every choice, from the film they'd see to the time they'd meet, had been deferred to her. Damn it, she thought, tears stinging her eyes, why couldn't he remain a mouse. Now she was confused again. She felt all her new-found confidence ebbing away like sawdust trickling from a splitting doll. Making one last desperate effort, she tried to retrieve the initiative. Clamping her arms round his neck, she kissed him fiercely and said: 'Take me to bed, Ronnie. And if we like it, we'll discuss marriage in the morning.'

She thought the direct approach might disconcert him. When he carried her into the bedroom and she saw that the bed-covers had already been stripped down, she knew she'd lost.

It was still early when she woke. Bird song and sunlight poured through the curtains in equal parts. Moving Ronnie's arm, which lay heavily across her waist, she slid out of bed and pattered towards the bathroom. Her foot knocked against a discarded condom.

'Do you always carry those?' she'd asked, when he'd paused in his enthusiastic exploration of her body to fish his jacket from the floor and take the packet from the top pocket.

'Yes. Want to put it on for me?'

With a wicked smile, Phyllis had obliged. He'd fitted the second one himself.

It was only afterwards, when they were lying quietly in the dark, exhausted and sated, that the stories had come tumbling out of him. The bleakness of the freezing Nissen-hut barracks. The desperate homesickness. The struggle under the rough grey blankets to choke back the tears and avoid the taunts that fell on those who didn't manage it. The stupid, cruel practical jokes that were played on those who appeared soft. And the women they'd sneaked into camp.

'One of the blokes, he had a cousin in town who fixed us up with a couple of tarts a few times. We all had to have a go. You couldn't say no, Phyl.'

Stretching lazily, she had assured him she understood.

Rubbing a circle on the steam-filled mirror now, she examined her own body, still red and blotchy from the bathwater. It wasn't bad, she thought complacently. Wrapping a towel round herself, she returned to the bedroom, opened the curtains and sat on the bed.

The movement woke Ronnie. Twisting over, he smiled sleepily at her and reached for the towel. She evaded his hand. 'Are we engaged then?' he asked, levering himself up on one elbow.

The question sent a shiver over her still damp skin. She took a deep breath. 'I'd like to marry you, Ronnie. But there's something I have to tell you. And once I have, perhaps you won't want to marry me.'

He sat quietly, making no comment whilst she spoke. He'd eased himself up against the headrest, leaving his chest in the shaft of sunlight that came through the gap in the curtains, but placing his face in darkness. She couldn't see his expression.

When she'd finished her confession, there was a moment's silence. Then Ronnie slid his hand across the sheet and covered hers. 'It's all right, Phyllis. You couldn't really call it murder, not properly. I'll stick by you.' He drew her one-armed against his chest and kissed her tear-stained face. 'Fix us some breakfast, then we'll go round and face Mum.'

For the first morning in a long time, Phyllis found the smell of frying eggs made her ravenous. She ate with as much enthusiasm as Ronnie. Afterwards she dressed with a light heart, fixed the straw hat at a provocative angle, and faced the world on her fiancé's arm in a haze of light-hearted joy.

It was a mood that lasted until they reached Junction Cut. Despite the early hour, there was a small collection of welcoming neighbours to call out to Ronnie. To the accompaniment of a chorus of good wishes, he dropped his kit-bag to the floor and inserted his key in the newly fitted lock at number four. Twisting the tumblers free, he pushed the door.

It swung inwards for a foot, then stopped.

Ronnie shoved harder. The door refused to budge. Ronnie's startled gaze met Phyllis's. 'I think,' he said, in the hesitant, apologetic tones of the pre-call-up Ronnie, 'that there's something caught behind the door.'

'Oh Gawd, Ronnie,' squeaked Minnie White, who'd flitted across the road unnoticed. 'That's 'ow they found your Val.'

Chapter 22

Jack's Saturday had started badly. He was a selfish, uncaring, ignorant copper who didn't deserve to have a friend in the world and probably wouldn't have if he didn't get his head out of his flaming cases and start taking a bit of notice of what was going on in the world.

At least he wouldn't according to Eileen O'Day.

Jack was left contemplating the cream paint of her front door, the wood still vibrating from the force with which she'd slammed it in his face. All he'd done was knock and ask if she'd bought any eggs for him yesterday. Before he could recover his voice, the door opened again and Sammy's face peered round the two-inch gap. It looked white and pinched, as if he'd been sucking lemons for breakfast.

'Post 'as come, Mr Stamford,' he hissed. 'And there ain't nothing from our Brendan again. Mrs Clark got a card from her old man on Thursday. And Micky Simmons called the pub on Friday so someone could take a message round to his mum. They were both in our Brendan's lot in France. Mum stopped by your phone all day yesterday. Me and Maury had to go up the market for her. Sorry about yer eggs. We dropped 'em.' He flashed a quick look over his shoulder, reassured himself his mother was still in the kitchen, and said: 'Reckon the Germans have got Brendan, Mr Stamford?'

'No,' Jack lied gallantly. 'It's easy to get separated from your unit in a retreat. Brendan will be all right. He'll have joined up with someone else. Got on a different boat. Tell your mum that, Sammy. And tell her . . . I'm sorry.' It wasn't the time to tell her himself. Later, when she was calmer, and feeling guilty about what she'd said to him, even though, God knows, she had every right, he'd make his peace with her.

He ate breakfast in the station canteen. The appetizing sizzle of frying bacon tempting him to eat more than he would normally. He was just mopping up the last of the egg yolk with a slice of fried bread when the young constable who was so friendly with Sarah McNeill came in, collected a cup of tea, and stood hesitating. Jack's table was the nearest. It had three spare chairs. But Stamford was a chief inspector.

Jack solved his dilemma, using one foot to push the chair opposite a few inches from the table. The constable took the hint.

'Thanks, sir.' He threw back a swig from the thick china cup, disposing of half the contents in one gulp.

'Thirsty work, the early shift,' Jack said.

'Not too bad this time of year, sir. It's a real sod in the winter though.'

'I remember. Falling out of bed at five o'clock and finding the water's frozen in the pipes so you can't shave. Then realizing you've forgotten to polish your spare pair of boots and by the time you've tramped through the snow in the other pair they won't be fit to be seen on parade.'

The constable grinned. 'You come up through the ranks then, sir? Fancy that. We all thought you were one of His Lordship's lads.'

'Bit long in the tooth for that, Constable,' Jack said ruefully. 'I got made up to inspector two months before the College opened.'

When Lord Trenchard had opened the Metropolitan Police College seven years ago, Jack had felt a pang of envy for those who were going to spend fifteen months receiving a proper training for inspector's rank, instead of foot-slogging it out in the job and praying they didn't fall flat on their faces before they got the coveted leg up from station sergeant. Having heard, however, of the College's obsession with skills in sports, he was now inclined to think he'd had a lucky escape. Organized games had never really been his forte. He preferred to work alone. With the possible exception of a good sergeant. Which reminded him of his current sergeant's last encounter with this constable...

'How's Felonious?' he asked.

'All right, sir. As far as I know. I ain't heard anything to say Oggie's got to him. Mind, what with Fel working for Mr Bowler now, I don't suppose Oggie's runners would be stupid enough to do him any real harm.'

'Why would they want to?'

'Dunno, sir. Nobody's saying. Not to a copper anyway.' He finished his tea and scooped up his cup.

Pushing his chair back, he made to return to the serving hatch, then turned back to Jack: 'Reckon the Germans will invade now, sir?'

Jack considered responding with the usual pacifying, non-committal reaction, then shook himself mentally. The boy was bright enough to recognize a line when he heard it. 'I don't know,' he said honestly. 'But it seems quite probable. Now that the Expeditionary Force has been withdrawn, the logical step would be for them to carry the fighting on to British soil.'

The constable visibly brightened. 'I hope they do, sir. I could do with seeing a bit of action.' He nodded, returned his cup and marched out of the canteen with a definite spring in his step, wishing a cheery 'Good morning' to Sarah McNeill who'd just entered the room.

Sarah slid into the chair that the constable had recently vacated. Without bothering with any preamble, she asked bluntly: 'What now, sir? Hadn't we better push on as fast as possible? In case we get over-run before we solve the case?'

She was looking at him with that slightly critical frown between her eyebrows. Jack had the uneasy feeling he had a piece of egg adhering to his chin. 'Sorry I'm not working fast enough for you, Sergeant. In answer to your question, we're going round to Junction Cut to see if Edith Yeovil has left any clues in number four as to her present whereabouts.'

'Do we need a search warrant?'

'And waste all that precious time?' He was sharper than he'd intended because he knew her implied criticism was justified. It was all taking too long. He was used to stepping in when the crime was no more than a few days old at most. When consciences were still raw and alibis less firmly embedded in their owners' minds as definite facts. And when half his mind wasn't across the Channel. He knew he hadn't done well by this investigation. Instead of driving it, he'd allowed it to lead him.

Detective Constable Bell held the door open for them as they left the station and set off up Kentish Town Road.

'Does he usually work on Saturdays?' Jack enquired. A scan of the current CID load at Agar Street hadn't suggested to him that over-time was necessary.

'No. Not usually, sir.' Sarah was struggling to pin her hat into place as she trotted beside him. 'He must have something special on.'

'He doesn't look too pleased about it.'

'Ding Dong always looks like that. He has wife problems. His keeps disappearing.'

Leaving Jack grappling with the idea of Mrs Bell fading and re-constituting in a cloud of ectoplasm, like some kind of spiritual conjuring trick, Sarah succeeded in anchoring the hat then increased her pace, taking several steps in front of her boss.

They arrived in Junction Cut to find that a small, vociferous crowd had already collected around the front door of number four. Apart from the inevitable collection of Whites, a couple of small boys, and several housewives who were blessing themselves and shrieking advice in equal parts, Dolly Toddhunter was standing slightly aloof on the pavement outside number two, drawing on a pair of gloves.

Stamford headed for her on the theory that he was more likely to get sense and a quick calm explanation from her. She didn't disappoint him.

'Ronald Yeovil has returned home on leave. I gather they have just found Edie. I believe I informed one of your constables that she was away. I apologize for misleading you, but since she hadn't been seen for some days, it was a natural mistake to make.' She touched the navy blue arm-band, painted with the white letters WVS. 'Normally I would offer to help, but I'm expected at Charing Cross Station. My group are manning a canteen. However, I understand Miss Nettles is with Ronnie. She has always struck me as a capable young woman. I'm sure she'll be able to handle Edie once she has ceased to be scared of her.'

She left them with a swirl of her coat skirts. Watching her click briskly out of sight, Sarah remarked: 'It's sad, isn't it, sir?'

Jack raised his eyebrows.

'I mean,' Sarah explained, 'that it takes a war for Miss Toddhunter to be appreciated.'

Jack couldn't help wondering if she was having a sly dig at the Met's normal attitude to female detectives.

A small, grubby hand tugged impatiently at his sleeve.

'Have you come to take M'ssus Yeovil away to the loony bin?' Queenie asked, her eyes alight with excitement at this novel Saturday morning entertainment.

Jack felt in his pocket and located a florin. 'Not today, Queenie. Here, treat your boyfriends to the Saturday morning house at the Forum.'

Queenie indignantly informed him that the collection of dirty-kneed boys trying to push past the adult legs for a better view of the hallway of number four were not her boyfriends nor not ever likely to be. But basically she was a fair-minded child. And having been told to share, she reluctantly issued the invitation. The under-tens quickly lost interest in Edie Yeovil and galloped off in a noisy argument on the merits of spending the change on lemon drops or a bottle of Tizer.

The adults were not going to be so easy to disperse. Told to move back by Sarah, they reluctantly shuffled a few steps to the rear then re-grouped outside number six.

Jack stepped into number four. He was confronted by Phyllis Nettles. The neck of her blouse was open at the throat, a button, hanging by one thread against her breast-bone, rising with each shallow breath. A clump of hair had escaped from its roll and fell into the curve of her throat; the pin that should have secured it dropped with a ping to the hall lino as Stamford stared at her.

Holding a lace-edged handkerchief to the scratch on her left cheek, Phyllis said: 'She was behind the door. She went berserk when we tried to move her. Ronnie's seeing to her. You'd better go through. I just make her worse.'

She disappeared into the parlour. Stamford called Sarah, who was still resolutely keeping the neighbours at bay, and told her to keep Miss Nettles company. In an undertone, he added: 'And see if you can get her to open up about the blackmail business.'

Once the front door was shut, it took his eyes, still adjusted to the brilliant sunlight outside, a few seconds to cope with the gloom in the windowless hall. Shuffling forward he found that the kitchen was also in semi-darkness. He tried the light-switch. It clicked fruitlessly back and forth.

'Meter's run out.' The young man bending over a figure sitting at the kitchen table jingled a handful of change, extracted several coins, and offered them to Stamford. 'Meter's under the stairs. Would you mind, sir?'

It wasn't until he returned to the room that Jack realized that Ronnie was immobilized by his mother, who was holding on to his hand with an intensity that was draining the blood from her fingers and bringing a purplish tinge to her son's.

'Thanks,' the boy said. 'If you could get the blinds up we could turn the light off.'

'No. No, Ronnie. Not the curtains. I don't want them to see me. They're all looking at me.' Edie's voice rose in a protesting shriek. She rocked her son's arm back and forth, clawing at his chest with her free hand.

'It's all right, Mum. There's no one out in the yard.' Putting an arm round her shoulders, he rocked her soothingly, murmuring reassurance.

Taking down the blackout, Jack opened the window for good measure. It would help with the smell of stale alcohol and body odours that pervaded the room. Turning back to the scene at the table, he regarded the tableau.

Edie still wore her Daniel's uniform of white blouse and black skirt. But instead of the crisply pressed perfection demanded by Daniel's, it hung around her in crumpled folds; the blouse stained with yellow half-circles that spread from beneath her armpits and the skirt's drooping hem decorated with festoons of escaping black threads. The fair hair, its greying roots showing at the scalp, hung in rat's tails, the passage of the scalp grease marked by a tide line halfway down her skull. Her arms were locked round her son's waist, her face buried in his diaphragm.

'She got the sack,' Ronnie said, by way of explanation. 'She was drunk by all accounts. Reckons it was all your fault. If you're the copper who's investigating our Val's murder, sir?'

'Yes. I am. Detective Chief Inspector Jack Stamford. The officer with your fiancée is my assistant, Sergeant McNeill.'

The mention of Ronnie's fiancée had an electrifying effect on Edie. She pushed herself away from her son, skewing round on the chair and spitting at Stamford: 'She's not his fiancée! Ronnie's going to stay with me. He doesn't need her. He's going to get me a nice house. I shan't be fitting any more corsets on fat, rude women who stink of face powder and lavender water. This house is just temporary you know, Inspector.'

Plums of purplish black had flowered beneath her staring eyes. The bloodless skin was gashed by a slash of red lipstick across her mouth, dragged into a lopsided grin by the restlessly sawing hand she regularly passed across her face. It reached an ear and sought the straggling hair, patting it automatically into a bun that had long since collapsed.

Jack took a seat opposite her. He smiled. 'Yes, thank you, Mrs Yeovil. Tea would be very acceptable. Kind of you to offer.'

It worked. For a second, Edie's mouth pulled into a doubtful pout. Then her expression cleared. 'Of course, tea. Where are your manners, Ronnie?' Her tone became high and arch. Chatting inanities about the pleasant weather they were having, she took a Vesta from the packet by the gas stove and attempted to light a ring. The unflickering match-flame burnt brightly.

'Gas has gone too,' Ronnie hissed. 'I'll get it.'

He disappeared into the cupboard beneath the stairs, whilst Stamford discreetly blew out the burning match. Once the supply was restored, he lit a ring with his own lighter.

Edie bustled around the kitchen, filling the kettle, laying the table cloth, and counting out crockery and spoons with painful concentration. She stopped at three. The two women in the parlour did not exist as far as she was concerned. The slight hiatus when she discovered she was out of milk was solved by Ronnie seizing the jug, opening the front door, and thrusting it at Minnie White with a curt order that she fill it. Lost for words for once, Minnie did so without protest.

Once the bizarre tea-party was safely established at the kitchen table, Jack broached his first question. He directed it at Ronnie.

'No,' he said promptly. 'I didn't know she wasn't my full sister. I knew Mum preferred me, but you don't question things like that when you're a kid. I liked being the favourite. Never thought why. Just thought I deserved to be. Being such a loveable kid.' He directed a self-deprecating grin at Jack.

'Did you like Valerie, Mr Yeovil?'

'No, I can't say I did much. I didn't *dislike* her. We got on all right. But she was a lot younger than me, so we never really played together or anything. But we didn't fight. Just left each other alone.'

Like two acquaintances sharing a house, Jack decided. With a twittery, self-conscious mother, desperately worried by the world's opinion, blaming one child for her miserable situation and clinging to the other one whom she firmly believed would provide the respectability that his father had failed to bring to her life.

'How did you feel when you heard Valerie had been killed?'

'Sick to my stomach. I mean you would, wouldn't you? Thinking what that bastard had done to her before he'd finished her off. Val had never had a boyfriend. She was still innocent about that sort of thing.'

Which was, no doubt, what most brothers thought

about their sisters. If Ronnie had been a girl, they might have obtained a clearer picture of Valerie much earlier in the investigation, Stamford realized. A sister would never have fallen for that butter-wouldn't-melt performance.

'You never had any doubts that Billy Zimmermann was responsible?'

'No. Why should I? Your lot said he was. And he ran, didn't he? Shows he had a guilty conscience.' He watched his mother who was fussing with a tea strainer, holding it first this way and then that over the cup. 'She's not been right since.'

Edie's hand continued to pour a steady stream of golden brown liquid into the cup. She was unmoved by the turn of the conversation. They might have been discussing a distant acquaintance. Which was a pity, because she was the only one who could answer Jack's next query.

Accepting his cup and a gracious invitation to take milk because, most unfortunately, she seemed to be temporarily out of lemon, Jack said: 'So you don't think Valerie was too upset to discover who her real father was?' He held his breath, wondering if she'd take the bait.

'Oh, no,' Edie responded calmly, adding a dash of milk to her own cup. 'But if she had been it would have been entirely her own fault. If she was going to persist in pestering me in that truly nasty way, then she really deserved to be told.' Edie laid one hand over her son's. 'She wasn't like you, darling. You can always see when

Mummy's got a headache and doesn't want to be bothered. But not Valerie. She'd just go on and on and on.'

'So you told her. And she went to see him?'

'Did she?' Edie looked vaguely at the inspector, as if she was surprised to find him still there.

That was one that Stamford couldn't answer. He was just guessing. It seemed a logical step for a fledgling blackmailer.

'Did you know she'd visited your husband several times last summer, Mrs Yeovil?'

'Dad? You mean, she visited the grave?'

Stamford remembered that Ronnie Yeovil hadn't been informed of the true facts. 'Where do you think your father is buried, Mr Yeovil?'

'Up north somewhere. Outside Huddersfield, isn't it? He was working up there for the bank when he died.'

He took the truth well. Jack was grateful for his calm acceptance of the situation. 'I could give you the address if you wish.'

'Best not to bother,' Ronnie replied. 'I mean, he obviously weren't – *wasn't* – bothered what happened to me. Best leave it.'

'He was always a disappointment,' Edie announced with a dismissive wave of her hand. The nails were black with ingrained dirt. 'I thought marriage would be different.' Her only experience of love had come from Gothic novels and the flickering, silent images of the moving picture shows. She'd imagined it would involve being caught up in a crescendo of music, lights and uncritical adoration. Exactly like the scenario that her son had recently dismissed. Instead she found herself living with a virtual stranger. Only a stranger whose dirty linen she was now expected to wash; a stranger whose minor habits, such as breathing through his mouth whilst he ate, now drove her mad; a stranger who wanted to go to bed with her. 'He made no effort at the bank, you know? With just a little application he could have been made up to head clerk. We could have afforded to employ a parlour-maid.'

'Did Valerie's father promise you a parlour-maid?'

'A man like that doesn't need to promise. It is taken for granted.' She shot a coy, sideways glance at Stamford. 'One had only to look at the way he lived to appreciate that Valerie's father was a gentleman.'

Not so much a gentleman that he was prepared to stand by a pregnant mistress, Stamford reflected. 'I'd very much like the opportunity to observe the way the gentleman lives, Mrs Yeovil. Does he still live in Kentish Town?'

'Good heavens, no.' Edie gave a titter.

It made Jack's teeth itch and judging by Ronnie's expression it hadn't done a great deal for his dental work.

'Kentish Town is far too common. He lives in Hampstead. I'm sure you must know him, Inspector. He is such a public benefactor.' She looked at the two men with complacent smugness. 'You must know Mr Bowler.'

Chapter 23

'I don't believe it!' was Sarah's first reaction. 'Even when she was young I don't see Edie as any great beauty. And Leo does like to get value for money.'

'You think looks are the only criterion for a relationship?'

'What else would have attracted him? Her wit? Her vivacity? I mean, let's face it, Edie Yeovil is just ordinary.'

They were both silent for a moment, recalling how often that description had been offered about Valerie Yeovil. Only in her case it had been false. Valerie Yeovil had been extraordinary. Edie Yeovil wasn't. So what had attracted Leo Bowler?

They'd returned to the station to collect the car. Turning out of Agar Street yard, they encountered DC Bell again. Waving and offering a tentative twitch of his lips that might have been intended as a smile, Ding Dong raised one thumb.

Jack responded in kind. Double-declutching as he pulled into traffic, he had the uneasy feeling that perhaps the DC was pursuing some line of enquiry that he himself had ordered. Except he couldn't, for the life of him, remember what it was. He found himself praying that Ding Dong's good spirits were related to a recent manifestation of Mrs Bell.

'I just can't see this affair,' Sarah protested. 'It's got to be a figment of Mrs Yeovil's imagination. Can you honestly see Leo Bowler with her?'

'No. But on the other hand, her lover abandoned her when she was pregnant. And, judging by her financial circumstances, made no effort to support her or their child. I can see Leo Bowler doing that.'

Sarah snorted. 'I can see nine men out of bleedin' ten doing that!'

She caught Stamford's eyes in the rear-view mirror and flushed, aware that her carefully suppressed working-class accent had fought to the fore with a vengeance. 'And before you ask, no, I've never been caught that way myself.'

His sergeant was in a mood. Jack justified his appointment to Central CID by pin-pointing the probable cause of her suppressed anger. 'Phyllis came across then?' he deduced. 'And you don't like what you heard.'

'Yes.'

'Yes?'

Sarah stared through the windscreen, refusing to turn. 'She had an abortion,' she said shortly.

'When?'

'Last October.'

'Ronnie's baby?'

'No. There wouldn't have been a problem if it had been. It was a former lover. By the time she found out, he'd already gone abroad – with his wife.'

'And she was frightened that Ronnie would find out and break off the engagement?'

'It wasn't just Ronnie. In fact,' Sarah said truthfully, 'I got the impression that Ronnie was the least of her worries. It was her parents' reaction that worried her most. That and her employer's.'

They'd reached the junction with Haverstock Hill. Jack attempted to turn right and narrowly missed a cyclist who was overtaking on the inside. His vision could have been obscured by the ten-foot ladder balanced on his left shoulder. Alternatively, perhaps he just had a death wish. In any event, his vocabulary was mainly anatomical.

'Go on,' Jack ordered. 'I take it that was what Lily Hendry meant when she implied someone at number four had broken the law?'

'She supplied the name of the abortionist. Phyllis said she was the only person she could think of who might know that sort of thing. She couldn't exactly place a "wanted" advertisement in the newspapers.'

'And Valerie?'

Valerie had been the worst thing in the whole sordid business. Fate had picked the weekend for Phyllis: her parents were to transport her middle sister and her toddler twins to the safety of a maiden aunt's house in Cornwall; Susan was spending the two days with her fiancé's family; even Hatty had asked for the time off to visit a sick cousin. For two whole days in late October Phyllis had had the unaccustomed luxury of an empty house and no one to check on her movements. She'd visited the abortionist on Saturday.

'Something went wrong,' Sarah told her boss. 'The woman wasn't one of the usual crochet-hook butchers.'

She'd dilated Phyllis by the insertion of some soaked bark that had swollen on contact with water, and flushed the uterus. 'Should come away by itself now, ducks, like you was having it natural. Just move around a bit.'

Phyllis had moved around. She'd jumped, strode and danced around the woman's basement flat. But the foetus had refused to be dislodged. The woman had become more agitated as time passed. 'I'm sorry,' she'd said eventually. 'Me old man's due back any minute. He don't know I make a few extra bob on the side. You'll have to go. If nothing's 'appened by Monday, come back after nine and we'll 'ave another go.'

'She delivered it herself on Sunday morning,' Sarah explained. 'In the hall.'

'The hall?' Stamford repeated blankly.

'That's where the phone is.'

Crouched on a nest of sheets on the polished floor as the pains gripped her, Phyllis had made silent bargains with herself. If it doesn't come by the time the clock strikes the half, I'll telephone the doctor. Each shuddering contraction had led to another deal with her conscience: one more minute and she'd definitely start dialling; just another few seconds until the gilt minute hand on the delft clock that stood by the telephone touched the gold-leaf VI.

JUNCTION CUT

The jangling door bell had made little impression. It wasn't until a draft of air had blown over her cheeks, cooling her as it played across the sheen of perspiration, that she had been aware that the letter-box flap had been pushed inwards and a pair of eyes was framed in the oblong opening.

'If there's a god of blackmailers,' Sarah said, 'Valerie probably had something on him too. Ronnie had sent her with a note. It was the only time she'd ever called at the Nettleses' house uninvited.'

Phyllis had crawled across the floor and pushed the spare key through the slot. She'd finally delivered the tiny embryo holding tightly to Valerie's hand. Afterwards they'd disposed of the foetus and bloodstained sheets in the boiler.

'And Valerie started blackmailing her.'

'Yes. Although in a funny way I think Phyllis almost welcomed that. She wanted to be punished for killing her baby.'

Despite her upbringing Phyllis had listened to enough whispered conversations in ladies' rooms to know what the results of a back-street abortion could be. She would have welcomed a uterine fever as a penance. Even sterility if that was to be her punishment. But the abortionist's boast that she was worth her thirty quid fee held good. Phyllis had remained in perfect health. Her periods had started again the following month and, as far as she could judge, her body was ready and willing to play host to her next pregnancy.

'She's still suffering dreadfully, sir. It's worse now, of course.'

'Why? Because Ronnie's home?'

'No. He knows. He's standing by her.' An edge of definite exasperation crept into Sarah's voice at this display of male obtuseness. 'Because,' she explained, 'it's May.'

It was obvious that Stamford wasn't following her. 'Which,' she said slowly, 'comes seven months after October. It would have been born this month.'

'But she didn't want it,' Jack protested.

'She couldn't have it,' Sarah corrected. 'That doesn't mean it wasn't wanted.'

'Did you get the abortionist's address?'

Sarah finally twisted in the passenger seat to face him. Her body rocked with the rhythm of the car, causing the shadow of her hat brim to dip over her eyes one second and unveil them with the next movement. It was whilst they were hidden that she said: 'What abortionist would that be, sir?'

The muscle at the side of Jack's jaw tightened. 'It's a crime, Sergeant.'

'Oh no, sir,' she corrected. 'It's an uncorroborated and unwitnessed statement.'

'A medical examination would prove it.'

'It would prove she'd lost a child. She could have had a natural miscarriage. Like I said, the woman wasn't a run of the mill "grit your teeth while I hook it out, love".'

'You have a very idiosyncratic view of your job,

Sergeant. And it won't do. You can't just enforce the laws you happen to approve of and ignore the rest.'

'Well, sir, if you think you can get Miss Nettles to repeat her statement under oath...'

'No, fortunately for you, I don't.' He swung into the kerb and parked the car with a vicious jerk of the handbrake. 'Let's tackle Mr Bowler – a gentleman whom, I assume, you'll have no scruples about putting up before the Beak?'

Leo Bowler lived behind the High Street, in a tall, narrow Georgian house. It was reached via a stone staircase which led to a small courtyard surrounded by half a dozen such houses. One of which, Stamford knew, contained Bowler's councillor son, John, and his family. The whole place had a slightly eerie air of isolation and past lives; it held insinuations of sedan chairs, powdered wigs and unwashed bodies covered in white-lead paint and mouse-skin patches.

Rumour had it that Leo had a substantial estate, complete with private shooting and trout lake, somewhere in the West Country. The young footman who opened the door to them would certainly have looked more at home there.

Close to, his strange colourless eyes beneath girlish lashes were even more disconcerting. He'd swopped his chauffeur's uniform for black knee breeches and a yellow and black striped waistcoat. The air of eighteenth-century elegance was further enhanced by the catching of his fair hair at the nape of his neck with a black velvet ribbon, and the faintest hint of rouge on the paper-white cheeks. Only his hands, thick and misshapen by swollen knuckles, spoilt the pose of effete languor.

His reaction to their warrant cards, an instinctive closing of the door, was frustrated by Jack's shoe. Resigning himself to the inevitable, the footman led them along the hall corridor. The door to the left was open far enough for them to see furniture covered in dust sheets and bare walls. A muted light played over paler squares where the pictures had once hung. It suggested blinds had been drawn over the unseen windows.

He left them in a study at the back of the house with a languid promise to see if he could find Mr Bowler, as if his employer might be lurking under one of the dust sheets.

It would have been pleasant to dismiss Leo Bowler as just another crook with more money than taste. Unfortunately, Stamford admitted to himself, to do so would be gross self-deception.

The room had been painted in a pale eau-de-nil shade. It created a cool, restful feel that was further enhanced by the cream lawn curtains, sprigged with stylized representations of British flora, that looped back from the floor-length windows. Furniture had been kept to a minimum: a writing desk and chair between the windows; a display cabinet containing a few pieces of creamware and a framed photograph of Councillor John and his wife, looking self-important in their robes and chains; a pair of high-backed easy chairs against the opposite wall and a small occasional table holding a statue of a negro's head.

Jack ran one finger over the cheek, noting with admiration the way the sculptor had captured the skin tones which varied from deep coffee to palest cinnamon.

'Magnificent, isn't it, Inspector? It's one of my favourite pieces.'

He must have had the door hinges oiled to allow him to make his entrances unnoticed. He was in his late-seventies as far as anyone could ascertain, but slim and active-looking as a forty-year-old. His face was finely etched with lines but his dark eyes were bright with intelligence and his silver hair full and luxuriant. Extending a smooth, white hand in a perfunctory handshake, Leo seated himself on the writing-desk chair and waved his visitors to the easy chairs with a fluid pass of those long fingers. It could have been the gesture of a well-mannered host seeing his guests were comfortably seated. It also, of course, meant the light was in the two police officers' eyes, whilst Leo's face remained in shadow.

'Now, how may I assist the Constabulary, Inspector? It is Inspector?'

'Chief Inspector Stamford, sir. And this is Sergeant McNeill.'

'A sergeant?' His tone was just sufficiently this side of incredulous to ensure that any smart reply from Sarah would look like over-sensitivity.

She removed Valerie's notebook from her jacket pocket and held it lightly, tapping it almost absentmindedly against her upper thigh. She had the satisfaction of seeing a stiffening in Bowler's attitude. It wasn't much, but it was there. She ruffled the pages just for the joy of seeing him lean forward slightly, attempting to read the rapidly flickering sheets.

It was Stamford who claimed his attention. 'You said you wanted to assist us with our enquiries, sir?'

'Of course, Insp . . . Chief Inspector. How may I help?'

'You can tell us about your affair with Edith Yeovil.'

The man's laughter was genuine and his relief obvious. Whatever he'd been expecting, it wasn't this. 'I'm flattered, Chief Inspector. Truly I am. But I fear you have the wrong man. I'm innocent of the charge.' His palms were displayed to the officers in a gesture of mock surrender.

'Yet according to Mrs Yeovil, you are the father of her younger child. The one who was murdered.'

Leo sighed. 'A sad business. I daresay the experience caused a decay in the poor woman's mental faculties. They were never very strong in the first place as far as I remember. I fear she has become confused.'

'You deny you're related to Valerie, Mr Bowler?'

'Not at all, Inspector. No, no. Not at all.' Even if they couldn't see his face clearly, they could hear the amusement in his voice. He was enjoying the game.

Jack refused to play. He sat silently until Leo grew bored and contributed further information: 'I am not Valerie's father. That distinction goes, or rather went, to my son John.'

He rose like a cat from his chair and walked across

to the display cabinet. The key was attached to his belt, amongst a cluster of others in assorted sizes and shapes. Evidently Bowler judged others' standards of honesty against his own. In which case it was surprising he hadn't got man-traps set around the house. Perhaps he had.

The silver-framed photograph was passed to Stamford. 'My son. Unfortunately he takes after his late mother.'

The plump, weak-willed face certainly carried none of his father's genes.

'Sixteen years ago John acted as my rent collector. He was useless at the job, as indeed he was at everything else. That's why I got him into politics. An inability to arrive at a definite decision can be such an asset in that profession. It's regarded as having an open mind.'

'Edith Yeovil?' Jack prompted.

'Ah yes, Edith. Shall I tell you why John had an affair with her?' His long middle finger tapped the picture glass. 'Because I informed him I had just arranged his marriage to Ruth.' Leo returned to his own chair and linked his fingers in the manner of a schoolmaster preparing to deliver a lecture. 'John occasionally suffers from delusions of free-will. He confuses stubborn petulance with resolve. I'm sure you know the type? Anyway, I told him I'd engaged him to marry Ruth. Her father had certain properties I was anxious to acquire. John was somewhat upset.'

'I'm not surprised,' Sarah said. 'What on earth made

you think you could tell a grown man of, what . . . ?'

'Thirty,' supplied Leo obligingly.

'Thanks. Tell a thirty-year-old man who to marry?'

'Well, the fact that he did marry her rather proves could, doesn't it, Sergeant?'

Stamford interrupted: 'How did he meet Edith Yeovil, sir?'

'She was, I imagine, the first available woman on his rent round that day.' He unlinked his long fingers to wave them dismissively. 'She was his gesture of independence. His grand romantic statement. So much more satisfactory than simply stamping his foot and crying that he wouldn't marry Ruth.'

Stamford could imagine their coming together. John Bowler desperate to stand up to his contemptuous, strong-willed father. And Edith – disappointed and lonely in her loveless marriage – seeing him as her passport to the wealthy world that she equated with respectability. He wondered whether they'd ever actually looked at each other. Whether, in fact, they would have recognized each other if they passed in the street six months later.

'Did you split them up?'

'Not at all. I wished them every happiness. Naturally I also informed John I no longer felt able to support him in the style to which he assumed he was always going to be accustomed.'

'Naturally,' Stamford agreed drily. 'How long did the affair last?'

'Several weeks, I believe.'

'Did you know Mrs Yeovil was pregnant?'

'She did approach me for help after the child was born.'

'Did she get any?'

'Certainly. I'm not totally unfeeling, Inspector. When she told me she could no longer afford the rent on her house, I arranged for her to move to a room in one of my houses in Warden Road. I felt it was the least I could do.'

'The very least,' agreed Sarah.

'I didn't ask her to have an affair with my son. I owed her nothing.'

'What about Valerie?' Stamford demanded. 'Did she think you owed her something?'

'Owe? No, Inspector. She made no claims on my conscience. Her approach was far more honest.'

He was interrupted by a loud crash from the corridor. With an irritated 'tsk' he rose and pushed the door shut, but not before Stamford had glimpsed the broken-nosed LDV sergeant and the wasp-like footman struggling to right a tea chest. Silver glinted between knobbly packages swathed in newspaper which were spilling from the open top. Evidently Bowler was carrying out his own preparations for a possible invasion.

'You were saying – Valerie approached you,' Stamford prompted as he reseated himself. 'How was she honest?'

'She attempted to blackmail me, Inspector. Came straight out with it – ten pounds a week or she'd tell everyone John was her father. I told her to go ahead, although it was hardly something most people would want to boast about.'

'She didn't attempt to approach your son?'

'He and Ruth were in the country that weekend.'

'Which weekend?'

'The one before the girl was killed.'

'Did she make you angry, sir?' It was hard to imagine anything ruffling that urbane calm, but you never knew.

'Not at all, Inspector. In fact, I rather liked her.'

'Even though she was asking you for money?'

'I ask people for money all the time, Inspector.'

'Yes,' Sarah interrupted. 'But a great many of them don't like you, sir.'

Leo held up one hand. 'Touché, Sergeant. Nonetheless, I assure you, Inspector, I harboured no violent feelings towards Valerie. Quite the contrary. Ruth has proved to be an excellent daughter-in-law in many respects, including, I would point out, the ability to see which side her bread was buttered on and to treat a brief affair by her husband, prior to his marriage, with the indifference it deserved. However, she has disappointed me in one respect – both her sons, despite the most rigorous attentions of the English public school system, take after their father. Valerie, on the other hand, took after me.'

It was true. As soon as Bowler said it, Jack could see the truth of the statement. The bold, mocking, intelligent eyes that stared out from Margaret's sketches were Bowler's. She was an even finer artist than they'd credited.

Leo had become quite animated. 'She was mine. My own flesh and blood, I could see that. The way she came straight out with what she wanted ... ten quid or I tell. I could see myself sixty years ago.' He shook his head regretfully. 'If only she'd been a boy, I think I would have been tempted to adopt her. What an heir she'd have made for my business! But, of course, I couldn't leave it to a girl.'

'I'll bet Henry the Eighth said much the same, sir,' Sarah remarked coolly. She waved the notebook again. 'But you did pay her blackmail money, sir. Fifty pounds. It's entered under "G.D." – for Grand-dad.'

'Really? How charming. Yes, as you say, Sergeant, I gave her fifty pounds. I liked her. She gave me the best Saturday afternoon's entertainment I'd had for a long time. I also informed her that was all she was getting. Now, if you'll excuse me?' He rose. 'I have matters to attend to. The man will show you out.'

The man was busy attempting to keep someone else out. One arm was hidden behind the partially open front door as he hissed instructions to the unseen caller to: 'Shove off.'

'Please, let us in. 'E won't even know I'm 'ere,' demanded a familiar voice. 'I could sit quiet in the kitchen.'

Jack cleared the corridor in two strides and pulled the door from the man's hand. He beamed. 'Hello, Felonious. The sergeant and I were just on our way back to Kentish Town. Want a lift?'

'I . . . er . . .' Felonious glanced over his shoulder. He looked back at the two officers. It was obvious he was weighing up the lesser of two evils. 'All right,' he said eventually. 'Yeah, ta, *Inspector*.'

'Splendid.' Jack put one arm around the little man's shoulders and led him towards the stone stairs. Two men in cheap suits, their faces shaded by caps pulled down over their eyebrows, preceded them into the High Street.

'It's lucky we ran into you, Felonious. Otherwise I'd have had to send the sergeant to pick you up. There's something you can tell me about the day Valerie Yeovil died.'

Chapter 24

Stamford took the wheel again. Sarah found herself in the back of the car with Felonious. He moistened dry lips and said in a transparent attempt to fish for information: 'You bin talking to Mr Bowler then?'

'We've been hearing about his idea of Saturday afternoon entertainment,' Sarah muttered, half under her breath, slamming the door shut.

'That right?' Felonious's taut body relaxed back against the upholstery. 'You know about that then. Cor, fancy that. Didn't know you was on the list. Still, nothing wrong with making a bit extra, is there? It's not like a real crime, is it? Not like he was asking you to look the other way while they done a bank or something.'

'Tell me something, Felonious,' Jack invited, his voice as casually conversational as the crook's, 'why did you collect the rent from the Caves on Friday the week Valerie Yeovil was killed? Thought you might not get round in time on Saturday morning, did you?'

'Yeah. That's right. First fight started at two. I mean, it don't make no odds to the shops whether I collect on Friday or Saturday, does it? It's not like they're waiting

393

for the old man to fetch his pay-packet home.'

'Did you manage to see the first bout?'

'Nah. All over in the first round, weren't it? Knockout.' He bounced on the seat, one fist curled to protect his face, the other jabbing mock punches at the back of Jack's neck. 'Wouldn't think he had it in him, would you? Looks like a Nancy boy.'

'Oggie didn't think so, did he?'

'No.' Felonious chuckled. 'What a choker, eh? Twenty to one. You should 'ave seen the look on his mug.'

'I don't see why he needs to put the squeeze on you this time. Not now he knows the lad's form.'

'He ain't worried about him, is he? Mr Bowler's got a couple of new boys. Brought 'em in from Ireland. Got 'em in hiding somewhere. Oggie reckons I must have seen them working out. But I ain't.' A thought occurred to him. 'Did Mr Bowler tell you to give me police protection?'

They were gliding down the Prince of Wales Road again. Stamford pulled into the kerb. 'I'm afraid not, Fel. You'll just have to keep your head down until the fight's over.'

'Don't know why I bother with this working lark,' he grumbled, climbing over Sarah's legs. 'Reckon I'll go back to thieving. It's safer.'

The last sight they had of him, he was scuttling up Malden Road.

Sarah flopped back with an audible: 'Phew!'

Jack twisted round and rested one arm over the back of the driving seat.

JUNCTION CUT

'So,' she continued. 'Bowler's been organizing boxing matches.'

'Probably bare-knuckle,' Jack said. 'Certainly illegal. And by the sound of it, he's paying back-handers to some officers to look the other way.'

'Not from Agar Street!' Sarah protested angrily.

'That remains to be seen. We'll turn that particular problem over to uniform and let them deal with it.' He drove slowly into the back of Agar Street, ignoring the impatient hooting behind them, and drew to a halt next to the wireless car. Instead of getting out, however, he tilted back his hat, folded his arms and stared out of the windscreen, apparently lost in contemplation of the unremarkable three-storey building.

Sarah waited. She felt they were on the brink of something remarkable. Any second now Stamford was going to astound her.

He didn't let her down. In actual fact, he managed to leave her spluttering for breath.

He said: 'Sex, Sergeant.'

'What! I mean, er . . .'

Stamford continued to contemplate the flat face of the police station. She realized his remark hadn't been intended as an invitation. And was annoyed with him.

'That's been the problem with this case,' he said, still apparently addressing the windscreen. 'It's got in the way from the start. First as the supposed motive, then as a reason for people to alter the truth slightly in order to protect their own secrets. And each lie nudged us a little further off the path. Edith and John

Bowler; Valerie and Billy Zimmermann; Phyllis and her lover... they've all muddied the waters and stopped us seeing the truth. Listen...' He finally twisted round and faced her. With his chin resting on his folded arms, he told her how he thought Valerie's murder had occurred.

When he finished, she shivered. What he'd outlined made sense, but if it were true... 'That's horrible, sir,' she said. 'It's so cold-blooded. But can you prove it?'

'Not at present. But if I'm correct, I think I know how to do it.'

It took four calls to find the right shop. Eventually they located it in Dartmouth Park Road. Fortunately the proprietor was anxious to maintain his good relations with the police and, once he'd been assured he wouldn't be figuring in their enquiries, provided the records they asked for without protest. Jack copied down three numbers, with their corresponding entries, and showed them to the man.

'Do you remember these items?'

The man nodded eagerly. He pointed to the third one. 'That's Margie Wilkes. Lives in Cathcart Street.'

'Are you sure?'

'Dead certain. She's a regular. Now that second one I hadn't seen before. But I remember because it was such an unusual piece. Don't get that quality around here normally.'

'We know about that one. What about this first entry?'

'Came from the north.'

'What? Like Golders Green?' Sarah asked.

'No. The real north. Up there.' His inky index finger indicated the ceiling. 'Yorkshire or Lancashire or some such. I remember her 'cos it was her first time in. Her man had just been called up. Told me her whole life story. Some of them do. Like they've got to apologize for being here. Bit posh she was.'

'Did her life story include her present address?'

'The Montagu Tibbles flats.'

'You've a good memory.'

'It pays,' he said modestly. 'People like the personal touch. Makes them feel a bit special even in a place like this. Number one came back several times after that. Haven't seen her recently though.'

'Thanks.' Jack handed him the closed ledger. 'It would be best if you didn't mention this visit to anyone.'

The man tapped the side of his nose and winked. 'Don't worry, officer. I know the form.'

Tracing Mrs Wilkes proved to be relatively simple. Her house was pointed out to them by a postman on his last round of the day. Their knock was answered by a girl of about ten with a grubby toddler clamped on one hip who informed them her mum was at work.

'Where's that?' Sarah enquired.

'Sainsbury's, miss.' She took in their official appearance. 'Have you come about the cockroaches?'

'No. Sorry, love.'

The girl sighed philosophically. 'I'll keep jumping on them.' The door closed and they heard her skipping back down the passage in a game of insecticidal hopscotch.

Margie Wilkes didn't look like a woman bothered by pests. In her white overalls, with her hair bound back in her muslin cap, she wielded the cheese wire through the waxy slab of Cheddar with the clean precision of a surgeon amputating limbs.

Her welcoming smile, however, drooped to openmouthed terror when she saw their warrant cards.

'Oh, mercy,' she gasped, a hand sliding to her throat. 'It's not one of my boys, is it?'

For a moment Jack was thrown. In his excitement at closing in on the killer, he'd forgotten what was happening in the rest of the world. Then something in the expression of her eyes brought back a picture of the misery in Eileen O'Day's. 'No,' he said quickly. 'It's nothing like that, Mrs Wilkes. We just need to ask you some questions about last January.'

She had to hold on to the marble counter until her breathing returned to normal. Eventually she was able to ask a trainee to take over the cheese while she led the officers outside.

'You don't mind talking out here, do you, sir? I need a breath of air. The smell of the bacon's been turning me queer all day. I 'ope I ain't got another one in the oven.'

'I'm sorry,' Stamford apologized again. 'I really am. That was thoughtless of me. Would you like to sit down somewhere?'

'No. I'll be all right now I know it ain't me boys.

JUNCTION CUT

What was it you wanted to ask me, sir?'

Jack showed her the entry in his notebook. 'Do you remember taking that in? It was the twentieth of January. A Saturday.'

Not only did she remember, but in her relief Margie became garrulous. Of course she remembered. She could recall the day quite clearly because it was her sister-in-law's birthday. 'I invited her to come round for a bit of tea, sir. I wasn't working then. First she said she couldn't come. Then she turns up on the doorstep with her old man and their four kids. And I didn't have nothing special in, so I popped up Dartmouth Park with the clock, same as I usually do.'

'Can you remember what time you got there?'

'Five o'clock exactly. Clock started chiming as I went in the door. The old man was down under the counter and he said, without even looking up: "That's Margie Wilkes, ain't it? I'd know that chime anywhere." Because it's a bit of a joke between us, sir . . .' In her relief, she obviously wanted to talk. Jack felt even worse cutting her short, but he needed to speak to number one on his list as soon as possible.

Montagu Tibbles House was in Queen's Crescent.

'Do you think Councillor Tibbles's parents disliked him or did they just have a sense of humour?' Sarah remarked as they walked down to it. 'I mean, sounding like you're descended from a long line of house cats must be bad enough. But *Montagu*? Why couldn't they have done the poor man a favour and christened him Fred?'

'Perhaps he likes it. It's the sort of name you can't forget. Which has to be an advantage in politics.'

'Tibbles for Prime Minister?' suggested Sarah, pushing through the entrance doors.

'Could scrape in by a whisker.'

'Ouch.'

Several of the flats were, or appeared to be, empty. In any event there was no answer to their knock. Those tenants who were in varied from surly to effusive, but their information was largely useless. Murphy's Law had come into operation and dictated that it was the last flat they tried whose occupant was able to provide any definite clue as to the identity of the young woman from north of Golders Green.

'I think you must mean Jean. You'd better come in.' The door was opened wider to admit them to a pleasant flat, well furnished in pastel shades and smelling deliciously of mimosa. 'Please sit down. May I offer you some tea? I was just making a pot for myself.' In proof of this statement, the imperious whistle of a kettle screeched from a room to their right.

'Thank you, Mrs . . .'

'Grayson. Myra Grayson.'

The tea was presented on a silver tray. The service was a translucent porcelain, rimmed in gold. Myra Grayson poured three cups with plump but competent fingers. She was, Jack supposed, what would be described as 'handsome'; a large-boned woman with strong features and an ample figure encased in a tailored black suit and white silk blouse.

Once they were settled, Jack prompted her: 'You think we must mean Jean who?'

'Jean Healey. She lived next door, that way.' Her head of thick black hair, streaked with grey, indicated the left wall. It was one of the empty flats. 'But I'm afraid she left in April.'

'Do you know where she went, Mrs Grayson?'

Myra Grayson took a sip of tea. She regarded Stamford over the rim of the cup. 'May I ask why you wish to know, Inspector?'

'Because she may have important information relating to my current investigation, Mrs Grayson.'

'But Jean isn't the subject of that investigation?'

'Should she be?'

Myra Grayson eyed him for a moment. Then her attention was transferred to Sarah. She seemed to be trying to read their expressions. Eventually she asked what they knew about Jean.

'Nothing. Beyond the fact she comes from somewhere in the north, and she was occasionally short of money.'

'Frequently, I'm afraid would be a better word.' Myra put her cup down. 'Jean married last December. It was an elopement. She was only seventeen. Her husband brought her to London and installed her in this flat just before he was called up. He couldn't afford a wife, of course, and I'm afraid the poor man felt he had to live up to Jean's girls' magazines' idea of married life.

She had, I'm afraid, no idea how to manage a budget.'

'You mean she skipped owing money?' Sarah said.

Myra nodded. 'Several weeks' rent. And she also had accounts outstanding with many of the local tradesmen. She was far too young to marry. I know some girls are quite mature at seventeen, but they tend to be working-class and used to helping out in the house. Not rather sheltered doctor's daughters who spend the money for the butcher's bill on a new hat because they're feeling homesick.'

'Did she go home, Mrs Grayson?' Jack asked.

'Not exactly.'

'But you do know where she is – exactly?'

Mrs Grayson walked across to a bow-fronted walnut chest of drawers. Sliding open the top drawer, she extracted a slip of paper. 'It's her grandmother's address. She left it with me in case there was any news of her husband. I believe she had visions of them delivering the telegram to an empty flat.'

Jack passed the slip to Sarah. 'Harrogate? You mean we've got to drive all the way up there!'

'I believe the natives are quite civilized,' he said, and couldn't resist an inward laugh. His sergeant had a real Londoner's attitude to the outside world. Allingham had been as country as she wanted to get. Anywhere beyond Welwyn Garden City was regarded with the suspicion of a Roman legion preparing to walk into an ambush by woad-painted Celts. 'But I believe we'll rely on the telephone and the Yorkshire constabulary. Thank you for this.' He stood, and offered his hand to Myra Grayson.

She took it and wished him luck with his investigation. He was grateful to her for not asking any salacious questions under the guise of concern.

The Harrogate station operator informed Jack that the CID officer had gone home because he finished at noon on Saturdays. He ended up leaving the details of the case with a station sergeant who insisted on ringing him back at Agar Street: 'Just to check this's not some bugger's idea of a leg-pull, sir.'

Jack agreed solemnly that you couldn't be too careful these days.

'Hopefully it shouldn't take more than a couple of hours to get a statement from Mrs Healey, if they can spare a uniformed constable to go round directly,' he said, resettling the receiver on its handrest.

'You'll think they'll do it tonight?' Sarah asked.

Jack glanced at his watch and was startled to see it was nearly half-past seven. 'God,' he said. 'I'm sorry, I'd no idea it was that late.' Something else occurred to him. 'You haven't had a weekend off since this case started, have you? You should have told me I was a slave-driver.'

Sarah shrugged. She'd perched herself on a desk and was swinging one leg to and fro. It was one of her more tomboyish habits that she kept telling herself she ought to have outgrown. 'I don't mind. I can always take days off in lieu later. I've enjoyed it. It's nearly over, isn't it?'

'Yes, it is. But I suspect you're right about Harrogate.

I doubt they'll bother to interview Mrs Healey tonight. My guess is we shouldn't expect to hear much before say ten o'clock tomorrow at the earliest. Will you meet me here at nine thirty?'

'Of course.' She used both hands to push herself off the desk edge.

'Do you fancy a drink before you go home?'

Sarah's face lightened.

'The Assembly Rooms are handiest, aren't they?' Stamford said.

He wasn't to know he'd inadvertently trodden over an Agar Street taboo. The Assembly Rooms had been the haunt of Inspector Kavanagh and his sergeant. The rest of the station had made a point of avoiding this particular pub. Not from any delicacy of feeling but because if the inspector's drink started talking (or singing, or swearing) they didn't want to be the one who had to nick him on a drunk and disorderly. Even though the man had been dead for months, the Assembly Rooms still carried an invisible 'out of bounds' sign as far as Agar Street was concerned.

Stamford knew none of this. He simply saw the dismay on Sarah's face and assumed he'd put her in an awkward position vis à vis socializing with a senior officer. 'Or shall we leave it until tomorrow and make it a victory toast?' he said, giving her a get out.

'Fine,' Sarah beamed. Her mouth stretched wider and wider because she was aware he'd misinterpreted her reaction and now she couldn't think of any way to retrieve the situation without making it sound like she was desperate for a drink – or a date. She knew she looked like the Cheshire Cat. Embarrassed, she turned away and started fitting her hat, twitching and positioning it far more than was necessary. When she turned back, Stamford had gone.

Chapter 25

Sunday 2 June

He was shaving, dragging the razor over the prickly stubble that was black rather than auburn, when the telephone extension in the bedroom rang. Assuming Harrogate had already been in touch with the duty officer at Agar Street, he answered with a terse: 'Stamford!'

'Well, hello, Mr Stamford. Beautiful morning, isn't it? Makes you glad to be alive, don't it?'

The cheerful voice was naggingly familiar, but he couldn't place it. 'Who is this?'

'Oh, come on now, Mr Stamford. You've not forgotten me so soon? Me feelings are hurt.'

'Look, I'm waiting for an important call on police business. Now either tell me who this is, or get off the line.'

'Oh, sorry, Mr Stamford.' The bumptious tone was instantly subdued. 'Didn't realize. It's me, Brendan O'Day.'

'Brendan!' Jack rubbed lather off his jaw with the towel, whilst struggling into a shirt. 'Hang on. I'll fetch your mother. Where are you? Are you out of France?'

Daft question. It was unlikely Brendan was ringing

from a public phone in Calais. 'Don't go away.' Flinging open the front window, he bawled to the startled milkman, 'Hey! Knock at the O'Days'. I've got their Brendan on the phone.'

The man had only got halfway up the path when Eileen hurtled out of the front door, followed by Patrick, Maurice and Sammy. 'Don't let him go,' she called up to Jack. 'Don't let him go.'

She'd forgotten her key. Jack reached the front hall just as her assault on the knocker set all the neighbourhood dogs barking out a ferocious challenge. Eileen thrust her way in as soon as he slid the bolt off and seized the extension on the hall table.

'It's dead.' Angrily she rattled the receiver. 'He's gone.'

'It may just be the extension. Hang on, I'll check the bedroom phone.' Jack took the stairs two at a time. Flinging himself across the bed, he scooped up the receiver which he'd left lying on the bedside table. The steady burring note of the dialling tone told him that Brendan had, indeed, hung up.

'Is he there?' Sammy demanded. He'd followed Jack up the stairs, scrambling up the treads on all fours like an excited terrier. When Jack shook his head, Sammy shot back to the hall banisters and bawled the news to his mother, before leaping astride the rail and sliding to the bottom. For once nobody told him to pack it in if he didn't have a pressing need to get his ear clipped.

'I'm sorry,' Jack said, descending at a more sedate

pace and taking the opportunity to button his shirt. 'But if he rang, it means he must be in this country somewhere.'

'That's what Pat says,' Eileen sniffed. 'But they've got telephones in France, haven't they? He could have found one.'

This was, Jack conceded, remotely possible. Paris hadn't fallen yet, maybe some of the telephone lines were still intact. Perhaps Brendan wasn't with the BEF at Dunkirk, but for some reason had been trapped the opposite side of the advancing German Army? Even as he thought about it, he saw the flaw. 'It was a direct call, it didn't come through the operator,' he said.

'Was he on a public phone, Mr O'Day?' Patrick asked.

Jack struggled to remember whether there had been any tell-tale bleeps before Brendan spoke. And found he couldn't.

'Oh, well,' Eileen said, wiping away a tear. 'Best to look on the bright side, isn't it? At least he's alive. I'll make some tea.'

She bustled around Jack's kitchen, setting places for five, cutting bread and tutting abstractedly when she found the egg dish empty.

'You've already got the pan on in our 'ouse, Mum,' Sammy reminded her.

'Oh, lord. So I have. I've left the gas on under it. We'll be burnt down.'

'It's all right. I turned it off,' Pat reassured her. 'The lads at the fire station would have a right laugh if they had to turn out to a blaze at my house.'

'Go get it for me, Maury, there's a good boy.'

'Sorry, Mum. Got to scram. Bit of business. Why don't Mr Stamford go over to our place? Be easier.'

'Because Mum wants to eat here, that's why,' Patrick informed his brother. 'Now Mum asked you to fetch the frying pan and eggs. So get!' A large hand twisted Maury's collar at the scruff of his neck and propelled him towards the front door. He was thrust back into the street with an instruction to bring the bacon as well.

He returned, scowling angrily, with the blackened frying pan in which fat was already congealing back into a solid slick, a basin of cracked eggs, and a solid joint of bacon which, to Jack's eyes, looked a great deal more than the ration for four people.

Maury saw him looking. 'Got to go now,' he muttered. They heard his footsteps clatter along the linoleum then cease as he stepped on the door mat. 'Bloody hell!'

'Maury!' Eileen dropped the bread knife with a clatter. 'I'll wash your mouth out with soap when I get my hands on you . . .' She made for the kitchen door, then stopped with a cry between a moan and a scream.

'What you all doing over here?' Brendan asked. With a fine disregard for the paintwork, he swept his kitbag off his shoulder, dropped it to the floor, and swept his mother up in his arms instead.

He was lost in a welter of cries and demands for explanations. Once he'd told them he'd phoned from the tobacconist's on the corner just to make sure someone was up when he arrived, he was punched and slapped on the back by his brothers, and ribbed and teased on the single white stripe sewn on his sleeve. Eventually he managed to extricate himself and tell them he'd landed in Margate yesterday. 'Just banged right into the bleedin' pier. Sorry, Mum,' he added hastily. 'I mean, we lost the engine and drifted in. They put us in the Winter Gardens. Remember the theatre, Mum? We went there nineteen thirty-seven, weren't it?'

'Never mind seaside trips, Brendan. What happened to you? Are you all right? You're not hurt, are you?'

Jack saw Patrick surreptitiously squeeze his mother's arm and shake his head slightly.

She pushed Brendan away and smiled brightly. 'Well, never mind about all that. You can tell us later. I don't suppose you've had your breakfast?'

'There were volunteers at the stations along the line. Gave us tea and wedges. Mind, I wouldn't mind one of your breakfasts, Mum.'

'Sit down then. I'll get the bacon on.' Taking up the knife she attacked the flitch with enthusiasm, hacking off an uneven rasher. 'It was kind of your friend to give us his rations, Maury. But I wish you'd told him to get it sliced. Maury's got this new Jewish friend, Brendan. Thirteen in the family and none of them can touch bacon.'

'Oh, ain't that a shame for them?' he sympathized. 'And ain't it wonderful how they've taken to Maury. Giving you all them ration coupons out of the goodness of their hearts.'

Maury glared, scuffed back his chair and announced he'd got to go.

'How long's your leave ticket?' Patrick asked.

'Ah.' Brendan's expression started to resemble Maury's.

'Brendan, you haven't!'

'Haven't what?' Eileen asked, vaguely attempting to crack an egg into the teapot.

'I'll do that,' Jack said, taking the pot from her hands and busying himself with the kettle. It gave him the opportunity to turn his back on the table and pretend he couldn't hear the hissed conversation on the subject of daft idiots who went absent without leave.

'Couldn't resist it. What with the tube being so close an' all. Couple of lads from Bow did the same. I'll nip back to Victoria soon as I've eaten and hitch on to the next batch that comes through. Everyone's mixed up higgledy-piggledy anyhow. I ain't seen nobody from my own lot since last Wednesday. Don't suppose you've heard anything?'

They were able to tell him what they knew, whilst he tucked into fried eggs, bacon and bread.

'Did you kill loads of Germans, Brendan?' Sammy asked, miming a machine gunner and spraying particles of half-chewed egg across the table. 'Eeoow! What yer do that for?' Drawing up a knee into his chest, he massaged a calf that had just been soundly kicked by his eldest brother.

"Fraid not Sammy. Walked up and down that beach for days. And we just couldn't find a German to shoot

JUNCTION CUT

anywhere.' Brendan swallowed his tea and pushed his cup forward for a refill. His chin showed signs of a hasty shave and his hair was freshly combed. But he hadn't been able to disguise the deep purple circles under his eyes or the pungent smell of dried salt and oil that emanated from his crumpled battledress. It would be some time before Brendan could talk to anyone about what had happened at Dunkirk. At present, he just wanted to bury himself in the normality of life in the Square. 'So what you lot been up to?' he asked, wiping up the last of the yolk with a slice of bread. 'On a good investigation, are you, Mr Stamford?'

'What!' His watch said it was nine-fifty.

The O'Days found themselves talking to an empty chair as Jack snatched up his hat and coat and sprinted for Prince of Wales Road.

Sarah had gone when he arrived.

'Went out about twenty minutes ago,' the station sergeant said. 'Had a phone call. Seemed excited about something.'

Jack felt a cold trickle of horror go down his spine. Surely she hadn't decided to tackle the murderer on her own? A murderer who had nothing to lose by killing a policewoman. They could, after all, only hang you once.

Sarah had arrived at the station at nine o'clock. Surprisingly DC Bell was in before her. In response to her joking remark regarding his usual aversion to overtime, the constable had waved a file triumphantly at her and announced he'd finished.

'Finished what?'

'Checking all them alibis. It's taken me days, me bunions are killing me. But you know me, Miss McNeill, I've never been one to shirk me duty – even if it means ruining me 'ealth and neglecting the lady wife. When I can find her to neglect, that is.'

Curious, Sarah twisted the file. Stencilled across the top were the words: 'Junction Cut – Alibis'.

'Checked 'em all out. Everywhere they said they all went, I went too.'

Sarah was horribly certain that Stamford had forgotten all about that instruction which had been issued in the midst of his misery and worry over the possible fate of his family. But she hadn't the heart to tell Ding Dong the truth. 'All tally, did they?' she asked.

'Far as I could tell. Except one.' He shuffled papers like a pig rooting for a particularly succulent truffle. 'There! Carey Meeks. Said he finished work at half-five. But he didn't. Clocked off at four according to his time card.' He laid the neatly typed report in front of Sarah with what might have passed for a smile in anyone else.

She didn't know what to say. The telephone bell saved her. Harrogate had located Jean Healey and, rather than take a statement on what they suspected might be an elaborate joke, had brought her into the station to talk directly to Agar Street (on the grounds that she could waste their time instead).

It was a difficult conversation. However, between

bouts of hiccups and sobbing, intermingled with tangled explanations of why Jean hadn't been able to settle the bills before she left and promises to send the money as soon as her husband came home, Sarah was finally able to extract the relevant information from her. Her timing was, she insisted, accurate. She'd walked up and down the street for ten minutes trying to pluck up enough courage to go in. And she'd looked at her watch several times during that period.

Sarah re-cradled the phone and beamed at DC Bell. 'Looks like we've caught a murderer, Ding Dong.'

'That right?' The DC fingered his report doubtfully. 'And he looks like such a harmless runt, don't he? We going to pull him?'

It was nine-twenty. 'Chief Inspector Stamford will be here in ten minutes. He'll want to make the arrest himself.'

'Fair enough.' Ding Dong unrolled his newspaper and turned to the back page. He'd been in the job too long to take arrests personally: careless motorists or mass murders, they were all the same to him. Nick 'em, book 'em and forget 'em, was his motto.

Sarah wandered restlessly around the room, picking up and discarding papers. She checked her hat (the second best), reapplied her lipstick and rolled a powder-puff over her nose, blotting an imaginary shine. The minute hand ground past the half hour with infuriating slowness. And still there was no sign of Stamford.

She touched the telephone longingly then changed her mind. If he was late, no doubt he had a good reason.

It wasn't up to her to pull up her boss for bad timekeeping.

Unable to keep still, she wandered out into the street and peered along Prince of Wales Road. There were several couples in Sunday-best hats and gloves obviously on their way to church services and a uniformed nursemaid pushing a large pram, but no sign of Stamford. Just as she was re-entering the station a shout stopped her.

'Miss, miss! Wait! Please wait.'

There was a squeal of brakes and a stream of invective followed Queenie as she darted and weaved between a bus and a brewer's lorry.

She gained the kerb, sprang across it and hurtled towards Sarah. A scrap of paper was thrust into her hand. 'Letter for yer, miss.'

Sarah unrolled the note and read:

I should be grateful if you could call on me at once.
There is a matter that is causing me some concern.
D. Toddhunter (Miss)

Queenie was probing a gap in her upper gum where she had recently lost a tooth.

'Did Miss Toddhunter say what she wanted to see me about?'

'No, miss. Just said I was to give the letter to you or that inspector who give me the money. And if you weren't here I had to ask if there was another lady copper and give it to her. And if there weren't I had to find a nice copper and bring him round straight away.'

So whatever Dolly Toddhunter wanted to tell her, it was obviously urgent. It was now nine-forty. 'Wait here a minute, Queenie, and I'll walk back with you.'

'Y'ss, miss.'

She scribbled an account of Jean Healey's testimony, pinned Dolly's note to it, sealed them both in an envelope marked for Stamford's attention, and told Ding Dong to see he got it as soon as he arrived.

'Going round there, are you?'

'Yes. Miss Toddhunter wants to speak to me.'

'I'll come with you.' Ponderously rolling his paper, Ding Dong heaved himself to his feet.

Sarah experienced a pang of exasperation. Even Ding Dong, who'd be hard put to out-punch a ten-year-old, thought she needed his protection. Then she remembered all that tedious leg-work he'd just put in. 'I'm only going to have a word with Dolly Toddhunter,' she warned. 'There won't be any action until Inspector Stamford catches us up.'

As it turned out, she was wrong.

They heard the sound of raised voices, one shrill and female, the other male and accusing, before they turned the corner into Junction Cut.

Pearl Scannell stood on her parents' step. Her youngest child was in her arms, the three girls huddled behind her back.

'Just stay away! You hear me, girl? We don't want your sort in this house. And take them thief's spawn with you.'

'Don't be daft, Carey, let her in. She's family. Only one we got now.' Irene pulled down her husband's arm. 'Come in, Pearl love.'

Carey squared up to his daughter, apparently prepared to throw her bodily back into the street if she tried to cross the step. Then, suddenly, he sagged. 'Oh, come in if you must. It don't matter now, does it?'

He shuffled back. Irene waved her daughter and the four wide-eyed children in.

She'd left the front door open. Before Sarah could speak, Ding Dong followed the family down the passage. Reluctantly, she went after him.

Edie Yeovil was seated in one of the two easy chairs. On the officers' appearance, she smiled graciously and informed them she was considering taking lodgings with her good friends as a paying guest. 'Just temporarily of course.'

Raising his eyebrows, Carey Meeks flopped into the seat opposite her, folded his arms, and dared the world to intrude.

Irene had taken a seat at the table, opposite her daughter. Between them was a collection of tinned meat and fruit, half a pound of butter and a pound of dried fruit. The children shuffled closer to the table, gripping its edge and staring with awe at this display of luxury.

They were forced to part as another woman, whom Sarah vaguely recognized as being Minnie White's next-door neighbour, entered the kitchen, produced a shiny blue package of sugar from beneath her cardigan and placed it on the growing pile.

'If you need a hand, you've only got to ask, Irene. You know that.'

She departed as quickly and silently as she'd arrived.

Sarah understood the significance of the food. 'Joey?' she said gently.

Irene nodded, her lips trembling with the effort to stem the next outburst of tears. Pearl reached across the table. Wordlessly their hands gripped together.

"Ad the letter yesterday,' Pearl said. 'A munf, a whole munf since his ship went down, and they only just told 'em. Disgraceful, ain't it?'

'Now, Pearl. I expect they wanted to be sure.' Irene had been a peacemaker all her life. She couldn't give up the role now. Picking up a tin of pineapple, she turned it doubtfully in her hand. 'It's kind of people, I'm sure. But I don't see how we can have a funeral tea if we ain't had a funeral. I don't think it would be proper, would it?'

Both women's eyes turned to Sarah, as a representative of authority. 'Well . . .' She appealed silently to Ding Dong for help.

Displaying a rare presence of mind, he suggested they ask the vicar to hold a memorial service for Joey. 'Then you could 'ave the tea after that. That's what they did for my uncle when they lost him off South Africa. Works a treat, you'll see. Better than the real thing. You don't 'ave to stand round getting your feet wet in the graveyard.'

'That so, sir? You hear that, Carey? We can have a service for our Joey. That'll be a comfort, won't it?' Her voice was determinedly cajoling, in the manner of someone trying to coax a small child to eat another spoonful of an unwanted meal.

Carey didn't answer. His crossed arms tightened across his chest. They could hear his restricted breathing against his self-inflicted strait-jacket. With a low keening sound, he started to rock back and forth.

Ding Dong placed one hand on Carey's shoulder in the time-honoured manner of the arresting officer. 'You lied in your statement to the police, Mr Meeks. Gave a false time.'

'What!' Carey shrugged the restraining hand off angrily. 'What d'you say?'

'Lies, that's what I said, sir. Told the inspector you left work at five-thirty the night of the murder. Didn't though, did you? I've seen your time card. Four o'clock you knocked off. That's an hour and a half to be accounted for.'

Carey sprang up. His face suffused with anger. 'You want to know where I was? Church! That's where I bleedin' was.'

'Carey! Language!'

'Shut your mouth, girl.' One finger waved uncertainly under the DC's nose. 'On me knees, weren't I, praying that our Joey'd be kept safe? Hours I've spent asking the Lord to look after our Joey. Telling him I was sorry for abandoning him like. Promising him anything if he'll just bring our boy home to us. And what's he do? Let's 'em take Joey and looks after scum like Edgar Scannell.'

'My Edgar ain't scum! He's unlucky.'

But Carey wasn't listening. With a deep sob, he seized a cup from the shelf and crashed it against the floor. 'Well, sod the Lord! That's what I say. Sod 'im! I was right. He don't exist.' He ground the pottery fragments beneath his heel. Another cup then a plate went the same way.

Edie smiled placidly. The children backed nervously towards the scullery, giggling at the excitement but prudently keeping the grown-ups between them and this madman.

This was a situation that Ding Dong could recognize. He'd been in uniform for years. Domestic disputes were bread-and-butter to him. 'Now, now, sir,' he said, advancing at a slow march. 'We don't want none of that language, do we? Now you give me that plate.'

Carey responded to this instruction by slinging it at the DC's head. It exploded harmlessly on the wall behind him. Pearl screamed.

Sarah felt a tug on her skirt. 'Miss,' Queenie pleaded, 'Miss Toddhunter says to come *now*.'

Sarah assessed the situation in the Meekses' kitchen. Carey was half-mad with grief, but he was a small man and she thought Ding Dong could disarm him if he picked up anything more dangerous than crockery. A tin of custard powder, pitched over-arm, lost its lid and covered the advancing copper in a cloud of yellow dust. Ding Dong walked on as if it were an everyday occurrence.

Sarah took the small girl's hand. 'All right, Queenie, let's go.'

Dolly was on the pavement, her back against the wall, but one elbow thrust into her own front door to prevent it closing.

'Thank heavens you've come. I wasn't sure I was right to bother you. But now I'm quite certain there's something wrong. I believe Lily is in serious danger.'

Chapter 26

Sarah drew Dolly away from the door. 'Tell me,' she instructed, her voice low but her lips moving precisely so the older woman could lip-read easily.

Dolly explained quickly and concisely. After manning a WVS mobile canteen at Charing Cross on Saturday morning she'd returned home and made her weekly visit to the Public Baths. 'One of the attendants knows me – and Lily. She said she'd seen Gus dragging her along the road on Friday morning. I thought very little of it at the time. They sometimes have quite violent rows and Lily usually gains the upper hand eventually. But I knocked on their door when I came in, just to ensure that Lily was all right.'

'And?'

'Gus opened it. He said she had a headache and was lying down, although that was plainly a lie since I could see the bed reflected in the dressing-table mirror and it was empty. However, since I could hardly interfere between man and wife, I dropped the matter and went down to Weaver's for my tea . . .' A gust of air from the closing door caught her on the back of the neck. Sarah gripped her arm and said urgently: 'Go on. What then?'

'Later that evening I made a pretence of wanting

change for the meter. This time I tried the kitchen door. It was locked, which is highly unusual. And when Gus eventually answered he came out of the front room, although I'm sure he was in the kitchen originally. I could see his shadow moving under the door slit.'

'So you haven't seen Lily since – when – Friday morning?'

'Oh, yes, I have. That's one of the reasons I'm so worried. You see, I slept in a chair by my window last night. I felt sure if she was there, she'd have to use the lavatory some time.'

It had been two o'clock before her silent watch was rewarded. Huddled against the wall, her cheek pressed to the fading wallpaper, she'd peered through the slit she'd left in the carefully arranged curtains and seen Gus standing in the back yard. 'He looked up to my window, then he went back into the house.' And a minute later he'd emerged, leading Lily by one arm. 'It was difficult to see clearly because I didn't dare move in case he saw me but I think her hands were tied behind her back. And she was gagged, I'm sure of that.' The white slash of the handkerchief had caught the moonlight as Lily had turned and backed into the lavatory. 'He kept the door open with his foot. He was standing in the entrance watching her while she did her business.'

'And afterwards?'

'He took her back into the house.'

'Why did you wait until nine-thirty to send for the police, Miss Toddhunter?'

'Because, despite appearances, I'm not completely inexperienced in sexual matters. I am aware that some couples' proclivities lie in strange directions. I did not wish to intrude if that was the Hendrys' usual method of obtaining gratification. So this morning I called and ask if Lily wished to accompany me to church. When there was no sign of her, I paid several of the children to take turns at knocking on the front door then running away. Whilst Gus was occupied chasing them off, I dragged the dustbin up to the house and looked in the kitchen window. The curtains don't quite meet at the top.' Balancing precariously on the ribbed lid, she'd peered through the two-inch slit. 'I saw legs, Sergeant. A woman's legs, on the floor. The top half of the body was out of sight. That's when I sent Queenie with the note.'

Sarah made a quick decision. Luckily Edie had left her own front door unlocked. Moving quietly, Sarah entered the alley at the back of the houses. The back gate to number two was bolted, but the cross-beam on the wooden planks gave her sufficient foothold to scramble over. 'There's a plain-clothes constable in number six,' she said to Dolly, who'd followed her into the alley. 'Tell him what you've just told me and get him round here.'

Slapping the door with an open palm she called loudly: 'Open up, please. Police.'

There was no response.

'Come on, Mr Hendry. I know you're in there. I just want to talk.'

Inside the house somewhere a baby whimpered and was shushed.

For the first time since her temporary transfer, Sarah found herself longing for the old-fashioned blue serge uniform with its stout skirt, leather shoes and solid truncheon. She took a quick scan of the yard. The only likely object was a besom broom propped against the lavatory wall. Seizing it, she drove the handle into the kitchen window. The glass shattered and fell inwards with a crash of cascading fragments.

Flicking her jacket over the jagged stubs that formed a vicious row of teeth along the edge of the frame, Sarah hauled herself on to the dustbin and thrust her shoulders cautiously through the flapping curtains, expecting to receive a knock on the head at any second.

At first glance, the kitchen appeared empty. A muffled cry demanded her attention. She felt the sharp pricks of glass slivers jabbing into her folded jacket. One went into her knee. Dragging the leg awkwardly round at a side angle, she managed to kneel on the top of the cupboard which lay under the window. The cry came again from the direction of the floor.

Looking over the edge, she met Lily Hendry's eyes.

'*Mmmmm* . . .' Lily repeated, her eyes pleading above the gag. She squirmed, jerking her head back in repetitive nods.

Sarah dropped to the floor. The other woman's arms were tied above her head, the wrists rubbed raw where they'd been bound to the leg of the heavy iron cooker with a leather belt.

Bending down, one eye on the connecting curtain to the parlour, Sarah located the knot of the gag in the tangle of Lily's hair, and managed to loosen it sufficiently to pull it down over the chin.

'I didn't think nobody was ever going to come,' Lily coughed and gasped, spitting in an attempt to rid herself of the taste and fibres of the gag. 'The mad bastard's had me trussed up for two days. I don't mind a bit of a thumping for what I done, but this ain't natural.'

He'd woven and twisted the belt together. Her fingers were slipping on the greasy leather. Cursing as her nails ripped, Sarah struggled to release the squirming Lily.

"Urry up, can't yer?"

'Keep still.' Sarah saw blood on the skirt of her dress. The scraped knee was bleeding in a thin but persistent steam down her leg. And still there was no sign of Ding Dong.

Realizing that the back door was still bolted, she left Lily for a moment to release the catches. Behind her the parlour curtain rattled back on its rings.

'Leave her be,' Gus yelled. 'She's my wife, and Gussie's my kid. I can do what I like with them. It's no business of the police's.'

'I'm afraid it is if you imprison your wife against her will.' Sarah stepped away from the door. She tried to smile. 'This isn't like you, Mr Hendry. I thought you were a family man? My dad now, he couldn't have given a damn what happened to us once the drink was inside him. But you're not like that, Gus. I could tell soon as I saw you with him, you love your kid.'

Whilst she was talking, Sarah had moved back into the room. Not looking down, she stepped over the recumbent Lily, and positioned herself between Gus and his wife.

Gus's hands were bunched threateningly. His shoulders and neck hunched, thrusting forward his head like a suspicious bulldog. 'That's right, miss,' he growled. 'I love my kid. I ain't having him going to America.'

Since Sarah was unaware of Lily's emigration plans, this statement momentarily flummoxed her. But not Lily.

'It was Canada. An' if you really loved the kid you wouldn't want him stopping here where 'Itler can drop bombs on his head.'

'It's got nothing to do with the war. You were going off with that Yank.'

'He's Canadian, you stupid bastard!' The experience might have terrified some women but it had left Lily blazing mad.

'Shut up!' Sarah shouted, panting partly from her exertions and partly from anger. It looked like the Hendrys' situation was no more than a domestic dispute that had got out of hand.

Lily had succeeded in pulling her wrists free from the partially loosened straps. Grabbing Sarah's arm, she nearly pulled her over, using her as a prop to stand upright.

'Steady,' Sarah advised. 'Here. Sit down for a minute.'

'I don't want to sit down. I want my kid.' She walked unsteadily towards the parlour door where Gussie could be heard rattling the bars of his cot and demanding: 'Ma, Ma, Ma.'

Gus blocked her way. 'You're not taking him, Lil. He's stopping here. You both are. I wrote to that last pub we saw. Said we'd take it. We'll be moving end of the week.'

'Sod yer rotten pub! You can keep it. I ain't going with yer, and neiver's Gussie. He ain't your kid. You ain't got no right to him.'

'I got every right, after what I done for you.'

'What?' Lily challenged him, one hand on her hip, her chin raised in a provocative tilt. 'Go on. What have you ever done for me that Joe can't do better?' For the moment she'd forgotten that Joe had finished with her.

Colour suffused Gus's pale face. 'I kil—'

He bit the words off, but it was too late. His eyes had met Sarah's across Lily's head. And they both knew.

The speed of his attack caught her by surprise. Thrusting Lily aside he lunged across the kitchen and had his hands round Sarah's neck before she could gather her thoughts. Instinctively she reacted by jerking her arms between his and pushing outwards. It broke his grip sufficiently for her to back away, but her foot slipped and skidded on the discarded leather belt. He seized her and clasped her to him in a bear hug, pinioning her arms to her sides and preventing her from using her knees effectively. She did what she'd seen her father do many times when he was fighting drunk. Drawing back her head, she smashed her forehead against Gus's nose with all the force she could manage.

He dropped her with a roar of rage: a spray of bright red droplets spurted from his nostrils and splattered her frock.

For the first time she was aware of voices outside in the yard. The square of the window darkened as another body climbed through it.

'Unbolt the door,' Stamford ordered. 'Constable Bell's outside.'

Gus tried to stop her but Stamford was already inside, his forearm locked round Gus's neck, bending him backwards. Attempting to loosen the grip, Gus put both hands over Jack's arm and tried to drag it off. Stamford responded by seizing one of the man's wrists and twisting his arm behind his back.

'Get the cuffs on him,' he panted, as Ding Dong rushed through the door.

'I haven't brought them,' Ding Dong was forced to admit.

'Get mine out of my inside pocket,' Stamford said to Sarah. 'And then get back to the station and whistle up the Black Maria.'

She left them pinning the wriggling Gus down over the table, and limped through a crowd of interested spectators. This wasn't how she'd imagined the arrest. It had no glory. It didn't even have any dignity. It was more like being in a second-rate stage farce.

And the situation didn't improve when they got back to the station. Ding Dong was trailing clouds of custard powder and a brown mist which left the taste of chocolate on her lips.

'Cocoa,' he explained, beating ineffectively at his trousers. 'Carey had most of the store cupboard on the floor, before we stopped him.'

'Is he all right?'

'Bawling on his missus's shoulder when I left. You want to get the Matron to look at that bruise.'

Sarah put her hand up to her forehead and winced as her fingers encountered the spot that had been in contact with Gus's nose.

A glance in the mirror in the women's lavatory told her the worst: in addition to the swelling bruise over her eyebrow, her hair was hanging in rat's tails over one shoulder, the top of her dress was spattered with Gus's blood and the bottom had a swelling splodge from her bleeding knee. Hitching up the skirt to examine the wound, she discovered a large hole in her stocking which was spreading in ever-widening ladders towards her shoes.

After dabbing ineffectively at the oozing knee with her handkerchief, she made her way along to Matron's office. On the way she encountered Stamford who told her she'd had no business going into the Hendrys' before he arrived.

'Bollocks,' muttered Sarah rebelliously under her breath.

Once she'd been bandaged up and dosed with Matron's all-curing remedy of hot, strong tea with three sugars, she went in search of Stamford.

He was in the cells, facing a truculent Gus Hendry.

'It was an accident,' he whined. 'I never meant to kill her.'

'Notebook,' Stamford said briefly as she went in. 'You slipped into the back entrance from the pub yard,' he said, returning his attention to Gus.

'Yes. I just wanted to talk to her.' He looked appealingly from Jack to the scribbling Sarah.

'About her bet? It was her bet, wasn't it? Not yours.'

'She asked me to put her stake on. Oggie wouldn't take a bet from a kid. She gave me five quid to do it. I thought she was crazy. Oggie thought it was his birthday. A hundred quid on a dead cert loser.'

'But she won.'

'Yes. Don't know how she knew. Nobody else rated him.'

Because she had inside knowledge, Sarah thought to herself, writing furiously. No doubt gleaned by eavesdropping on her visit to Leo Bowler.

'So you decided to kill her before anyone else found out it was her two thousand pounds, not yours. It must have been quite a shock, finding the house empty. Standing there in the dark, wondering how long you could afford to wait before the governor from The Hayman came out into the yard to find out where you'd got to. How long did you wait for her, Mr Hendry?'

Gus's eyes filled with tears. 'Only a couple of minutes. She came in in a real spate. Cussing and swearing. Terrible words. Then she started slinging clothes and things all round the kitchen.'

'Did one of them hit you?'

'Some kind of silky stuff. It went over my head. I put it up on the washing cradle.'

Sarah exchanged a look with her boss. At least that explained away the slip.

'Go on,' Stamford urged. 'Did she know you were there?'

'Not until I hung the underwear thing up. The washing cradle started swinging and creaking.'

'Was she scared?'

'No. I told you. She was angry about something.'

'So what did she think when she found you in her kitchen?'

'Thought I'd come about the bet. She was really happy when I told her we'd won.'

'We?'

Gus's mouth twisted into a pout. 'That's what she said. *We?*' He mimicked a high, girlish voice. '*We* haven't won. *I* have.'

'Is that when you killed her, Gus?'

'No! I told you, I never meant that. I said we could share it. Half for her, half for me. I told her Oggie would never pay out if he knew a kid had put the bet on.'

'And Valerie wouldn't play?'

'Said she'd rather tell Oggie herself than give me a farthing.'

He looked pleadingly at them. 'I only wanted half. For my pub. So I could go home. I told her. A girl that age has no business with all that money. What use was it to her?'

'But she wouldn't agree?'

'No risk, no gain, that's what she said.' His voice changed to a girlish tone again. ' "I took the risks, Gus, so I take the gain. You're just a loser like my mother. I've paid you for your trouble, now go get my money." '

'Is that when you hit her?'

'She pushed me, in the chest. Told me to get out.'

'So you pushed back.'

'It was only a tap.'

Jack asked: 'Was she scared then, Gus? Did she run?'

'Not 'xactly.' He was refusing to meet their eyes now. 'She went into the corridor. Said she'd use the front door if I wouldn't let her past.'

'And you followed her, didn't you? Hit her on the back of the head. But not hard enough. She turned round. Put her arm up. She must have been crying by then, Gus. Did she plead with you to stop?'

'Called me stupid. Well, I ain't stupid.' For the first time a hint of the cunning buried within his slow intelligence sparked for a moment in his expression. 'I fooled you all, didn't I?'

'Yes,' Jack agreed. 'You fooled us.' He stood up. Sarah felt sick. She guessed maybe Stamford did too. 'We'll leave it there for now. I'll have a statement typed. Are you prepared to sign it?'

Gus gave a non-committal shrug.

'In the long run I think we've got enough circumstantial evidence to nail him,' Stamford said to Dunn.

Sarah heard the crackle of static as the Chief Superintendent, dragged from lunch to take the call, demanded further reassurance.

'Yes, sir. The pawn-shop records are conclusive. Mrs Healey and Mrs Wilkes pawned their items at four-forty and five o'clock respectively. Gus's ticket number was between theirs. Which means he pawned the brooch over two and a half hours after the fight he'd supposedly staked the hundred pounds on. I should have got on to it sooner. But like everyone else, I assumed the bet was on a dog race.'

There was another burst of crackling from Dunn.

'No, I'm sure it was premeditated, whatever he chooses to believe now. Maybe he did have a belated burst of conscience at the end and offer to split it with her, but all his previous actions indicate he intended to kill her. Not only did he pawn the brooch to provide a plausible source for his stake money, he even made himself late for work changing into his suit so that he could put the waistcoat and jacket on after the murder. He must have realized his shirt would be splattered by Valerie's blood... No, I don't think he knew about the relationship with Zimmermann. That was just a piece of tremendous luck for Hendry.'

A uniformed constable appeared at the door and hesitated when he saw the chief inspector on the telephone. He proferred a piece of paper vaguely in the direction of the coatstand. Jack signalled for Sarah to take it.

'A jemmy,' Jack was continuing. 'They used it for opening crates. We won't get any forensic evidence off it after all this time, but the pathologist may be able to match it to the shape of the wounds. Yes, fine, sir. I'll see you in the morning then.'

Jack replaced the phone. Sarah waved the opened letter at him. 'From Fran Jolly. James died in his sleep two days ago. We never did find his mystery woman.'

'It was Pearl. She nicked her dad's watch while her mum was in the bath. Don't you remember? Gus loaned Irene fifteen pounds to redeem it. That's why Carey and his daughter aren't on speaking terms.'

'They were the last time I saw them.' She told Stamford about the scene in the Meekses' kitchen. 'It must be the worst pain in the world – losing a child,' she said. A second later she was scanning the tattered carpet, praying that the first recorded earthquake in NW5 would rip a hole in it and allow her to slide quietly out of sight for ever.

'Yes,' Stamford agreed quietly. 'It must.' He unhooked his ankles from the desk where they'd been crossed, and returned his chair to the upright. 'You'd better get your notes typed up and then we'll see if Gus is prepared to sign a confession. Then maybe we could . . .'

He was interrupted by the jangling phone bell. The voice over the crackling static was lighter this time. A woman, Sarah guessed.

'Yes,' Stamford said. 'Yes, yes. I understand. I'll come at once.'

Vaulting the desk, he snatched up his hat and grinned at Sarah. 'I have to go. They've found her. My daughter. I'll see you later.'

'And your wife?'

He didn't answer. He was already sprinting past the startled desk sergeant.

Sarah looked at her notes without enthusiasm and decided she'd take a walk up to Parliament Hill before she got started on the typing. Reaching for her own hat, she realized she must have left it behind in Junction Cut.

'I stuck it in the scullery,' Lily said. 'Get it for us, will you, Doll?' Her normally pale complexion had turned pasty. The rouge and lipstick looked like clown's make-up. The shock of learning she'd been living with a murderer, and realizing the danger that she'd been in ever since Gus had found out about Joe, had just begun to sink in.

Lighting another cigarette, she said: 'They'll all blame me, you know.'

'Why should they? You didn't know what he'd done.'

'Don't matter. They're bound to say he did it for me. I'll 'ave to move.' She flicked ash into the saucer. 'What'll happen to the money? The two thousand quid?'

Sarah didn't really know. 'Since it was Valerie's, it

ought to go to her next of kin. Which would be her mother, I suppose. But the bet was illegal anyway. So I suppose Oggie might have a claim, if he's got the cheek to make it.'

'And he 'as. God, ain't that typical? Gus never could get anything right.'

Dolly returned with the hat. The crown was crushed flat. The imprint of Ding Dong's size eleven boot, outlined in vanilla custard powder, was clearly visible.

'Life's a bitch, isn't it?' Lily said.

Sarah agreed. Setting the hat on at a jaunty angle, she stalked back to the station to finish her typing.

Epilogue

She sat facing him over the kitchen table. Solemnly taking a tiny portion of Eileen's rice pudding on to her spoon, she probed it with her tongue.

'Is that good?' he asked.

She didn't answer. Her little pink tongue twisted and licked experimentally. She hadn't spoken for the past eight days according to the WVS worker who'd brought her to the house. Ever since a group of Belgians had found her clinging to the dead body of a young woman after their refugee column had been strafed, the whistling hail of bullets striking indiscriminately into the stream of civilian refugees and army trucks. The British passport she'd been clutching then was on the table by her bowl. She'd refused to be parted from it. She still did.

'It's as if she'd been told not to let it go,' the volunteer had told him.

The Belgians could offer no further information. They'd only had time to snatch her up and take cover before the planes had returned. Afterwards, they'd struggled on to the coast and found a ship. She'd not said a word during all that time.

Jack wondered whether she even remembered any English now.

'Do you remember her, Annaliese?' he asked, holding up a grubby knitted doll that had been overlooked when Neelie left.

The back of the silver spoon was massaged up and down the glistening tongue. She stared at him, then back down to her plate.

'Have some jam in it,' Sammy advised. He'd invited himself in and was now seated next to Annaliese, watching the rice pudding with envy. Ladling out a tablespoon of strawberry jam, he said: 'It's sweet, see?' And to Jack's horror he ate half and lobbed the remainder into Annaliese's rice.

'J . . . A . . . M. Go on, you say it. J . . . A . . . M.'

Annaliese took a deep breath. '. . . am,' she whispered.

Sammy beamed. 'There yer are. Don't worry, Mr Stamford. I'll soon learn her to speak proper again.'

The grave was already looking neglected. The stone letters were pristine in the marble headstone; a fine, high-quality Italian stone paid for by the outraged public. But the grassy mound was overgrown, the bindweed exploring the edging stones and the sunken metal vase with increasing confidence. Moving aside the crumbling remains of wreaths woven into circlets, crosses and prayer-books, Sarah poured water from the rusting can she'd found by the water tap outside the church, and slotted her own few flowers into the vase.

A shadow fell over her shoulder, its elongated shape

sliding over the white stone. A young girl's shadow.

With a start, Sarah fell back on her heels.

'Sorry,' Margaret said. 'I didn't mean to startle you.' She sat down next to Sarah. 'I just came to talk to Valerie. I do that sometimes. I can sort of hear what she'd say. I do miss her, you know.'

'Yes,' Sarah said slowly. 'I can imagine if you'd had Valerie Yeovil as a friend, it must leave quite a gap.'

'That's it.' She snuggled a shoulder against Sarah's companionably. 'Do you know, I thought you'd understand. Even though I didn't really like her, Val made me feel strong. You sort of felt that if Val was behind you, you could do anything.'

Reaching forward, she tweaked Sarah's flowers into a more artistic arrangement.

She read the inscription that flickered beyond the girl's waving hair.

Beloved daughter and sister.

It was a lie. She knew instinctively that Valerie Yeovil would have despised the choice of words. She hadn't been loved by anyone – her mother, her natural father, her supposed father, her grandfather, even her brother. All had treated her with loathing or indifference. Most girls would have withered and retreated into themselves without anyone to care what became of them, but not Valerie. She'd fought back. Maybe she hadn't fought fair, but then the world hadn't been fair to her. So she'd paid it back in its own coin. At fifteen she'd clawed her way to a decent education and enough money to start her own business. She'd foundered against a man with an even stronger dream and the brute strength to realize it. But she'd nearly made it. Sarah thought she'd have liked Valerie too.

Putting her arm round Margaret's shoulder, she said: 'Come on, I'll walk you home. You can talk to me instead.'